White Highlands

White Highlands

JOHN McGHIE

Little, Brown

LITTLE, BROWN

First published in Great Britain in 2017 by Little, Brown

1 3 5 7 9 10 8 6 4 2

Map © John Gilkes 2017

Lines from 'Night and Day' by Cole Porter. Lyrics © Warner Chappell Music Inc.

Extract from 'Disobedience' by A. A. Milne from *When We Were Very Young*
(Methuen, 1924) © Trustees of the Pooh Properties

A CIP catalogue record for this book
is available from the British Library.

Hardback ISBN 978-1-4087-0856-9
C-format ISBN 978-1-4087-0855-2

Typeset in Baskerville by M Rules
Printed and bound in Great Britain by
Clays Ltd, St Ives plc

Papers used by Little, Brown are from well-managed forests
and other responsible sources.

Little, Brown
An imprint of
Little, Brown Book Group
Carmelite House
50 Victoria Embankment
London EC4Y 0DZ

An Hachette UK Company
www.hachette.co.uk

www.littlebrown.co.uk

To Sarah, Tom and Olivia

What turns a weak creature into a sadistic bully behind a barbed-wire fence? What strange twists of thought made the security forces think they always had God and right on their side whatever crimes against humanity they committed?

Josiah Mwangi Kariuki, *'Mau Mau' Detainee*

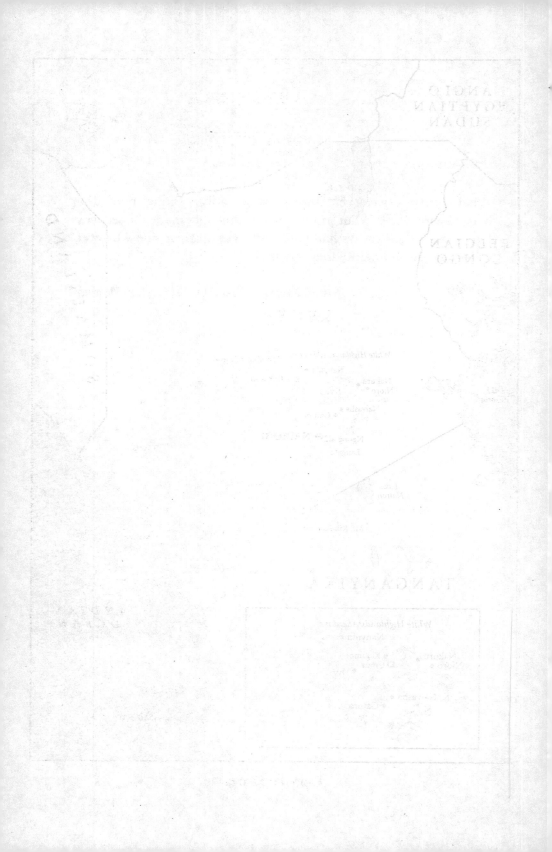

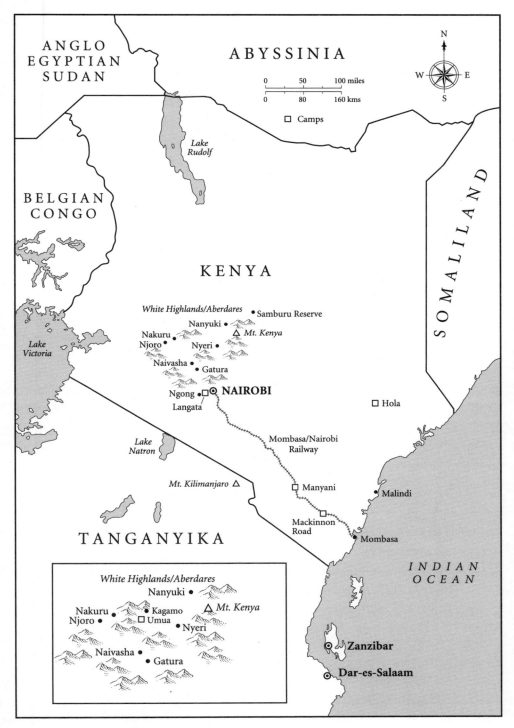

Colonial Kenya

Prologue

White Highlands, October 1952

For men of Empire, a sacred time.

As the orange sun dissolves behind the mountain bowl, for the fleetest of moments before forest clamour crescendos into shrieking night, a small hiatus of peace.

It is the period Cedric Cunningham loves best. Soft armistice with the day.

On the cusp.

The silence is welcome, inside and out. The Overseas Service sustaining Connie with its crackling whisper of home is finally muted. Cedric has heard all the news he can bear. Now the dusk is his, cares of the day temporarily shelved.

Indoors, houseboys light candles, arrange mosquito nets, lay the table. Baby is down and Connie is at her vanity table putting on her face, whisky to hand. Although she drinks this first one quickly, before condensation can form a ring on the teak, Cedric still has five minutes before she joins him on the veranda to take 'the other half' and Jomo, head houseboy, brings his second Tusker.

When his wife arrives, Cedric rises to greet her. Wafting Chanel, Connie presents a cheek, sits beside him on her own rattan chair, drink resting securely on hunting-patterned coasters. They discuss what they did, Connie first, describing a day of ordinary purpose that makes Cedric feel things are right in one part of his universe at least. He nods, half listening, pleased with the tone, happy with the rhythms, the cadence of normality restored.

Servants and flowers, Nyeri Club gossip and the wicked doings of Ayah with baby. Connie is retelling *that* story – how lucky she found them where she did, when she did. The bloody python, Cedric, it's still there in the rockery. Garden boy has to be told or something

1

very unfunny is going to happen; Ayah just doesn't care. Cedric shrugs. Connie is exaggerating and she's wrong about Ayah. He's told her often enough: there are other servants to ensure nothing really terrible happens. She might not see them, but they're always there. Or thereabouts.

Tonight Cedric is too tired to reopen this. Instead he mutters 'I know, I know,' dutifully twitching the corner of his lip in amused assent, trying to hit the right note. But her eyebrow arches. He's getting it wrong. Again. The part of him that still cares cavils against this unfairness. They've been here nearly a year; she must understand snakes and wildlife are part of their lives, part of the package. This is Africa. He knows she's read the manual, positively pored over it on the three-week voyage out. Pythons and errant ayahs are common fodder for the ladies of St Andrew's Presbyterian Church. If it's not in their *Kenya Settlers' Cookery Book and Household Guide* it's not worth knowing

On another night, depending on mood, Connie might suggest a quick rubber of two-handed bridge. Or they could sit on in varying degrees of companionable silence until the dinner gong, watching the velvet sky needle into brilliance. This evening, however, she wants to take it further. Cedric doesn't know anything about what happens at home. He's never there! He goes on about how wonderful the servants are, but these days they're nowhere to be seen. Why can't he accept she probably knows just a teeny-weeny bit more about the people who share her house twenty-four hours a bloody day than he does?

Connie's tirade is a prelude to the old campaign, the tiresomely suburban fear that African nature, in collusion with most of the household staff, wilfully desires to trespass across their cultivated English lawn with the express purpose of harming baby Charlie, herself and every other white person within fifty miles.

Cedric wants to understand, desires only to shelter in the familiarity of her worries, the quotidian trivia of her life. But given what's going on, his mind can't quite focus. Besides, he emphatically disagrees about the servants. He knows Jomo; chose him himself. Capable and dependable. That's what the references read. And it's true. Jomo is both – capable *and* dependable. Connie should be grateful. There are few enough of them around today.

Connie's view of this stubbornness is that, like other husbands,

2

Cedric has an obstinate myopia when it comes to the running of the house. As the cooling vent of evening blows in – cardigans soon – she sighs. Really, doesn't she have enough to do without keeping an eye on everyone? It's obvious Ayah can't be trusted for a second, and Jomo is definitely selling sugar to his nephew. That very afternoon she's seen the two of them, heads together, behind the back door, both looking guilty as Satan. Honestly, anyone would think they aren't being treated decently, but the whole valley knows the Cunninghams pay higher than strictly necessary. Besides, Cedric has never shouted at them once.

Once this is off her chest the talk turns his way. Given the times, there are minefields here too. When she asks how his day has been he can only mumble: 'Oh, you know, the usual.' She pretends to want to know more but doesn't push it. She's heard a thing or two from other wives at club lunches and knows better. Give him time. He may tell her later, when they're both under the mosquito nets, his head on the dampening pillow, eyes closed, intoning the most frightful stories. He's been doing this more recently, a lot more, and her duty is to listen, not talk. Some husbands never say anything, but it only comes out in other ways. The Wilkins woman may wear dark glasses all the time, but everyone knows what lies behind. This is better. The two of them, three now with Charlie, making a life; keeping on top. Doing their bit. Isn't that why they're here?

But tonight something is not quite right.

Connie has returned to her room to check on baby one last time before dinner but Cedric has heard something. From outside. Normally by now Cedric's boots and socks are off, hot feet cooling on the veranda rail. Tonight the boots stay on and Cedric's fingers brush the holster on his Sam Browne belt, not sure what he's hearing but glad of the weapon. They've all had refreshers on the firing range at Nanyuki. No point in having the damn thing if you don't know how to use it.

Cedric hears something again. Beyond the lawn.

He's told Connie many times they're safe out here. She always reassures him she isn't worried. Her only desire is that he takes care of himself. She's loyal, that one. But he's seen the look in her eyes and knows the second drink is now followed by a third. The tone she takes with Jomo doesn't help. Jomo is always calm and shows no expression during her harangues but it's obvious he doesn't like it. Cedric won't intervene, but it really doesn't do to talk to the head houseboy like that. He wonders how she'd cope if she knew the true scale. It's not just the cattle slashing. He remembers how she went to pieces when news came in about the Carters. Poor Judith, the ghastliness made worse by the pregnancy and what they'd done to her son, hunting him down in the dark. Only six years old.

Cedric shivers, unable to stop himself from looking into the house, thinking of the kitchen where Benson is chopping chicken for tonight's meal.

He catches sight of the family-sized trunk in the hall, already filled with the exotic Africana a man is supposed to take home on furlough – salad bowls, masks, an ostrich egg.

Leave is still over a month away yet Connie's been packing for weeks. Cedric wonders if she's given thought to not coming back. It would be wiser all round to stay in Surrey with her parents. He could move into a bachelor flat with one of the junior ADOs. But he knows she'll say no, affronted he could even suggest it. Her place is by his side, thank you very much. And that will be that. Although Cedric will protest, he'll be secretly glad because frankly he doesn't know how he's going to face another two months, let alone the two years left on his posting. It's coming. Everyone can feel it. The Office is frantic. Wives not to be told. Don't show anything; hold the line.

Cedric paces the veranda and thinks about smoking a cigarette. He's left them inside and is heading towards the door when he hears a scream, high-pitched, ending in a wail that cuts off suddenly. It lasts no more than two seconds, stopping almost before it begins. He swivels his eyes to the forest. It is not a human noise, but it belongs to no jungle animal he can recognise. The Morgans' dog? The hairs on his arm rise up as his body registers alarm before his brain can articulate what is happening.

They're here.

Dark shapes from the tree line, loping across the lawn. Four, no, five of them.

Out of the forest they will come.

Cedric's hands are trembling violently and he cannot undo the catch on his holster. Where's Jomo? Loyal Jomo, loyal Kikuyu. One of the best. Together with Benson and the other kitchen staff they

4

might see them off. A tendril of hope: the patrol is due later! Or
Morgan might pop over for one of his chats. At work Cedric has
been on the offensive so long he's almost forgotten how to defend at
home. He needs to move. Christ, they're almost here, black figures
running low across the ground. He can hear panting breaths and
the rhythm of a running chant. They'll be over the veranda rail in
seconds.

At last Cedric sprints, heavy boots clumping on the wooden
boards, adrenalin pulsing him into the living room, past a copy of
Horse & Hound messily thrown on the floor, into the hall. Where's
Connie, where's Jomo?

'*Jomo!*'

Cedric knows he must get Connie and Charlie out of the house.
They might be able to run to the Morgan place – less than half a
mile from here – while he and Jomo hold them off. There is whooping and a low moaning, the anticipation of the chase. They are
vaulting the veranda rail.

At this moment Cedric understands he is lost. There is just one
chance – for Connie and Charlie.

He bursts into the bedroom, relieved to find Jomo there, already
guarding Connie. Dependable. Loyal. He calls her name but Connie
doesn't look right. Her face is pinned back in some private horror,
not moving. Jomo isn't turning round either. Time slows. The
window is open and he can see more black legs running fast across
the lawn. Cedric looks at the cot. Empty. He sees Connie's eyes turn
involuntarily toward the bunk bed. He follows her gaze, seeing she
has hidden Charlie underneath the bed. He mustn't wake now. Jomo
needs to do something, immediately.

Cedric issues the only order he can.

'Connie, take Charlie and run. *Now, Con, now!* Through the
window. *Go!*'

But Connie isn't moving. Jomo turns. He is carrying a panga.
Good – they'll need that. The head houseboy stands to one side to let
Connie pass, but Connie is behaving oddly, clutching her stomach.
And now Jomo has moved, Cedric can see blood seeping through
her fingers, the white blouse slashed through half a dozen times.
Cedric is reminded of a chicken breast scored for marinade. Nothing
is right; his view off kilter. He looks at Jomo, finally absorbing the

5

fact there is blood smeared on the curved blade of the panga held at Jomo's side; held by Jomo. Head houseboy. Loyal Kikuyu. One of the best.

Even with the evidence before him, Cedric cannot put it together. The implications are too immense. Simply not possible. Connie groans and looks at him desperately, legs buckling as she falls on the bed. He starts to move towards her but Jomo checks his way. Again, so slowly, everything happening through a deadening haze. The men running to the house pause in the living room before starting up again, pounding along the corridor. It is too late, everything is far too late. This is so stupid. All for nothing. They are clambering into the room – into his precious baby's room – silent now except for their breath, panting and gurgling, excitement bubbling ammonia into their sweat glands; the closure of the hunt.

Cedric takes in leopard skins, more pangas, a monkey's head cowl, blood smeared on shiny faces. The sour stench of forest grease. One sawn-off shotgun. A smell of burning, flames flickering in the living room behind – the sofa alight. Finally Cedric opens the catch on the holster but his thumb refuses to work and he cannot find the safety. His hand falls to his side, service revolver pointing uselessly at the floor.

'Jomo.'

The blast from the sawn-off catches Cedric in the midriff, blowing him backwards over the low chest of drawers where Connie usually changes baby Charlie. Through the mist Cedric hears the high keening of his wife, then Jomo is standing over him. Normally expressionless Jomo. Not now. The last thing Cedric sees is his servant's teeth, lips peeled back, a rictus of hate – or fear. In the moment before the second shell destroys his chest wall, Cedric knows it has to be fear.

Of course, no one is immune to that.

Chapter 1

Lincolnshire, February 2008

Samantha Seymour was tired of waiting. And, she was forced to admit, just a little nervous. She shivered, pulling a black cardigan tighter around her shoulders. Thin cashmere might be suitable for court, but visiting a country house in winter required something altogether more robust, especially if the house in question belonged to Magnus Seymour. The proprietor and senior partner of Seymour & Co. hadn't made his fortune by wasting money on fripperies like heating, and old Magnus was not a man to retreat from that axiom in his own home.

A home that wasn't even a real country house, she thought, surveying faux art nouveau lamps, false gables and fake mullions. The armchairs were cosily chintz, but the primary motif was hunting; riding to hounds on paintings, on tapestry cushions, on coasters, even on the magazines scattered artlessly on the ugly glass coffee table. To Sam's certain knowledge Magnus had never sat in a saddle in his life, or pursued anything wilder than a disobedient Labrador.

She brushed a strand of dark hair from her shoulder, eyeing a brace of hounds whimpering in front of the fire. It might have been more sensible to have worn the horrible Barbour sweater her mother had laid out, but at twenty-eight Sam was too old to take instruction – from that quarter certainly. Magnus should see it as a tribute. She never wore this kind of outfit outside work, but she hadn't seen her great-uncle properly for almost a year, and given what might be coming it seemed sensible to dress up a little.

The grandfather clock listlessly intoned another quarter hour, her life sentenced to hard labour in fifteen-minute instalments. How much longer was he going to spend in his study before she was summoned into the great presence? Susie, Magnus's latest wife – his fourth, if you were counting: one divorce, two deaths – was in the kitchen fetching yet more tea. She'd spent an age in there fussing over a new pot, shouting apologies for the cold leaching through the Spode. Sam was grateful to be spared her attempts at conversation. The Gauleiter, as Sam called her for the excessive zeal she brought to guarding her new husband, was at least thirty years younger than Magnus, and although Sam fought hard not to judge on looks, especially with her own gender, she made an exception for Susie. It was impossible not to regard the powdered, jutting chin and dark puffed eyes as anything other than outward signs of the snarling pug within.

Sam ran her finger down the inside of the window pane, where condensation trickled into the lead frame. She tried sketching a happy face but the line of the smile dribbled down, giving it a horror-clown expression. She wiped it away with her sleeve and gazed through the hole. Flat fields of frost-flecked mud terminated in a dark hedgerow scoured of colour by February gales. Although it was Sunday, the orange lights of a tractor blinked in the furthest field, where piles of clay-encrusted roots were clumped at irregular intervals. The Campaign, as Fenlanders called the sugar beet harvest, was nearly over.

A large group of crows pecked disconsolately among the beet heads. Sam wanted to look at her BlackBerry, but knew if Susie came out of the kitchen it would provoke the lecture on how her generation was losing its way, never read a book, couldn't correspond in the real world and so on and deathless so on. Sam sighed, and as if they'd heard the birds suddenly took off together, sweeping into the sky in a dark mass, wheeling and darting in unison. How did they do it? She was fascinated by the way vast flocks seemed to know when to move without any outward sign of communication, rippling across the skies as one living organism; an airborne shoal of black herring, pulsing and pivoting in harmony with themselves and their element.

A coughed grunt from the Gauleiter broke her train of thought. Susie was standing at the door, pointing down the hallway, every inch the praetorian stewardess.

'You can go in,' she barked. 'Magnus will have finished by now.'

'Thanks,' Sam said, amused at how much Susie really did

resemble an air hostess indicating an emergency exit. Which, in a way, was actually true. It *was* an emergency exit – or at least Sam hoped it would be. Susie took a step to accompany her, but Sam headed her off.

'I know the way.'

She was annoyed with how returning to the house had squashed her back into childhood. The corridor was long and she tried to imagine what the soundtrack to this scene would be. The Recalcitrant Returns. Slo-mo drift along the hall, Daft Punk on audio. Close on the face. Expression dreamy but purposeful, tinged with anticipation – or was it anxiety? Even as she thought it Sam felt a butterfly twirling. But it was only Magnus. What could he say in those gently modulated tones that her father hadn't already shouted, that her head of chambers hadn't insinuated? She passed the loo. Maybe do a little line? She had the remnants of one in her purse, the powdered reminder of her night of shame. *Stop it*, Sam admonished herself; it was thinking like that which had led her here. Childish things needed to be put aside. Magnus had promised a way out. *Behave.*

The study door was ajar but out of habit she knocked anyway, before walking in to the familiar book-lined room.

Magnus was sitting behind his desk, head lolling, book folded on a concave stomach. Spidery legs were propped up on the table, trousers folded back well above the sock line, revealing pale shins. She hadn't seen him properly since her return and felt a stab of tenderness. He was cadaverously thin, his gaunt face tinged with yellow. The wrinkles on his forehead had multiplied alarmingly, the skin on his face compressed, squashing lines and crows' feet together like whorls on an ancient thumb print. Suddenly he snorted and jerked awake. His clear blue eyes flapped open, instantly transforming him back into the Magnus she recognised.

'*Sam!*'

He padded over on shoeless feet to hug her, almost lifting her off the ground.

'Sam – *Sam!* How wonderful to see you.'

He stood back from the embrace, looking up at her from underneath the famous Seymour coxcomb. Her father Robert had it too, all the male Seymours did apparently, a band of hair that stood up proud from the rest, though in Magnus's case the hair had thinned and lost its strength, flopping to one side with unseemly languor.

'You look marvellous, Sam. Quite the prettiest girl in Lincolnshire – Lincoln's Inn too, I would have thought. Ha ha. Sit, sit.'

He pointed to a leather armchair underneath a watercolour Sam hadn't noticed before. She was surprised to see it depicted a forest scene somewhere in Africa, a green canopy under an impressive rainbow. He brought his own chair round to sit opposite her.

'How *are* you Samantha? You look well, but I gather not too happy to be back. Not fighting with your father already I hope? Not already, Sam?'

He'd tipped his head to one side, radiating concern. Sam suspected he did this with all his clients.

''Course not, Magnus. I've only been back a couple of weeks. Give me a chance.'

'Good, good. Susie been looking after you? Excellent. Well, let's have a proper drink now, you and I. A Christian drink. Man cannot live by tea alone.' Magnus sprang up, rummaging among the bottles arranged on the lower ledge of the bookshelf. 'Six o'clock somewhere, I'm sure. Whisky water? Half half?'

'Please.'

'Good, good.'

Sam had forgotten the double-tap staccato delivery. A bird pecking on a lawn. They clinked glasses and he sat back, peering at her.

'You do know you grow more like your grandmother every time I see you. It's unnerving sometimes. Uncanny. Especially when you smile – which you don't do often enough, by the way. I shouldn't say this about your parents, but I'm rather glad that looks have skipped a generation. Ha ha. Well, well.'

They sat in silence, sipping their drinks while Magnus did what Sam thought of as his twinkling act, beaming and nodding, his eyes alive with merriment. She wasn't taken in. She'd seen the same eyes snap to ice in a heartbeat.

'Magnus,' she said. 'You know I love seeing you, even if I do have to sit with the Gauleiter for the best part of an hour while you pretend to work. But really, why did you summon me? And what did your note mean about a "way out"? It sounds awfully dramatic.'

'Quite right – straight to the point.' Magnus frowned. 'But my darling, you mustn't tease Susie. I know you don't mean it, but when you speak like that I rather understand what your father says he's going through—'

'Oh come on, Magnus . . . '

'Yes, well, you can be rather hurtful if you choose – as well you know. Believe it or not, Susie's a good woman. Dotes on you. Thinks you're the bee's knees. Yes, Sam, the knees of a bee no less, *no less.*'

'No she doesn't,' Sam laughed. 'Anyway, you're evading the question: what *am* I here for? You're brimming over with one of your schemes, I can feel it.'

Magnus paused and twirled the liquid round his tumbler. He really did look tired, thought Sam. Was he ill? Her parents hadn't said anything, but then they wouldn't.

'Right, OK,' he said. 'We'll just get to it.'

He sighed and looked so grave Sam feared there might have been a death in the family. But there couldn't be – there weren't many Seymours left. She had no siblings and apart from two cousins on her mother's side whom she rarely saw, she'd seen all of the remaining family members in the last twenty-four hours.

'*So,*' he said forthrightly. 'First of all, Samantha Seymour, I'm obliged to enquire whether you are happy in your work here. The pace of helping out in a country practice like ours must be a little different to the hectic demands of London. It goes without saying that Seymour & Co. is lucky to have snared someone of your calibre, but if what I'm hearing is correct you are – how shall we say this diplomatically – a little *bored*, perhaps?'

'Well, not bored exactly, but it's not terribly inspiring. I mean . . . ' Sam stopped, realising how churlish that sounded. 'But actually it's all fine, really. I don't think I've ever thanked you properly for taking me on. Do tell me – how *is* the Pullingdon fertiliser deal going?'

'No, Sam, sorry,' Magnus said. 'Now it's you who's being evasive. I'm afraid it's time for one of those serious talks I usually manage to avoid. That was always your father's job, though I note he wasn't much of a one for that either.'

Sam tossed down the remains of her drink. It was the kind of speciality malt she could never afford. The smokiness invaded the back of her throat and she felt tears coming to her eyes. Magnus saw them and misunderstood, lowering his tone.

11

'Look, Sam, darling, you really can't go on like this. The Bar foul up is something I can understand. We've all concealed things about our past we don't think are relevant to our present. But getting drunk and taking two days off without telling anyone where you are is not really the stuff of a country solicitor's practice.'

Sam bridled.

'I found all the bloody loopholes in your tedious Agro-Beet contract, didn't I? None of your other lackeys spotted them. Christ, Magnus, those people – they're so dull.'

'Which is precisely the point. They're meant to be. So are you if you work among them. And I don't think that's possible any longer, is it?'

'I can do dull.'

'No, you can't. Take it from me: you really can't. Honestly, Sam – what were you thinking of?'

Sam suppressed a grin. What she'd actually been thinking of were the delicate hands of a rather attractive Polish boy, a worker from the processing plant up at Deeton's. She'd slipped into the Plough after being despatched to buy printer cartridges in town. She'd only meant to have a quick glass of wine – it was the firm's bloody fault, they should have had clerks to buy ink. How was she to know the pub would be packed with night-shift workers in the final stages of an epic pool tournament, first prize a monkey – a real one, with a red ribbon on its tail? Sam defied anyone to resist when the alternative was ploughing through agricultural contracts. In retrospect it was probably not such a great idea to have spent all the afternoon and most of the evening drinking. And possibly a slightly worse one to have ended up in a migrant workers' caravan with Cibor – or was it Tibor? But what the hell, she deserved some fun after all the shite.

Magnus was looking at her with a worried expression.

'Are you going to sack me, Magnus?'

'Should I?'

'Probably.'

It was Magnus's turn to suppress a smile. He was glad she felt this way. It would make it easier. She looked vulnerable, yet smart and defiant. So bright it was painful, always wanting more: attention, time. Love. If she didn't get it, off she went and bugger the

12

consequences. First that business at Cambridge, then not telling her employers about it and getting booted out of chambers. And now the disappearing act. There was probably more Magnus didn't know about; didn't want to know. But what he did understand, had seen too often in court where, despite Sam's derision for the county legal scene, all life eventually swam before it, was that certain patterns of behaviour inevitably led to serious tears.

Magnus blamed himself. Sam's father, the wretched Robert, simply hadn't stepped up to the mark. When he saw the neediness in his daughter he felt the gulf of his own and ran a bloody mile. Hopeless, thought Magnus, though in a sense it was all *his* fault. Robert would never have had a void if he'd had a real father. Magnus had done his best, but severing an eight-year-old child from his parent wasn't the best basis for a relationship. Might he have left the boy? It was inconceivable. To have abandoned Robert in Africa would have been neglect amounting to cruelty. Quite apart from the matter of those criminal charges. Serious ones too, the type that could put a man inside for the rest of his natural, and in a time of war, perhaps worse. He'd found out about that one when he was over there. Hadn't told anyone, not even Susie. Fewer who knew the better. He wasn't even sure if Robert was aware. Sam certainly wasn't. All something of a mess but he wasn't going to let the fallout travel down the generations and get to his precious Sam.

As he looked at her, scowling and pretending not to be hurt, he felt a fierce surge of love. She might not be his daughter or even his granddaughter, but by God she felt like it. She was headstrong and reckless, capable of spectacularly stupid acts of self-destruction, but the flip side was an awesome fearlessness. Sam was nothing like Robert, and though she might resemble Tansy physically, it was Johnny she really took after. Sam had spirit enough for all of them.

Which is why she had to leave. She did not belong here.

When Magnus died – sooner rather than later, if the results of the latest prostate test were to be believed – he would do so content in the knowledge that he'd done his bit: fashioned some order, scraped a living from the same flinty soil as the farmers who were both his clients and his community. For Sam, however, this kind of life was not even a beginning – more a slow death. Immurement by county.

13

Magnus thought back to the meeting with his consultant during which the subject of his own death had been addressed with no one actually mentioning it – all very English, which Magnus was grateful for. No sense in getting emotional about an inevitability, but it had certainly provided a spur. Which is why he needed to attend to personal matters – starting with Sam. With no children of his own, she was not only the future of the Seymours but also its link with its past. One part of the past, anyway. The part that had always been missing.

Magnus itched to go himself. If he were younger, fitter, there'd have been no question. But he'd left it far too late.

It was up to Sam now.

'No one's going to make you leave,' Magnus said finally. 'Not sure it's ever been possible to force you to do something against your will.'

Sam smiled tightly but didn't move, conscious he wasn't finished. He was leaning forward on his chair, his eyes neither merry nor scolding, more like a doctor at a Swiss clinic about to offer the big injection goodbye.

'Tell me, how do you fancy swapping the delights of February in Lincolnshire for warm sun and exotic vistas?'

Sam didn't respond. She'd seen Magnus operate and knew there was more. Her shoulders tightened.

'What do you know about Kenya?' Magnus continued, floating the suggestion as if it was the most natural thing in the world.

'*Kenya?*'

She could barely believe he'd said the word. *Kenya?*

'I think I might have found you a job,' he said, trying to sound jaunty. *Keep it upbeat. Casual as you like.* 'Have you ever heard of Mau Mau?'

Magnus blew out his cheeks, taking advantage of Sam's silence to launch into a rapid explanation about how he'd run into an old chum in London who'd told him about a vacancy. There was a legal mission going to Kenya. Could be interesting. An investigation into compensation claims being made for old Empire sins going back fifty years or more. Someone had dropped out. There was a vacancy – had he said that already?

Sam heard the words but couldn't take them in, not able to match what he was saying with his ludicrously jovial expression. It was so

unlike him. Magnus had never talked about Africa in his life. No
Seymour would ever talk about Africa out loud.

Now he was proposing she go there, to the heart of the family
darkness.

Dinner. The echoing sounds of a family restrained: scraping of plate,
jaw-click chewing, dull thud of wine glass returned to table. Too often,
in Sam's case. The air heavy with the absence of words. A meal, then,
like a hundred others chez Robert and Alice. So good to be home.

There was absurdly little time. The team of government lawyers
was heading out to Nairobi next week. When Magnus had learned
someone had pulled out he'd advanced her name as a last-minute
replacement. If she expressed interest she'd have to go for an interview with the Foreign Office tomorrow, Tuesday at the latest. Sam
was, to put it mildly, a little confused why her name should have
been put up in the first place. The Magnus she knew rarely acted
on impulse and his meeting with the lawyers seemed more than
providential. A deeper purpose would hopefully reveal itself soon
enough, but until it did, the scheme was mired in uncertainty.
Besides, she was hardly suited to the task. She knew next to nothing
about human rights law, even less about historical jurisprudence, and
the little she'd learned of Kenya's history had been hoovered from
between the cracks of family silences.

Like the ones round the table tonight, she thought, where conversation was as stilted and meaningless as ever, punctuated by false
politesse – pass the gravy, pass the salt. She wanted to pass her father
a bloody cattle prod and jolt him back into the present. Magnus had
said he'd already informed her parents, so their omertà was wilful
and perverse.

Sam waited until pudding to put the question. She had no great
hopes for a real answer, but if ever her father was going to discuss
anything to do with his past it might be tonight. Seeing him sitting
there with his dull grey tweed jacket matching his pale grey face,
Sam was torn between hating him and feeling sorry for him.

Robert affected not to hear her question, squeezing his eyes shut
for a beat longer than normal before looking down at the book
beside his plate. Small-talk at dinner was not exactly a family tradition, and while Sam and her mother might chat occasionally her

15

father invariably hid behind a newspaper or book. Tonight it was a volume of poetry by Tennyson. Sam could feel the old anger rising but was determined to suppress it.

'Father,' she said, using the formality she reserved for cross-examination. 'I'm aware this is not a matter you feel comfortable with, but could you please do me the service of replying just this once. This is a big decision and, strangely, I would welcome anything you might have to say.'

Across the table, Alice shifted uneasily in her seat, shaking her head in warning. Sam ignored her and when her father still made no reply she carried on.

'I know you've been told what Magnus asked me. And I'm also pretty sure I know what you'll say. But wouldn't it be nice, for once, to talk about this?'

Robert ignored his daughter's question and turned a page of the book, his head bobbing as if he were declaiming the verse in his head.

'I mean,' said Sam, raising her voice, 'is there anyone I should speak to if I go there? Anyone you might want me to look up? Anywhere I might go—'

'*Go?*'

The word spat from him and Sam waited for the tirade. At least he'd be talking. But there was nothing else. He looked down at his book again and Sam had to fight the urge to pluck it away and throw it into the fire.

'Father, *please.*'

He turned another page.

Sam exploded.

'Why can't you bloody answer me? For once in your life will you please just recognise there are other people in this family? Put that fucking book away.'

'*Sam* – stop it.' Alice's gentle voice could be loud when it had to be. 'Do *not* use that language in here.'

'Why not? He can't hear me anyway. Just look at him! He can't even meet my bloody gaze. What is it about Kenya he can't come to terms with? It's pathetic. Why can't he just pretend this is a normal family for one evening and give me a civil reply? I'll be gone soon enough.'

'*All right!*' Robert shouted, knuckles whitening on a drab olive napkin. '*Enough*. I'm sorry I don't meet your high expectations, Sam, but believe me it's not easy. Especially when your own daughter gets charged for criminal damage at university and then fails to tell her employer about it.'

Robert wore his blond hair cut short but it could not tame the Seymour coxcomb. Whenever he was angry it rose up into needle points, bristling like a dog's hackles.

'No wonder they kicked you out,' he said, his voice thickening. 'You go on about the need to be *open* and how we should talk about our *feelings* all the bloody time but when it comes to the test you fail spectacularly, unable to reveal a basic truth. And then when we pick you up off the ground and give you a job, you go walkabout. So don't you dare lecture me about family when that's the way you repay us.'

As he was talking his face flushed, growing somehow rounder. The lines around his mouth filled out, making him appear much younger. Sam was struck by the thought he might actually be regressing into childhood before her eyes.

'I'm sorry,' Sam said quietly. 'I just wanted to talk about what could be a new job like any daughter would with her parents. But because it's about Africa you won't – can't – listen to me. It's so bizarre.'

Robert stood up quickly, his chair tottering behind him, threatening to fall.

'I do *not* have to endure this in my own home. Sam I hope to God you know what you are doing. If you persist with this *reckless* idea it is entirely on your head. And if you are that stupid I'll ... '

He let the sentence fold into its own rage as he crashed from the table, hurling the napkin onto the sofa and striding, white-lipped, upstairs. Alice began to cry and Sam mumbled an apology and headed for her own room, thinking how sad and inevitable it all was.

Lying on her bed, Sam found herself on the verge of tears. She must have been mad to think she could live at home for more than a day. No one could be that repressed and plain bloody weird. She punched her pillow, remembering how often she had done exactly the same thing in the past. Christ, maybe it was her who was regressing. She looked round at the room that had always been her sanctuary. It was the same as when she'd left it ten years earlier, a shrine to late-teendom: photos of schoolfriends on a corkboard, Knebworth '96 wrist bands, cut out images of Jackie Kennedy and Noel Gallagher. A couple of Labour election posters from '97, her first-ever vote.

That had turned out well. Like everything else.

She sat up and drummed her fingers on her thighs, urging herself to pull herself together and come to a decision. She hadn't realised how much the Cambridge episode still rankled her father. She shouldn't be surprised, though: every time she thought about it herself, she felt daggers of hot embarrassment. Why on earth hadn't she told Wheatcroft? Her head of chambers was nothing if not worldly. As he'd said in his little speech when he was 'letting her go', the original sin was petty – it was the cover up that was so stupid. 'Nixon didn't get impeached because inept burglars broke into the Watergate,' he'd said. 'It was the lies afterwards that did for him. Should have told me, Sam.'

So she should. But how could she have foretold that a student prank would have had such consequences? All she'd done was glue a giant brassiere to the statue of her college's alleged royal patron. When she'd discovered it wasn't the king but his wife who'd put up the money to found the college, it had been important to make the distinction that it had been a woman – not a man – who should be celebrated, especially as he was lording it over everyone from his giant plinth on the pavement. A bra on the statue of the monarch seemed a light-hearted way of doing it. Unfortunately that hadn't been the view of the Cambridge constabulary and less than a month later Sam was found guilty of criminal damage and fined two hundred pounds. It hadn't worried the college authorities, so when she was interviewing for jobs in chambers it had seemed prudent not to mention it.

What Sam hadn't reckoned on was the intense rivalry in chambers. The porous interface between lawyers and police meant it had been no great effort on someone's part to access her criminal record. A word in the right ears and it was only a matter of time before Wheatcroft heard about it and been obliged to act. Who had done the deed? Sam had her suspicions. For a year she'd had an on-off relationship with a colleague, a charming enough chancer – someone to pass the time of night with but nothing serious. It was within a week of her moving on from him that she'd been summoned and found her past re-emerging to strike her out of chambers, out of the Bar and, until Magnus had picked her up, bloody nearly out of the law entirely.

So there wasn't much to stay in England for. And yet going to Africa was such a decisive leap. Given her father's lifelong abhorrence of all things African, a move to Kenya would make a difficult relationship infinitely worse. Perhaps she needed to stand up to him, but it did make it rather more than just a normal career choice. For someone who prided herself on her decisiveness, Sam was disconcerted to find she couldn't see which path to take.

One thing that she did know was that she urgently needed a cigarette. But they were in her coat downstairs and she couldn't cope with the idea of running into the legions of the hurt and mad again. Instead, she let her eyes run along her bookshelf, pleased that her younger self at least had the good sense to read well. Atwood, Austen, the Brontës, Harper Lee, Virginia Woolf. Simone de Beauvoir. And there, next to *The Second Sex*, was the blue spine she realised she'd been searching for. The only material thing in the whole house from or about Africa.

It was a child's book, *Flora and Fauna of Africa: A Young Naturalist's Guide,* by Charles Marlow. She pulled it out, opening it at random to inhale the musty pages. Her childhood rushed back with the scent, damp and mysteriously sweet, and she remembered hours of lying on the bed getting lost in its tales of the dark continent. She traced her finger along the worn lines of the cover picture etched in faded gold. A lion, his jaw open in a mighty roar, was standing on his hind legs, looking more like an heraldic device than something a naturalist might actually see. How she'd loved this book. *'If the lion is King of the Savannah then the great grey hippopotami are the unquestioned Monarchs of River and Marsh. If we rise early enough we can often hear these magnificent beasts booming sonorously across riverbanks, their deep calls silencing even the mischievous vervet monkey forced by the bassoon notes to stop and pay homage.'* The words brought back the enchantment of discovery, picturing the great, grey Monarchs of River and Marsh, wishing she could have witnessed the cheeky vervet stopped in its tracks by bassoon notes.

19

Leafing backwards, she found the page near the front where all the boring dates of imprints and editions were lodged. There, above it, were two inscriptions she'd forgotten about. The first, in fountain-pen ink read: *Happy Seventh Birthday Bobby – my darling Man Cub. May you never forget this magical land. Your ever-loving father.* The only remnant of Johnny Seymour and, Sam realised with a start, proof that his son Robert *had* once enjoyed the love of a real father.

Then, underneath, another inscription, this one in pencil.

Sam, it is time for you to have this now. I hope it gives you as great a pleasure as it gave me. Happy birthday. Father.

She really hadn't remembered that one.

'*Fuck.*'

She thrust the book aside and put her head in her hands, stretching back the skin at her temples. He was human. But such a bloody mess. Why did he have to take it out on her? Perhaps not going anywhere near Kenya would be the kindest thing. Was a job opportunity really worth sacrificing her family's feelings? It was the only family she had. Yet she couldn't stay here a moment longer, that was clear. Sam felt a decision edging closer. A friend of hers in London was about to go travelling and she'd ask if she could crash on her sofa for a week or so. Get a temp job. Travel, think – be free of this place without bringing the house down. Anyway, why would she want to get involved with government lawyers – government lawyers, for Christ's sake – on a case about which she knew nothing and cared even less?

She lay back on the bed and stretched out her legs. It was nearly ten. Good, her parents would go to sleep soon and she could sneak down for a cigarette. Another reason to get out of here. An adult, but still forced to hide in her bedroom. It was pathetic. *Really.* She groaned aloud, trying to make the noise stretch out for as long as possible until her breath ran out. Another thing she'd done when she was a child. Suddenly she expelled the remaining air in one sharp burst. Someone was knocking on the door.

The head jutting apologetically into her room was not one she wanted to see. Sam sat up and folded her arms defensively. Her mother took a couple of paces inside the room, looking wretchedly nervous. What had once been pale beauty now seemed haggard, Sam thought cruelly, the skin stretched too tautly across cheekbones.

'*Yes?*'

Alice was writhing in her indecision. She was carrying something in her hands and her upper body was twisted, half turning back towards the door, uncertain whether to proceed. Not for the first time Sam wondered how she could possibly have been born to this woman to whom she bore no resemblance, physical or otherwise. Why hadn't her mother helped earlier? It seemed to Sam she was complicit in the gaping lie that lay at the heart of her husband. Never once had she seen Alice try to open him up – or stand up to him for that matter. She sat there in ghostly silence, an emotional sponge-wraith soaking it all up, never facing up to anything real, weeping quietly like a bloody convent martyr when it kicked off.

'What do you want?'

Alice hesitated and looked so abject Sam was immediately annoyed at herself. Her mother's passivity always managed to provoke her to aggression. She uncrossed her arms, gesturing for her mother to proceed.

Alice approached the bed, standing quietly until Sam moved her legs. Perching neatly on the edge, she placed what she'd been carrying in the space between them.

'Sorry. Don't want to disturb you, but I thought it was time you saw this, Sam.'

On the bed lay what looked like an ancient scrapbook, bulging with papers and photographs. It wasn't anything like Sam had seen before, too large for A4 but smaller than A3, and covered in some kind of animal skin. Several leather thongs bound it together, wrapping the contents tight inside. It smelled faintly musty, even gamey, as if it had belonged to a zoo keeper or animal warden. She made no move to touch it.

'What is it?'

'It was given to your father,' Alice said, adding quickly, 'he doesn't know I've got it and you mustn't tell him.'

Sam looked at her mother sharply. Exchanging girlie secrets of the 'don't tell Daddy' variety was as far from their routine as it was

21

possible to get. She'd have been less surprised if she'd suggested they do mushrooms together.

'Why, what's in there?'

'Just have a look, darling. It's quite important actually. *Please.*'

Darling? It must be serious. Sam poked at the scrapbook, feeling the bristles of the animal fur. Some species of deer, she thought. Gazelle. Her grandfather had written his name on the inside cover – John Lawrence Seymour. *Lawrence?*

'You're behaving oddly, Mummy,' she said, turning the book around in her hands, still not opening it. 'I'm feeling a little freaked.'

To her surprise, Alice laughed softly.

'But Sam, you're always *a little freaked*. You mustn't be quite so suspicious. I'm really not the enemy. Go on, take a look.'

The edge of an old photograph jutted from the scrapbook and Sam extracted it cautiously. Holding it under the bedside lamp she was startled to see a black and white image of herself staring out from a foreign beach. The woman had the same oval face, the same slightly too large nose. Her hair was long like Sam's, but wet and tousled from swimming. In the background waves crashed onto deserted sand and a line of palm trees swayed in idyllic holiday poster style. The picture only showed the woman's top half – slender, tanned shoulders emerging from a dark bathing suit. She was hiding a smile and Sam knew that the woman was on the verge of saying something to make the photographer laugh.

'Is that my grandmother?'

'Yes, Tansy Thompson. She's lovely isn't she?'

The mystery grandmother almost never mentioned, yet here she was staring up at her like a model from a fifties fashion shoot. What had she done to be excised so thoroughly from family history?

'She's beautiful.'

'Well so are you darling. And now you know why. By all accounts she was rather formidable. As are you!' Alice laughed again, before adding sadly, 'They had to be quite tough in those days, but I think that despite all your bravado you're gentler than her. I think – *hope* – that at least is one thing you got from me.'

Sam glanced at her mother with a sudden twitch of sympathy. It must have been hard to have a child who looked and behaved nothing like you; to put up with a husband who had whole areas of his life you could never enter.

'I get lots from you, Mummy,' Sam said gamely.

Alice shook her head.

'I don't think so, but it doesn't matter, darling. Perhaps you'll know if that's true when you've looked at the rest.' She pointed at the scrapbook. 'It's from your grandfather. It's full of his old things. The pictures are particularly interesting. I hadn't seen any of them before and I don't suppose you have either.'

Sam flicked through. It was stuffed with photographs, cuttings, maps, documents and even some letters. She pulled out another photograph. In this one a blond man was trying to evade the camera lens. He had an air of flying above it all, of not belonging; a wedge of hair aggressively pointed skywards. A camera was slung round his neck. *Johnny.*

Another picture was of a scene at a party. A short man in a dinner jacket staring out through thick spectacle lenses that magnified his eyeballs alarmingly. He was flanked by a smiling Tansy in a glamorous ball gown and Johnny in a dull suit, looking to the side and wearing a look of deep embarrassment. On the back someone had written *Grogan Littleboy and his protégés, Oct '52.*

Next Sam picked out a yellowed newspaper cutting. She scanned it and saw it was about an investigation into a murder of a family, the correspondent describing a scene of barbarity and 'dark horror' too upsetting to repeat. A large picture showed a policeman standing in front of an old colonial bungalow. The headline read: GOVERNMENT MAN HACKED TO DEATH BY SERVANTS. WIFE AND BABY PERISH IN FRENZIED MAU MAU ATTACK. Underneath the picture the caption stated 'Police scour Cunningham house for clues – picture taken by J. Seymour, Information Department'.

She hadn't even known he was a photographer. These pictures were the only images of her grandparents she'd ever seen. And the scrapbook was swollen with more.

'Where did Daddy get this from? I didn't think Johnny ever came back.'

'He didn't,' her mother replied. 'I think Magnus gave it to your father after he went to see Johnny back in the mists. Don't know when – or the details, I'm afraid.'

'But why are you showing it to me now?' Sam asked. 'I've asked endlessly about all of this and now you've produced this collection from my own grandfather that's been hanging around for decades but which I never knew existed.'

'I only found out about it myself a couple of days ago,' Alice said. 'Your father must have kept it hidden and taken it out again after he learned what Magnus was up to. I found it next to his bed last night. I've only had time to look at some of it, but if you're going away it might be a good idea to go through it.'

'But I haven't decided that I *am* going yet. I was trying to talk about it at dinner but you saw: he just won't have it. I don't know what the best thing is to do.'

'*Really?* You genuinely don't know?' Alice was shocked. 'Of course you've got to go. Samantha Seymour, tell me you haven't decided to stay.'

Staring at her mother, Sam wondered if she'd strayed into a parallel life, one in which casual intimacy between mother and daughter was the norm. Her own mother never came to her room. Never shared confidences about her father, never expressed strong views.

'What does Dad think?' Sam asked. 'He must be opposed to me going.'

Alice took hold of her daughter's hand, stroking the back of it with one finger just like she used to when Sam was little. Sam didn't pull away. Her mother's lips were moving silently, struggling to say more.

'To be honest, Sam,' she said, finally meeting her daughter's gaze, 'that's the real reason I'm showing you this. He would never say so, but *of course* he wants you to go. More than anyone. This whole business about his past has been killing him. He doesn't sleep, he hardly eats. He . . . ' She paused again before adding quietly, 'It's killing all of us, actually.'

They sat in silence. Was that really how her father saw it? He'd never given a single hint that was what he felt. But then he was hardly likely to talk about something so intimate. Sam sighed, removing her hand from her mother's to leaf through a bundle of documents fixed inside the scrapbook with a decaying rubber band.

'Well, I'll leave it with you,' Alice said, smoothing her skirt as she got up from the bed. 'But promise me you won't make any decision until you've looked at it.'

'I'll try,' Sam said.

Her mother tentatively opened her arms for a hug. Sam stepped awkwardly into the embrace, realising with some shock it was the first time she'd been hugged by her mother for a very long time. In a night of surprises this was probably the biggest. The smell in the crook of her mother's neck was exactly as Sam remembered, a hint of perfume, homely echoes of kitchen and garden. A safe smell, she thought; a smell she'd missed.

'Thank you,' Sam said. 'For that as well as the scrapbook or album or whatever it is.'

'Well, it's your family history,' her mother said quickly, their intimacy over. 'And if anyone's going to deal with it, it's going to have to be you.'

Alice took a few steps down the hall before turning.

'I won't be here tomorrow morning. I've got to run Magnus up to the hospital – endless checks, poor man. Waterworks, apparently. Anyway, I doubt I'll see you before you go.'

She gave a tight wave, her hand barely raised higher than her hip. She stared at her daughter, for a moment giving the impression she might be preparing to impart some final advice. Her mouth began to open but after a stutter of hesitation her lips neatly creased together and whatever she was going to say vanished behind the familiar antiseptic smile.

Sam took the scrapbook and separated it into its different components. Placing the photographs to one side, she arranged the documents on another and put bits and pieces like maps and receipts in the middle. She scanned the titles, wanting to get a sense of what was in there before plunging in. The papers were a strange assortment of press releases from the colonial government's Information Department, railway timetables, lists of building equipment and oddities like a call sheet of names for a punishment roster and an old ticket for a liner from Southampton to Mombasa. There were disappointingly few photos. Shots by a pool; a group of men in an office; several rural scenes containing zebras and one of an elephant with her baby. The rest were divided up into those of Tansy in various poses on a beach and a separate, grimmer bundle of snaps of some kind of African work detail.

After being starved of information about Kenya and her grandparents for so long, the wealth of material spread out before her was so overwhelming, so intimate, it almost felt an intrusion to press on.

Before her mother had come to her room, Sam had been veering towards staying in England. Now the main reason not to go had been removed. If her mother was right, her father actually needed her to go to Kenya. There was obviously unfinished business that neither he nor Magnus could deal with. Though how Sam could help was beyond her. Perhaps there would be clues amid these photos and scraps of written detritus that had drifted onto her bed from another age.

She ran downstairs and fetched her cigarettes. Propping herself up on the window sill, she eased open a pane and lit one, exhaling the smoke out into the freezing Lincolnshire night. She held up the photograph of Johnny with his camera round his neck, shifting it in her hands so that it caught the light. That she resembled Tansy was without question, but it was her grandfather's eyes which fascinated her. Johnny's were more hooded than her own but the message they emitted, of not wanting to be there, of having some secret place he'd rather be, was exactly like hers. His stare was directly at the camera and as Sam peered back she tried to read what his eyes were signalling. Come? Stay away?

Sam drew deeply on her cigarette and put the photograph down. Neither, of course. They were the eyes of a dead man from a long time ago in a very different land. It was absurd to think she'd garner any message from them. Yet there was something. She picked the photograph up again, studying the image once more.

And there it was. She'd missed it the first time; too absorbed by the eyes. It was the mouth. At first glance it seemed to be set against the world, almost in a grimace. But now she saw the lips were slightly angled down at one side, in a kind of lopsided grin.

She threw her cigarette out of the window and although the air was sharp with cold she hardly felt it, her thoughts already soaring away from frozen beet fields towards the heat of an Africa where her own grandfather could visit bungalows and witness scenes of barbarity, and yet still look at a camera and smile.

26

Chapter 2

Nairobi, October 1952

Grogan Littleboy abhorred disorder. Of all things he detested, it was mess. What Africans did by the side of the road was their business. But this was an office – *his office* – not a latrine, and when he'd left here last night it had been in pristine condition, fit for purpose. Now it was a filthy hovel. Papers everywhere, desks not cleaned, a grotesque cartoon of an African's head superimposed on the official photograph of the young Queen. Press cuttings were strewn over the floor, a map of Kenya half ripped off the wall. The ceiling fan lumbered slowly, wasting valuable generator fuel, but the room still smelled of sweat and stale cigarettes.

Impossible as it seemed, it looked to Grogan as if someone had been holding a party.

Grogan was by no means a tall man, nor was he thin, yet when he moved he did so lightly and with surprising fluidity, like an outsize ballerina sidestepping off the stage. Now he picked his way, if not daintily, then gingerly around desks, afraid of what he might discover, almost tripping over an empty bottle of South African Stillpot brandy. He grimaced at the staccato buzzing of a fly trapped drunkenly among the fumes. There was another noise from behind the stationery cupboard.

Snoring.

Grogan marched over and his small mouth pursed at the sight of a man lying on the floor, head lolling on a pillow fashioned from the *East African Standard*. The sleeping man's mouth opened and closed in an ugly sucking motion. Grogan bent down, putting his lips close to the man's ear, and bellowed:

'*Get up!*'

It had an immediate effect. A tall man in a rumpled jacket

27

stumbled to his feet, hands held in front of him, palms up, as if he were warding off a threat. Which, to some extent, he was, though he was still too befuddled to understand its precise nature, his body merely reacting with the instinct for self-preservation that had helped him emerge from worse predicaments.

'What the hell is this?' Grogan said over his shoulder, already striding towards his office. 'Clear it up and come and see me. In fact, clear yourself up too. You look rough as a badger's arse.'

Johnny Seymour swayed where he stood, not yet awake, but beginning to be aware of how ill he felt. He looked round in confusion and saw a pair of knee-length socks ending in sandals heading away from him. There was only one man who always wore shorts and socks, whatever the weather, whatever the occasion.

The previous night strobed in Johnny's head. Had she gone? Yes, thank God. He felt dizzy and in great need of water. What time was it? *Christ*, not even eight. Didn't Grogan ever sleep? He grabbed the brandy bottle and made it to the toilet. He filled the bottle with tepid water and drank deeply before fishing in his trouser pockets to produce some aspirins. He downed them quickly with the rest of the water, not noticing the fly in the bottom. He splashed his face and tucked in his shirt. From a jacket pocket he found a tie and half a cigarette. Could be worse, he reckoned, staring at his bloodshot eyes in the mirror, trying to straighten the unkempt knot of hair protruding from the back. No new bruises, at least.

Grogan was trying to get off the phone, and waving at Johnny to sit down.

'Right,' he was barking in his official voice. 'Of course. That's why we're here ... Don't worry, we'll deal with it ... Yes, sir. Straight away.' He placed the receiver back with care and glared at Johnny with Cromwellian intensity.

'Thought you said you were going home.'

'I got distracted. Shouldn't have brought her here. Sorry. It was rather late.'

Johnny's voice was melodically reassuring, the tone conveying precisely the right ratio of apology to complicity – don't be a bore, where's the fuss? It wasn't practised, but that's what made it effective. He ran his hand over the back of his hair. Rueful yet unapologetic.

'But what the hell are *you* doing here?' he laughed. 'When I left you were wrapped around Tansy. Weekends are meant to be for fun, Grogan, didn't they tell you?'

If it had been anyone else, Grogan would have quietly and with great precision had their guts. Quiet was Grogan's way, but so too was evisceration. There were few in the office who hadn't felt the acid of their boss's displeasure. But Grogan took a different line with Johnny. Most thought he'd simply succumbed to the famous Seymour charm, though Porter and a few others believed there was more to it. It was known they went back a long way, but no one had yet unravelled the trail so nothing was said. Overtly at least.

'Quite so,' said Grogan dryly. 'Tansy's something, isn't she?'

Johnny lit his half cigarette and inhaled deeply. *Fuck yes*, he said to himself, because swearing had come naturally in the army, and afterwards the only people who swore more than soldiers were journalists and the satellites who aped them: his new, but in all other respects deeply uninteresting, colleagues, the Government Information Officers.

Yes in-fucking-deed. Tansy Thompson certainly was something, though what she saw in Grogan and his long socks was beyond any of them. But then Tansy was unusual. Most nurses spent their leave by the pool at the Norfolk but Tansy slept all day, rising at cocktails to sing at the piano in the Night Bar. She should have been – usually was – just the type for Johnny but he obviously didn't appeal; no one did. Now she only had eyes for Grogan. It was unlikely. In fact, looking at his boss sitting behind the desk with his crisp, short-sleeved Aertex shirt and prematurely balding head, it was preposterous. She was far too good for him, far too ... *attractive*. The whole thing was wrong. Not natural. Like imagining your parents at it. More than wrong.

Johnny shuddered and extinguished the cigarette on the sole of his shoe, noticing a hole developing in the Italian leather. He flicked the butt into the wastepaper basket, reluctantly tuning back into what Grogan was saying.

'Put the office back together again and I'll stand you lunch at the Stanley,' Grogan said, levering his short body up from behind his desk. 'You'll need something in your stomach before this evening's do. I can't give you a lift up there so you'll have to make your own way. Should only take a couple of hours on that machine of yours.'

Johnny hadn't been planning to do any work today. The world of information and the absurd apparatus of lying for Queen and country could surely wait until Monday morning. Anyway, he was aware of having arranged to meet the girl again. Grogan peered at him impatiently.

'Don't tell me you've forgotten? Jesus, man, get a grip. Six o'clock sharp. Nyeri Club. Best bib and tucker.'

Johnny shook his head. How much had he drunk last night?

'Sorry. Forgot all about it.'

Grogan paused at the door and looked over his shoulder, owlish eyes magnified through the thick lenses of his spectacles.

'C'mon, Johnny. If you're going to understand anything about this snakepit you need to appreciate the farmer-settler perspective. Life looks a lot whiter from the White Highlands.'

Johnny had already met some of the farmers at their Nairobi watering holes and mixing with them en masse in their own habitat was not something he'd envisaged doing voluntarily. Not that an invitation from Grogan could ever be classified as voluntary.

'Sounds unmissable.'

'Don't be like that,' Grogan said. 'Might even be fun. One or two coming from the office. Mattingly certainly. Not Porter, I hope. But there'll be a sprinkling of Old Kenya too. You should bring your camera – there'll be lots to snap.'

The idea of settlers being fun seemed extraordinary, but even more so was Grogan displaying any hint of what might constitute enjoyment.

'Think of it as a means to an end,' Grogan continued. 'It's what any of this is really. You won't be working for Her Majesty for ever. It may seem early to be contemplating, but in my experience it pays to think ahead.'

Johnny smiled to himself. This was more like it. He'd only been in the country two months and already his boss was proposing an escape route. Vintage Grogan.

'All right, so what kind of a party is it?'

Grogan grinned. '*What kind?*' The spontaneous smile revealed a younger man, less sure of himself, more vulnerable, and Johnny began to understand what a woman like Tansy might see in him.

'The valley may be a little less happy,' Grogan said. 'But there's only one kind of party Old Kenya throws. I suspect you'll need some more of those aspirins before the weekend's out.'

It was less than a hundred miles to the club at Nyeri but Johnny felt every yard. There should have been a romance to riding the open road but it had been absent in Kenya so far. A thousand potholes lurked in every mile, bigger and harder to avoid since the rains. He was torn between driving quickly and risking the suspension or dawdling to protect his beloved 1950 Triumph Thunderbird.

He'd decided to take it easy. They hadn't lingered over lunch as even on a Saturday there were meetings Grogan was mysteriously obliged to attend, and Johnny calculated he could afford to be careful and still make good time. Endless nonsense from Customs at Mombasa meant the Triumph had taken six weeks to arrive. He didn't want to put her in a garage immediately. It seemed as if no one had ever seen a motorbike before, although it was probably true they hadn't seen one as beautiful as this, Johnny thought, easing the throttle to stay clear of a line of Kikuyu women, graceful despite the weight of firewood on their heads.

Going slowly gave him the chance to see the countryside. Once he'd cleared the fumes of Nairobi the views were flawless right up to the Aberdares, the high hills at the centre of the White Highlands. In the short time he'd been here he couldn't get enough of the scenery, a fluency of emerald and red everywhere he looked.

Off the main road, he wound through miles of European coffee, tea and sugar-cane plantations. Here countless green bushes were tiered and layered upon the warm red earth of the most fecund land in Africa. It was said that if you left a stick in the ground overnight it would have spread roots by morning, produced leaves by the end of the week. Europeans were proud of transforming the territory into one of the most productive on the continent and their plantations defined the landscape. If Africans were present in the White Highlands at all nowadays, it was mainly as servants. Many of the Kikuyu had been moved onto native reserves, though some had remained in illegal squats, growing banana and sisal on small *shambas* dotting the route up into the hills.

At a bend in the road he pulled up to ease his stiff back. He'd made good speed and there was time for a cigarette. He parked the bike in the shade of a Mopani tree and strolled to the verge. The hillside below was covered with the green shrubs of a tea plantation. The air was sparkling and fresh. In the distance smoke from a few *shambas* wisped into the clear blue but otherwise there was no sign of anyone, just hills and green and sky. It was serenely peaceful and Johnny understood why people of all races coveted this place.

It was always about land in the end.

He arrived at the club an hour later, relieved to have made it before dusk. Travelling by night wasn't officially dangerous but he'd heard rumours of lurking roadside gangs and had no desire to find out if they were true. Despite the relatively early hour, festivities were already in full swing. Cars overlapped on the driveway with African drivers standing by, smoking or polishing bonnets. He placed the Triumph in full view of the club's front windows, not wanting it to be pilfered overnight. Retrieving his camera and holdall, he heard jazz and laughter tinkling from the rear lawns. Europeans here liked to take their parties outside, levering floral-print sofas and armchairs into a wide circle around a fire, echoing the span of wagons and rings of thorns their grandparents might have built. A group of younger men were running about on a neighbouring stretch of lawn, jackets and ties off, playing a game with cricket bats and what looked like a large beach ball. They were braying and sweating, urged on by the cheers of some of the women. Johnny slipped past, praying he wouldn't have to join in.

The club's sleeping quarters were in a series of smaller houses a short stroll from the main complex. Like so much colonial architecture, these buildings were an echo of a certain sort of English home, a confusion of mock Tudor and country cottage with a dash of the veldt to wild it up. Floral cushions and zebra skins, hunting prints and antelope heads.

Yet despite its Home Counties camouflage and evasions, Nyeri was a long way from Surrey. Almost straddling the equator, it stood some five and a half thousand feet above sea level. It got cold at night, a blessed relief for Nairobi swamp-dwellers like Grogan who came alive when he saw his own breath, but an ordeal for Johnny who hated the cold. He shivered, feeling as if he'd walked back in time to the camphor chill of his prep school. There was a reason why he'd spent the last five years moving ever southwards.

His bedroom seemed determined to shut out any warmth, as if admittance of the African sun constituted a betrayal of pale principles. A pair of fraying blue gingham curtains looked as if they'd not been opened in half a century. The only light was provided by a dim bedside lamp, its cream shade yellowed by decades of nicotine. A smell of mildew sweetened the room and he feared there might be something rotting beneath the floorboards. Johnny threw his bag on the bed and snorted. What would Kenya's golden generation think about their fabled watering hole now?

He flung open a window, savouring the clean air. The room looked out on a side lawn where a couple was walking the grounds, stopping occasionally to appreciate the view. A tall man strode past, greeting them cheerily. God – Mattingly. One of the dullest people he'd ever met. Johnny shared a desk with him and had already grown heartily sick of his cherubic red face oozing with unreliable benevolence. Thankfully Mattingly had taken to slipping out of the office at lunch, returning hours later smelling of booze. Rumour was he kept a native girl in town but Johnny didn't believe he had the balls.

He forced himself to stop thinking about the office. Out here and beyond was where he should be. The club was on top of a hill, and where the lawns ended the real Africa began – coils of shrubs and dense forest as far as the eye could see, sweeping down to a river valley that swelled on the other side towards mountains shimmering blue in the dipping sun. He yearned to be in amongst it, not here with settlers and farmers, knocking back *chota pegs* and *stengahs*, complaining about servants or the impact of the crisis on seed prices.

It wasn't even that much of a crisis. Apart from the terrible one-off business with the Carter family last month, the reported upsurge in violence was all tribal – Kikuyu on Kikuyu – and a curfew in some of the outer suburbs seemed to be quelling that. And while it was true the murder rate had shot up in the native quarters, for Johnny, as for most Europeans, that was just a statistic in a newspaper. Aside from dealing with tremors of intent from African labourers and servants, life for the British, in Nairobi at least, was continuing as normal. Perhaps it was different in the bush; everyone said the capital was like another country.

Through the window he watched the couple complete their circuit of the grounds, and as they wandered nearer he recognised Grogan. It was the first time he'd seen him without the famous long socks. He was arm in arm with a woman whose dress covered her feet, so she appeared to be floating across the lawn. She was tall, and when she leant down to talk to Grogan their shadows on the grass fused, the dark hair coiffed high on her head mutating into the horn of some misshapen beast. She laughed and he was mesmerised by the sound. A glissando that ought to have been flowing across an opera stage. But it ended in such a raucous, throaty chuckle that, as absurd as it sounded, he thought Grogan must have been telling a dirty joke.

Tansy.

Johnny wanted to hear more, was envious, he realised, not to have made her laugh himself. He continued watching, but when Grogan pulled Tansy to him with a stubby forearm and reached up to caress her neck, an image of an old painting he'd once seen in Venice snapped unbidden into his head and he saw a priapic old satyr coupling with a nymph. He forced himself to look away. The move caught Tansy's eye and she broke off, peering in his direction. Annoyed, Grogan followed her gaze, but when he saw Johnny he brightened.

'Johnny!' He waved. 'You made it. Good.'

'Hello, Grogan. How did you get here so fast?'

'New driver. Kikuyu fellow – knows all the back roads. Quite competent for a change. Macharia something. Dig him out of the pool next time you go into the field.'

The couple advanced towards his window. Johnny was concerned they'd think he'd been spying on them. He reached in his pocket for a cigarette, searching for a smokescreen. He didn't need one. It would never have occurred to Grogan that Johnny might be staring at him. And even if he'd noticed he wouldn't have minded. Grogan Littleboy was a man who enjoyed being examined.

'You've met Tansy Thompson?' Grogan asked.

'Of course.'

He allowed himself to look at Tansy properly. She was standing about a foot away, near enough for him to catch wafts of an expensive perfume. Her evening gown was clasped at the neck with a precious green stone. Unruly dark hair was piled high on her head,

34

make-up accentuated her cheekbones and she exuded an air of classi-cal elegance. Suddenly the sophistication evaporated as she lurched, grasping Grogan's arm for support.

'*Bugger!*'

Johnny stifled a laugh as one of her heels sank into the lawn. Tansy fumbled under her dress to remove her shoes.

'That's better,' she said, beaming at Johnny. 'Hello.'

Grogan frowned, clasping the lapels of his dinner jacket, as if he might address them both. But he changed his mind and peered inside Johnny's room.

'See you've found yourself a cushy billet. So, when you've changed, get yourself a drink and come and find me. Mattingly's about somewhere – have you seen him?'

'No.'

'Well, Tansy and I won't be staying long as we've got an early start tomorrow, so make it quick.'

'Oh?' Johnny asked, but Grogan was already marching off, draw-ing Tansy away. She tugged against him, turning back towards Johnny.

'Clinic,' she said, smiling lopsidedly. 'His Lordship needs to attend the clinic.'

'Is he ill?'

'Oh yes. He's a . . . *very* . . . sick . . . man.'

She giggled, and though the gaps between her words might have been for emphasis, Tansy was swaying and Johnny suspected she'd been drinking.

'Very funny,' Grogan said, moving off. 'See you later, Johnny. Come on, Tansy.'

Tansy stuck her tongue out at his retreating back.

'Honestly, Grogan, sometimes you're so *bloody* . . .'

She left the sentence hanging and glared, placing the hand clutch-ing her shoes defiantly on her hip, continuing to stare at him after he'd gone. Abruptly, she turned to Johnny.

'My dear Mr Seymour. Johnny. I do hope you're not going to be a bore as well.'

'I can assure you, I shall endeavour not to be.'

Tansy gave a short laugh.

'Well, you'd better watch it. You already sound like him.'

35

'I'm nothing like Grogan,' Johnny snapped.

Tansy, who'd moved away a couple of steps, stopped and smiled. Sadly, he would think later, but for now he was happy just to be caught in her beam.

'Well that is a relief,' she said. 'Not sure Kenya could cope with any more Grogans. See you later, I hope.'

The minute Johnny had seen Grogan's dinner jacket he'd feared he was seriously underdressed. And so it proved. Most of the party had moved inside the clubhouse and were sitting around Formica-topped tables or congregating in standing groups, the chatter growing louder as champagne cocktails were thrown down sunburned necks. Without exception, the men wore dinner jackets while the women were in glamorous long dresses with glittering jewels to match. Amid all this formal evening attire, Johnny thought his suit resembled something a manager of a bank might wear. He might as well be naked; the humiliation would be the same. Actually, that part probably wasn't true. If any of Old Kenya really were here they'd probably prefer a birthday suit. Johnny grinned. Like everyone, he'd heard the scandalous stories: wife-swapping, cocaine, jealousy and murder amid the plantations. Some of the big houses where the orgies had taken place were not far from here, on the other side of the valley out towards Naivasha. High Veldt was the nearest, a vast ranch house now owned by a South American millionaire, where the libidinous former hostess was said to have luxuriated in the nude in front of unbelted earls and unbuttoned ladies, offering drugs and sexual favours to all comers.

Johnny couldn't see Grogan but Tansy was standing near the piano, talking to a couple of men. To his annoyance, he realised one of them was Mattingly. He couldn't believe Tansy would give him the time of day but she appeared to be laughing at something he'd said. Johnny grabbed a champagne flute off a passing salver and threaded through the party, determined to head that one off. But halfway there he heard his name being called. Grogan was waving him over. He approached reluctantly and his boss grimaced, indicating his suit.

'Sorry,' Johnny said. 'Didn't get the message about the uniform. Hope they're not going to chuck me out.'

A lean, older man on Grogan's right grunted 'They might,' before thrusting out a hand.

'How d'you do. Sullivan.' His grip was hard and he maintained it longer than would have been polite in England, appraising the new arrival. He gestured towards his companion. 'This is Crawshaw. He keeps cows and I've got a place over there' – he nodded towards the air behind Johnny's head – 'where we try to grow something in this pest-ridden paradise.'

'What he means,' Grogan said, 'is that Crawshaw operates one of the biggest cattle concerns in Nyeri, while Sullivan here runs coffee and pyrethrum plantations of – what is it Jack? More than forty thousand acres, I think. Suffice to say Jack Sullivan is one of the largest landowners north of Naivasha.'

'We do what we can,' Sullivan drawled. 'So what brings you to Kenya, young Seymour? You've picked a fine time to arrive. Are you attracted by trouble or just plain ignorant? You certainly have the look of an ignoramus – you're dressed like a fucking Pondicherry clerk.'

Johnny estimated Sullivan had to be in his early sixties. Crawshaw was younger, over-groomed, a cloying aftershave clinging to cheeks starting to mottle. Sullivan's hair was white, standing out from sun-basted features like sheepskin on a mahogany floor. There was a glint in his eye, impossible to tell if it was humour or malice. Grogan was playing with the stem of his glass, avoiding eye contact.

Johnny ran his tongue over his front teeth before pursing his lips. It was an unconscious gesture that made him appear more reflective than he felt but it gave him time, a literal pause for thought. He knew he should say nothing, but he couldn't stand the way Crawshaw was leering.

'Well, it's kind of you to ask, Mr Sullivan. The truth is, and I'm sorry to break it to you like this – you too Grogan – that my job at Information is just a cover. I've actually been sent here by London to report on you red-necked bastards to see whether you need your hand held in a crisis or whether we should just give the entire country to the people who deserve it, what are they called? Mau Mau, isn't it?'

Grogan's eyes narrowed.

'*Johnny . . .*'

Sullivan stared at Johnny, his grip tightening on his glass. Suddenly he clapped Johnny on the shoulder with a mighty thump that knocked him sideways, spilling his drink. He tossed his white mane back and roared. Grogan joined in with an unconvincing titter while Johnny stood, grinning defiantly through his embarrassment.

'Your man's all right, Grogan,' Sullivan declared. 'Good for you, Seymour, you'll do. Now have a proper drink.' The settler drained the remains of his champagne and looked round the bar, shouting 'BOY!' until a waiter appeared.

'Whisky all round. Strong. And hurry up about it. *Haraka!*'

When the drinks arrived Sullivan said *'God save the new Queen and may the ladies always oblige,'* and they all clinked glasses. Grogan spotted someone over Johnny's shoulder and moved away, raising a warning eyebrow as he passed behind Sullivan's back.

'Not often you find a government man with a sense of humour,' said Sullivan, still chuckling. 'You're going to need it. You find yourself in interesting times, young Seymour. The natives are stirring. Are indeed decidedly restless.'

'Too bloody right they are,' Crawshaw said. 'Did you hear about Fitch? Thirty of his cattle destroyed this morning. Wogs cut their hamstrings. Animals were in so much pain he had to shoot them. Brought them up since calves. Cried like a baby.'

'You'd better report it to the district officer,' Sullivan said. 'Add it to the tally. Cunningham should be here tonight. Haven't seen him yet.'

'Connie's probably taken him off to the Nanyuki hunt ball,' Crawshaw guffawed. 'She likes a younger crowd. Either that or she's three sheets to the wind. By now she—'

'Who was it that attacked Fitch's animals?' Johnny interrupted.

Crawshaw turned to Johnny, as if he'd noticed him for the first time.

'Interesting question,' he answered slowly. 'Fitch did turn a couple of his milk boys over to the police. Doesn't know if they did it, but he felt they should've been protecting the cows. Even if they weren't guilty it doesn't really matter: Mau Mau bastards have infiltrated every bloody estate in the Highlands. Can't trust a single one of the hands now.'

38

Sullivan looked grave, and added, 'That makes five farms in the last fortnight. God knows what happens when they get bold enough to take on the people who run them. No disrespect, Seymour, but when the government gets involved things always take a turn for the worse.'

'Not sure I follow?'

'No good outlawing Mau Mau after you've closed down all the Kyukes' legitimate organisations. They need to be talking to these buggers, not just arresting them all. Simply drives them underground.'

'Don't agree,' Crawshaw said. 'Talking to the wogs never achieved anything. Government's trouble is doing too little too late. Speaking of which, Sullivan, some of the chaps have been talking to the Zebra. He wants to form a commando to stand guard; sort the bastards out. Interested?' He turned to Johnny. 'We know how to handle them without the government's help. If they want to play, we'll give them a fucking game.'

Sullivan grunted.

'Vigilante nonsense won't cut it. If we're going to sort this out before the kettle starts boiling blood, we'll need the cooperation of the African. That means listening. Not that you cattle men know how to listen to anything but the sound of your cows farting in the fields.'

Crawshaw reddened and put his drink down. He nodded curtly to Johnny and strode uncertainly towards another group, who opened their circle to admit him. A tall man, whip-thin with a red face and hair slicked back in the old Happy Valley style, was holding court. He looked across and nodded to Sullivan, who returned the gesture respectfully before draping a giant arm round Johnny's shoulders and shepherding him towards the door.

'Ignore Crawshaw. New breed. Been here five minutes, took over land that was already worked and made a lot of easy money. Now they think they understand the African. Treat the labour like dirt. If I worked on his farm I'd be a fucking Mau Mau. Right, come and look at this. I'll show you a slice of the real Kenya. Never ceases to amaze.'

Outside the air was cool, the dew already beginning to form on the grass. Sullivan looked back inside and shook his head.

'Can't understand why the Zebra puts up with fools like Crawshaw.'

'Zebra?'

'Tall chap talking to Crawshaw. Real name's Graves. Ewart Graves. Now, he really is old school – his family have been here since the ark – but he can't be bothered with coffee or cattle. For him Africa's about enjoying the wild, not taming it. Sold his farm before the war. Been a hunter ever since.'

Johnny thought that if he stayed in Kenya he might want the same, though he wasn't sure how he'd take to hunting. Shooting with a camera was probably all he was good for now.

'One of the best trackers in the business,' Sullivan continued. 'Tough as a Masai. No wonder Tansy bats her pretty little lashes at him.'

'*What?*' Johnny almost shouted. 'She can't have. I mean, surely . . . '

Sullivan laughed again, not unkindly.

'Did she catch your eye too, Seymour? Well beware. Take it from an old campaigner, there's a wild streak in those Thompson women. Playing one silverback off against another is par for the Tansy course. I remember when her mother was younger she . . . ' He stopped himself with a snort.

'Anyway,' Sullivan said, pointing up. 'Look at that. Takes your breath away doesn't it?'

Johnny had seen the Southern Cross from the window of his Nairobi hotel room, but it had not prepared him for this. The sky seemed infinite, undisturbed by any artificial light. A rolling black curtain punctured by pure white stars and a perfect crescent moon starting to rise. Ten thousand candles flickering in an endless cave.

'It's magnificent,' Johnny whispered.

For the next twenty minutes they watched the stars multiplying until the heavens were more glitter than darkness. Sullivan knew his stars, naming the constellations for Johnny, the Hero, the Hunter, the Twins, and when they walked back inside, he stuck out a hand.

'Glad we've met, Seymour. When Grogan said one of his boys was coming up here to learn a few things, I admit I was prepared to despise you on sight. Grogan's a tricky bugger and I imagined one of his disciples to be even trickier. But you're not really one of them are you?'

Johnny wondered if he should be confiding in a near stranger. But his instincts told him Sullivan might be a man he could trust.

'Well no, I'm not really "one of them",' he said. 'But I do owe Grogan a lot. He was my old CO during the war. Giving me this job allowed me to pull myself out of a stupid mess I was getting into after it all ended. I had a bit of a . . . I'd seen a lot . . . a lot of . . . '

Johnny couldn't finish the sentence. There was no way of describing what he'd seen.

'No need to explain,' Seymour said. 'Nothing wrong with loyalty. Anyway, no one has to know why. You're in a new country now. Chance to reinvent yourself.'

Muraya Macharia had stopped polishing the official Austin some hours ago. Unlike most of the other drivers, he didn't smoke and had no desire to chat to the female kitchen servants. Yet he was not bored. Apart from foraging a cup of tea, he'd remained at his post. There was much to observe. Besides, *Bwana* Grogan might appear at any time. Macharia had been working for the Information Department for less than a week but already he knew his boss to be both unpredictable and demanding. He'd never been rude, nor raised his voice, but the other drivers warned him that the instant Macharia put a foot wrong the *Bwana* would have no hesitation in sacking him. Then it would be back to being a filing clerk or, worse, expelled to the reserves. That could not be allowed to happen.

He was well qualified for the job but even so, he was lucky to have been taken on. The British were increasingly careful who they employed. Macharia was barely into his thirties but there were few men his age who knew how to drive and speak English. The one he'd learned from his brother, a mechanic in Nairobi, the other from the mission school at Gatura. He'd done so well there the Christian Brothers had tried to persuade him to go on to teachers' training college. But by the time he'd acquired the necessary grades, the world had moved on. The teaching profession used to be one of the few ways out for a man of his background, but now there were other possibilities. Mau Mau was strong, growing more powerful every day, and Macharia's learning had marked him out as someone who could take advantage.

41

The men who had inducted him into the Movement were delighted he'd slipped through Special Branch's vetting, anticipating how the Information Department was likely be at the heart of the struggle.

'Watch everything. Do not draw attention to yourself and wait for orders,' they'd said. 'Your time will come.'

And if that meant standing still by the car all night while *Bwana* Grogan and his woman cavorted among the decadence, that's what he would do. Through the windows he could see the whites at play and it did not seem much different from watching them at work, clumsily milling around, drinking, preparing to fornicate with each other's women. And through everything the *wazungu* played their games. Polo, cricket, riding, racing. Dancing. The elders talked about orgies and depravity in the old days, before the European war. It was not as bad now but there was still decadence here. And one thing Macharia had absorbed from poring over Gibbon and other English histories in the school library was that decadence in an Empire preceded its fall.

He hoped the call would come soon.

Inside, Johnny was also surveying the gathering. The atmosphere was more frenetic now, ties loosened, tongues looser, decibels mounting. Suddenly the sound of a glass being tapped by a spoon cut through. It was a noise people here understood well and almost at once the party fell silent. A speech was imminent, news or announcements on their way.

A handsome middle-aged woman near the piano raised her voice.

'Ladies and gentlemen, it is with great pleasure that the Nyeri District Country Club can announce the wonderful Miss Tansy Thompson has kindly consented to sing for us. Accompanying her on piano is the redoubtable Lionel Delaware. So, for a few minutes, I entreat you, stand back and enjoy the Voice of the Highlands. And when she's finished give her a bloody big round of applause or I'll make sure Mr Hillier doubles your chitties.'

Polite laughter died down while Tansy took her place behind the piano, hands folded demurely in front of her waist. She had let her hair down and it lay curved to one side of her neck. Someone turned off the main lights and the room quietened, but she remained motionless until the silence became almost oppressive.

Johnny felt nervous, but at the exact moment when attention was at its most acute she raised both hands and began to sing. Quietly at first, then louder, her smoky voice coiled round the room, wreathing the audience in a haze of Cole Porter.

Like the beat, beat, beat of the tom-tom
When the jungle shadows fall . . .

At the end of her first number her audience roared with delight and Tansy smiled in acknowledgement before leaning down to murmur to the redoubtable Mr Delaware.

For the next half an hour she kept the room spellbound. 'Don't Fence Me In'; 'Begin the Beguine'; 'I Get a Kick Out of You'. In between each song, while the cheers rang round the room, she whispered the next title into her pianist's ear. By the finale, 'Anything Goes', there wasn't a man in the room who didn't wish she was whispering into his.

The last sultry note melted into the heat of the room and cheering and shouts of 'More!' erupted from the audience. Tansy looked embarrassed and tried to wave it all away, politely declining an encore. Soon she was surrounded by young admirers, vying with each other to buy her a drink. The man called the Zebra, Johnny noted, was standing in the shadows, surveying her. He only watched him for a second but the Zebra immediately flicked his eyes Johnny's way, searching out who had the temerity to prey on the hunter.

Johnny looked away quickly and was thinking about escaping outside when there was a tap on his arm. Grogan had appeared, his large head glistening with perspiration. Over his shoulder Johnny saw that the Zebra had disappeared.

'Thought you were having an early night,' Johnny said.

'True, but Tansy's a very determined woman. Did you hear her? Told you she wasn't too shabby.'

'She's amazing. Did you know she could sing like that?'

Grogan smiled proprietarily.

'I did, as it happens. There's a group being formed to provide entertainment for the new troops and I was thinking about asking her to join. She'd be a real asset to morale.'

I bet she would, Johnny thought, baffled as to why anyone would

43

cast a girl like Tansy onto a circuit with thousands of young men for company. More fool Grogan.

He changed tack.

'Did you say *new* troops? Sounds a bit ominous.'

'Ominous times, Johnny. Guns going missing, Mau Mau suspects disappearing into the bush. To be frank, it doesn't look too pretty. Could get very nasty very quickly. Usual crew think it'll all blow over. It won't.'

Grogan dabbed at his forehead with a large yellow handkerchief.

'Best not say anything. Don't want to panic the buggers – they're spooked enough already. God knows how they'd react.'

Grogan began to deliver an impromptu lecture on 'winning hearts and minds', his phrase of the moment, culled from a recent visit to counter-insurgency officials in Malaya. Johnny pretended to listen, focussing instead on scanning the room for Tansy. She was in a far corner, a couple of determined admirers hanging on, puffing their chests out in extravagant courtship displays. But though she was smiling back he could see her heart wasn't in it. She kept looking over their heads, her eyes roaming the room. When Johnny's gaze finally intercepted hers, he felt a charge that jolted his entire body. His eyes stayed locked on Tansy's and though she was on the far side of the room, the distance between them seemed to vanish.

'Johnny, are you listening? I said you should come to lunch tomorrow at Tansy's parents. We'll be back from the clinic by noon at the latest.'

Johnny forced himself to shift his gaze back to Grogan.

'Tansy's? Yes, of course. Kind of her to ask.'

Grogan frowned.

'No, the invitation's from me. You could learn a lot from the Thompsons. Good farming folk, old school. Look Johnny, the chaps in the Nairobi office are OK but I don't know any of them, don't have a history – as we do. If the balloon's going up I'm going to need someone I trust, but there's no point if that person hasn't got a bloody clue.'

Johnny shrugged. Of course. He should have known. Grogan was the most practical man he'd ever met. Spontaneity was not his game. He did not invite people to clubs or lunches without good reason.

Chapter 3

The next morning Johnny rose early, invigorated despite having slept for only a couple of hours. Nobody was up except for the kitchen boys lighting the mobile stoves that warmed vast quantities of pre-cooked sausages and bacon. Like all hotels in Kenya, the food here was tinged with the smell of paraffin, and after last night's alcoholic intake Johnny wanted nothing to do with it. Instead he took a cup of coffee outside. Some garden boys were tidying up after the party while a peacock stuttered across the lawns, its mournful call echoing across the valley.

Apart from the peacock, the crisp air was utterly still, devoid of any sound. The dawn chorus had come and gone, and it seemed the entire land was holding its breath, waiting for the sun to rise from behind the mountains.

The dew was strong when he left and he had to get a hotel boy to wipe the seat. The Triumph started on the first kick and he glided down the long drive, feeling a rare exhilaration as the mountains came into focus and he realised he had the whole morning to himself. He was glad he'd seen a glimpse of Old Kenya and after meeting Sullivan he felt he had a better understanding of where the settlers stood. They were certainly not all carved from the same bone. He smiled, remembering Sullivan's reaction when he mentioned he'd been invited for lunch at Tansy's.

'*Ha!*' Sullivan had snorted. 'Wish I could be a fly on the wall. You should have seen Grogan's face when Tansy told him she'd asked the Zebra to come as well! Not quite sure what she's playing at but it will be entertaining, mark my words.'

Johnny was intrigued by the idea of Tansy playing games, and the fact she might not be welded to Grogan gave him a sliver of hope, ridiculous as that was. He looked forward to seeing her again but wasn't going to rush. He'd planned the route to her parents' place the night before and he intended to dawdle, stopping whenever he saw anything worth photographing.

It was going to be a good day, he could feel it.

The clinic did not really deserve the name. From the outside there was little about it that was medical. It lay down a track, a hundred yards from the main road, part of a row of peeling whitewashed buildings, their exteriors streaked red with dust. Probably built in the thirties when travellers might have stopped off here en route to Nakuru, the houses formed a small arcade of Asian shops selling baskets, shoes, cooking pots and toiletries. At the front Africans had spread blankets on the ground, covered with yams and other vegetables Tansy could not identify. In the fierce morning sun the air felt torpid and heavy.

Grogan was inside. The last building on the right had a spiral staircase running up to a second storey, where the clinic – two rooms jammed with mattresses – was located. Tansy had been there most of the morning and had become fatigued. She went outside, telling Grogan she needed air. A cigarette made her feel no better but at least she was away from the pitiful sights and smells of the clinic.

Cutting women's genitals was a foul business, and although it was possible to operate skilfully, if that was the word for it, it was often botched, leaving young girls – twelve or thirteen years old, sometimes younger – in a terrible state.

Europeans did not see the half of it; Tansy knew that. The problem was endemic and still growing. All that the nurses who ran this weekly drop-in could do was attend to those lucky enough to make it here under their own steam. Mothers and other older female relatives often didn't dare – or did not want – to bring in their own girls. Tansy used to believe it was due to shame but Grogan persuaded her otherwise, describing how Kikuyu men were putting pressure on their women not to attend. Circumcision had become increasingly political, a sign of the Africans' growing impatience with European interference in their customs.

Tansy had seen the suffering at first hand for years. As a nurse she'd been forced to confront the blood and infections and scarring, both mental and physical, that came from the cuts inflicted by the *irunya,* the wedge-shaped iron knives wielded by the elder women. The idea this should become a political tool for the Kikuyu was revolting. There were plenty of political issues she might support them on, but the cutting of their female children could never be one. Indeed, she'd joined the campaign running since the end of the war to get female circumcision on the agenda of the colonial administration – to ban it outright. Missionaries had fought the practice for decades but there had been little progress. Arguably the reverse. Many Kikuyu had left the mission schools in protest and the new educational colleges they'd started were now reputed to be hotbeds of Mau Mau ideology.

Grogan had surprised her with his support. It was not a fashionable cause for a Colonial Office man. When they'd first met it had been at a debate just after the war; Tansy was still almost a girl herself. She'd been passionate about the injustice of it and was surprised to see a man get up and, with no apparent passion at all, sweep the arguments of the pro-cutters aside. She'd remarked on it afterwards and remembered his reply to this day:

'Passion has its uses, but it is reason that wins the day.'

Ever since, despite the teasing of her sister and all her friends, she'd become certain there was more than cold reason to Grogan. When they'd taken to visiting the clinics together – there were two more like this one in Central Province – she enjoyed watching him interact with the children. She'd surmised long ago that when there were no officials looking over his shoulder he behaved more naturally. Like today, for instance, when he'd sat on the edge of the mattress of a girl aged no more than eleven. She was clearly in pain, with fat tears rolling silently down her cheeks, and Grogan had gently held her hand and offered her some chocolate. She'd nodded, but when he pulled the bar from his pocket it had melted, leaving sticky chocolate all over his handkerchief. If she'd imagined he might have been annoyed, she couldn't have been more wrong. In an elaborate pantomime he pretended to be very hot, wiping his forehead with the hanky, leaving chocolaty smears across his face. When the girl noticed and began to giggle, he said 'What?' and did it again. In a few minutes not only the girl but all her neighbours were laughing at the silly *muzungu*'s face.

47

He was coming out now, squinting against the sunshine, searching for his driver. The new man, Macharia, was efficient and had parked the Austin under the shade of some trees on the other side of the road. As he went to fetch it, Grogan beckoned her over. He looked worried.

'What's the matter, darling?' Tansy asked.

She didn't usually employ such an affectionate term, but when the two of them were alone, doing something so worthwhile together, it was impossible not to warm to him and she wanted him to know it.

'Chap inside, African male nurse in the other ward, told me something was brewing. Wouldn't say what but I gathered it might already have happened. He was most concerned that you and I return to Nairobi.'

'That's odd.'

'Isn't it? Still, let's get you to your lunch first of all. Then we can worry about getting back to Nairobi.'

In the back of the car, Grogan took her hand and put it to his lips.

'You have to promise me you'll look after yourself over the coming months. They are likely to be trying times.' He smiled affectionately. 'I'm not sure what I'd do if anything happened to you, my dear.'

To her consternation Tansy found herself blushing. She tried to make light of it.

'Thank you, Grogan, but aren't you being a teensy bit melodramatic? You forget that I was brought up in the bush, whereas you're almost a newcomer!'

'Of course. It's just that . . . Tansy, you do know I care for you very much don't you?'

She did know; he'd been making that increasingly clear. If that Johnny fellow hadn't been watching out of his window, she wasn't sure what the kiss in the garden might have turned into. But the problem was that she didn't know whether the prose could really connect to the passion. Grogan was clearly brilliant. *Electrically clever* was the term she'd come up with. He was so bright he sometimes crackled like one of those modern power lines, fizzing and shimmering with energy and cleverness. And it was good cleverness too. Others believed in God, but Grogan believed in Progress. The only question for him was how to achieve it. He was, as he liked to say, a means-end man. Since she'd come to her senses about his polar

48

opposite, the bushman Graves – how could she have let herself be pursued by that? – she'd arrived at the view that the mind could be the most important thing. But was it really possible to fall in love with a mind and not mind, as it were, about what it was attached to? She grinned, suddenly thinking of Johnny Seymour and how he'd suppressed a laugh when he'd seen her remove her shoes. Then she felt disloyal. Grogan was holding her hand, murmuring endearments, and she was thinking about the smile of another man. With a lurch she remembered having invited Graves for lunch. Oh God, why had she done that?

It really was time to pull herself together.

Despite taking his time on the journey, Johnny found he'd arrived at Tansy's parent's place long before the appointed hour. Glenmore had been easy to find and he was pleased to see the red roof of the farm house looking for all the world like a cottage somewhere in the Chilterns.

Patrick Thompson, Paddy to his friends, and to Johnny immediately after they'd shaken hands, welcomed him warmly, making straight for the larder to fetch a bottle of Tusker. As far as Johnny could see, he didn't look like his daughter at all. Stooping and with a slight limp, he was a head shorter than Tansy. He wore a shabby blue cardigan and as he passed the beer he revealed hands covered with rusty earth. It was only when he looked up, twinkling mischievously, that Johnny saw a resemblance.

'Sorry,' he said, examining his nails. 'Been pottering. The ladies have gone, so I've been taking advantage. They don't seem to think it's proper for an academic to be kneeling in God's great garden. But I'm an agrologist! What else do they think I do?'

He tut-tutted at this calumny and led Johnny out to the veranda.

'Sit yourself there, young man. Just us at the moment. Tansy's at some clinic with that odd civil servant of hers and my wife's visiting a neighbour who's had a bit of a crisis with her animals.'

'Cattle?'

'Yes, did you hear about it? It was over at the McIntosh place, on the other side of the valley. Bad business.'

Another one. Johnny realised he must have driven straight past it.

'How do you see things developing, Paddy?' he asked. 'There

was certainly a degree of unease among some of the farmers last night.'

'Perhaps. They tend to get alarmed at most things. What you've got to understand, Johnny, is there've been very few of these ghastly events. Most of the Kikuyu are wonderful people; love cattle much more than we do. Wouldn't hurt a fly, most of them. It's true there are a handful who're being difficult, but that happens every few years and then dies down. We mustn't make a fuss, d'you see? Whips it all up and plays into the hands of the extremists. Trouble is, the colonial admin chaps only stay here for five years and they move on to another posting. Can't see the long-term picture. Always wanting to make an immediate splash with their latest plans.'

Paddy was aware of making a speech and grinned ruefully over his pipe.

'But what about you? What brings you out Kenya way? Not often we get the fresh English perspective at Glenmore. Mary will be thrilled – though you mustn't let her pin you down with her endless questions about London and fashion.'

Johnny nodded and they chatted amiably for half an hour before Paddy looked at his watch.

'Good heavens – the soil temperatures! Forgive me, Johnny, but I'll have to leave you to your own devices. The ladies won't be back for an hour, so why don't you have a poke around the grounds. Get up into the forest. Nice and cool there. Tell me what you think at lunch – we'll see if you've acquired your Kenya spectacles by then. I wager you'll soon be seeing it like we all do. Some good, some bad. Mostly damn perfect!'

Paddy was right. As Johnny wandered among the trees on the edge of the forest, it was almost idyllic, the air pristine in the shade of the arching green canopy. For some it was the savannah with its galloping zebra and herds of wildebeest, but for Johnny it would now always be the forest that conjured up the real Africa. Perhaps it was the relative coolness, or the constant hooting and cackling. The forest was alive with profusion and possibility.

It brought back memories of an old book by a long-forgotten Victorian naturalist that he'd read on the voyage out. Damp-smelling with a picture of a roaring lion embossed in gold on the blue of the hard cover, the book had provided a real spark for nature, African nature. What a steamy paradise it had evoked with its poetic names for flowers and trees: hoop pines, bastard almonds, Nandi flames, cashew apples, jackfruit, king palms, sausage trees, pigeon-wood. Cape chestnuts, fishtail palms and jaggery palms. White stinkwood and buffalo thorn.

A swooping noise snapped him out of his reverie. He was astonished to see dozens of birds, darting and dive-bombing the forest floor. For a moment he stood motionless, hardly daring to breathe, even forgetting about his camera. It was only an instant in time but the scene was so alive he felt as if he had been immersed in a Petri dish of creation.

The birds passed swiftly overhead and he became aware that the forest had fallen absolutely silent. No bird calls or monkey shouts. Nothing. Very odd. The calm of a volcano on the eve of eruption. Then, on the edge of hearing, becoming louder as it approached rapidly towards him, a rustling. When Johnny explained it later that was the only word he could find, though it didn't really do it justice.

Rustling.

Up ahead, about a hundred yards away, the trail branched to the right. Like all others in these hills, the path was red. African-earth red. Cloying and sucking after the rains; choking with dust in the dry season. Damp and springy in between times. Like now: a vibrant leaf-mulch bounce. Except suddenly it wasn't red at all. The path was becoming dark, a roiling mass of blackness pressing towards him.

Fast.

A shoal of black energy driving everything before it. The hairs on his arms rose. As it approached he could make out insects pouring from the front of the column, trying to escape as larger animals might from a forest fire. It was now obvious why the birds had been present, taking advantage of a vast meal being produced by the advancing force. He saw an animal with quills, a small porcupine perhaps, struggling to get out of the way. Within a few seconds the whole body was overtaken by the column. Soon nothing was visible except the tip of a spine.

Ants.

No ordinary ants either. Johnny guessed these must be *siafu*, the

51

fabled army or driver ants. They moved in massive columns, eating everything in their path; even crocodiles had been known to be consumed, the ants ignoring the tough outer skin and swarming in through the jaws, past useless teeth into the stomach, devouring the beast from within.

He was rooted to the spot, appalled and fascinated. He might have stood like that all day, transfixed, until a sharp pain on his calf made him look down. A dozen outriders were crawling through his leg hair, nipping and stinging. That bloody hurts, he thought, slapping the creatures off, realising he should move. More of the ants arrived, phalanxes of them, racing up to his shorts. Red heads piercing his flesh again and again. *Jesus.*

Johnny jumped sideways off the path into the undergrowth. For a moment it seemed as if the column was swerving towards him. He ran for all he was worth, not looking back until he stood, panting, fifty feet away. Some stragglers were still clinging to him as he watched the main cadre march relentlessly past. He firmly patted his back, legs and thighs, sweeping off more ants clinging to his shirt. A few had made it to the collar and he swatted them while a sharp nip in his groin had him batting the front of his shorts. Ants in his pants! He began to laugh at the absurdity of the sight he must be presenting, alone in the forest, a crazed white monkey jumping and slapping his own groin.

But he was not alone.

A pair of eyes had been on him all the time, and when Johnny turned to go back to the house a man kept pace, slipping through the shadows, silently using a cane to part the vegetation as he followed.

Lunch was not a success. Tansy seemed withdrawn, watching warily as Grogan and the Zebra sparred. She barely acknowledged Johnny but her parents, seeing something was amiss, compensated by becoming more voluble than ever. For the moment, though, it was Graves who held the floor.

'You do know,' he said in his odd, reedy voice, 'that Johnny was lucky. A lot of people have been killed by those ants. *Siafu* don't stop for anybody. Columns might have fifty million ants in them. Consume everything in their path. Come right through a house, eat every living thing in it. Bloody good way to get rid of insects in the pantry or snakes under the floor. They're blind, you know, but can feel your tremors. When they've got you down they climb into every orifice. Most people die of suffocation before the stings get 'em.'

'Nonsense,' Grogan said. 'I happen to be conversant with the facts and there's only been one recorded incident of a man dying of ant bites, and that's because he was allergic.'

'Perhaps you'd like to take your "facts" out into the bush with me one day, Grogan,' Graves said, smiling tautly. 'See how far they get you.'

'It's my fault,' Paddy intervened. 'Sent him out into the forest solo. Sorry, Johnny, should have made one of the houseboys go with you. Got to be sensible out here or you'll come a cropper.'

'Don't be melodramatic, Paddy,' came a voice from the head of the table, 'he'll get the hang of it soon enough.'

Tansy's mother Mary beamed at her gathering, then turned to smile at Johnny. Tansy witnessed the exchange, not sure if she approved. She toyed with the raisin rice pudding, suddenly annoyed with her parents. Why had her mother insisted on this lunch? No one was on form after last night's party. And why did they have to eat this absurd English food? Mary always insisted on serving up sugary abominations at special occasions, having read that these were the sort of thing they ate in Surrey. If it was good enough for the Home Counties, they'd have it here too, thank you very much.

Mary Thompson was Kenya born and bred and had never visited England, never wanted to. Yet the distance from what she still thought of as the mother country only served to accentuate an imagined, often heightened, sense of Englishness. Other wives looked to Nyeri for gossip and Nairobi for news but Mary eschewed both, relying on the wireless and a surprisingly efficient postal service for back issues of *Home Chat* and *Woman's Weekly*.

The continual stream of news and views from England seemed to give her an inner core of strength. She radiated calm and good sense, deflecting her husband's eccentricities with a soothing balm of understanding and mild rebuke. She only needed to say his name – *Paddy* – and he would grin sheepishly, slinking away to check the barn or call the dog. But get between Mary and her wireless when the Overseas Service was on and the saintliness would evaporate. Her attachment to the radio was known throughout the house and no one — but no one — disturbed her after the jaunty notes of *Lillibullero* heralded the news from London.

The radio was never off in the Thompson house, and as the hour now struck two *Lillibullero* could be heard firing up in the background, cutting through the lunchtime chatter. Mary quietened when she heard it, only just stopping herself shushing the others as she would have her own family. At the other end of the table Grogan stiffened. For the first time Mary warmed to him, imagining that as he was now involved in its manipulation he must share her addiction to news.

The real reason would have shocked her. Since arriving in Kenya six years ago Grogan had grown to hate the tune, loathing the superior, portentous tones that seemed to symbolise everything that was out of date about a decaying Empire and the men who ran it. Though you might be the only white man in a thousand miles, the tune's rancid timbre seemed to shout, London was calling and, by God, your calling was still London. Whisky peg anyone? *Stengah?* Mud in your eye. Chin fucking chin.

Didn't they know it was over? Only one thing mattered now and that was a proper withdrawal before the real trouble began. A retreat with honour — if there was any left to salvage. Grogan scowled and Tansy was about to ask what was wrong when the phone rang. Ignore the bloody thing, Paddy said, but Mary told him not to be ridiculous; it might be important.

The office was calling for Grogan. On a Sunday. He took the call in the other room but they could hear his reaction.

'Right, I see. All of them? *Christ* . . . Oh no. When? Any arrests? Who else knows?'

The guests heard the click of the heavy Bakelite receiver. A minute passed before Grogan reappeared, pausing under the lintel of the dining room doorway, his small mouth clenched, quivering with efficiency and suppressed anger. Johnny thought he'd filled out, inflated to appropriate levels. He remembered that look from the war and could almost hear Grogan's old refrain: 'Cometh the hour, cometh the man.' It was intended ironically then, amid the immensity of what they'd witnessed, but the way he seemed to be swelling out now suggested he believed it might have come true. It was certainly Grogan's moment and all eyes locked on to him.

'Bad news,' he said quietly. 'It's the Cunninghams. They've been murdered. *Butchered.*'

'*My God,*' Paddy gasped. 'Can't be. *All* of them? Who would . . . ?'

'The baby?' Mary groaned, putting her napkin to her lips. Tansy and her father looked at each other, aghast.

'Sorry, I must go,' Grogan said. 'You too, Graves. Orders from Nairobi. We'll take my car; we can talk on the way. State of Emergency expected any moment. All leave cancelled. Johnny, stay here until you hear otherwise. Paddy, round up the cattle. Get the dog in. And for God's sake don't let the servants into the house. Tansy, Mary . . . do what Paddy tells you and on no account should any of you leave until you get the all-clear. Got it?'

'Why's this happening?' Mary asked softly. 'What have the Cunninghams ever done to anyone?' She stared at Grogan as if he might actually have an answer.

Grogan exchanged glances with Graves, who was already on the far side of the dining room, retrieving a service revolver and holster from his bag. Johnny was dismayed: he thought he'd seen the last of war but here it was again, waiting at the end of a phone line, its cold instruments coiled and ready inside an ordinary briefcase.

Chapter 4

Nairobi, February 2008

Sam gave herself the once over in the hotel room's wall mirror and took a generous swig of lukewarm minibar vodka and tonic. By some miracle she looked vaguely presentable: air-travel skin cleansed, eyes clear regardless of the noisy, dehydrating air con, tummy unbloated despite poor hotel food. Was she showing too much cleavage? She tugged her neckline higher but it wouldn't stay up. What the hell: she was sure the Ambassador or High Commissioner or whatever he called himself had seen worse.

In retrospect, though, the boots might not have been the best addition. Far too hot for Kenya and slightly tarty, but it had been them or a pair of Doc Martens. Given the rush to pack it was lucky she had anything even halfway smart. The heels gave her another three inches so she was going to tower over all the boring little lawyers. They'd probably love it. Too late, Sam discovered on the plane that she was the only woman on the mission. During the last three days, her new colleagues had presented a uniformly grey face: middle aged and middle class – pale, male and stale, though not so stale they hadn't noticed her. She'd already received one dinner invitation and another suggestion to take adjoining rooms, which earned marks for speed if not class. Sam hoped there might be someone more amusing at the reception. To mark the end of their induction the British High Commission was throwing a final briefing-cum-cocktail party and she was looking forward to escaping the confines of the hotel. In the last few days she'd virtually been a prisoner, forced to attend a succession of meetings in the reception rooms downstairs. There was a garden which she'd wandered around to smoke in, but apart from that and a quick dash to the chemist across the busiest road in Africa, she'd not seen Nairobi at all.

Satisfied with her look, she pressed her mouth on a tissue, scrunching her lips to blot any excess lipstick. She'd bought it at Jomo Kenyatta airport and it was much too glossy. Very African, though. She was ready, but had another quarter of an hour before joining the others for the minibus over to the High Commission. Just time for another drink.

It was the first occasion in days that she'd had any time to herself. It had all been such a hurry. After her mother gave her Johnny's scrapbook she'd spent most of that night delving into the contents, gripped by the pictures and fragments of a life that seemed far away and, despite an unresolved sense of Johnny not fitting in, intensely glamorous. Palm trees and ball gowns versus the February beet harvest. A difficult decision had turned into an obvious one: she could not stay in England a moment longer. She'd taken the early train up to town, heading straight to the British Library to cram some last-minute knowledge of Kenya before her interview. Reading about Africa had provoked the strongest desire to see emerald green plantations and feel the tropical sun prickling on her skin, and she was grateful to Magnus for finding a way for her to escape the grey, frost-heavy skies of England.

So far, Kenya was a bit of a disappointment. The hectic blare of modern Nairobi hardly sat with the vision stirred by Johnny. Hopefully the real version lay outside the capital. At least there'd be no Mau Mau gangs now, loitering about to hamstring any passing animal or panga to death any white settler. They'd all probably been done in by the wicked British, she thought, glancing at the pile of depositions she'd been wading through. And how very wicked they'd been. If these witness statements were to be believed there could hardly have been an innocent European in Kenya alive during the fifties and barely a single unwounded or un-put upon Kikuyu.

Was that too flip? Probably, but gallows humour seemed an appropriate way to deal with the litany of abuse contained in the depositions. For days now she'd been immersed in one horror story after another, trying to cope with what was being described. But she was aware that her levity masked something else too. As she'd been reading through the files it had become clear there might be problems with some of the accounts and, most uncomfortably, these involved allegations made by women. There were difficulties with

57

some of the men's stories too but the most awkward, certainly most consistent, set of discrepancies seemed to revolve around one particular female issue. One that couldn't have been more sensitive.

She picked up an affidavit at random and re-read it. Like all the others, this deposition had been taken a year earlier by lawyers acting for the Kenyan Human Rights Commission. The flat description of what had apparently been done was threadbare, but no less horrific for it.

I, Viginia Munyiri, a resident of Maraigushu Village, Karati sub-location, Naivasha Division, Nakuru District, Rift Valley Province in the Republic of Kenya hereby make oath and state as follows: –

1. THAT I am a Kenyan female adult of sound mind and holder of identity card no. 1872671.
2. THAT I was born in 1936 in Kigumo location, Muranga'a District, Central Province.
3. THAT in May 1953 I was shot in the left hand by a white man nicknamed Kan'eru.
4. THAT my left hand is now paralysed as a result of the shot.
5. THAT I lost consciousness for about two hours.
6. THAT after about 12 hours I was taken to Thika town where the said white man did as follows:

   a)   Shot my little finger which is now disformed (*sic*)
   b)   Inserted a bottle of hot water into my private parts

7. THAT they took me to hospital where I spent about 2 years.
8. THAT what is deponed hereinto is true to the best of my knowledge, information and belief.

Being shot in a police raid or army ambush was one thing, but the casual way the woman had slipped in how she'd been subjected to a form of sexual assault was quite another. When Sam had first read this she'd raced through the other women's depositions to find out if it had happened anywhere else. It had: not only to some women, but many. Sam had been shocked to discover how many claimed to have been raped by white men. But what was more extraordinary, not worse, not better – how could one possibly make that judgement? – were the large numbers who claimed to have been assaulted with a bottle. *A bottle, for Christ's sake.* Army soldiers, Kikuyu Home Guard, white settlers had all been implicated.

But there was just too much repetition and too little detail. Sam could not avoid asking how so many testimonies could be so similar, despite having occurred in different regions – and with anything up to four years between them. She found it horribly easy to believe that men would attack women, but the number and precise nature of so many of the sexual assaults, involving one particular implement, seemed harder to understand.

Though picking apart these women's stories seemed almost a betrayal, Sam had forced herself to put her lawyer's head on, trying to see them as evidence presented in a court case. It was vital to root out falsehoods, because false statements diluted the strength of those allegations that were true.

And if it turned out the allegations had substance, Sam felt it was her duty to make them as public as possible. It was the sort of human rights case she'd dreamed of championing when she'd started out in law, though she doubted the mission saw it that way. In their very first briefing the team had been assured they should proceed with open minds, shouldn't hesitate to call it how it was. But anyone with half a brain could see that one particular verdict would be infinitely more acceptable.

Perhaps she shouldn't be so cynical. The urbane chef de mission, Pugh, seemed like a reasonable human being. And why send so many out here – there were six lawyers in all – if the authorities didn't want to get to the bottom of it? It occurred to Sam that at a time when British soldiers were almost daily being accused of barbarities perpetrated in Iraq, it might even be good PR to confess to some historical wrongs.

She wondered what Johnny would be making of it. Would he have been shocked, or might he have explained it away under the 'war is hell' defence? How much had he actually known? He'd worked in the Information Department after all, at the bloody heart of the establishment. Although that was precisely where she was now, Sam realised: not exactly the best location to practise campaigning human rights law. But surely it didn't matter where you sat – the facts were still the facts. If Kenyans had been abused by the British, the mission had to shout about it. The victims should be compensated, however late in the day. Justice demanded it.

She stared out of the window, allowing the alcohol to ease the tension she'd been feeling all day. The sun was going down and the city appeared washed of colour, smeared in a yellowing light that should have been romantic – the sun setting on a balmy African night. But in the mood she was in, Sam saw the glow for what it was: dust and exhaust fumes produced from endless streams of polluting traffic.

Tomorrow couldn't come soon enough. They were travelling to Nyeri District to start the real investigation. Not only would she finally be seeing the countryside of Johnny's pictures but she'd be able to address some of her doubts by dealing directly with the people who'd sworn the affidavits. They were leaving early so she'd better not drink too much tonight. Although, actually, why not? A bit of light relief amid the gloom.

Someone knocked on the door. Opening it, she was surprised to find Pugh adjusting his tie and fiddling strategically with his cuffs.

'Mind if I come in for a moment?'

He didn't wait for an answer before gliding inside.

'Getting to grips with it all I see,' he said, indicating the pile of depositions on the bed.

'Kind of.'

'Excellent, time spent in reconnaissance is very rarely wasted.' Pugh issued a watery smile and pointed to the drink still in Sam's hand. 'You're aware, of course, that any minibar costs have to be paid yourself?'

'So I guess you'd like one then?'

Pugh smiled properly.

'Thanks. Just a quickie, perhaps. I'll buy you one in return before the mission's over. Somewhere nicer.'

Sam watched Pugh sip his vodka and tonic and could imagine him working the room at a cocktail party. It probably wasn't the first time he'd slipped into a female colleague's bedroom for a drink either. He was very much at ease with himself and his surroundings. In his mid-forties, with fashionably greying temples, his eyes were slightly hooded, conveying an air of assurance and experience. Underneath a certain fussiness, he might be quite attractive. Although, Sam thought, he was so dapper he resembled one of those sleek business travellers in adverts for expensive watches.

'You missed the briefing about tonight's event,' he said. 'Wanted to bring you up to speed.'

'I thought the do was a briefing in itself,' Sam replied. 'Are you saying there are now briefings about briefings?'

Pugh laughed.

'There have been rather a lot, haven't there? And you're right: I don't really need to tell you about tonight. Though there was one thing, actually. Wanted to have a quiet word about it before we left.'

Sam brought her drink up to her lips, conscious there was no liquid left in the glass. Quiet words were never good.

'No need to be anxious,' he said. 'It's just that I had a call from London this morning. As your arrival on the team was so sudden we didn't know much about you beyond your stellar degree and excellent experience. Not to mention your ability to pick up a brief so rapidly.' He smiled again. 'That was quick work, mugging up on Kenya, by the way – very impressive and half the reason I took you on.'

He put the empty tumbler down on the dresser, taking a quick glance at himself in the mirror.

'Seems like you have history in Kenya, Sam. At least your family does. There are likely to be several people from the old days present at tonight's do – H.E. is very keen the mission gets a sense of perspective of what it was like back then. Wants the old crowd to fill us in on what was really what.'

Sam's eyes opened wider. Did that mean people from Johnny's day? How amazing that would be. What if she met someone who'd known him? What if . . .

Pugh's voice became serious and she forced herself to listen properly.

'Look, there might be a problem, Sam. You're going to have to be bloody careful. Not sure how to put this, but apparently your grandfather was not a popular man in these parts. Most records

61

have gone from that period but from what our people can gather, a former Information Officer known as John Seymour was alleged to be responsible for some sort of crime . . . '

Sam shook her head.

'*Crime?* What kind of crime? No one's ever mentioned a *crime* in my family. Where on earth did you get that nonsense from?'

Pugh looked apologetic.

'Powers that be, Sam. Those whose job it is to know these things. They didn't give me the details, I'm afraid. All I know is that it happened towards the end of the conflict and may well have been a little messy – their words, not mine. The point is, some of the veterans being wheeled out this evening might react badly if they find out you are anything to do with him. Thus, for tonight at least, I should be very grateful if you could belong to another Seymour clan – deny all connection . . . I say, are you all right? You look horribly pale.'

'No, no, I'm fine,' she said, suddenly feeling sick. 'Thanks for the warning. I just need to freshen up a bit. Perhaps you should join the others. I'll be down in a minute.'

Pugh approached and for one horrible moment Sam thought he was making a move, but all he did was gently touch her shoulder, patting it in such an avuncular manner she realised she was safe enough for the moment.

'All right? Drinking on an empty stomach after being holed up in a place like this is never a good idea. Come down when you're ready. There's no need to hurry. I'll make the others wait – privilege of rank.'

Sam smiled gratefully, but the moment the door shut behind him her mind crawled over Pugh's news and she knew that vodka had little to do with how she felt. Could Johnny really have been involved in anything 'messy'? Despite the lack of communication at home, she would surely have heard about it. Try as she might Sam could not put the man she'd seen in the scrapbook photographs in the same frame as the victims from the depositions. It was inconceivable that whoever had done such things could be a member of her own family. At the very least Magnus would have hinted at it – wouldn't he?

Not totally convinced by her own logic, Sam put the matter to one side, now more determined than ever to get to the reception. If there were any answers she had a hunch they might lie there. She needed to get a move on. In the bathroom she washed her hands, peering at a reflection that suddenly looked tired. She splashed water on her face.

'Tonight you are not a Seymour,' she said to the mirror, drying her cheeks with a towel.

Oh yes you are, she heard her own answer. And you bloody know it.

And so will they, she thought, strangely pleased with the idea. So will they.

The party was in full swing by the time they arrived, delayed both by Sam and by rigorous checks at the gate. The heightened security had taken Pugh by surprise and he mumbled something uncomplimentary about the Americans and their ability to deal with terrorists.

'Ten years ago,' he said. 'The American Embassy bombings here. Bad business, but because the Yanks couldn't keep the bloody jihadis out we've all had to suffer. Should have handed it over to us – we're quite good at counter-insurgency, as I've no doubt you're learning.'

He'd sat next to Sam at the front of the minibus, squashing her in against the window, and Sam had the impression of being carved off from the herd by the lead male lion. When he pressed his thigh against hers she moved it away smartly. 'Sorry,' he'd said, as if it were the motion of the van. A coward's pass. If he wanted it, at least he should have the courage to declare himself. She ignored whisperings from the back. Let them, she thought. Biggest thrill of their evening.

Pugh stood by her side for the first ten minutes, and as the second chilled white wine began to take effect Sam rediscovered her equanimity, almost happy to have the attention. The room was a symphony of grey and white: grey carpets, off-white walls, grey lamp shades, cream blinds, white lilies, grey ceiling fan. Suits the suits, she thought, seeing her grey team dissolve into the party, becoming indistinguishable from their hosts. There were flashes of colour: purple cummerbunds marking out waiters; an African woman's dazzling headdress; scarlet and blue dresses on the younger European

63

women. And of course, the striking red sash girding Elizabeth in the royal portrait looking down on them from high on the wall. The atmosphere was not raucous, not angry, as she'd seen at some drinks gatherings in London. Not even that festive. Pleasant was probably the word, humming along briskly. Smiles and small-talk, courtesies exchanged, strong views left at the door. Consensus, agility and laughter – the weapons of choice for British diplomats. Not fake exactly, but definitely manufactured.

'I'll just be a sec,' Pugh whispered, waving at a woman in the far corner of the room. 'See you on the other side.'

His place was immediately taken by a young man, no more than twenty-three or twenty-four, deposited with her by an older colleague from the High Commission. He introduced himself as Jules, Third Secretary Commercial. Sam guessed it had been discussed beforehand: you're the nearest in age, you take her. He did his best, and was actually quite amusing, dispensing the questions others had asked before providing his own answers:

'Good flight? *Lovely thanks.* First time here? *Yes it is actually.* Going on safari? *Really hope so.*'

'Very good,' Sam said. 'I see you've done this before.'

'Occasionally.' He was a few inches shorter than Sam, and looked up at her with a smile that threatened to make him quite appealing.

'Do you know all these people?' she asked. 'They don't seem old enough to have been part of the colonial gang.'

'Ah, you mean the veterans of the honourable struggle to keep Kenya safe for the Kenyans. They're just over there – sitting down. Most of them must be in their eighties by now. I'm amazed so many are still around.'

Sam looked over to the far side of the room, where a sofa and some hard-backed chairs held half a dozen or so elderly white men and one woman. Always one, thought Sam.

'Was it that honourable, though?' Sam asked. 'The struggle?'

'Yes, well – isn't that what your lot have come here to find out?'

'Perhaps. But what do you think? What's the view from the exalted heights of the very High Commission?'

'My goodness – talking shop. I'm sure there are rules against that.'

'Aren't you senior enough to know then, Jules, Third Secretary Commercial?'

His smile faltered and Sam could see him struggling to impress her while needing to hold the party line.

'OK, well, if you insist. What I would say is that if, as we all suspect, there had been activities of a less than salubrious nature, then firstly it would have been regrettably normal in a wartime situation, and secondly it would probably be impossible to prove one way or the other so far from the events, as it were. Thirdly, I'm not sure HMG really wants to be paying out unspecified sums for something that happened so long ago, which may or may not provide precedents for Malaya or Cyprus or any of the other colonial difficulties ... Sorry, have I said something funny?'

He'd noticed Sam was smiling and taken it for amusement, not knowing it was how she looked when moving in for the kill.

'You *all suspect*? What do you mean? Suspect what, exactly?'

'Sorry?'

'You said that you all suspect there were activities of – what did you call it? A less than salubrious nature. Why do you all suspect that? And what could possibly be less than salubrious? Come on, Jules, give it up.'

Jules reddened and laughed awkwardly.

'Ah, very good. I see where you're going with this. Look, Ms Seymour ... '

'Oh, Sam, please,' she said sultrily, moving nearer, closing the gap between her and the unfortunate Third Secretary Commercial to breathing distance. Kissing distance. She was rather enjoying this vamp role.

'OK, *Sam*. So there have been reports, papers really, that indicate there may well have been quite a few – well, some anyway – incidents back then.'

'You've seen them, these papers? These reports?'

Jules looked over his shoulder and tried to take a step back but his progress was impeded by a large rubber plant.

'Not exactly, no, just the summaries. Not really a commercial matter. But look, Sam, I'm not sure we should be talking about this. Your team has been provided with all the relevant papers and if you don't know about them maybe it's something you should take up with your people.'

Sam pushed forward again, aware of her breasts lightly brushing

65

his chest, smiling at him from close range. She almost felt sorry for him. He was leaning so far back either he or the plant was about to topple over.

'But I'd much rather take it up with you, Jules. Wouldn't you prefer that?'

'Ah, I see. Well, of course. But I really think—'

'Well, what *I* really think, Jules,' she interrupted, pulling gently on his lapel, 'what *I* think is that you should tell me all about them. It's not as if we're not on the same side here.'

'*Sam – put him down.*'

Sam took a step back, disappointed to see Pugh beside her again. Jules muttered goodbye and slipped past her to safety. For the rest of the night Sam saw him watching where she was, moving away at the slightest hint of an intrusion into his airspace.

'What on earth were you doing?' Pugh laughed. 'Poor boy looked terrified.'

'Just playing,' she said, holding out her glass for a refill. 'By the way, do you know if there is any documentation we haven't seen yet that might support the complainants?'

'Not sure what you mean.'

'Yes you are. Is there?'

'Well,' Pugh said, 'if there is – and I'm not saying there is, or indeed there is not – it wouldn't constitute proof or even supporting evidence. Besides, I'm sure that if any other documents did exist and were relevant they'd be in play.'

He looked at the retreating figure of the Third Secretary Commercial.

'Not sure you should be interrogating the staff, Sam. Not really what we're here for.'

'I thought we were here to find out the truth.'

Pugh smiled thinly.

'Truth's an interesting concept for a lawyer, you know that, Sam. *Assess* is the term I'd prefer. As with any case, we need to assess the strength of the opposition. Strength and truth are not always the same thing . . .'

He broke off, looking over her shoulder.

'Don't turn round, but there's an old boy over there giving you an old-fashioned look and a half.'

Sam did turn and saw a man with a white beard, stooped, leaning on a stick about ten paces away. He was swaying, staring at Sam, his mouth slightly open.

'Nothing old fashioned about it,' Sam said, earning a snort from Pugh. The man gestured at them with his stick and began to limp over.

As he drew nearer Sam was struck by the colour of his skin – a dull burgundy speckled with lighter liver spots. His hair and wildly profuse eyebrows were snow white, giving him the appearance of a louche Father Christmas. He was panting slightly and though supported by the stick it was evident that if age allowed him to uncoil he would be a tall man.

Ignoring Pugh, he lumbered towards Sam, never taking his eyes off her.

'What are you doing here?' he breathed.

'I'm sorry, do I know you?'

The coolness of Sam's tone brought him up short and he stopped, just inches away.

'Name?' he barked, oozing sour wine and tobacco in her face. 'What's your name?'

'Samantha,' she said, issuing her most charming beam while noticing that, close up, the fringes of his snowy beard were stained yellow. 'Sam, if you prefer.'

'Sam who?'

Sam glanced at Pugh, who was slowly shifting his weight from one foot to another, trying not to look pained. He moved his shoulder in front of Sam to face the questioner, cutting her off.

'I'm not sure it's polite to insist on a lady's name,' Pugh said. 'Especially when you haven't introduced yourself.'

Sam had a flashback to Pugh on the minibus. She would not be cut out or shepherded, driven into a bloody pen.

'Seymour,' she said, pushing past Pugh's shoulder with some force and putting out her hand. 'It's Sam Seymour.'

The man looked at Sam's extended arm with shock. For an uncomfortable moment it appeared he might leave it hanging. But he took her hand and Sam felt her palm held in a strong, dry grip.

'Mattingly,' he announced and Sam smiled at the use of the single name, wondering if it was a generational thing or just men in Africa.

She realised she had no idea of Pugh's first name either. Mattingly clicked his fingers without looking round and a waiter appeared with a tray. He swept up a flute of champagne and downed it, replacing it with another before the waiter could move away.

'Does anyone know you're here?'

'Well, the mission does, of course, but anyone else? Don't think so – no. Why do you ask?'

Pugh intervened again, his tone more clipped.

'I'm afraid we have to get going. It's been really nice to meet you, Mattingly, but—'

'Are you two together?' he asked, cutting across Pugh to direct his question at Sam.

Sam laughed.

'No way. We work together.'

'Then why don't you tell him to piss off so you and I can talk?'

'That's not very nice, Mr Mattingly,' Sam said.

He took a sideways look at Pugh before turning his gaze back to Sam.

'You're Johnny's girl, aren't you? Have to be. You look exactly like Tansy. Extraordinary. That bloody smile. Can't be anyone else.'

Sam felt an electric tingle. *Johnny's girl.* He was so old he must be confused about the generations. It didn't matter. Pugh's earlier admonitions were rendered pointless. Mattingly clearly saw the family resemblance, so it was ridiculous to deny it. He seemed incredulous that she should be at the party; could he really still be angry about whatever Johnny had done?

'Come along, Sam,' Pugh said firmly, tugging her elbow. 'I'm afraid it's time to go. Good evening, Mr Mattingly. Sorry we can't stay, long day tomorrow. Off early.'

Sam drew her arm away sharply. If Pugh wanted her to leave he couldn't have said anything more calculated to make her stay.

'No, it's fine, thank you. Why don't you mingle – oh look, that nice-looking *old* woman you were talking to earlier is all on her own.' Pugh raised his eyebrows, too long in the game to cause a fuss. 'You sure?'

'Absolutely. Don't worry – I remember what you said earlier. It's fine.'

'Let's go to the bar,' Mattingly said.

They moved to a long table placed along the wall, where another African waiter dispensed a whisky for him and a wine for her. There was only one chair free but Mattingly declined to take it.

'Prefer to stand – not dead yet.' He raised his glass and tossed the drink back in one, tottering slightly as he held out his glass for another.

'So tell me, *Sam* Seymour, what the hell are you doing with this lot?' There was a faint Midlands burr to his accent. Perhaps that's how you sounded if you stayed in Nairobi long enough.

'I'm a lawyer,' she replied. 'You know – the mission. The one you're meant to be educating us about. Telling us how tough it was in the old days.'

'*Tough?*'

He paused and looked at Sam as if she'd suddenly come into focus.

'Ever seen a man dragged behind a jeep? Skin comes off awfully quick. One moment it's there, the next – smeared all over the road. Doesn't look black when it's in strips. More red really. What about someone being burned alive? A tyre round the neck, fill it with petrol, light it and up she goes. Takes at least five minutes of jumping and running around. They think they invented that little one in the Jo'burg townships but we saw it here first. Nice smell, burning rubber and flesh.'

He paused, eying Sam unsteadily.

'Yes, I suppose you could say it was tough.'

He finished his drink.

'Care for another?'

The cosy protective atmosphere of the party had slid away from Sam and she shivered. So, underneath the smiles and ball gowns, this was her grandfather's generation. No wonder Johnny was never spoken of at home.

'No thanks. Was that what you did then? Burn people alive?'

A wheezing, racking laugh crackled out of the white beard.

'What if I did?'

'Seriously?'

'Long time ago. No one can remember what they did yesterday, let alone fifty years ago.'

'There's no statute of limitations on war crimes, Mr Mattingly.'

'Just as well I was only an Information Officer then. Bystander.'

'Couldn't you have stopped it?' she asked. 'Reported it?'

The laughter returned.

'Of course not. It was war. You didn't check your own side. Not to their faces. Wasn't the done thing at all. You've heard the phrase – "play the white man". Christ, you've got a lot to learn.'

Sam put down her glass. She'd drunk enough and needed something to eat but the idea of food nauseated her. Mattingly had a fresh drink in his hand and Sam wondered how the old bugger could possibly still be standing. She needed to get the facts out of him before he toppled over.

'Was the Information Department where you met Johnny? Did you know him well?'

Mattingly gazed at Sam as if she'd uttered something incredibly stupid. His eyes were beginning to go, one of his pupils intermittently disappearing into the lid.

'Know him? Of course I bloody knew him.' The words were an effort now. 'Everyone knew Johnny. Lucky man, wasn't he? Got his girl. Grogan's girl. Least that's what people thought. Everyone loved her. Beautiful Tansy. Too bloody good for him. Lovely Tansy.'

Mattingly stretched out a hand towards Sam's face and though she recoiled he kept going until he found her cheek, stroking it with the back of two fingers, his eyes filmy with moisture.

'*Tansy, Tansy,*' he whispered. 'He should never have done that. Never have taken you away. So beautiful.'

'All right, old friend. That's enough now.'

Transfixed by Mattingly, Sam had been unaware of the approach of another of the veterans' brigade who now stood at Mattingly's side, gently coaxing the hand away from her face.

'Time to call it a night. Come with me. Esther's here – she can drive you home. Come on.'

The new arrival summoned a woman who'd been standing by the wall. A minute later Mattingly was leaning on the arm of an elderly and anxious-looking African woman. She was short and round and carried her weight with difficulty, rolling along as if she were balancing on a ball. She had a magical effect on her charge, shushing him like a baby as she escorted him to the exit, discreetly going round the side to avoid cutting through the main throng.

'Good woman that Esther,' said the man. 'He's lucky to have her.'

After Mattingly's performance Sam thought it extraordinary that such an unpleasant old drunk would be able to keep hold of any servant. She switched her attention to the man who stared up at her through unfashionable eighties-style glasses. He was much shorter than Mattingly and she looked down on a smooth pink crown lightly covered by wisps of sun-bleached greying hair. His face was round and surprisingly unlined and he wore a broad smile that beamed reassurance and energetic good humour. The thick lenses of his glasses exaggerated two startlingly blue eyes. When they weren't trying to pierce her armour they raked the party, marking out the contours of the room.

'Sorry about that,' he said. 'Mattingly's a good man but he has a weakness for the booze I'm afraid. Problem of the post, as we used to say. Sorry, I haven't introduced myself. I'm—'

'Grogan Littleboy.'

He was exactly like she'd imagined from the scrapbook picture of him standing between Johnny and Tansy at that party, springing to life like a rotund genie conjured from the past. Short, dapper and bustling. Though he must have been in his eighties he didn't look much more than sixty-five, and when he heard his name from Sam's lips he laughed pleasantly, which had the effect of subtracting another few years.

'My goodness they brief you well these days. Yes, Grogan Littleboy. And you, I think, must be some kind of Seymour.'

'I certainly am,' Sam laughed. 'Please call me Sam.'

He held her hand and again Sam was struck by the natural way these older men touched her. The Third Secretary Commercial's grip had been transitory, weak and slightly clammy. Like Mattingly, Grogan's hand was dry and firm, pressing hers for just long enough to be polite – and to convey the power of the person behind. A man used to being in charge.

'I'm sure you've been told this all night,' he said, 'but the similarity really is astounding. I am right in thinking Tansy was your grandmother?'

Sam happily explained where she fitted into the Seymour firmament, warming to Grogan immediately and glad to have found someone relatively normal she could talk to about Johnny. The

71

friendly, open way he was listening suggested he'd be all right with any questions. And before Pugh turned up and tried to shut down conversation again she was determined to find out what had happened to Johnny.

'By the way,' she said casually, slipping it into a gap in the conversation. 'Did you ever hear about any trouble that Johnny might have got into? Something he might have done towards the end?'

'How much do you know about his life?' Grogan countered.

'Not much at all,' Sam said. 'I've been given a few pictures and some bits and pieces in an old scrapbook but they don't really tell me anything significant – about him or his role here. I take it you knew him quite well. I've seen a picture of you together. Tansy was in it too.'

'Tansy *and* Johnny?' A small smile wiped quickly over Grogan's face. 'Must have been at the Nyeri Club. That really was a long time ago.'

'Tell me about it,' Sam pressed. 'I'd love to hear about what you all did back then. From what I've been reading it does sound like a very difficult time.'

'Yes, it was certainly that. You know, few people these days have ever heard of Mau Mau, let alone know what we had to do to fight them. With this legal action brewing, I'm rather worried people back home are going to get a one-sided view. Not sure it would be entirely fair to leave all the history to the losers.'

'Who was it that lost?'

'Mau Mau of course,' Grogan said. 'They didn't get the Brits out – we elected to go at a time of our choosing. And we left the country in good hands. Mau Mau didn't get a look in with post-colonial Kenyan governments. Kenyatta was never really one of them, nor were the current crop. But you don't want a history lesson from an old fool like me,' Grogan laughed, 'you need to see it for yourself – hear from all sides. Isn't that what you're here for?'

'I suppose it is,' said Sam, aware that Grogan hadn't given her the one answer she wanted. Grogan shrugged, raising his palms in appeasement.

'Look,' he said, smiling genially. 'Everything was a lot more complicated then. Can't really be explained over cocktails. But I'd love to tell you more about Johnny and Tansy – just not here. Why don't you come to my house? I can send a driver or tell you how to get there: it's slightly off the beaten track, four or five hours' drive from town. We can have a full and proper discussion about it all.'

Grogan had been polishing his glasses, and he replaced them on his nose with a flourish, pleased with his own suggestion.

'What do you say, Sam? It would give me huge pleasure to have you under my roof. I have to say that when I was asked to come and brief you lawyers, I never imagined I'd be meeting the granddaughter of two of my dearest friends. It would mean an awful lot – do say yes.'

'Well that would be fantastic,' Sam said. 'If you're sure?'

'Of course! Never been surer. We'll do it next week when you know your schedule.' Grogan looked at his watch apologetically. 'But now you'll have to excuse me, it's getting late and I'm afraid I can't seem to stay up as long as I used to. Where are you staying? I'll send a card with the address. Good night, my dear.'

He leant forward and Sam had to dip her head for a peck on the cheek.

'It's wonderful you've made it to Kenya after all these years,' he said quietly. 'Your grandfather would have been so proud to have seen you here.'

Sam watched him march benevolently away around the cocktail drinkers before she moved back into the party to find Pugh. He was scowling, talking to a group of officials from the High Commission. When he saw Sam he broke away and came to her at once.

'Have you heard? There's been a cock-up with the transport. We can't go anywhere tomorrow. No drivers. They claim they were told the day *after* tomorrow, so they've buggered off back to their families. The Commission is insisting we use fully vetted locals so we're stuck in Nairobi for another bloody day. I need a proper drink – shall we go somewhere else? I can buy you the one I promised.'

Over Pugh's shoulder she saw Grogan in the reception hall, waiting for his driver. He'd caught up with Mattingly, who'd broken away from his servant and was lurching about, waving his stick. They seemed to be having a furious argument.

Pugh stepped into her line of sight.

'Well?'

He looked vulpine, ears flat, sniffing the scent of his quarry.

'Don't think so, thanks,' Sam said, annoyed it had even crossed her mind. 'I'm feeling rather tired, to be honest. I might just get a taxi back to the hotel.'

'Suit yourself.'

Pugh's face regained its even demeanour and he loped away with a sidelong grin.

By the time Sam reached the reception hall the two quarrelling veterans had gone. As she waited for her taxi it struck her how Grogan and Mattingly resembled one another. They might have been conjured from a previous era but these old men weren't figures from a history book. Compared to the ranks of suave, suited professionals from her own time these men were fully three-dimensional: greyer of hair and stouter of stomach but also more drunken, more charming, more querulous. In short, more real. *Present* real, not like history at all.

Chapter 5

The Cunningham homestead was typical of the European bungalows studding the Aberdare hills. Cedar and teak, corrugated-iron
roofs, whitewashed walls and verandas looking out over English
gardens. A long drive ending in the kitchen, as settlers liked to say.
The settlers liked to say a lot of things, Johnny had noticed, most of
them banal. What would they have said about what he'd been asked
to take pictures of? Nothing commonplace about that. It was a fucking mess and he wanted to be far away from it.

Grogan had rung the Thompson place the following afternoon,
speaking to Tansy for several minutes before summoning Johnny to
the phone. Grogan had cut straight to it, enquiring if Johnny had his
camera on him.

'Good – this is where you earn your stripes,' he said, sounding
pleased. 'Huge flap on down here. Colony's in shock. Wants answers
and reassurance. That's where we come in: need to show the police
and armed forces working hand in hand to root out the menace – stopping at nothing to apprehend the culprits, turning over every stone.
Get in and out as quick as you can, Johnny. Talk to the Cowboys and
squeeze a quote or two out of the neighbours if they haven't barricaded
themselves in or drowned in their pink gins. Are you up to it?'

Johnny responded dryly that he might just be able to manage.
Truth was, he would be glad to be doing something. Paddy and
Mary had known the Cunninghams well and, ignoring Grogan's
strictures not to leave the house, they'd gone to Nyeri to see what
they could do. Tansy had risen late and immediately occupied
herself with the servants, before wandering down to the crossroads
where the squatter camp lay. Johnny thought it the most foolish thing
possible, but when he tried to raise an objection she'd cut him short.

75

'I'm afraid you know little about Africa and nothing at all about the people who share this land with us.'

He'd hardly seen her since, so when the phone call came it was a relief. Grogan had apologised for having to despatch him but claimed everyone else was up to their eyeballs and Johnny was nearest of them all. Then he'd added a final rider and Johnny had felt the stirrings of unease.

'Try and get into the house and take some pictures of what's happened inside. Unpleasant I know, but it might be extremely useful. You've seen worse. Don't think – just click and go.'

Johnny parked beside the police vehicles and the *garis* – extended, militarised Land Rovers – noticing there was an army lorry too. He thought about turning round and driving back; hang the consequences – but this was not something he could avoid. He retrieved his camera and notebook from the Triumph's pannier and made for the house. A well turned out askari wearing a King's African Rifles slouch hat saluted as he walked up the steps to the veranda.

At the top he recognised the tall figure of Graves. The hunter hailed him, sticking out a hand to crush Johnny's in a shake that could either have been friendly or the opening of hostilities. In his other hand he carried a long bamboo pole, half cane, half swagger stick. He looked at home here, far more comfortable than at the club or Tansy's parents' house.

'Hello, Seymour. Grogan got hold of you then. Thompsons all OK?' Graves spoke softly, with a settler inflection.

'Everyone's fine,' Johnny replied.

Graves nodded, turning to bark an order at an African in Swahili. The man stopped in his tracks, said 'Yes, *bwana*' and ran off in the other direction. Askaris were scouring the lawn while men trooped in and out of the house. Graves was every inch the man of action, directing proceedings with quiet authority. He moved languidly, giving the impression of being ready to spring into a sprint at the drop of a panga.

'Been here long?' Johnny asked.

'Arrived last night. It's bloody ugly in the house. Outside too, for that matter. You sure you want to go in?'

Johnny was very sure he didn't but had no desire to let Grogan down in front of his rival. He noticed Graves had changed into a khaki shirt with braid on the epaulettes. He pointed at them.

'Police or military?'

'Does it matter?' Graves snapped. 'It's all designed with the same end in mind.' He pointed his whip-stick towards the house. 'Be my guest – be good for a backroom boy to see what these vermin actually do in the name of freedom.'

He smiled thinly. 'We can chat later. It's about to get a little hectic here. Some of the squatter-camp nigs are being brought in.'

Johnny turned at the sound of a vehicle approaching. A pickup truck with half a dozen Africans in the back stopped and two Europeans in civilian clothes jumped out and started pulling them down, slapping and kicking until the squatters were all cowering on their haunches at the side of the truck.

'Get them away from the house,' Graves shouted, using his stick to point down the hill. 'This bit doesn't concern you,' he told Johnny over his shoulder, setting off towards them. 'You don't want to know.'

He was right about that and Johnny shivered slightly before picking his way slowly along the veranda. An odour of charred meat and wood smoke snaked out of the house. In the hallway a trunk was on its side, the contents smashed and strewn over the floor. The remnants of what might have been an ostrich egg crunched underfoot. The source of the wood smoke was a blackened settee in the living room. White walls were smudged but the fire hadn't caught. All of the other furniture had been broken or chopped up. A painting of an English thatched cottage was hacked through, the canvas half ripped from its gilt frame. On the floor was a photograph album, individual pictures torn out and scattered randomly. Johnny picked a couple up. One showed a man in shorts and a peaked hat standing in front of a black official saloon car. On the back was some writing: 'Cedric Cunningham, Government Building, Fort Hall 1950.' *Christ* – a district officer. Another picture showed a black and white portrait of a family – the same man in a linen suit, arm round his wife. The woman was blonde, well-built, wearing a headscarf and dark glasses. In front, a smiling ayah held a wrapped bundle with a baby's head peeking out.

Johnny felt sick with dread.

77

A low murmuring of men working stopped when he entered the bedroom. One kneeling, dusting for prints, looked up angrily.

'Who the hell are you?'

As Johnny had swiftly discovered, Grogan's Information Department wasn't universally loved and his answer met the usual growl of disapproval. The deviousness necessary to generate propaganda seemed wrong, un-manly even, a hint of perversion about it. Greasy back-room boys making things up, laughing at the idiots on the front line, never getting their hands dirty.

The man who'd challenged Johnny stood and told the other policemen to take a break. 'Wouldn't want to be interfering with the real work, would we boys?'

While the detectives were in the room Johnny had been able to keep his gaze on them. Now they were gone he was forced to confront what was here.

They were as they'd fallen. The man bent backwards over a chest of drawers, his torso blown open, white bones of his spine visible through dark congealed blood. It was impossible to connect the district officer in the pictures with what he saw now. Johnny put the camera to his eye, shooting pictures of the body from above. Then, instinctively, he knelt near the head for a close-up. Johnny's hands trembled as he depressed the shutter, his right thumb automatically pushing the winding lever, moving the film forward. Shoot, push, refocus. Shoot, push, refocus. It was gloomy in the room and he should have attached the camera bulb but it would have been too fiddly and he didn't think his fingers would stay still long enough. He didn't care if the pictures came out anyway.

He worked in silence. Then, for a second, Johnny forgot where he was, lowering the camera to see where else he should be shooting. With the camera away from his face the room came into a different type of focus and his other senses picked up. The smell was revolting, high meat and rotting faeces. It left a foul metallic tang in his mouth. Cartridge casings littered the floor.

A noise was thrumming out of the man's body. Flies, dozens of them, crawling along his chest and head, some in his nose and eyes. Until now they'd been hidden, their black thoraxes blending in with the darkened blood. Johnny waved his hand violently. The flies buzzed away, some coming straight for his own face. He stood quickly and retched.

It was only then that he really noticed the woman. She'd made it to the bed, legs on the floor, body twisted to one side, one hand up by her head still warding off blows, blonde hair matted and scabbed with dried blood. Her skirt was up by her waist and Johnny couldn't stop his eyes from glancing between her legs. White pants soiled, stockings ripped and stained. Might have stopped them raping her. From the photograph he'd found next door, she'd once been rather lovely. Then Johnny thought: why the fuck am I thinking about this? But he knew why. Bastard Grogan. How dare he put me back like this? *Get out. I must get out.* Her white blouse was black with blood. Johnny put the camera up quickly and squeezed off a few more shots, retching every few seconds. There was meant to be a baby somewhere. He wasn't going to stay and find out.

Outside the detectives looked on as Johnny gulped in clean air and fumbled for a cigarette, flapping at his pockets for a lighter, not finding one, panic rising. The man who'd growled at him inside came over and lit it with his own matches, a peace offering, solidarity established with the viewing of the dead.

'Deep breaths, mate. And thanks for not being sick in there. Bloody awful smell. Poor sods have been lying there for a while. It's fucking horrible the first time but it goes – it will go.'

'Thanks,' Johnny said, managing a half-smile.

But it was a lie. It did not go. One thing Johnny knew for sure was that it never went.

He walked back to his bike, uncertain whether he had the stomach to stick around and get quotes. He was the snapper, the shutter man, not the writer. There were plenty of those in the office and they should have been here, not him.

Down the hill, further along the drive, he could hear voices. A group of Africans sat in a ring on the ground around an acacia tree. Graves was leaning over one of the men; next to him was a youthful KAR officer and some other plain-clothes whites. Reflexively Johnny put the camera to his face and focused, bringing the scene much closer. The officer was very young, no more than eighteen or nineteen. It would be a good portrait. England in defence of eternal values, out in the bush, taking on the evil African perpetrators of unspeakable atrocities. Johnny shot a few pictures and zoomed in on the officer's face. A study in concentration; stern but fair, the very epitome of young justice. Grogan would love it. Suddenly the officer recoiled; he took a step back, disappearing out of frame. Johnny lowered the camera and saw Graves move. Once, twice, his hand darted towards a sitting African's face. From this distance it seemed to Johnny as if Graves was flicking something off the captive's neck. A fly perhaps. Johnny re-engaged with the camera, focusing in quickly on the men, firing off some more shots.

The African had collapsed sideways, his legs twitching. Graves was wiping something on a handkerchief. Johnny zoomed in on the man lying down. There was a thin line across his throat. Through the monochrome viewfinder the blood pooling on the earth looked black. He switched the camera back to Graves and something about the movement prompted Graves to look up. For a second Johnny saw him large in the frame.

Flat, expressionless eyes staring back at him. Johnny Seymour had been marked.

Then it all began to happen at once. The men on the ground, arms tied behind, were scrabbling backwards on their haunches, away from Graves and the body. A rising wailing noise, high-pitched, like nothing Johnny had heard before, rent the air. Three of the men got to their feet and began to run. Two down the hill, one up towards Johnny. Graves and the officer were reaching for their weapons. An askari raised his rifle and fired. One of the men running away fell. The other zig-zagged. By now other soldiers and the young officer were all firing down the hill, the crackle of shots sounding like a fairground contest. White men shouting orders. Frenzied wailing. Then Graves walking without any hurry to the captives who had not run. His pistol out. His pistol to the head of the nearest man, who was pushing his head and shoulders backwards into the earth to avoid the gun. A sharp crack. The man went still. Graves advancing on the others. Three more shots. Three more bodies.

Johnny was paralysed. He knew what he was seeing but could not believe it, the gap between perception and cognition absolute. He raised the camera and depressed the shutter release, reality distanced by the lens; false calm behind the camera.

Picture after picture, no time to focus, no time to frame. And then in the viewfinder, no more than a few yards from where Johnny stood, was the anguished, sweating black face of the captive who was running up the hill. Near the acacia tree, a line of soldiers were pointing their guns in his direction. For some reason the fleeing man was running straight at him. Johnny realised that the moment he went past, the soldiers would open fire. Graves's voice boomed up the hill.

'*Out of the fucking way!*'

Automatically Johnny took out the film and put it in its carton, replacing the roll with a fresh one. Old habits. The camera was on a strap around his neck and he pushed it over his shoulder. There was no choice. He stepped to one side, waited until he was parallel before launching himself into a flying tackle reminiscent of unwelcome days on the rugby field. He grabbed him and there was a sharp pain in his temple as a knee struck his head. But the man went down and Johnny hung on to the legs thrashing in desperation.

Within seconds the struggling ceased as the fugitive was lifted to his feet and an askari's rifle crashed into his face. One of the plain-clothes whites, whom Johnny had seen earlier in the *gari* with the prisoners, pointed his gun towards the bleeding African, finger on the trigger.

'*What the hell* . . .' Johnny shouted, scrambling to his feet. 'That's enough!'

The man glanced at Johnny before moving his pistol to the prisoner's head, point-blank range.

There was no lens between them here, no excuse not to act. Johnny forced himself to take a step forward. The European's eyes moved his way again but the pistol remained pointing at the African.

'Stay back! This Mick's mine.'

'Are you serious? What the hell are you playing at? And who are you anyway?'

The pistol, pointing at the man's ear, did not waver.

'Kenya Regiment. And you are interfering with an officer in the execution of his duty . . . so I suggest *you stay . . . the fuck . . . away.*'

Johnny froze. He'd assumed it was only police and army up here, but of course the settlers and part-timers who made up the Kenya Regiment, the Kenya bloody Cowboys, weren't going to miss this. A white official murdered by Mau Mau – they'd want their pound of flesh. What was he going to do now, kill his prisoner in front of him?

Then Graves's quiet voice at Johnny's flank. He hadn't heard him approach.

'Put it away, Creed. We can take it from here.'

'My Mickey, I think, sir.'

Graves advanced to within a few inches of the KR man, narrowed eyes boring into him.

'All right, Creed, I want you to think very carefully about what's about to happen here. This one stays alive. Do you understand?'

Graves's tone was velvet and compelling, smoothly insinuating into the man's consciousness. Like a snake, Johnny thought. Creed looked uncertainly behind him. Graves's men were all around. Graves raised an eyebrow, cocking his pistol. The man lowered his weapon.

'OK, fine. Keep the fucking wog. It'd be a waste of a bullet anyway.'

He strode back down the hill towards his companion in the truck.

'Good choice, my friend,' Graves said softly, holstering his own pistol.

He ordered a police sergeant to lock the prisoner inside one of the *garis* before turning his attention to Johnny, who was trying to light another cigarette.

'That was a fine tackle, Seymour. You should try out for the Tuskers.'

The tension had eased but Johnny was still in shock. He realised he should say nothing, hop on his bike and ride back to Nairobi. Get a drink; get ten drinks. Let Grogan sort it out. But he couldn't stop himself.

'For fuck's sake, Graves! There was no need for any of that. *Christ, man.*'

'Is there a problem?'

'They were tied up, for God's sake – they weren't going anywhere. You didn't have to bloody *shoot* them. That's not war, that's . . . '

Graves cut him off.

'Yes, that's what? Go on.'

Johnny's lips open and closed, goldfishing, searching for a word to describe what he'd seen. Nothing came out. Graves sneered angrily.

'I don't know who gave you the right to fucking lecture me. You know nothing about how this works. Any of it. These are not ants we're slapping, Seymour, and it's about to get worse, a lot fucking worse. So you'd better be bloody sure about your facts before you say any more.'

Johnny looked down, unable to keep eye contact with the older man. Graves was seething.

'Still don't get it? Then come with me.'

Johnny shook his head.

'No bloody way.'

He began to walk away, but before he was aware of Graves even having moved, the policeman slid in front of him.

'It's not a request man. We're not at a fancy club now. You asked about these,' he said, pointing at his epaulettes. 'Means you do what I say. Take orders like the rest of us. So shift your arse and follow me.' He tried to soften his tone but it only evolved into satin menace. 'It really would be in your interests. You need to see something. Get your camera ready.'

Graves took Johnny's arm in an iron grip just above the elbow and steered him, making for the side of the house before turning away across the lawn. Halfway across Graves stopped and stood in front of him, holding his bamboo stick out at arm's length. For a moment the cane hovered over Johnny's stomach while Graves stared at him. Then it began to flick from side to side, up along the buttons of his shirt towards his face. It did not hurt but the effect was shocking, Johnny's skin become an animal hide prepared for flensing. A touch of whip here, a mark there; the cane crept up until it was parallel with his eyes.

'You weren't taking my picture back there were you?' Graves asked casually, the cane dancing in front of Johnny's face.

'No.'

The tip quivered. It would be a second's work for Graves to turn the flick into a cut, take his eye out. Johnny blinked and backed away but the tip moved too, maintaining the same distance.

'Just using the telephoto to see who was down there,' Johnny added. 'No photographs.'

'Certain?'

'Of course.'

'Then you won't mind giving me the film in your camera.'

'No problem, Graves. We're on the same side here.'

Graves looked at him for several long seconds before slowly nodding and finally lowering his stick.

'Good. I want to trust you, Johnny,' Graves said. 'Any friend of Tansy's is a friend of mine. And anyone who can bring down one of the nigs without a gun has my respect. Keep your film. But if by some accident you were taking my picture and it ever found its way into the public domain ...' Graves paused and stared, unblinking, at Johnny. 'Well, as this is an Emergency, Emergency rules would apply. It might be argued you were giving succour to the enemy and I would be obliged to regard you in a certain light. I would have, well, certain thoughts. So, are we clear on this?'

Graves was near enough for Johnny to feel sour breath on his face.

'Yes, there's nothing to worry about.'

'Oh, I know that. Just wanted you to know where you stood.'

Graves continued to lead Johnny across the lawn.

'If you're going to survive the war we've undoubtedly found ourselves in, you're going to have to wrap your handsome little head around a few realities. You want to understand why we do things differently out here? Why a smile and a pat on the Kyuke's back aren't going to work? Because *they're* fucking different – that's why. Take a good long look, Johnny boy, see what these Mickeys can do.'

They'd stopped at a flower bed. A typical English flower bed: roses at the back, petunias and well-tended perennials at the front, to one side a jumble of climbers twining up sharpened bamboo staves. Mrs Cunningham must have had green fingers. They might have been in Surrey or Kent; might have been standing in the cottage garden of the house in the picture he'd seen earlier, slashed and hanging out of its frame.

But he wasn't in Surrey or Kent because in the English Home Counties you did not find a baby's head stuck on a sharpened stick next to the clematis.

'Why don't you take a photograph of that?'

Johnny felt as if someone had punched the air out of him. He couldn't look, couldn't look away.

'Pretty isn't it? It's what those animals do.'

Johnny had a desperate urge to run, anywhere. Escape.

'Go on man – take a bloody picture,' Graves hissed. 'People have to see what we're up against. That's your job, isn't it?'

84

Slowly Johnny raised his camera, snapping the shutter four or five times from chest height. It was enough for Graves who took him by the arm again, marching quickly and furiously.

'Make sure they see those when you get back. Especially Grogan.'

Johnny tried to pull free but Graves restrained him easily. '*Woah* boy – where're you going? We're not finished yet. More to see Johnny, more to understand.'

Johnny walked alongside him in a daze as the policeman led him past the house and down the hill to the acacia tree. The bodies of the prisoners lay where they had been killed.

'Open your eyes and look properly for once.' Graves used his bamboo stick to point at one of the corpses, a young African man, blue serge shirt open to the waist, dirty fawn trousers. It was a dead body, Johnny had seen those before. He shrugged at Graves, not trusting his voice.

'The shoes, man. Look at the bloody shoes.'

They were Church's by the look of them, a pair of newish English brogues. In good condition, they probably cost around thirty pounds, the best part of a year's salary for an African. They didn't fit and the African's sockless heel had half come out of the shoe; it was raw from rubbing.

Graves pointed to the next body.

'And him.'

This one wore a woman's necklace, a string of what looked like rubies. The dead men were Mickeys – Mickey Mouse. MM. Mau Mau.

Graves put his head even closer to Johnny's, almost spitting in his ear.

'You make me sick. How dare you presume to judge what I do to protect you and your little lily-white friends? Do you really think I'm going to let baby-killers and murderers have even half a chance of running?

'And if I did, where do you think they'd run to? I'll tell you where – to your fucking house, that's where.'

Chapter 6

Nairobi, March 2008

Sam's plans to do very little on her unexpected day off lasted as far
as the lie-in and a long bath. By the time she was downstairs it was
past eleven and she'd missed breakfast. She wasn't hungry; she felt
curiously energised by last night's encounters with the old guard and
was looking forward to exploring this city where the past merged
into the present. Pugh and the others had scuttled away so she was
very much on her own. In truth, she preferred it that way; she was
used to amusing herself. Surveying her tourist options, Sam decided
to give the Snake Park a swerve but thought the Nairobi National
Museum looked interesting, even for someone not exactly into fos-
sils. She'd seen enough of them last night. In the afternoon she would
enjoy a bit of animal-watching at the safari park. It was a good idea
and it kept her buoyant for the entire three minutes it took to get a
map from reception and make her way to the doors.

'Miss Seymour? Miss Samantha?'

The voice was deep and African, and Sam was surprised to see it
coming out of the tiny woman who'd appeared at the party last night
to whisk away the drunken Mattingly. It was his servant with the old
biblical name – Esther. She was resting her round form against a
wall as if she'd been waiting.

'Can I help?' Sam asked.

Esther must have been in her seventies and she approached slowly,
listing and rolling on the balls of her feet in the exaggerated gait of a
sailor on shore leave.

'Excuse me, Miss Sam, excuse me,' she said breathlessly. 'Did you
not get the message?'

'No, sorry.'

Esther was taken aback. She herself had delivered it *in person* on the telephone to a nice young lady on reception at seven this very morning.

'Joseph is so ashamed,' Esther said. 'He wants you to come to the house. Today. For a talk.'

'Joseph?'

'Yes, yes – you were speaking to him last night. Joseph Mattingly.'

Sam's heart sank. This was not at all what she had in mind for her day. She was looking forward to seeing the other veteran, Grogan, again next week. But a talk with Mattingly was hardly enticing. Besides, she'd had the distinct impression he was angry with her for something Johnny might have done.

'Well, that is kind,' Sam said. 'But I'm afraid I was just on my way out.'

Esther took hold of her arm.

'Please, Sam. We do not get many visitors. It would mean so much to him. Just for a short time.'

Sam walked on but Esther kept pace. Mattingly had been up most of the night, Esther explained, worrying he'd been rude, knowing he'd drunk too much. He used to drink in the old days but for years he'd resisted. This business of the past coming back had not been healthy.

'Last night – all those faces. And *that man* being there. Then you – you he was not expecting to see and yet of all the people you were the one he would most liked to have spoken to properly – and when he did he ruined it . . . he is so unhappy . . . oh dear.'

Esther took out a tissue and dabbed an eye.

'Please,' she implored, 'it will only be for an hour or two at most – he gets very tired these days. Afterwards I will drive you wherever you want to go. What do you say?'

What could she say? Ten minutes later Sam was clinging on to a seat belt that wouldn't buckle, pinned to her seat as the African woman took off at speed, slewing through the capital's traffic, hand on horn, cursing her fellow drivers while peppering Sam with questions about her family and her life.

'Not married? No boyfriend?' Esther tut-tutted. It was not right that someone of Sam's beauty and status was still single. A lawyer would be a fine catch for any man. Perhaps she would meet someone here.

Sam answered tersely, still annoyed that her day had been hijacked. But Esther cackled and laughed, answering her own questions, her short arms flailing and slipping round the wheel as if it were covered in grease. Sam tried not to look as the car veered onto the pavement or swerved to within a paint-thickness of other vehicles. Esther didn't notice, continuing to hoot and snort, her small head only just poking above the dashboard.

Forty minutes later an ashen Sam was deposited at a whitewashed building in a nondescript suburb while Esther found somewhere to park. Mattingly must have been watching as he opened the door immediately, sheepishly ushering her in.

The house was small with bright light streaming in from a pair of rear doors opening onto a courtyard. On a teak table outside, a polished silver jug that would have sat well in an English country house steamed with fresh coffee, the aroma mingling sweetly with a scented mass of fleshy, white gardenias tumbling over a low garden wall.

'So glad you could come,' Mattingly said. 'I had rather feared you wouldn't. Terribly sorry about last night. Not really myself. Not every day you bump into a ghost.'

Mattingly had made an effort. He'd combed his beard, his short-sleeved white shirt was newly pressed and his blue cotton trousers had a smart crease down the front. Sitting opposite Sam, he seemed more in control of himself, and not having to lean on a stick made him appear stronger. His face was less ruddy and his gaze was steady, though his hands trembled as he poured the coffee.

They managed some stilted small-talk but it was clear Mattingly – Sam found it impossible to think of him as a Joseph – was waiting for Esther. Thankfully she appeared a few minutes later and he brightened.

'Did you find somewhere safe to park?'

She came to sit with them, making a clicking noise with her tongue that suggested the question was unworthy. Mattingly smiled at Sam.

'As you no doubt discovered, my wife drives like a fiend, but I can tell you she parks even worse – like the very devil. Never seen anyone with so little regard for the division between road and pavement.'

Sam sat up.

'Your wife? You're married?'

'That's usually the tie that binds one to a spouse.'

Sam felt her cheeks reddening.

'Of course. I thought . . . '

'We were merely cohabitating? Living in sin? Frightfully modern of you, Sam.' He put his hand on Esther's shoulder. 'Actually, perhaps not that modern – reminds me how people reacted when we announced our engagement. Long time ago, thank God. Fifty years, to be precise.'

He paused before smiling brightly.

'Anyway. Happier times! It's our anniversary in June. Never a cross word.'

Esther picked a nut from a bowl, narrowing her eyes at her husband before unleashing a torrent of Swahili at him.

He laughed and stroked her arm fondly, saying something back which made her smile. Through the prism of their delight in each other's company Sam saw how they might have been when they were younger, and also what they really looked like now, the stereotypes of drunk and servant banished to her own shameful hall of embarrassment. On the way through the house she'd seen a couple of framed pictures showing the couple from a few years ago, a beardless Mattingly next to a handsome, beaming Esther. No children. But after her crass error Sam wasn't going to ask about that.

'Now,' said Mattingly, pouring Sam another coffee. 'You had some questions last night which I don't think I answered well. Sorry, there were a lot of people there I hadn't seen for a long time. Strange to be so forcefully reminded of a period we've all been trying to forget. So now, if there's anything you'd like to know that could help, Esther and I would be happy to try and fill you in.'

Mattingly watched Sam carefully. She was sitting perfectly still except for a forefinger which flicked against her thumbnail. Again he marvelled at the likeness. This morning, in the early hours, he'd come to consciousness thinking of Tansy. Couldn't shift her from his mind. He'd no clear recollection of the evening before but woke with the strongest of feelings, the direct opposite of foreboding. He hadn't thought of her like that in years.

Sam wasn't nervous but she was hesitant. There were a dozen things she wanted to know, but where to start? If Mattingly really had seen what he'd claimed, he would be invaluable. As a European his testimony would surely be worth more than ... She stopped, glancing at Esther. More than a black voice? Another stupid assumption and she regretted it immediately, conscious she was turning into a version of what some white South Africans were still like: wrapped in a rancid cloth of colour and race.

'My grandparents,' Sam said. 'Tansy and Johnny. What were they like? You said you knew them?'

Mattingly nodded slowly.

'We weren't what you'd call friends, Johnny and me. Not at the start. I knew Tansy first, everyone did. She was so natural, a force of nature. Kind too. The nurse with the voice. Sang beautifully – did you know that? Took some courage to stand up and sing in front of a lot of squaddies. "Curves and nerves," they used to say! As for Johnny, he was more difficult – to know, that is. Shy, you might say. Towards the start he had to deal with the aftermath of a really nasty murder. An entire family killed by Mau Mau. Turned him. When he came back he was very concerned about some pictures he'd had to take. Horrific stuff, apparently. We all knew he'd had a bad time during the last war but whatever he saw up there changed him. Soon after he took off with some others. Went into the bush for months. Then later on, whatever he did or didn't do— So sad. He could have ... '

Mattingly's voice faltered and Esther took over.

'Perhaps there was something specific we could help you with,' she said. 'Regarding these cases you're investigating.'

A number of different thoughts occurred to Sam. Given his position in the Information Department, was Mattingly someone she could trust to tell the truth? Similarly, was Esther someone to have any confidence in after she'd turned her coat to marry a member of what was then the oppressing elite? Or, on the contrary, was it *more* likely they'd tell the truth because they'd both presumably endured the hostility of their own tribes to be together?

She decided to test them – Esther in particular.

'Perhaps there is,' Sam said. 'Something's been bothering me about quite a few of the cases of alleged abuses against women. It's quite sensitive, I'm afraid.'

Esther nodded and Mattingly inhaled deeply, closing his eyes.

Sam took it for assent and spent several minutes describing the difficulties she was having with some of the testimony. As she said it aloud, it seemed to Sam that she was answering her own question. How could so many women have been intimately assaulted with the same implement? It really was not credible. So was it organised? Were the witnesses being led? Worse than led – conspired with? She inspected Esther carefully for her reaction but beyond the merest hint of a flinch at the word bottle she betrayed nothing, her dark eyes fixed on Sam's.

'So what I need to know,' Sam summed up, 'is whether it's remotely possible that these things were done to women or . . . '

'Or whether they are making it up?' Mattingly pursed his mouth, hiding it behind his beard. 'What do you think, Sam? What's your experience in these matters? You've been here – what? – a week, is it? Learned enough to believe that when the natives need a bit of cash they are happy to lie about what was put up their—'

'*Joseph!*' Esther slammed her hand down on the table, making the discarded nutshells jump into the air.

'This is a reasonable question and it will be dealt with reasonably.'

She shook her head despairingly at Sam and Sam recognised the universal expression that said in a flash: 'Men are crass, men are boorish. But we love them anyway and I love this one particularly so please forgive him.'

'But it's true,' Mattingly protested. 'How can she possibly ask that?'

'Joseph, I am taking Sam now. These are matters better discussed elsewhere. The place we talked about. Sam – please come. There is something you need to see.'

There was little in her tone that brooked dissent. While Esther went ahead to fetch the car, Mattingly limped into the living room to pick up an envelope.

'I'm sorry,' he said over his shoulder. 'Esther scolds me for being too protective. I try not to be but I can't help it. You can deal with things if they happen to others, to strangers, but it's almost impossible if you love them.'

'Here,' he said. 'You need to see this as well. Open it later – it's self-explanatory. And please, Sam, do not tell anyone where you got this from. Use it but – do they still say this? – never betray your sources. Truth is, I live off a government pension. It's not much but it's all we have; can't afford to lose it. I know I'm not being very brave but my time for that passed a long time ago. You'll find Esther is much braver.'

He handed Sam the large white envelope. His eyes had taken on the filmy surface Sam remembered from the previous night and she half feared he was going to cry.

'We have not spoken enough of your grandparents. Johnny would be, would have been, very proud of you. He was very concerned about the sort of things you are looking into. Please ring me after you return to Nairobi. The number's on the back – you'd better destroy it when you get to the hotel. There are still people around today who would react badly if they knew what I'm giving you.'

He gave Sam a meaningful stare.

'What are you saying?' Sam said. 'We all know this is important, but surely you're not suggesting anyone is going to try and stop the truth getting out? I'd like to see them try.'

Esther was outside, the car half on the pavement, beeping the horn.

'Look,' Mattingly said, taking hold of her forearm, surprisingly strong fingers wrapping tight around her flesh. 'This is not a game. Far from it. It may all seem a long time ago to you but if this unravels it's going to be bloody serious. You have to be careful. Some people alive today have got a lot to lose, and they won't mind how they protect it. I trust you with this because of your grandparents. Once you have read it and I know you understand we can talk further – about Johnny, about everything. Meanwhile Esther will answer your questions in her own way. Be gentle with her. I love her so much. It was not easy for her. *Is* not easy. Remember that.'

'And if Grogan Littleboy contacts you,' Mattingly went on, 'you have not seen me. Do you understand? We have not met.'

'Grogan? But I thought he was Johnny's friend.'

'Did you?' Mattingly shook his head sadly. 'Grogan likes everyone at the beginning. And everyone likes him. Just use your instincts, Sam. There's so much you're not aware of yet.'

Sam suddenly felt very young and out of her depth. She smiled meekly, earning a last squeeze from Mattingly before he retreated inside.

As Esther hit the accelerator and the car careened away Sam looked back and saw Mattingly at the window. He was smiling and she could have sworn he had raised his fist in farewell; not aggressively, but clenched near the side of his head in the old salute of comrades through the ages.

Chapter 7

Nairobi, December 1952

When Grogan rode in the back of the Austin he always wore his cap. Most of the officers Macharia ferried between government buildings in Nairobi took them off, glad to use the privacy of the car to relax and wipe a perspiring forehead. All whites sweated, except Grogan, who seemed unperturbed by the heat, sitting in the back of the car with the windows wound up. Macharia had not yet fathomed his passenger. He knew him to be important, recognising this was an opinion certainly shared by the man himself. The moment he had swapped civilian clothes for khaki, Grogan's body had stiffened, as if the new outfit impressed a military bearing through its very fabric. Other drivers laughed at the diminutive *muzungu* with his perfectly pressed short trousers, joking that it was all for show, his military regalia designed to impress bystanders as he swept from meeting to meeting. But Macharia knew it was ludicrous to imagine he was preening for the public. The Emergency might only be a few months old, but the capital was already full of uniforms. The reality was Grogan was truly dedicated, and from Macharia there could be no greater compliment.

Macharia turned the Austin into a government-only parking space behind the Ngong Road, two minutes' walk from the Law Courts. The Information Department had started life as a tin shack on the top of the court building, but thanks to some smart moves by the new director, they were now situated in spacious rooms in the old library opposite.

In the back of the car Grogan was finishing a conversation with his fellow passenger, one of the cohort of linen-suited young men streaming into the capital on the coat-tails of the military. At first they'd all looked too similar to distinguish, but Macharia was beginning to notice the small differences among the European tribes. By the shininess of his briefcase and the excessive mopping of his forehead, it was clear this one was new to the country. Macharia surmised he must be a reporter as he was taking notes using strange symbols instead of letters. Shorthand, the Information Officer Mattingly had called it. A code for journalists and secretaries.

He could see the notebook balanced on the reporter's knee. It was a major part of Macharia's assignment to find out what his passengers were doing, and he'd devised a way to adjust the side mirror so that a casual glance would reveal everything that was going on in the back. He'd learned the hard way not to use the main driver's mirror when another passenger, the one they called the Zebra, had caught him looking.

'Keep your fucking eyes to yourself, boy,' the white officer had snarled, using his cane to poke him hard in the back of the neck. It had been a shocking blow, not for the pain but as a reminder he was not as invisible to the *wazungu* as he believed. Usually days could pass before a white man or woman acknowledged his presence. Only the younger one, Johnny Seymour, the man whose white hair stuck up on his head like the crest of a crane, regularly said hello.

Of all the whites, Graves was the one Macharia least enjoyed transporting. He leached threat as others might smell of body odour or fear, and when Macharia informed his superiors that the Zebra often rode in his car they'd been alarmed, warning Macharia to be especially careful. They knew of him and what he could do. It would be wise not to arouse this man's suspicions.

As it happened, the Zebra had not been in the car for some weeks. Guerrilla activity was increasing both in the city and out in the Aberdares and the British were responding, bustling around Nairobi, attending more meetings, talking urgently behind their papers. From overheard snippets Macharia understood the Zebra was away, at the forefront of 'intelligence gathering' and not likely to be back soon. He was glad. It seemed hotter in the car when Graves rode in it.

The reporter put his notebook away. Grogan was still talking, not allowing the man to escape.

'And the last sitrep is at nine to coincide with evening deadlines in London. If you need anything at all come and see me or one of my chaps. You know where we are now.'

95

The man nodded, muttered thanks and jerked the door open, glad to get out. Grogan wound down the window.

'Don't forget, Adams, it gets dark at six precisely. Make sure you're safely squared away by then. Some of the crazies come out at night so you really don't want to go wandering off. Impossible to find your way around after lights out here. Isn't that so, Macharia?'

'Yes, *bwana*. Six o'clock sharp. African night comes very soon. Very fast.'

As Grogan waved a curt farewell to the reporter, Macharia realised he had just made a bad mistake. It was his abiding fear that a stray remark would give away how educated he really was. Whites feared Africans with learning, suspecting an education led logically to sympathy with independence. They were probably right about that but Macharia knew he'd played the role of innocent, smiling driver boy well. His mistake lay not in the way he had spoken but the readiness of his answer. Unless he'd been listening to Grogan's conversation how could he have known what was being said? It was a serious error. He loosened the collar of his shirt and risked another glimpse in the side mirror. Grogan was still staring into the back of his head. Macharia tapped the steering wheel nonchalantly, the hairs on his neck tingling.

There were at least a couple of hours before Grogan emerged from the evening situation report. The driver's duty was to stay with the car, ready to leave at a moment's notice. After what happened earlier, Macharia needed to be especially responsive to Grogan's needs. But he had missed several rendezvous already and his superiors in the Movement would be getting nervous. Macharia was a link in a chain of Mau Mau operatives. Because he had more freedom than many Kikuyu in British service, he'd been entrusted with a postman's role, delivering notes all over town. He seemed to be invisible to all whites – except the Zebra – and this worked in his favour. No one noticed the smart young man with white shirt and tie wandering among them, casually leaving a newspaper at the barber's, leaning against the wall next to the cinema, strolling into the Information Department. No one batted an eyelid as the handsome new driver stood by the filing cabinet, fiddling with the stapling machine while his long fingers secreted a message inside page four of *Baraza*.

The shoe shop where Macharia received these messages was not far from where he'd parked, and although it was dark he knew the way blindfolded. It would be risky. Security forces seemed to be everywhere, stopping every black face, demanding to see passbooks, the *kipande* that all Africans were now obliged to carry. But if it was bad in the capital, it was even worse on the reserves. Rumours reaching Nairobi were scarcely credible: men arrested without reason, tied to jeeps and dragged behind, flogged and beaten by traitorous so-called loyalist Kikuyu from the new Home Guard.

As he passed a sign warning whites that the area was out of bounds, Macharia thought about the danger to his brother, Gatimu. Skilled men, especially mechanics like Gatimu, had been among the first to be rounded up, suspected of being quartermasters for the forest fighters. Mau Mau didn't have many guns yet and so had to arm themselves with homemade weapons, rifles from bicycle tubes forged in covert metal shops. Was his brother one of these armourers? Macharia hadn't seen him for over a year but knew in his heart it must be so. Despite the peril it would bring, he was pleased at the idea.

Macharia paused in an alleyway as a patrol of soldiers marched past. There was no formal curfew yet, but any African seen out after dark was liable to be picked up. He didn't mind the soldiers so much; they were dull with their questioning and his knowledge of the back streets and secret alleys meant he could probably outrun them. It was the Kenya Police who knew Nairobi as well as he did that Macharia feared. If you fell into their hands, it would get ugly very fast.

As he waited for the soldiers to disappear, he reflected on how extraordinary it would have seemed to his younger self to be here now, skulking among the city's shadows, carrying messages that could have him shot on the spot. It had been a long journey, but not inevitable.

The day it began he and Gatimu had skipped school to see Jomo Kenyatta at the famous meeting in Njoro. Hearing the leader in exile had returned and was performing oratorical wonders, the brothers walked for hours to a nondescript field where a crude stage of planks on oil drums had been erected. Wriggling their way to the front, they'd been yards away from the great man, watching in awe as he mesmerised the crowd with his rich, deep voice. His baggy brown

97

leather jacket had looked enormous in silhouette against the setting sun, but it was his words that provided protection from the evening chill. Macharia and Gatimu had looked at each other in amazement: it was the first time they'd ever heard anyone speak about things as they really were. About what needed to be done.

The white men had arrived in Kenya as strangers, Kenyatta boomed, and Kenyans had looked after them as guests. Fed them, housed them, even carried them on their backs. Now these guests claimed the land belonged to them. When Africans had joined British armies to fight and die in their war in Europe, they'd been promised land and freedom. But on returning they'd found villages burned, land confiscated and people forced onto worthless reservations. Despite this, Europeans had nothing to fear from an African government. But first, Kenyatta cried, pointing his carved walking stick into the air, guests had to learn to behave like guests and give the house back to its rightful owner.

Macharia and Gatimu had both been captivated by the moment, the roar of the crowd throwing a mantle round their shoulders, cloaking them in the joy of revolt. Who would not have dedicated themselves to the struggle on the spot? Macharia knew the course to take. Everything he'd learned from the Europeans' own history showed how change could be wrought peacefully by ordinary men and women, through the ballot box, through demonstration and argument. And while Gatimu was frustrated not to be involved in something immediate, Macharia returned elated from seeing Kenyatta. Teaching could wait; he would earn a living by selling his labour like most Kikuyu while he dedicated himself to the struggle, employing the same methods as the great British reformers: arguing, discussing, reading and learning.

But the democratic path was not open to black Africans. Kenyatta was taken into custody, African organisations declared illegal, arrests followed arrests; many of Macharia's schoolfriends disappeared. A line was drawn. Families were divided, between those prepared to take the next step and those who bartered favours from the British by proving their loyalty. Men hounded in the reserves melted into the freedom of the forest. Old soldiers who'd served in the British forces passed on their training to hundreds of new African recruits. *Mau Mau.*

Still Macharia prevaricated. He was cautious by nature. A career in education beckoned; a non-violent approach surely still had to be an option. And although he declared he had no time for such matters, there was even a girl, the niece of a neighbour, who was said to look favourably on him. There was, in short, a life to be led that might be comfortable, might even lead to a certain prosperity and standing.

But while Macharia dithered, Gatimu had known how to act, secretly joining the Movement. It was only after their favourite uncle was arrested, dragged off in front of his wives to be beaten and questioned by the new Kikuyu Home Guard, that Macharia allowed himself to be persuaded. Gatimu was right – no one was safe. The armed road was all there was. That night Gatimu led his younger brother through the sacred banana-stem arch to take the Mau Mau oath.

Now here they both were, dedicated to overthrowing the white rulers. Macharia in his European tie and collar, driving the white elite to meetings that plotted his people's destruction; Gatimu hammering out weapons on the anvil of revolution, producing the only thing the British would now listen to. Who was making the greater contribution? Macharia knew the messages he delivered were important, but he yearned to do more. If he could not manufacture guns, at least he should be allowed to use them.

As the British patrol passed by Macharia realised it was foolish to think like that. The Movement had earmarked him for something higher and that moment was coming soon. The British were planning a new offensive and he'd been ordered to bide his time and collect every scrap of intelligence. When this stage was over, there would be a job in the forest for a man of his capabilities. For now, stay patient. Maintain vigilance. Deliver the messages.

Macharia eased slowly out from the alley, turning down a minor road running parallel to Victoria Street. It was darker here. Away from the main shopping areas, there were fewer street lights and many had no bulbs; those that did sputtered a baleful yellow glare that was easy to avoid. If he kept to the shade he should be all right. The shoe shop was near, only a couple of streets away.

'*Stand still!*'

The voice came from behind. Macharia's heart dropped into his stomach. He didn't glance round, increasing his pace in the hope they might be addressing someone else.

'You there! Stand still or we will shoot. Hands in the air. *Now!*'

The metallic click of weapons being made ready echoed through the night. Macharia put his hands up, his lungs pumping as if he'd run a mile. He cursed himself for his stupidity. He had kept watch ahead but forgotten the most basic rule of all, to make sure he wasn't being followed. He heard footsteps running towards him. *Concentrate,* he told himself, the messages you carry are verbal. Just thank Ngai they didn't catch you on the way back.

'What have we got here?'

A white man with a tie too wide for his lapels had taken off a panama hat. He stroked its brim as he circled his captive. By his side were two askaris, their rifles pointed casually at him. Another man was standing behind, his breath close to Macharia's ear.

'Why were you running, boy?'

'Not running, sir, merely hurrying, sir.'

The man with the hat moved his head to one side and looked incredulously at Macharia.

'I'm sorry? Did you say *merely?* I could have sworn you said *merely.* Merely fucking what?'

Macharia smiled his widest *yes-bwana* smile.

'Yes, sir. Not running. Just hurryi—'

The man nodded and Macharia was suddenly on the ground, his words hovering as the askari behind him smashed a rifle butt into the back of his leg. Macharia gasped, putting his arms out on the pavement to steady himself. It was the wrong thing to do. Still stroking the brim of his panama, the white man placed his black leather brogue on Macharia's left hand and transferred all his weight onto it, swivelling the toe slightly as if he were grinding out a cigarette.

The pain from the blow to his leg was just coming through but the sheer agony of his knuckle popping made Macharia howl. The man bent down, putting his face to Macharia's.

'You don't fucking run from me, boy. And don't ever make jokes. Now stand up and give me your *kipande.* Chop chop, no funnee-funnee.'

Macharia stood, slowly handing over his *kipande* with his good hand. The man took a cursory look at the papers but seemed uninterested. He flicked Macharia's tie.

'Why are you wearing this, sambo? Did you steal it? You think you're important, is that it? Too fucking important to stop and chat with the likes of me?'

'But, sir, I work for *Bwana* Littleboy. Grogan Littleboy, sir. He demands that I look smart, sir.'

Grogan's name had an effect, pushing the man's eyebrows up into an exaggerated arch on his forehead.

'The director of the Information Department? You work for him – that what you're telling me?'

'Yes, sir. I am his driver, sir.'

The man took a few steps to the side, examining Macharia from a new angle, looking down at the photograph in the *kipande*.

'If that is so,' he said, putting his face close to Macharia's ear before suddenly screaming. 'Then what the *fuck* are you doing here and not waiting by his car?'

Macharia remained silent. Anything he said would make it worse. He held his damaged hand, feeling it swell agonisingly under his fingers. The man put the panama triumphantly onto his head, pushing the peak high on his forehead before opening his jacket to reveal a shoulder holster. He saw Macharia looking and smiled as he withdrew a large service revolver.

'We're going to have a long chat, you and I – *Mr* Macharia.' He leaned in to within a few inches of his prisoner, smearing the gun's barrel slowly down Macharia's cheek before bringing it to rest on his lips.

'If you try and run for it I will personally ram this down your fucking throat, pull the trigger and blow your black guts all over the pavement. Understand me, boy?'

Johnny Seymour was standing at the back of a fetid National Theatre. The windows were open and a ceiling fan flapped slowly, barely disturbing the cigarette-sodden air folding damply through its blades. A single spotlight cut through the smoke to reveal the star of the show performing her encore: the Nyeri Nurse herself, the one and only, the *sensational* Tansy Thompson.

The audience, mostly male, mostly uniformed, all European, was not making a sound. Not a cough or a dropped programme was interrupting this finale as the svelte voice slid round the mournful chords of the blues. African music via America, given life by a long-gloved white beauty.

Johnny smiled in the darkness.

This was the third and final night of the African Broadcast Service's Entertainments Spectacular. Tansy and he had barely crossed paths since that sticky lunch at her parents' house, she busy with her touring and he tied up by Grogan's frenetic work regime at the Information Department. In fact, he was only here tonight on Grogan's say-so. There was another flap on and his boss feared his meeting might over-run. For the foreseeable future the city was likely to be more dangerous after dark, so if Johnny would be kind he'd escort Tansy back to her hotel after the show. Trusting of him, Johnny thought, but conceding there was little reason not to be. On the few occasions he'd seen Tansy on the circuit, she'd seemed happy enough with Grogan and he was beginning to think that moment of eye contact at the Nyeri Club hadn't happened. She'd probably been looking at someone else.

As the audience stood to cheer and the first bouquet of white lilies landed on the stage, Johnny left the auditorium, making his way to the back entrance. He found a pillar to lean against and lit a cigarette, braced against the sounds of Nairobi uncoiling into another oppressively hot night. A couple quarrelling, the clicking of secretary heels rushing to beat the darkness, men shouting in the distance, scuffling; floating notes from a party, sundowners on the lawn. Further away, a siren. Dogs barking. Dogs everywhere. Always the mournful howling. How different it was here compared to the wild cacophony of the Highlands forest. Johnny flicked his cigarette onto the street, watching the glowing butt arc into the gutter.

He was fed up with Nairobi and missed the cool of the Aberdares night. The city had changed. When he'd arrived almost a year ago it had been hot then too. But it had been the heat of possibility; the warmth of motion, loosening ties, shedding memories as fast as inhibitions.

Africa!

How hot the tropics had been then. The night rhythms, the cocktails, willing typists by the pool, a wife in town with a husband in the bush. Cicadas and smiling waiters. *Jambo bwana! Jambo!* A film set of a modern colony at play. Passenger jets and cinemas, coffee and air conditioning, a veneer of modernity skating on the barely frozen, still mischievous, pool of the golden epoch.

Perfect for a man in between.

But the mood had putrefied since then, the country developing a stench that was impossible to ignore. Something rotten in its cellar, wafting inexorably into all quarters, even Johnny's. The one time he had glimpsed it for himself still haunted him. At day's end, when he fought for sleep underneath the mosquito nets, no amount of whisky or cheap perfume staining the pillow offered salvation. The baby's head, little face blackened in the sun, would blink sightlessly into Johnny's dreamscape, dragging him panting and sweating to wakefulness.

Thankfully, nothing he'd seen or done after the Cunningham episode had been as bad. Grogan had noticed the effect, removing Johnny from the front line of press photography and allocating him to Porter's film unit. Porter, old hand that he was, didn't seem to care much what he did as long as his own work burden was eased. So far, Johnny had made short films on the Archbishop of Canterbury's visit, the proper management of cattle and the declining power of witchcraft. At least the last two had taken him into the bush where it was possible to pretend the Emergency had gone away.

In the city the military was everywhere, tangles of wire dividing up Nairobi into no-go districts, impossible to move without being stopped by a soldier at a checkpoint. The ghostly presence of Graves didn't help either, he thought, recalling how the Zebra would slip unseen into the office to visit Grogan, suddenly emerging to nod at Johnny with menacing civility.

Thinking of Graves reminded Johnny that he still didn't know what to do with the film he'd kept back from Grogan. They lay in his room, impossible to ignore. If developed, they could put Graves in the dock for murder. Not even the Crown in crisis could sanction the cold slaughter of prisoners.

He'd done nothing with them. Not because he didn't hate Graves's actions and not even because Graves frightened him; Johnny would gladly have stood up to the policeman's threats if he'd thought there was any point. But that was where the problem lay – *if there was any point.*

Johnny could not muster sufficient energy to see the purpose in it. It was, the army psychiatrist had once explained, as if the initial wound in Europe, that first horror, was so great it had traumatised everything round it. Like a sharp pain in the back deadening surrounding muscles to prevent further injury.

Johnny sighed. He wondered what Tansy would say if he told her. She might side with Graves; she came from settler stock after all. No, that was absurd. She was different, he was sure about that. He wished he'd taken a picture of her. He was good at portraits, believing the best ones revealed truths that belied the surface. He was certain Tansy was concealing something beneath her superficial girl-about-town gaiety.

She was walking towards him now, fobbing off the last of the admirers who'd crowded round the stage door hoping for an autograph or something more. Compared with the sophisticated entertainer he'd just seen under lights, this version of Tansy was fresher. She looked younger without stage make-up. She smiled shyly.

'Hello, Johnny, sorry to keep you waiting.'

Johnny laughed.

'What's the matter?'

'Nothing. It's just that your carriage for this evening is my Triumph. Not sure you're quite dressed for a motorbike.'

'Nonsense. You forget I was brought up on a farm. I can ride anything. Now give me a cigarette and tell me what you thought of tonight. You were there. I saw you.'

Johnny lit cigarettes for them both, noticing she was leaning on the same column he'd just vacated.

'*You were fabulous darling,*' Johnny drawled in affected theatre tones, adding more seriously, 'You know you were.'

Tansy's smile was brittle. 'Well actually,' she said, 'you may not believe this but sometimes it's hard to tell how it's going. When you're standing out there – do you know, I sometimes have the maddest thoughts. All I could think of tonight was coming off stage and having a drink. A gin sling, as it happens. Couldn't stop imagining what a lovely cold glass full of soda and ice would feel like against my cheek.'

Johnny smiled. He could read a cue.

'Shall we get one then? I'm sure the night bar at the Stanley will be open.'

'Was I being that obvious? Sorry, it's been a long night. Long nights plural, actually. Getting a bit tired of it all.'

Tansy pushed herself off the pillar and faced Johnny, folding her arms, cigarette smoke wreathing her bare shoulders.

'Is it worth it, Johnny?'

'Is what worth it?'

Tansy took a deep drag before exhaling impatiently.

'All this . . . all this *effort*. I mean, it's not as if we have a God-given right to own everything. I sometimes wonder if we should just say, here you are, thanks very much and take the keys. We jolly well enjoyed ourselves but now it's time for you to run things again. We're not all as awful as you think, so if some of us could stay on we'd be terribly quiet and wouldn't bother you with anything except our farms and maybe the odd trip to town.'

Johnny examined her, not able to tell whether she was being serious. Suddenly she grabbed his arm, staring fiercely up into his eyes and Johnny experienced a touch of vertigo, overly conscious of her nearness and the pressure of her hand.

'Do you know what I saw last week?' she asked, her voice urgent but distant.

'We were on the way to Fort Hall to sing to the Air Force boys – by the way, had you heard the planes they fly are called Vampires? *Vampires*, isn't that charming? Anyway, we were at one of these endless bloody roadblocks, a couple of cars back so the soldiers didn't notice us. And as we sat there we all became aware of this frightful wailing and crying. It was inhuman. So I got out and, casual as you like, sauntered over towards the noise. And I really wish I hadn't because there was a Kikuyu chap lashed to an oil drum . . . they'd actually tied him up . . . and the soldiers were taking it in turn to beat him with their belts. Not the leather bit, the buckle end, Johnny. They were laughing and the man was screaming, I mean really bellowing. Blood was flying everywhere. It looked as if they wanted to whip all the flesh off his bones. I felt so sick, it was a scene out of Dante or some disgusting Bruegel painting. Then this man. I say man but he was a boy really; can't have been more than eighteen or nineteen. Anyway, he notices me and says, 'Oh hello, miss, can we help you?' And he laughs and his mate laughs and I'm feeling dizzy and awful but I'm determined not to be sick in front of them. And I tell them to stop it this instant but all they do is laugh more and tell me to fuck off back to the city. And there's something about this boy I recognise. Then I remember: he was the handsome one at the last show in Meru. Asked me for an autograph, to be signed to his mum. And of course I'd signed it and we'd chatted a bit – he was from London – and I'd asked him about rationing and was it still as bad.

'So the thing is, Johnny, the *boy* who I'd sang for and given my autograph to and chatted to about his mum and meat coupons was standing in front of me flogging a man to death.'

Tansy's eyes didn't leave his for the entire story and Johnny was aware of the grip on his arm growing tighter, until her fingers were digging into his flesh. She let go suddenly, turning away.

'So yes, it has been a long few days actually and when I'm thinking of that gin sling I'm not really imagining it against my cheek, I'm thinking how quickly I can get it down my throat before I order another one.'

Johnny didn't know what to say. It had been so unexpected he felt as if he'd been struck himself. Tansy was pirouetting away, laughing to herself, muttering *'God'* in a long drawn-out way.

'Sorry, Johnny,' she said. 'But that's why I'm getting a bit tired of it all. In fact, I'm thinking of stopping this whole singing charade. I just can't carry on with it. Looks like nursing again for me.'

'What does Grogan think?'

'Grogan?'

Tansy laughed harshly.

'I haven't told him about giving up the singing yet. As to the rest – well, let's just say Grogan thinks very differently to you and me, Johnny. *He* believes it's all vile but says it has to get a lot viler before it gets better. Describes himself as a "big-picture" man – he's told me that often enough. Which means in a funny way that he wouldn't care a jot whether one African should be lashed to an oil barrel and beaten half to death in full view of the main road from Nairobi to Fort Hall.

'So, if you don't mind, I don't really want to talk about Grogan just now. Shall we go?'

Tansy solved the problem of riding a motorcycle in a tight pencil skirt by pulling it up so high she might as well have not been wearing one. She held on to his hips when the bike cornered, but it was her thighs and the inside of her knees sandwiching him that Johnny was most conscious of. Unless there was a particularly violent bend they did not touch him, yet they felt as if they did all the time, hovering an inch or so away, so near he imagined he could feel the heat of them the entire journey to the hotel. When she tapped on his shoulder to point out a police patrol or a roadblock he barely noticed, trying not to think about her proximity, the nearness of her legs and that smallest of warm spaces separating what lay between her legs from his own body.

They ordered gin slings – two each, at Tansy's request – and Tansy led him to one of the Stanley's private booths. Johnny had the wit to sit opposite her. If anyone who knew Grogan had seen them squashed together on a banquette it would have been difficult to explain. For a second, as they clinked glasses, Johnny thought about loyalty. He realised he didn't care. If there were any codes left over from Europe they did not involve two consenting adults enjoying each other's company. Sitting opposite was tactically better anyway. He knew where he wanted this to go but Tansy was veering towards the reckless and he knew of old that reckless could go either way. Besides, he wanted to stare at her green eyes while she caressed her glass, running it over her cheeks.

Slowly, he warned himself; this was something that could be precious. It had to be taken gently or not at all.

'So what happened to you after that ghastly lunch at my parents?' Tansy asked. 'Sorry for involving you in that, by the way. I seem to remember having invited everyone.'

'Is that why Graves was there?'

'Maybe. But of all people, I'm not going to talk about him.' She bent her head and Johnny saw how many freckles there were on her cheek. Abruptly she looked up. 'So, come on, tell me then, Johnny Seymour, what happened to you? I know you had to go to the Cunninghams'. Grogan said you behaved very well.'

'Did he?' Johnny felt discomfited that Tansy should have been talking about him with Grogan. 'It was pretty unpleasant actually.'

Tansy grimaced and Johnny changed tack, saying it was all a long time ago, making the aftermath into a story about Grogan running around the office in his long socks bossing everyone about.

She smiled and he was pleased to see the sparkle in her eyes return, enjoying the easy way her generous mouth laughed.

In reality the days following the Cunningham murders had been anything but funny. Grogan had been delighted with the photographs, especially the ones of the baby. He'd hung round the dark room when Johnny returned, impatiently snatching the contact sheet, still wet from fixative, to circle the pictures he wanted. It was as if the killings and subsequent declaration of the Emergency had been a starting gun for his energy. If there was any member of the press corps who hadn't published a Mau Mau atrocity story, Grogan relentlessly pinned them down until they capitulated. It was, after all, spectacular copy and the pictures topped everything. Grogan had insisted the photographs do the rounds, knowing the horrific scenes would stiffen the sinews. All of the press, even the liberal papers, had duly obliged with exquisite depictions of Mau Mau evil, though not even the *Daily Sketch* dared show the baby's head.

Government Family Brutally Slaughtered. Headless Horror at Farm. Child Decapitated. Bestial Slaughter. Baby Butchered.

Porter had kept a tally of what he called the three Bs – the number of times the words brutal, bestial and butchered were used. As far as Johnny could remember, bestial had won, though brutal was not far behind.

He didn't want to think about any of that now. Tansy was insisting on a third drink. She was not singing tomorrow, she said, and didn't see why she couldn't enjoy herself when the world about her was clearly going to hell. But the more Johnny saw and listened, the less he wanted this evening to end up like the others. So instead he asked how her parents were.

'My parents?' She giggled. 'Gosh that's romantic.'

'All right,' she continued when Johnny didn't reply. 'If you insist. *My parents.* Well, life goes on as normal, though when I went back last weekend it was a little unsettling to see Mummy blaze away at the scarecrow in the meadow with a pistol. Did you know, *everyone's* got a gun up there. It's mad, as if Mummy could hurt a fly! Meanwhile Daddy is insisting on building a strong room in the cupboard next to his study. Mummy of course is furious and keeps saying that if they need a strong room to survive she'd rather move back to England.

Which is a bit odd as she's never lived there in her life. Daddy asked after you, by the way. I think he rather liked you. Which again is rather odd because he's never liked any of the men I . . . '

Tansy stopped and blushed. But she held Johnny's eyes and in the long moments that followed he felt the nearness of her as a kind of heat, pulling him in. Tansy's palm lay open on the table and he moved his hand towards hers. It was halfway across the table when he felt a tap on the shoulder.

'Mr Seymour, sir?'

Johnny shot his hand back as if he'd been scalded. Tansy grinned. An African bellhop stood by the table with an envelope.

'A message for Mr Johnny Seymour, sir.'

Johnny nodded his thanks and sat upright to take the envelope. Divine intervention. Inside was a brief note. He read it quickly, shaking his head. Tansy looked at him questioningly.

'Seems one of our drivers has been detained,' he said. 'Arrested earlier this evening. Currently languishing in the central police cells.'

'Really, it's so stupid,' Tansy said. 'They're arresting anyone they see. It only fuels resentment, swells their bloody ranks. Who is it?'

'Chap called Macharia. You might have seen him driving Grogan. Seems a pleasant enough fellow. Very quiet. Can't imagine him getting caught up in Mau Mau.'

'Nor can I. I remember asking him once whether he got bored driving us around and he gave a funny reply. He said that what looked like nothing to us was always something to him.'

'Grogan wants me to get him out.'

'How are you meant to do that?'

'Suppose I'll go down to the station and fetch him in the morning,' Johnny said. 'Let them know he's working for us. Unless they have any evidence, they'll have to release him.'

'*Tomorrow?*' Tansy exclaimed. 'Have you any idea what goes on in those cells? I tell you, Johnny, if you'd seen what I did by the side of that road . . . Look, we should get him now. Before they do him any damage.'

'*We?*'

'Well, yes.' Tansy was already getting to her feet. 'You can't wander into one of those police stations on your own. They'd eat you alive.'

Johnny frowned. He didn't want the evening to end, but he certainly didn't want it to end in a police station. Then he thought of Graves and the soldiers outside the Cunningham farm. He couldn't claim to know Macharia but he was about the only African he'd ever spoken to. He seemed a gentle soul and his eyes shone with intelligence. Tansy was correct: the idea of him being interrogated all night by Kenyan security was unspeakable.

'You're right. Tomorrow's too late – I'll get him now. But I'm afraid I can't let you tag along. If you want to wait here, perhaps later we could meet and have another drink?'

'*Can't let me?* If you think I'm going to sit here leaving that nice man alone in a police station, you don't know me. I'm coming with you and that's final.'

Johnny hesitated, but before he could formulate further objections Tansy slipped her arm through his and leaned gently against him.

'Don't worry, Johnny. I won't get in the way. I might even be able to help. *Please.* I'm fed up with sitting on the sidelines.'

When they reached the lobby Johnny stopped, preparing to make one final protest. Before he could say a word she cut him short, kissing him softly on the cheek.

'Besides,' she murmured in his ear. 'I rather enjoyed riding on the back of that motorcycle of yours.'

Johnny held her gaze before putting his hands on her arms just below the shoulder, literally holding her at arm's length. Normally he would have kissed her then but this was not normally. He stared at with such intensity Tansy feared she was being committed to memory.

'All right,' he said finally. 'But don't play with me, Tansy. I can take pretty much anything, but not that. Please. Do you understand?'

Tansy nodded slowly. In the few seconds it had taken to walk from the table she was aware of something having changed. It was certainly not to be played with. Away from the bar's giant fans the air felt heavier and yet she felt lighter than ever. Not the lightness of the coquette role she hid behind, but a kind of weightlessness that made it possible to glide away from images of laughing soldiers flaying a man to death with their belts towards something better.

Johnny saw a difference in her and knew the exchange of glances at the Nyeri Club had been for him then and was for him again now.

To a casual observer the pair might simply have been a couple on the verge of parting, innocently saying good night. But to Grogan Littleboy, standing unseen near the concierge desk, looking for Tansy after his meeting, the way they looked at each other was as far from innocent as it was possible to get.

Grogan prided himself on his ability to read people and what he had just read might have amounted to the biggest betrayal of his life. But there was one redeeming feature: it was highly improbable anything had yet happened. The two might have been oblivious to their surroundings but there was still a reserve behind the intimacy that led Grogan to believe it was not too late. As he knew very well, events were not immutable; they were not written in the stars or even blood. On the contrary, as the director of the Information Department understood better than almost any man in Kenya, with the right type of intervention, events could be altered, outcomes changed.

It was all a question of perspective.

And timing.

Normally there were twenty double cells and eight singles at Nairobi's central police station. Within a fortnight of the Emergency another two large cages had been constructed in the old toilet block, which were meant to hold a dozen men each. If every place was taken there was room for seventy-two prisoners. Tonight, according to the staff sergeant's register, there were more than two hundred and fifty Mau Mau suspects jammed somewhere inside the station.

Last night there had been almost three hundred, so it could have been worse, although Macharia failed to see how. He'd been allocated a double cell, squashed in with a dozen others. As the newcomer he was shoved nearest the piss hole, which meant he was sitting in a puddle of urine, his smart trousers absorbing the product of the men crammed in with him. When he was first thrown in he'd been barely conscious, but relieved to be out of the interview room. A fellow prisoner had thought to lift his head out of the piss and the stench of ammonia was so rancid it had acted as a smelling salt, lurching him nauseatingly into full wakefulness.

The other men had all been through it but even so their grimaces told Macharia his face was not pretty. He couldn't remember much. He'd been dragged to the interrogation room where the man with the hat had enjoyed his turn for a while, splitting Macharia's face open with meaty pink fists, firing questions that were unanswerable but which made his young white assistant laugh. Why was he such a black cunt, why did he whimper like a dog, why was his mother the vilest whore, did he want his cock cut off and shoved up his own arse. And so on.

Macharia had been forewarned. Think of it as an initiation test, they'd said. Had he not already experienced pain during the circumcision ritual? During the oath itself? He was a man; he was Kikuyu. He could cope. The real questioning would come later. That was when it would get dangerous. He would be tired and disorientated, hurting. The questions would be like a knife slicing into his lies until the truth was cut open. He had to bide his time, cling to the rightness of what he was doing and say nothing.

So he'd been patient, learning to curl away from the blows to diminish their force just a fraction. The man with the hat had become bored, and gradually the punches carried less force as he panted more. When he stopped, rewarding his prisoner with a last kick to the kidneys, Macharia had thought he had survived.

A short while later the door opened and another man entered on his own. Through swollen slits Macharia saw the cane.

Zebra.

Since the episode in the car, Macharia had tried to find out about the man his superiors had warned him of. What he learned had not made his fear any less. When he discovered why he was called the Zebra he'd promised himself he would run if he saw him again. But there was no running inside a police interrogation room.

Like the Kikuyu people, Europeans enjoyed giving nicknames. Bomber Harris, Taxi Lewis. Monkey Johnson. For Kikuyus the name would often refer to the physical attributes of an animal – as with Johnny Seymour, whom the drivers all now called Korongo, the crane, because of the long white crest of hair which flowed when he drove his motorcycle. In the case of the Zebra, Europeans also believed his name came from the animal, deriving from Graves's speed in the bush, the way he could turn immediately at full run when being pursued.

But the true reason, the Kikuyu reason, was very different.

The Zebra liked to leave his mark.

Graves carried a cane of hardened bamboo. When he whipped he did so with great precision, leaving a trail of stripes along the back and thighs. Like a zebra. Graves was patient. In order to get a perfect set of stripes he would take his time, perhaps an agonising hour or more with a single man. And now he was here.

'*Stand up.*'

Macharia was scared and in considerable pain, and in the next second he made a decision that would save his life. It was the logic of the desperate. If he stood he would be whipped. If he were whipped he would break. And if he broke he would die, hanged like so many others.

So he lay, refusing to move.

Macharia calculated Graves couldn't possibly recognise the beaten face at his feet. It was beyond a mess, engorged and split like an overripe melon, streaked with red, his eyes swollen like a foetus's. From the outside it would be impossible to tell if he was conscious. He let his body go limp. If he was unconscious, he could not answer anything.

He heard the Zebra walking quietly towards him. The footsteps paused and there was silence. Macharia had to fight the urge to open his eyes. He was slumped against the wall and the fingers of the hand that had been crushed by the policeman lay under him. He held the damaged knuckle in his good hand and surreptitiously squashed it, forcing pain to ooze from it until he could hardly bear it. When the inevitable blow from the Zebra arrived, slicing without warning, whistling past his ear to strike him on the side of the face, Macharia was already so far into pain that he did not flinch.

Graves grunted and spoke angrily over his shoulder.

'You knocked him out, you stupid bugger. I told you to prepare him, not fucking beat him half to death.'

Macharia was dragged back to his cell and for the next three hours he lay, not bothering to get up, refusing to talk to any of the other inmates. Everyone knew there were always loyalist traitors planted among them and he would not be tricked into providing any information now. There was no chance he would survive the next interrogation. At least there was time to think what he would say.

When the cell opened and two askaris hauled him out, he was as ready as he could be. He knew the men in the shoe shop were as good as dead: he would give them all up in the end, all except for Gatimu. And that was his plan. He would never speak of his brother, however bad it got, whatever else he confessed. Holding on to that thought made him feel calm, and as he was being moved he let his body go limp so it was more of an effort for the dogs who led him. A small act of resistance. But in truth that was all his work for Mau Mau had ever been. Small acts of resistance. He was sad there had been no time for more. He closed his eyes, willing himself to think about Gatimu again and how he could make his brother proud. There was a sound of keys, a door opening, a gust of air, sweet and fresh. *Wazungu* voices. Then he was dumped on the floor.

'*Jesus!* Yes, that's him,' said a voice that was vaguely familiar. 'I'll take him now.'

Macharia felt his arm being tugged and he was gently pulled to his feet. Peering with difficulty though slitted eyes, he was amazed to see the European man with the hair of the crane. He was in a room near the exit. An askari sergeant was signing something on a desk and Johnny Seymour was shouting.

'What the fuck have you done to him? Who did this? Was it you? He's just a driver, for God's sake.'

The one they called Korongo was furious. Macharia had not thought he'd had it in him. There was a white policeman standing by, not looking amused while Johnny banged the desk with his fist, calling the officer a lot of names Macharia had never heard before.

It made him grin, but the expression tore open his lip and blood trickled down his chin. To his side a white hand holding a handkerchief dabbed at his lip. To his further astonishment Macharia saw the concerned face of Tansy Thompson. What was Grogan's woman doing in a place like this? She was clucking as if he were a child, trying to make him keep still so she could wipe the blood away. The scent on the handkerchief was delicate but unmistakably feminine and he surrendered to the sensation of being looked after.

'Thank you,' he croaked.

'Don't be ridiculous,' Tansy said. 'We're going to get you out of here, put you in some clean clothes and take you to a clinic. Johnny – stop that and help me get him out. We can deal with them later.'

'Don't you worry,' Johnny said tightly. 'We will. This is not going to be forgotten.'

And before he knew it, Macharia was outside, hobbling along the street being supported by two white people whom he barely knew and yet who had certainly saved him from torture and possibly death, not to mention avoided a serious setback for the Movement.

The world was indeed a strange place. Had he made it to the shoe shop and received an order there to kill either one of these whites he would have done so without a moment's hesitation. He looked at them in turn, suddenly suspicious. Was it a trick? What did they know? But Johnny was merely angry, muttering with rage at the behaviour of the police while Tansy's features were tear-stained and remorseful. They were not the faces of tricksters.

Nor were they, Macharia realised with a spin of thought so unexpected it made him reel, the faces of his enemy.

Chapter 8

Nyeri District, March 2008

Sam hadn't a clue where she was. Or why.

They'd parked by the side of a road leading out of a featureless village forty minutes or so north of Nairobi and were now on foot, had been for nearly an hour. Esther beckoned Sam to follow, refusing to engage with any questions, swatting them all away with a grunted 'Wait and see.'

The sun was meltingly hot, sticking Sam's dark-blue blouse to her skin, creating attractive armpit rings. She wished she'd worn a lighter top. With long sleeves. Her forearms were reddening under the stupidly low-factor sunscreen she'd applied when she'd thought this was going to be a normal morning. She was thirsty too. Properly thirsty, like she could down a litre of cold water without thinking. Esther was racing ahead, rolling through the grass with her curious gait, like a ball propelled by the wind. She stopped only occasionally to wave Sam onwards, shaking her head at her not keeping up. This aimless trek through dry grass and scrub was not at all how Sam had imagined her first trip into the Kenyan countryside.

At last Esther slowed and allowed Sam to catch up. For the past fifteen minutes they'd been climbing a gradual incline and the scrub had given way to some kind of plantation. Row after row of shrubs with sharp leaves resembling the kind of giant cactus found in the Mexican desert. Sisal, Esther said, the only direct question she'd consented to answer. The sisal rows didn't seem ordered; the plants were scattered haphazardly in clumps, forcing Sam to zigzag around them, increasing both effort and annoyance.

By the time Sam reached her, Esther was standing quite still, looking down at a valley covered with more of the plants. Sam got her breath back and approached, ready to give vent to her impatience with this seemingly purposeless route march.

Then she saw the tears sliding silently down Esther's cheek.

'Hey – are you OK? Esther, what's wrong?'

Esther's breath was coming in stutters and suddenly she crumpled, her legs no longer able to function. Sam squatted beside her, her arm instinctively wrapping around the small woman's shoulders.

'Hey, hey, it's all right,' she said, hushing her quietly. Esther herself had used the same tone when she'd soothed Mattingly away from the party.

'I am sorry,' Esther said, wiping her eyes roughly. 'I thought it would be OK but it is not. To be here once more is truly painful. Please forgive me.'

Esther began to weep again in small hiccups, folding her head into her chest, hands bunched into tight fists at her side. Eventually she sat up and pushed back her tears with the side of her hand.

'I brought you here,' she said, 'because I need to tell you a story. About what happened here.' She gestured towards the land spread below them. 'This valley is a place of slaughter.'

She turned to Sam.

'Joseph has given you something that will help you with the wider issues you have come to Kenya to investigate. The giving of it may have a cost, so I hope you appreciate what he is doing. I know this is hard for an outsider to understand, but for us, for my generation especially, the past lives with us today and has lost little of its power.

'Or its danger. And it was dangerous to be a Kikuyu then. Very dangerous. Equally so for the few white men and women who helped us.'

She shifted her position on the ground and swiped at an ant crawling over her ankle. Sam nodded, willing Esther to go on, conscious of the effort it was taking.

'The story I will tell you now I have never spoken of before. Joseph knows, but I have never given a deposition to a lawyer or told even my best friends.'

She paused and pulled out a stalk of grass, waving it in the slow breeze, before using it to point towards a distant spot in the valley where the earth sloped into a flat plain the size of a football pitch.

'Down there,' she said, 'over to the right of that line of trees edging

117

the sisals was where I used to live. It was my village. My home. It does not exist today. Not a hut remains. All that is left is that square field where nothing grows.

'This morning you were asking about what happened to the women. Whether it is true that so many could have been assaulted in the manner you describe. With an *implement*. I cannot say what happened to women in other villages but I can tell you what happened to mine. To one family on one day. The last day.

'Are you sure you want to hear this, Samantha Seymour?'

Sam's mouth was dry and she was hotter than perhaps she'd ever been. She could almost smell her skin roasting as the sun drilled down. But nothing on earth would induce her to move from that spot now. She nodded slowly.

'Very well,' Esther continued. 'It will not take long and at the end you can make up your own mind about how things stand with these other women who you have read about. And if you meet any of them, I hope this will inform you. What is it Joseph likes to say? Set the tone. That is it. *Set the tone*.

'*So* – where to begin?'

As she began to speak, Esther's voice became calmer and soon she was measuring her phrases with care before allowing them out. At times her sentences would dip at the end as if some words were fighting to stay in and Sam would be forced to lean in to hear properly.

'My village was small. No more than twenty huts, some of them empty because families had been forced into Nairobi to look for work. My father had gone a long time ago. I never really knew him; cannot today describe his face. He must have moved out before I was three. That left my mother, my sister Agatha and me. Agatha was older than me by two years. At the time I am talking of she was eighteen and quite striking. Unlike me, she was tall and she had a voice that was melodious and graceful. Men used to love listening to her tell stories or sing; our mother was so proud of her, she used to say her words were like molten silver, flowing and pouring into the most beautiful shapes. Agatha was considered to be a prize and had many admirers. I loved her very much.

'She was singing, I remember, when the soldiers came.

'You have to understand that this spot where we are sitting is only a short walk away from another place, a haunted and terrible place. It is called Lari. The name may mean something to you? Perhaps its notoriety has not crossed the years. Or maybe just the sea. It is still well known here. The tale of what happened in Lari has been rehearsed and spoken of many times. I have not a single doubt it was as bad as they say.

'The headman there, Luka Wakahangare, was friendly with the British. His association with the *wazungu* was said to have brought many benefits to him and his family. The village too. Whatever the reason, Mau Mau thought he was an appropriate target. It was one of their largest operations of the war. Several hundred gathered there and on the night of the twenty-sixth of March 1953, a Thursday, I believe, they surrounded Luka's hut and the huts of his wives and of every Home Guard family in the village. They made it impossible to open the doors and then they set fire to them. When people struggled out of windows they were hacked to death. Many of the men were away patrolling so most of the victims were women and their children. Mau Mau spared no one. How many died? One hundred? Two hundred? No one really knows. Many. Too many.

'So that was the Lari massacre and it was truly an awful thing and it is justly infamous. But what is not described so much in the history books is what happened afterwards.

'Some call it the second Lari massacre. This whole valley and the lands surrounding it, almost back into Nairobi, became a hunting ground. The Home Guard Kikuyu were maddened by the attack, the British equally so. Not a village was spared; not a Kikuyu living here untouched. Remember, this was early in the Emergency, just one year in. The British had never been challenged in such a significant way. Up to that point Mau Mau had only attacked a few isolated farms, killed individual loyalists. Lari was much bigger – a serious threat that had to be countered. The way they did it was to let their African loyalist hunting dogs go anywhere, do anything. And those holding the leashes, the white British soldiers and white policemen and their vigilante groups, they went everywhere too.

'Did everything.

'Our turn did not come until four days later. We had heard of terrible things happening all around us, of course we had – but where could we go? This was our home. There was nowhere else. There

119

was no one in our village who was Mau Mau so we thought we might be spared. Some of the boys I knew from the mission school had taken the oath at the beginning but they were long gone. In fact, most of the men had gone.

'My cousin Victoria was visiting with her new baby boy. He was only six weeks old and she was so proud of him. He looked like a little man, his face so serious as he wriggled in his sling. We had decorated her *kanga* ourselves; our birth present, and Victoria loved it. She hardly ever took him out of there, carrying him on her back or turning him round onto her stomach to feed.

'So there were four women and one baby in the hut that day. Not much of a threat, you might think. Not to armed men; not to any man.'

Sam didn't dare move. Esther was speaking even slower, picking her words with an awful inevitability.

'We heard shouts and a neighbour screaming but by the time we realised what was happening it was too late. There was nowhere to hide. They entered the hut very quickly. Five or six of them, askaris from the Home Guard. With guns. One had a whip. Then the white officer. They were all screaming, yelling at us to put our hands in the air. We did so immediately, but not fast enough. They used their rifle butts on all of us and we all went down. I didn't feel any pain then. It was a blow here.'

Esther patted her shoulder without looking.

'My mother recovered first and tried to shield us with her body. She put her arms out like this – like a cross. But they knocked her over. Two of them stood over her, crashing their rifles into her, again and again.

'She was too old for them. They had no use for her body. So they broke it instead.'

Esther stopped and bowed her head.

'I'm sorry,' she whispered.

Sam put her hand on Esther's arm. It was burning hot and rigid, whipcord tight from clenching her fist.

'*You* are sorry? God, *no*,' Sam said. 'Listen, you don't have to go on. You absolutely don't. Not for me. Really, not.'

'No. I *must*. It has to come out. It has been like a slow poison all these years. Yet it is still so fresh in my mind . . . I didn't realise how much it would ... I have tried for so long to put this behind me. Perhaps I should have spoken of these matters before. I did not ever think I would be back here.'

She looked hard at Sam.

'I understand this is difficult for you to listen to, Sam, but for some reason you have been chosen to be a witness. *My witness.* I am being selfish because I am telling you this for my sake when really it ought to be for the others. Worse was done to them, much worse, but if you can get some justice' – she waved her hand at the valley – 'for the ones who have gone. Then it will be worth it. Do you see, Sam? It is important you understand this.'

The air was still and the heat flickered in a lazy haze above the sisal plants. A fly buzzed in front of Sam's eyes and landed on her leg. It was the only sound in the entire valley. She made no move to brush it away.

'Yes,' Sam said quietly. 'I understand.'

'Very well. So, when they had finished beating my mother they started on my beloved sister Agatha. We had a small table and they bent her over it, face up. One man at one end, two at the other. They whipped her, then took turns. I couldn't look, couldn't listen, but when I put my hands to my ears to silence the screams the British officer slapped me until I put them down. My mother was on the ground not moving and the askaris stood on her, trampled on her body to get at Agatha. One put his foot on her face. His sandal had come off and from my position on the floor I could see his filthy yellow toenails digging into her cheek, gouging her nose, as he pushed to drive himself into my sister.

'I am glad my mother was dead. No parent should see ever such a thing.

'I was next. They kicked Agatha off the table and levered me onto it. Two of them. They ripped my clothes off with a bayonet, cutting my skin. Then they ... then they ... *oh ...* '

Esther's face was wet, her mouth tight, fighting for air, shallow breaths pumping in and out as if she were giving birth, rocking her head from side to side.

'*No. No. No. I cannot say, I cannot.*'

Sam was crying now. She put her arms round Esther again and pushed her face into the other woman's, forehead to forehead, crushing against her, wanting to push the pain away, desperately soothing, trying to kiss it away. Shield it with gentleness and love.

But it could not be. There was no shield against what Esther had endured.

Together they sat, their tears mingling, ragged breaths joined. No words, just a low keening and a shushing, animal noises, universal noises, at a distance impossible to tell from which woman they came.

After a while, Sam had no idea how long, Esther broke away and stood, blowing her nose and wiping her face with the back of her hands. She shuddered and the movement rippled the entire length of her body. Without looking at Sam she began to walk down the hill towards the site of her old village.

'Come,' she said over her shoulder. 'Perhaps it will be easier if we move.'

Sam caught up and held the woman's hand as they paced slowly down amid the sisals. Esther was so short she almost had to reach up to join hands. She spoke to Sam as they walked, slowly and with great precision.

'If you ask me – as you should, as it is your right to do – whether the men in the hut put an implement inside my sister or my cousin or me, I would have no answer. I do not know; even for myself I do not know. I bled enough and I have never been able to bear children, so maybe they did. There were things lying around our home.

'But perhaps a better question is why wouldn't they have done? They did everything else.'

She halted and faced Sam.

'There is another point. What they did that morning was so terrible, so inhuman, that if any woman could survive such an attack they might say it was a bottle rather than admit the truth of what was done to them. That is my answer to your question.

'As for the rest – I cannot tell you what they did to my cousin because I passed out after they had finished with me. All I know is that it did not matter that she carried a baby on her back. They left us for dead. Four women and a baby still strapped in his sling. And among us only I was alive, with so much blood on my face and body they must have thought I had died too. And in a way I had. Truly, I was not properly alive then or for years afterwards.

'Perhaps not even now.

122

'It was Joseph who found me. You know, he was my salvation. A white man – yes, it is strange. He had come up to Lari to record what had happened there for the British propaganda people he worked for – Grogan Littleboy and his men.

'I'm not sure how long afterwards he found me. I have no memory of it. He took me to hospital. Watched over me. Truly, the Lord moves in mysterious ways.'

She looked hard at Sam.

'Perhaps in telling you this, so that you can repeat it to the world, there may be some purpose to my surviving after all. Until now I have never seen the point.'

She took her hand from Sam's and marched purposefully up to the right, past several trees until she reached a group of sisals, clustered in a rough circle, set slightly apart from the rest.

'Here,' she said. 'This is where we buried them.'

The sisals looked no different from any of the others surrounding them. Esther dropped to her knees and crossed herself at the base of one of the plants, the tears coming again.

'I should have moved them. We were Christians. They should be in consecrated ground. But I could not, Sam. I could not come back here . . . to this place.'

Esther held her hands together in a steeple and began to pray, mumbling the words as she rocked on her knees. Sam stood back, numbed and empty. She was an intruder, did not know where to look or what to do. Only when she wiped her eye did she realise she was still crying. Esther finished praying and rose unsteadily to her feet. She broke off a rosette from under one of the sharp leaves and tucked the flower head into the pocket of her skirt, closing her eyes in one last private prayer.

They headed back the way they had come, in silence at first but then Sam could not stop herself. She had to know.

'Why Esther – why did you bury them here? Alone, so far away from anyone?'

'Alone? *Alone?*'

Esther stopped, gazing at Sam, slowly shaking her head. Taking Sam's shoulders, she pushed her round in a circle, pointing.

'Look around you, Sam – *look*. They are not alone. Will never be alone.'

Sam did look and all she could see were sisals, clusters of the plant for hundreds of yards in all directions. A numberless plantation of sisals.

Then she understood.

My God, the sisals.

Each one a grave.

Chapter 9

Nairobi, January 1953

The low pink buildings of the Muthaiga Country Club, with its discreet service and charming gardens, was a civilised location in which to take stock. No longer the rowdy meeting place for the Happy Valley set, it could still become lively enough at night but during the day its library and imported walnut desks were an oasis of calm amid the growing clamour of the city.

Johnny knew he should watch his intake but today he wasn't working, ordered to take the day off by Grogan. Sitting at the lunch bar he allowed himself a couple of whiskies. Any more and he might do something foolish. Such as head out for Mombasa and the ocean, never to set foot in Kenya again. Or ring Tansy Thompson. That would be better. But that wasn't allowed.

Tansy.

It had been less than a month since they'd rescued Macharia from the police station and there'd not been a spare second when he hadn't thought about her. It was, as Tansy had pronounced, all too confusing. *Confusing* – what did she mean?

They'd left his bike at the police station and found a taxi to take Macharia to a private clinic Tansy knew. Afterwards they'd strolled back to her hotel, talking so intently neither of them noticed they must have walked three miles. It was not small talk. Seeing Macharia had released something in Tansy and she had come to a conclusion: she was no longer going to sing.

'I have to do something! I live here, this is my home. I won't stand back and watch it get destroyed while I prance about on stage singing songs for a cause I can't believe in.'

'So what do you believe in then?' Johnny had asked.

'Don't know. People? One thing I am sure of is that you can't beat a whole country into submission. Even if we won, how would we control the peace? With a gun and a whip?'

She'd return to nursing. There was a hospital in Central Province called Kagamo where she'd seen a vacancy for a senior sister. Not glamorous, but at least she would be using her skills to heal, not stoke the fires. Johnny listened admiringly, conscious of how little he knew her. She was a different woman from the one he'd watched from the back of the theatre and a different one too from the flirtatious girl he'd been drinking with at the Stanley. With every footstep he realised how much he wanted to discover the real version.

But when they reached the hotel and he'd leaned in for the kiss he'd stupidly imagined was inevitable, she'd pushed him gently, but firmly, away.

'No, Johnny. I had a lovely evening and I think you're very nice but this is wrong.'

'How can it be wrong if—'

'Please,' Tansy said, refusing to let him articulate it. 'I can't do this. Not now. Besides, there's Grogan to consider.'

'*Grogan?*'

'Yes. Other people do exist, Johnny. Look, it's terribly confusing and the timing couldn't be worse. There's too much going on and to be truthful I'm not really sure about anything at the moment. I'm so sorry, but I really should go. I *have* to go. Good night.'

She had left him standing, walking through the hotel's night entrance without a single glance back. So phoning Tansy really was a non-starter. *It was all terribly confusing.* Fine. He could wait.

He flicked a finger towards one of the Muthaiga's legendarily efficient bar boys who immediately scooped ice into a pre-prepared measure of whisky. The drink arrived on a silver coaster with a small bowl of peanuts but Johnny didn't touch them; he was trying to concentrate on a book of African wildlife Porter had lent him. A picture of a lioness bringing down a kudu on the plain made him sigh. That's where he wanted to be now.

He brought the whisky to his lips, pleased to see the ice hadn't melted, when the unlikely sound of men chanting floated in through the window. He cocked an ear. The only marches that took place in Nairobi were by Africans, but what were they doing near the club, in this white area of town? Kenya wasn't South Africa – there was no formal system of apartheid, but informal colour codes were hard to avoid. Africans were permitted by law to drink anywhere they liked – even the New Stanley or the Muthaiga – but no black man would dream of going inside uninvited, and if he did there were large bouncers on the door to prevent any such impertinence. Nairobi was divided by colour. Native locations in Eastlands; Asians to the south and west; and Europeans in the Muthaiga district. It had been shocking at first, though now Johnny hardly noticed.

But Africans meeting together in plain view in a white suburb, now that was noticeable. The photojournalist within him stirred and he wondered whether there was time to fetch his camera. He hurried outside to see if there was a taxi he might hail back to the office. But on the street he was met with an astonishing sight.

There was barely a black face to be seen. This was white Nairobi on the move. A column of hundreds, perhaps thousands, of marching and chanting Europeans snaked down Thika Road heading towards the city centre. Men and women in their Sunday best, drill shorts, jackets over shoulders, hats pushed backwards, shouting: '*Baring out! Baring out!*' Faces were strained and red as they spat the words into the air.

The colour of the protestors was so unusual Johnny forgot about fetching the camera, deciding immediately he should tag along in case he missed anything. He was off duty but a story was a story.

Walking beside a group of couples about his age, he asked what was happening.

'It's a neck-tie party,' one of the men slurred. 'We're going to tie one on Baring at Government House.' A hipflask protruded from his jacket pocket. Another man, his neck settler-red, scowled when he heard Johnny's English accent.

'Are you fresh off the boat, man? Haven't you heard what those bastard Mickeys have been doing? The colonial government doesn't give a damn about anyone except themselves.'

Others joined in, talking loudly in slogans.

'Kyukes need a firm hand, not a fucking hand-out.'

'No bloody wog's going to run me off my land.'

'The only good Mick's a dead one.'

Johnny had heard these views before, ranted in bars when settlers took a few too many on board. Antipathy towards Africans had gone off the scale since the start of the Emergency, but until now the overt hatred being expressed by this crowd had been restricted to a few. It was shocking to find it being shouted in the open by the majority. He peeled away from the irate group only to find himself swept along with another section of the crowd, right up to the gates of Government House.

He wondered if Grogan was inside. Despite his own feelings for Tansy, Johnny couldn't help admiring him. It wasn't his fault they were attracted to the same woman. Showed he had good taste. Grogan regarded himself as a progressive on the question of race and would have been appalled by the sentiments articulated here. He'd once confided in Johnny that if he were African he'd probably be agitating for independence too, though 'not through the barrel of a gun'.

Johnny couldn't see any guns in the crowd but violence was not far away. People were shaking the iron railings and bottles were beginning to fly, cracking against the walls of Government House. Since the Cunningham murders, the colony had been on edge, reeling as its house journal, the *East African Standard*, pummelled them with one atrocity story after the other. Two more isolated homesteads had been hit; farmers these, not children. Two women in their late seventies had also been hacked to pieces and the white death toll now stood at eleven. The European community was reacting furiously: farmers and settlers forming militias, wives joining gun clubs, and chatter at the bar was about shooting every last Kyuke or herding them all off into camps. Lock the door and throw away the bloody key. Wild talk. Then yesterday, a bad situation turned worse. A Mau Mau gang raided a remote country police station near Naivasha; no one killed but a dozen Sten guns and a case of grenades stolen. The authorities seemed powerless. Something needed to be done – bloody soon.

The Governor, Baring, was doing too little; settlers wanted action now. The idea that Kyukes could be allowed to wander around, freely slaughtering old white ladies and young white children, was monstrous. Johnny shuddered to think how much worse the crowd's reaction would be if they'd seen what he had at the Cunningham home. Even Graves's methods might be seen as weakness.

Beyond a line of people carrying a banner, Johnny spotted a face he recognised. It was Crawshaw, the cattle farmer he'd met at Nyeri. He pushed over to him.

'Hello?' Johnny shouted above the hubbub. 'Seymour from Information. We met at the club.'

Crawshaw wasn't stopping. 'I remember you,' he said, 'you're Grogan's man. *Government* man.'

'What's this all about?' Johnny yelled.

'You're joking aren't you?'

Crawshaw wheeled on Johnny, but the crowd was pushing forward and he had to put his hand out to stop Johnny crushing into him.

'Didn't you hear what happened to Sullivan?'

Johnny shook his head, close enough to smell the beer on Crawshaw's breath.

'He's dead!' Crawshaw shouted. 'They buried the poor bastard alive! Head first into an anthill. Fucking monsters. Sullivan looked after his people, cared for them, God knows why. And look what they did. Only thing the African understands is . . .'

But Crawshaw's view on what Africans understood was lost as the cattleman was swept away on a surge of crowd. Johnny was shaken. He'd liked Sullivan; he was a good man. Why would Mau Mau kill people of his calibre?

A woman ahead of him tripped over a discarded placard and he thought of Tansy. She was a settler but she'd never come to an event like this. Like most people in Kenya, she was caught in the middle. At least she was going to be a nurse again – helping. Unlike him, he thought, skulking behind a camera, avoiding any form of commitment, still fearful of trapdoors to the past.

Johnny turned to go but found his way blocked by more protestors swelling forward towards Government House. A line of African police emerged from the residence, linking arms to form a protective barrier on the other side of the fence. Rather than calming the situation, the proximity to Africans seemed to enrage the demonstrators, the dark shade of auxiliary police skin a rebuke, a hateful reminder of settler impotence. Some of the crowd spat at the policemen while others screamed obscenities. A middle-aged woman in a brown dress sitting astride the shoulders of a bull-framed farmer was screaming over the fence towards officials peering out through windows: '*Filthy nigger-lovers!*'

A younger woman whose floral hat had been knocked askew was lighting one cigarette after another, passing them to her companions who reached through the railings, trying to burn the bare thighs of police officers. Another bottle went over, followed by a brick. One of the policemen fell to the ground, poleaxed by a large stone that struck him in the face.

Johnny felt lightheaded and recognised with some urgency that it was time to go. He'd never been good in crowds but this was more serious. There was a tightness in his chest and he thought he might faint.

He tried to back away, only to find his route blocked by an outsize farmhand stinking of cows and diesel. A woman to his left, slippery with sweat, half turned and Johnny scrabbled desperately past, sliding through a small gap. But all he'd managed was to get one row back from the fence. Again he was hemmed in, pressed against a heaving mass of rage. It wasn't the violence of the crowd. It was the anger. Inchoate and visceral, foaming into the air.

The image from the old sickness had knifed its way back to the surface. The picture was always the same. A person, small, screaming through wire at the top of their voice, clutching at Johnny. He'd never been able to tell the gender, however often the scene replayed. The spattered striped uniform hid everything but the anger. The voice was German with English thrown in. He hadn't understood then, didn't now.

Johnny shook his head but the image refused to leave, juddering and smouldering like film stuck in a projector. He'd thought he was over it. But here it all was again, surging back, threatening to become a full-blown fit. Panicked, he turned round to shove against the crowd but was pushed back by yet more people pressing forward; a furious tide smashing against the fence, wanting only to reach through and hurt the policemen.

Johnny lashed out. Facing the same way as the crowd, he dug his elbows back and forth, pistoning his way backwards. People shouted and one man threw a punch but the claustrophobic pressure drove Johnny on, heedless of the effect he was having on those around him. Not a moment too soon, he burst through. Any longer and he would have gone under.

He shivered in the heat, breathing deeply and slowly as the doctors had instructed. If he'd succumbed, submerged again into that

130

darkness, he might have ended up anywhere. He hadn't had a fit, or even the fear of one, for over three years and he cursed the fact there were still triggers that could claim him, however far he ran.

Tansy was late. She'd arranged to meet Grogan at the Stanley's café at four o'clock before they joined the others in the bar for drinks. Johnny would be there and she felt excited at seeing him again. The words that had tumbled from her at the end of their evening had been harsher than she meant. She hadn't wanted to put him off altogether, just not encourage him too quickly – yet. She needed to talk to him properly but it would be difficult with all of them being there together. She'd find a way. But, she told herself strictly, only if she'd been able to speak to Grogan first. She was dreading it but it had to be done, and this teatime tête-à-tête seemed the best chance.

Now, of course, she was late, which Grogan would hate and would make everything even more awkward. It hadn't been her fault – a stupid shortcut had found her in the middle of a dreadful settlers' march. She'd been appalled by the chants, and when she'd told a woman to behave herself she'd found herself accidently-on-purpose shoulder-barged to the ground as the crowd surged forward. It had hurt quite a lot and she'd needed time in the ladies to clean the scrape on her elbow.

When she eventually made an appearance Grogan was looking sourly at his watch.

She apologised and sat, trying to hide the graze. But her skin was livid and raw and she couldn't help grimacing. When Grogan saw the wound his sourness vanished and he countermanded her objections, calling the manager, ordering proper bandages at once.

Tansy tetchily reminded him she was the nurse here and knew the difference between a scrape and something more serious. But Grogan fussed even more, stroking her good arm, telling her how brave she was and how she should never wander off on her own. In her current mood, Grogan's concern was harder to deal with than his usual lack of it.

'Honestly, Grogan,' she said. 'You sound like that child's poem – *"You must never go down to the end of the town without consulting me."* Thank you, but really – I'm all right. Now shall we have some tea? I have something to say to you.'

131

Grogan sat back, looking so chastened Tansy didn't have the heart to blurt out what she really wanted. That they were friends and only that. She'd admired him but any earlier intimacy had been an error; the feeling of his fleshy hand on her bare thigh on the night of the party at Nyeri had made her sick.

Instead she put her toe in the water with a lesser admission. She'd decided, she said more gently, that singing was no longer for her. She was returning to nursing. 'Unlike you, Grogan, I'm actually quite good at it.'

'I see,' Grogan said, on firmer ground. 'That is a pity. I was reviewing your schedule only this morning. I'd promised the Air Wing chaps at Mombasa you'd make an appearance there in a week or so.'

'Well I'm afraid you'll have to cancel.'

Grogan poured a cup of tea for each of them and placed the strainer neatly on the edge of the tray.

'This has nothing to do with that business with Macharia?' he asked.

'How do you know about that? Did Johnny tell you?'

'You didn't really expect me not to hear about it when my, my ...' Grogan searched for the right word '... my *girlfriend* turns up at a police station in the middle of the night causing an uproar over one of my drivers? Can't think what Johnny was doing; police cells are no place for a woman.'

The word girlfriend made Tansy squirm. She needed to get this done quickly. But Grogan was pressing on.

'You had no business being there. I asked Johnny to take you home, not escort you on a Cook's tour of the war on Mau Mau.'

'Is that what it was? *Part of the war?* Doesn't it occur to you that might be the precise reason why I no longer want to entertain your wretched troops? I'm not completely naïve, Grogan. I know bad things sometimes happen but beating up an innocent driver is not what I'd call war. I've seen other things too. Being a singer seems a little bit too much like giving it my blessing.'

Grogan was smiling tolerantly, Tansy's words glancing off him. Mention of Johnny's name emboldened her. Her relationship with Grogan might have strayed beyond the borders of friendship but he'd no right to claim anything more. He'd be hurt but would come to understand.

'Look, Grogan, I have to tell you something else—'

'Hang on, speaking of Johnny, there's something I need to tell you as well,' Grogan said, urbanely pouring milk into the tea. 'Did you know he's moving on?'

'*Moving on?* What on earth do you mean?'

'I had no idea either until the other day, when he asked me if he could spend some time outside Nairobi. Says he's getting tired of city life.'

'He *said* that?'

'Yes. Suspect that business with Macharia's behind it. You know he went through a tough time during the last show? He was very young. Bit fragile even now, poor chap. So of course I said yes – sugar? Well, I want to be able to help those closest to me if I can. What's the point of rank otherwise? He seemed rather embarrassed, so I'd be grateful if you didn't mention anything to him.'

Tansy accepted the tea and sipped furiously even though it was still hot enough to scald her lips.

It couldn't be because she refused to kiss him. Was he really still that young? He must have known that if anything was ever going to happen between them it would have to be done the right way. Trivial affairs belonged to another age. She'd sensed Johnny believed that too. It was too ghastly. On top of everything else that had happened today. She felt so wretched she wanted to cry.

Grogan watched Tansy pretending to enjoy her tea. She was putting up a calm façade but he was confident he understood exactly what was going on inside her head. Infatuation versus love. Gratification versus duty. It was true he'd never experienced these conflicts himself, but he knew them when he saw them. She was, he thought to himself, thrashing around like a little salmon, and he loved her for it. Grogan was a great believer in facts and it was one of his unshakable tenets that a rational human being, when presented with a truth, invariably chose the right road, even if some of the consequences were unpalatable.

'I'm terribly sorry, Grogan, but I'm going to have to bathe this arm again,' Tansy said, getting to her feet. 'Perhaps I should have put on that bandage after all. I'm just going to . . .'

Tansy didn't finish the sentence, desperate to escape before he saw her face.

Grogan rose to his feet, admiring the curve of her thigh as she ran for the sanctuary of the ladies. He'd been planning to ask her this afternoon but that would have to wait. He didn't mind. Part of the art of persuasion lay in timing. Displacements made, there'd be plenty of time – and no distractions. He would make sure of it.

There were no taxis so Johnny set off towards the New Stanley on foot, trying to shed his atavistic hatred of the crowd, focusing instead on what Grogan might make of the march. He was sure the older man would despise it. While Johnny could never tell what his boss was working on behind the scenes, Grogan had always been clear the future lay in a shared Kenya. But with settlers in the mood they were, any notion of ceding territory was probably unthinkable now.

Johnny realised he'd never really examined the issue in any depth. The fact that Kenya was a British colony had always been a given. Neither fair nor unfair. If pushed, he would, like most Englishmen growing up with the map of the world splashed in imperial red, have accepted the usual reasoning that colonialisation could not possibly be exploitation as both sides benefited. Indeed, in the transaction it was Kenya that had the best of the deal. Health, government, roads, an end to tribalism – modernity, in short – exchanged for minerals, coffee and tea, a strategic port and the best farmland in Africa.

But having seen what was going on here, it seemed obvious to Johnny that the Europeans couldn't cling on. He thought Grogan believed this too, although on the few occasions they'd discussed it explicitly his boss was quick to point out practical difficulties. Who would the country actually be left to – Mau Mau baby slaughterers? Did any of the tribes have the machinery to run a national government? And what about the Europeans who'd been here for a hundred years; wasn't it their home too? Did they not deserve guarantees? Grogan's view was that only a nuanced approach would work. 'Kenya,' he would say with his annoying sphinx smile, 'is not a black and white issue.'

The Long Bar at the New Stanley was heaving and it took a while to find Grogan's party, who were ensconced at the table in front of the piano. Grogan was sitting between Tansy and a man Johnny didn't recognise. When he spotted Johnny, Grogan nodded and pointed at the hunched figure of Porter, who was at the bar and waving at Johnny to join him.

'What's your poison?' Porter shouted.

Johnny moved to the bar and asked for a gin; he preferred whisky but gin was what the colony drank before dinner and the Stanley was not a place to stand out from the crowd. This crowd anyway. It was noisy, even more frenetic than usual as it dissolved news of the settler riots. He was pleased to see Porter; the veteran had been looking after him, teaching him the dark arts of the Information game.

'Journalism without the exclusives,' he'd explained. 'Lie to everyone on an equal basis.'

Porter was ex-Fleet Street, mid-fifties, a shambling, foul-mouthed Yorkshire hack with a beard. Dark rings under his eyes and a permanently sour expression gave him the air of a hung-over naval commander called unwillingly to the bridge in the middle of the night. Despite his cantankerous exterior he'd been kind to Johnny, asking no questions about how he'd ended up in Nairobi. Porter had a past too – most of them had – but he didn't dwell there and was amusing company until about seven, after which he tipped into glassy incoherence. Johnny looked at his watch. An hour of lucidity left.

'How's tricks at the bunker?'

'Fookin' busy,' Porter said, clinking glasses and giving the curse the full northern vowel treatment. 'Boss class as nervous as a cat in a room full of rocking chairs. Heard what's occurring at Liars House?'

Johnny smiled. He felt comfortable with a man so formidably exasperated by everyone and everything. Rumour had it he'd been a first-class journalist in his day. Blotted his copybook with the wife of a trade union leader; allegedly caught in flagrante on a bench outside the marital home.

'The demonstration? Nasty business. I was caught up in the crowd,' Johnny said.

Porter grunted.

'So was Tansy. Roughed up apparently, by some of those settler cunts. Grogan's acting furious. Loves it really. Look at him – bristling with indignation. Very much the hero. Or would be if he'd actually been there.'

Johnny saw what Porter meant. Grogan's chest was puffed out, and in between loud and assertive declamations, hands bunched in chubby fists, he put out his arm to drape protectively along Tansy's shoulder. The trouble was that Grogan's arm was not long enough to fully encompass her shoulders and his fingers disappeared behind her neck as if he were stroking the nape. Tansy didn't like it and kept moving her head to one side. She looked up to see Johnny watching her and issued a half smile that could have meant anything.

Johnny felt hollow with shame and longing. Tansy was fooling around with Grogan as if nothing had happened. It wasn't that confusing, then. He'd been looking forward to trying to talk to her, but the way she was behaving suggested it might be better to avoid her.

'By the way,' Porter said. 'In case I forget, I need to discuss something with you. It's important, Johnny. Come and find me later.'

Porter marched off towards the table leaving Johnny to follow. Tansy smiled vaguely his way again, more out of toleration than warmth, he thought, and he did not return it. Grogan clapped him cheerfully on the back and Tansy deliberately turned to talk to Porter.

'Hello, Johnny – thought you might not make it,' Grogan boomed. 'Some kind of protest outside Government House. Rumours of something really nasty at a place called Lari. Half the bloody colony were in town. Didn't see it myself – in meetings all day. Poor Tansy felt the rough edge of the settlers' wrath, didn't you, darling?'

Tansy was bending a gloved arm towards Porter, showing him her sore elbow. Grogan leaned over the table, reaching for her hand to kiss. But Tansy was already withdrawing it to light a cigarette and he was left hovering.

'Does it still hurt, my darling?'

Tansy raised an eyebrow at Porter, who was trying to stifle a grin.

'Grogan, can we go soon, please,' she said languidly. 'This place is filling up with exactly the sort of people who were in the crowd. I'm not sure I care to go through it all again.'

The front of Grogan's shirt was untucked from his shorts and his cheeks were unusually red. Johnny wondered how long they'd all been in here.

'In a minute, my dear. I need to have a word with Johnny.'

Tansy stared pointedly in the other direction. Sitting in profile, with her bobbed dark hair and long black evening gloves she resembled a young Vivien Leigh. How many versions of her were there? She flicked her eyes Johnny's way before resuming her chat with Porter. He blushed, caught out.

'So, Johnny, I need to speak to you about . . . '

He couldn't hear the rest as Grogan was interrupted by a man shoving in between them, spilling Grogan's drink. A finger jabbed sharply into Johnny's shoulder. He recognised him as the Kenya Cowboy who'd put a gun to the head of the prisoner at the Cunningham place. *Creed*. He'd never forget him.

'Look who it is,' Creed barked down at him. 'What're you doing here? Shouldn't you be round the back with your wog friends?'

He was weaving unsteadily. Porter and Tansy had stopped talking. Johnny tried to stand but Creed pushed him roughly back into his seat.

'If you want to talk let me buy you a drink,' Johnny said as evenly as possible, fighting his instinct to punch him. To show off, an inner voice said.

'*Drink?* Think I'd take a drink off a filthy nigger-lover like you? Hypocritical bastard! You set us up to do the dirty work, but when you turn up you don't like what you see. Christ man, you're worse than they are.'

'Not sure I follow,' Johnny said. 'What do you mean, *set up*?'

'What I mean, you liberal cocksucker. Are those pic—'

Creed didn't finish the sentence. Johnny was aware of a flurry of movement and a second later Creed was bent double with Grogan standing beside him, pulling his head down by the neck. There was considerable strength in those short arms and Creed gasped in pain. Grogan's face was hard as he urgently whispered something into Creed's ear. The people nearest to their table had stepped back from the commotion but the action had been so quick the rest of the Long Bar hadn't noticed.

Grogan finished what he was saying before pushing Creed away. The Kenyan limped off clutching his side and Grogan watched him leave before turning back to the table. Tansy was standing, her face flushed

'You OK, Johnny?' Grogan asked.

'Absolutely,' he replied, annoyed Grogan had helped him out in front of Tansy.

Porter was cackling. 'Well played, boss,' he said, raising his glass to Grogan before draining it.

'Yes, well,' Grogan said, tucking in his shirt. 'Apologies all. An extremely rude man. Won't tolerate it. Ladies present. If they're the new master race we're all in trouble. Best if we go, I think.'

Outside the hotel they waited for a taxi and Johnny asked Grogan what he'd said to make Creed leave in such a hurry.

'Nothing really,' he chuckled. 'Told him I'd give his private address and the address of his family to some leading Mau Mau cadres I know.'

'Is that true?' Johnny asked. 'Do you actually know any?'

'Dear boy, you'd be surprised what you have to do in my line. Not always popular but got to be done, d'you see?'

Johnny had never witnessed his boss behave in a physical manner before and wasn't sure whether to be alarmed or impressed. Before he could say anything Tansy had taken Grogan's arm. She stroked his cheek with a gloved hand. Johnny forced himself to look away, walking out of her eye line. Had their evening together been a hallucination? She *was* playing with him.

'My hero,' she said to Grogan, with the barest flicker in her voice. Grogan didn't notice, pulling her to him with a short arm around her waist.

'Johnny, you'd better wait with Porter. See him into a taxi. And do try to avoid any more trouble with the Cowboys. Plenty more where that little shit Creed came from, alas. Meanwhile, as I was trying to say inside, from tomorrow I've been ordered on manoeuvres but I need to ask you something before I go. Important, actually.'

'I gather you're leaving us too, Johnny,' Tansy said. 'All very sudden?'

Johnny raised his eyebrows.

'Leaving? No I'm just—'

'Sorry, Tansy,' Grogan interrupted forcefully. 'Need to speak to Johnny now. Matter of some urgency, actually. So if you wouldn't mind.' A taxi had drawn up and he pointed at it.

Tansy's face deadened into a tight mask. Johnny feared she'd said something to Grogan about their evening. Grogan was always on manoeuvres and now it looked as if Tansy had joined him. She took a long final drag on her cigarette and pulled away from Grogan.

'Well, in that case I'll leave you gallant gentlemen to talk shop.'

Grogan opened the taxi door for Tansy. As she slid in he pulled Johnny to one side.

'Listen, I'll cut straight to it. Word's reached me you might be in possession of some pictures, some *damaging* pictures. From that time when you were at the Cunninghams'. There aren't, are there? I thought you'd shown me everything.'

Johnny looked blank.

'The day you returned from that mess,' Grogan pushed on. 'You developed some pictures, but did you keep some back? Come on, Johnny – this is serious. I'm sure they don't exist, but if they do they really have to stay a private affair – do you understand?'

'Not sure I do, actually.'

Grogan looked at Johnny steadily, small mouth set tight.

'OK, if that's how you want to play it. But you have to understand Graves is a grade-one shit. Very dangerous. Not to be meddled with. While I've some authority here I intend to use it to stop some of his barbaric nonsense. Already had a word with Monkey Johnson and he's minded to set up a task force within his African Affairs ministry to look into allegations of improper conduct. So the machinery's beginning to turn.'

Johnny nodded, relieved. He didn't have much faith in government machines but was glad a reason had come up to prevent him having to intervene off his own bat.

'Oh and by the way,' Grogan said, glancing towards the taxi before drawing conspiratorially close. 'I want you and Porter to get up to Nyeri. Rather short notice I'm afraid but there's no one else. I've had to send Mattingly to Lari – sounds as if it's gone damnably sour up there. A lot of people killed. Meanwhile the army's asking if we can help persuade the Kikuyu to understand that if they surrender they won't all get shot. Means a bit of filming – hearts and minds stuff showing how warmly they'll be received.

'You'd better pack a large bag, you'll be away for a while. Report to Porter tomorrow morning. He knows what to do. Don't worry, Johnny, shouldn't be too dangerous out there, whatever they say.'

'*Tomorrow?*'

'Yes. Sorry. Earlier the better.'

Over Grogan's shoulder, Johnny could see Tansy sitting in the taxi. Through the open door he watched as she carefully loosened each of her gloved fingers before slowly peeling the fabric down her arms to display the white skin beneath.

She looked up and caught his eye. There was no hint of apology in her expression but her eyes widened and if Johnny hadn't just seen how she'd acted with Grogan he would have sworn she was trying to tell him something. He was thankful it was dark and she couldn't see that for the second time that evening he was blushing.

In the taxi Grogan made a point of holding Tansy's hand. She didn't reject the pressure but neither did she return it, putting her head back on the bolster and closing her eyes.

'Are you all right, my darling?' Grogan asked.

Tansy smiled faintly and withdrew her hand. She was not all right but the last person in the world she wanted to talk to about it was Grogan. Today had been a nightmare. The riots, the teatime failure with him, the dreadful drinks with Johnny looking so hurt despite his apparent desire to flee the scene. What was the matter with him? Why had he been deliberately avoiding her? And now there was going to be the inevitable fumble when the taxi stopped. Frankly, she couldn't wait to get to Kagamo Hospital. At least the wounds would be visible.

There were few other vehicles in Nairobi at this time of night and as they drove Tansy turned to watch the empty streets flick by. The taxi's headlights picked up two men in the shadows who fled for cover as soon as the beam was on them. Everyone running from something. Reflected in the car window, she saw Grogan fiddling in his pocket and for one awful moment she thought he might be arranging himself for a lunge.

'Tansy, my dear,' he said, perching on the edge of the seat. If the car veered suddenly he would be thrown onto the floor. Tansy grinned at the vision of him on his back with his arms and legs waggling in the air like an upturned beetle.

'Do be careful, Grogan,' she said.

Then she saw that he held a small box in front of him, which he appeared to be offering to her.

'Ah, yes,' Grogan said, misinterpreting her words. 'This is indeed a moment that calls for caution. But I have thought about it long and hard. And not only do I believe it would be the most practical solution – which, as you know, would please me – but also the most affectionate, which I hope would please you.'

Tansy stared at the box, which Grogan had flicked open to reveal an elegant sapphire ring.

'It would be,' Grogan continued, 'a perfect union. Which is why, Tansy Thompson, I am humbly asking for your beautiful hand in matrimony.'

Before she knew it, he had taken her finger and slipped on the ring.

'What do you say, my darling? And please don't tell me you are flattered, I think that might break even my heart. And yes, I do have one, despite what people say.'

Tansy fanned out her fingers. The ring looked beautiful and fitted her perfectly. She looked at Grogan and realised he was so serious that for the first time in his life he was making self-deprecatory jokes. She stared at his earnest face, glimpsing something she'd not seen before. A vulnerability. It softened him, revealing a man beneath the surface she'd not met. And it was a man too; not a boy who ran away at the first sign of conflict.

'Do you really love me?' she asked.

Grogan was caught off guard, his petite mouth opening and shutting rapidly as he framed a reply.

'Well, yes, of course I do,' he said quietly. 'I should have said. I'm so sorry, I've never done this before. I'm not sure I'm any good at it. But yes, I absolutely do love you. I thought it was obvious.'

Tansy nodded slowly, in awe of how different he seemed. Hesitant and anxious. Like a real person. *My God.*

'But what about you, Tansy?' he asked, recovering his composure. 'If you have to ask, then I suppose I should too – told you I was no good at it. Do *you* love me?'

The taxi had reached their destination but neither made any move to get out. Tansy knew in her heart the answer to his question was the only important one. It was one she'd wrestled with over the past months while he'd been courting her. Was it possible, as she'd once imagined, to fall in love with a mind? And if you did, would the rest follow?

Whatever she said now would determine her happiness, or lack of it, for the rest of her life. She looked out of the window once more, searching for the truth. She'd thought she'd known what that was this afternoon. How quickly things turned on their head. The African taxi driver coughed quietly. He was waiting to end his shift, impatient to get going, back to his real life. Did he have a wife at home? She saw his eyes in the mirror and was reminded of Macharia. It made her think of Grogan's comment earlier. How much was he really involved in what he'd called his war? What was his actual role? Would he have been outraged if he'd seen what had been done to Macharia? Would he have banged his fist on the police sergeant's desk?

Like Johnny had done?

She reached out to stroke Grogan's cheek.

She had her answer.

Chapter 10

Nyeri District, March 2008

The big man who'd introduced himself only as Dedan was leaning against his bus, smiling laconically. It was a smile of impending victory and Sam was not entirely sure it helped. Every now and then his shoulders shook with aggressive mirth, confident there could only be one outcome. Reflected in Dedan's wrap-around mirror shades, the official driver looked tiny and didn't stand a chance. Why didn't he just admit defeat? It was annoying to be so late again. Yesterday had been a wash-out. A village with not a single Mau Mau veteran, even though the trip had been arranged by Pugh.

Sam pulled out the third cigarette of the morning and watched as her translator, Kamau, tapped at his phone. She wondered if he'd say anything to her today. Yesterday he'd grumpily ignored her, playing with his mobile all journey. She had been left in the back next to one of her fellow lawyers, the squashed-faced Gove, who managed to bore her for the entire trip with an unceasing monologue about lack of prestige and money among junior government lawyers.

This morning Gove was nowhere to be seen, thank God, having attached himself to another group. Pugh had offered to accompany her but Sam informed him she preferred to travel solo. The idea of him pressed against her, touching her knee all the way to Nyeri, had not been enticing.

Now here she was, enduring a spat over who was going to drive her. She didn't mind being fought over, but this was becoming tedious. She hadn't a clue who Dedan really was. He'd turned up half an hour ago, announcing that Mattingly had sent him, as if that were explanation enough. 'I will be better than this one,' he'd said contemptuously, before speaking menacingly to the official driver provided by the High Commission. Despite his manner, Sam had warmed to Dedan – there was something about his largeness that was reassuring.

'Right,' Sam said, crushing out her cigarette and advancing towards the quarrelling men.

'I'm sorry,' she said, turning to the official driver. 'We're going with this man. It's all been arranged. If you haven't had the paperwork that's a matter for you. Yesterday was a disaster and I'm keen to get going.'

She opened her palms in question to Dedan.

'Shall we?'

'Oh yes.' His deep voice rumbled with suppressed laughter and he slid open the doors of his van to let Sam in, giving a last volley to the driver before adjusting his dark glasses in the rear-view mirror.

No doubt she'd be reprimanded but she couldn't have borne another day of kempt courtesies. The official Nissan cruiser she'd travelled in yesterday was the same as every other air-conditioned, hermetically sealed car that whisked foreigners from safari to safari. The new mystery driver's carriage was a van. But not just any van. This was a *matatu*, one of the fabled psychedelic minibuses that flashed through Kenya's highways, blaring colour and noise. When Dedan had parked the *matatu* outside the hotel, its glinting curves garishly painted in green and red, Sam thought it was carrying a band. Ridiculously loud music pumped out of its speakers – including one attached to the roof.

There was plenty of room up front next to Dedan, but unlike yesterday Kamau allowed himself to settle in the back on a seat across from Sam's. They launched away from the hotel at ludicrous speed and Sam grabbed both armrests, happy to see that Kamau was anxiously clutching his seat too. She grinned at him and he returned a sheepish smile.

'It is not always the smoothest of rides,' he said.

'Too right it isn't,' Sam replied, wincing as the van leaned over to take a corner. 'It's like a bloody fairground.'

'Is this your first *matatu* experience?'

'Yes. Not yours, I take it?'

'Not at all, no,' he laughed. 'For Kenyans it is the most efficient – certainly cheapest – form of public transport. Everybody uses them. As you will see.'

He laughed again and Sam couldn't help laughing back, though he'd said nothing funny.

He grinned at her before putting on headphones to signal the end of the conversation. Being in the *matatu* had transformed him. He seemed happier and Sam thought it made him rather good-looking. He was a slender man and the fingers that tapped at his phone were long and elegant, reminding her for a moment of the Eastern European boy in Lincolnshire. Graceful and strong. And that laugh.

Kamau suddenly raised his eyes from his phone and Sam coughed in embarrassment, realising she'd been staring at him. As she rummaged in her rucksack looking for the depositions she scolded herself for even thinking about it. She was here to work and could ill afford any distractions.

She extracted the statements of the veterans she was going to interview today. In this new village she'd been promised at least half a dozen who'd recently signed affidavits about their treatment at the hands of the British. Shot and wounded; beaten and tortured; left for dead; sexually assaulted with an implement; raped. It went on and on.

Pugh wanted his team to 'assess' the strength of the claims – in other words, find discrepancies in their testimony. Two days ago Sam would have been happy to do just that. Pruning away inconsistencies was the sort of legal topiary she was well practised in. But after hearing Esther's story that approach seemed shallow, a narrow legal contrivance. Professional distance was impossible now. Ordinarily she might have recused herself as being too close to the case but this was far from being ordinary. The discrepancies in the testimony – if they were that – might matter in a fine legal sense but they had become irrelevant to a much greater truth. Sam was aware this might not be a view that sat well with Pugh. She would face that one later.

She sighed and looked out of the window, remembering the condensation she'd peered through at Magnus's house. She missed him. She'd rung yesterday but the Gauleiter had answered, so she'd put the phone down. Sam knew she ought to contact her mother but didn't feel up to that either. And as far as her father was concerned – he could wait.

Suddenly Sam felt tired and oppressed by it all. In some ways Esther's story had been so awful it seemed hopeless. How could you

145

ever get any real redress for that? Out on the road a woman carried a huge bundle while an elderly man limped behind. He had lost a leg and grimaced every time the makeshift crutches bit into his armpits. So much poverty and suffering here, nothing to do with the past or the British or colonialism. Or anything to do with her. Perhaps it might be best to let suffering dogs lie. If she wanted to make a gesture she could always work for a charity.

Just then Dedan turned up the volume on his sound system, grinning at her in the mirror. He had a massive shaven head and all she could see was the back of it, glistening and gyrating with the rhythms.

'Tony Nyadundo!' he shouted. 'You like him? "Isanda Gi Hera". Lovin' it!'

Sam laughed. She had no idea what he was talking about but his enthusiasm immediately lifted her mood. It became impossible to concentrate on her papers, the insistent beats of the drums and harmonica tattooing heavily into her skull. At least it was cheerful. Sam closed her eyes and before long the repetitive music and the motion of the *matatu* became soothing, swaying her into a hypnotic half-sleep.

As she dozed she couldn't keep her mind from straying over what Esther had described. Sam thought if anything like that had happened to her she would never have made it, never have been able to live with the shame and memory of it. Esther was so impressive, she had a heart of steel – refusing to remain a victim; moving on, even marrying a British man. Sam had found that curious, but on the way back from the sisal field Esther had explained how Mattingly had protected her for the rest of the Emergency. He'd found a place for her to live in the home of one of the Information Department's African clerks, every day bringing food and medicine, and when she needed them, false papers. Slowly bringing her back to life. To have been discovered sheltering a Kikuyu woman from the Lari district would have spelled the end of his career, might even have been dangerous. The security services suspected any white person who had a serious relationship with an African was a potential traitor. The stress had made him drink, a little at first then more than he could handle. She'd been able to assist him with that, which had helped redress the balance between them. Equality had been important as love hadn't come immediately for Esther. She'd confessed to Sam that her feelings only deepened much later. They'd married when the Emergency ended and been together ever since, if not happily ever after then with quiet affection on both sides. If they'd been able to have children that might have changed everything. But there it was.

The *matatu* came to a halt and Sam was jolted back into the present. As far as she could tell they were still on the outskirts of town. Dedan had leapt out and was helping two women and a small girl carry a pile of boxes and a large suitcase. Within seconds the women, the girl and all their belongings were crammed in next to Sam and Kamau. '*Jambo, Jambo*.' And off they rocketed, the music even louder than before. The *matatu* stopped twice more in quick succession, loading and unloading more people.

Sam tried to run through the depositions once more but the music and chattering passengers were too distracting. Then Dedan announced they would be arriving in less than an hour and she sat up in her seat, annoyed at not having used her journey time properly.

There was one task she could not put off any longer. Perhaps the most significant one of all. The extraordinary Mattingly documents. Too important to travel with, she'd left most of them behind in the hotel safe but taken a few key pages and a summary she'd made this morning. What she needed to do now was learn it inside out. It would be vital for when she questioned the veterans, though in truth it was far more significant than that.

The papers blew a hole in the entire British case.

When she'd first opened the envelope Mattingly had pressed upon her, the smell from the thick bundle of typewritten documents had been unmistakably from another era, a faint reek of stale cigarettes and dust conjuring the dry must of committees and confidentiality. In her hotel room, she'd read them with increasing shock, making notes immediately, recognising how explosive the information would prove. It occurred to her these might well be the same papers the luckless Jules had been referring to at the High Commission function the other night. No wonder Mattingly had been so paranoid, dramatically issuing his dire warnings of secrecy and peril.

They *knew* – they bloody knew!

The papers not only proved beyond doubt that crimes had been committed by colonial forces, but, more importantly in the current climate, they showed British authorities had full knowledge of them. The scale of the lying, or 'forgetting', was immense and in direct contradiction to the official line.

'Whatever we think about the colony,' Pugh had said, 'they were very good at one thing at least: bureaucracy. The British were famous for their efficiency. Every action had an order, every movement a chitty, every incident a report. It was inconceivable that abuse could have taken place on the scale being claimed by our human rights brethren because *it would have been known*. It would have been minuted in some bloody committee or another. And on that score, my fine legal eagles, the cupboard is bare. I know – we've looked.'

But Mattingly's papers gave the lie to that. The cupboard was not bare – it was groaning with evidence.

The documents were marked 'Most Secret' and contained complete, wonderfully unredacted minutes from a body called the Chief Secretary's Complaints Co-ordinating Committee. The CSCCC had been set up early in 1954 to deal with complaints of ill-treatment by any member of the security forces. It was attended by senior civil servants like the Deputy Public Prosecutor and the Under-secretary of Defence and up until 1959 was concerned with hundreds of cases of abuse. It didn't appear to make any recommendations for action, acting more as a scrutiny body. More interesting, thought Sam, was the circulation list. The minutes were forwarded to most of the senior colonial and army officers in Nairobi at the time, up to and including the Governor and all of his ministers. They were even despatched back to London for the attention of the Secretary of State for the Colonies – which meant right up to the Cabinet and, by implication, the Prime Minister.

They'd sat on it for half a century.

Although the Committee only heard those cases percolating up through the system – and therefore was probably massively underreporting the total number of cases – Sam found it highly significant to see the full range of abuses described in the depositions, including murder, torture and rape, finding their way to the Committee. The offenders reported to the Committee were from every branch of the security forces: Kenya Police, Kenya Police Reserve, Prison Service, Kenya Regiment, King's African Rifles and Home Guard.

The CSCCC papers, presciently kept by Mattingly for so long, were a summary of the case against the British state. It was extraordinary and again Sam reflected on the courage it must have taken for Mattingly to give them to her. If anyone from that period was still around today they would probably be facing a war crimes court. As Mattingly had warned, there were people who did indeed have a lot to lose.

For the rest of the journey Sam was engrossed in reading her summary. Again it struck her how absurd it was to think she could continue working for Pugh and the wretched mission. Yet she couldn't resign from it now – there was more work to do. Besides which, she had no money. Where would she stay if she had to leave the hotel? It would surely be better to carry on under the mission's banner until they returned to London. Then she would get in touch with one of the law firms active in this area. They'd know how to handle it. Might even give her a job. Sam brightened at the idea and raced through the papers to make sure she finished by the time she arrived.

The village was more of a small town. A central strip of shops and stalls, a small hotel and a red-dust market space where boys kicked a deflated ball around a woman trying to beat a carpet. Dedan got out and stretched, sauntering over to a barber's shop where he was welcomed with much shaking of hands in the African three-part, shake-grasp-shake manner.

'Does that man know everyone?' Sam asked Kamau, who had finally put his phone away.

'He seems to. Do you really not know him?'

'Me? No, he was recommended by a friend – that's what he told me. Should we be worried?'

Kamau smiled. 'No. I think he will do us very well. No one will mess with us if he is around.'

'Is that a possibility then – someone messing with us?'

Kamau pondered. Sam had already noticed his tendency to pause before giving an answer. She hoped he would not be as hesitant when the translation started.

'Not everyone claiming to be Mau Mau is genuine,' he said. 'When money and poverty come together there is always the possibility of trouble.

'Oh good,' Sam replied. 'I always love the prospect of trouble.'

'Yes, I could tell that about you. Dedan and I will have to be careful.'

Sam grinned. Apart from the tiniest sparkle in his eye the deadpan was faultless. Interesting. She was spared another exchange by Dedan, who gestured for them to come over.

'The people you wish to speak to have gathered over there,' he said, pointing to a field on the other side of the boys playing football. 'But quite a few of them have gone already. Someone's been here who they are concerned about, one of those leeches who suck on the blood of the reparations movement. Some of them weren't even born when Mau Mau started. If he turns up again I will let him know my views.'

'Is it going to be an issue?'

'I don't know. I shouldn't think so, but I will drive the *matatu* over there just in case.'

He shut the door and pulled away, leaving her to walk across with Kamau. Half a dozen chairs had been placed in a rough circle where four men and two women sat talking. When Sam arrived they all got to their feet, even a man almost bent double, leaning heavily on a cane. They all shook her hand respectfully and continued to stand, smiling hesitantly.

'I think you should invite them to sit,' Kamau whispered in her ear. 'They are not as young as you, you see.'

The deadpan again. She smiled and turned her attention to the Africans in front of her, bidding them to sit. She'd looked forward to this ever since arriving in Kenya. Finally she was out in the field, talking to real people. As they slowly eased into their seats, they seemed so dignified, two of the men sporting ties and the women wearing beautiful, crisply laundered dresses. They sat for a moment observing one another, and when enough stock had been taken Sam opened up with her questions, going round in turn, asking the same of each veteran.

It was hard going, and after forty-five minutes Sam feared it would prove unworkable. The veterans were halting and over-deliberate, and even though she asked short, easy to understand questions, Kamau's translations took forever and their answers grew ever longer. There was also considerable difficulty in trying to get

150

across the fact she didn't just want them to replicate their depositions word for word. They nodded and smiled as if they understood but then merely repeated what they'd said in their statements. Word for bloody word. On the third attempt she stopped and asked Kamau what was wrong.

'They are suspicious of you. They think that because you work for the British government you will not believe what they say,' he said quietly.

'They can also see that you are testing them. They are not stupid, Sam. They understand that if they deviate from their sworn testimony you, a British lawyer, will write down that they are lying. And so they stick to the words on the paper.'

Sam signalled she needed a brief time-out and went back to the *matatu* to look for her cigarettes. Dedan had parked in the shade of a building so she leaned against the bonnet, smoking and thinking. Two houses along a group of men sat on the stoop, watching their elderly compatriots. Watching her too, she realised.

Sam knew she had to clear the air. If she maintained her professional distance she would not get anything out of these witnesses. She put out her cigarette and walked back to the circle of chairs.

Time to come off the fence.

To Kamau she said, 'Tell them that I understand their mistrust. I too would not trust a government lawyer.'

Kamau raised his eyebrow.

'You really want me to say that?'

'Yes. And then you will tell them this . . .'

She whispered in Kamau's ear, conscious of how close she was. He must have been able to feel her breath on his cheek, yet he didn't move away; if anything, he shifted a little closer.

As Kamau began to tell the circle what she'd relayed, Sam closely monitored the old Kenyans. At first they did not react at all. Then they began to look at her, and when Lari and Esther were mentioned they stared openly while the words flowed round their heads.

Kamau came to the end and there was silence. Sam stood, self-consciously looking at them all one by one as she informed them, via Kamau, that the story they had just heard was personal, had come from a friend of hers. A friend she had promised to help by getting the tale to a wider audience. Sam said she couldn't promise there would be compensation – that was beyond her power – but she did know things that would make it more likely. She had been given evidence from the old days that made it far more possible there would be some justice for people who had suffered.

She had started as a government lawyer, she said, but the testimony she'd heard and the events she'd learned of had changed her.

'Now, before you, I swear that my interests lie not with the British state but with you. I need to hear your stories too, so that I can help. From tomorrow I will no longer have a job with the mission but I will still be a lawyer – just not a British government lawyer.'

After the translation no one spoke for a moment, then one of the men wearing a tie said something to Kamau. It did not sound sympathetic. She heard her name – Seymour.

Kamau looked up at her with surprise.

'He says they hear what you say but they have heard many promises from the British. What he wants to know – and I'm not sure why he is asking this, Sam – is that if your name is really Seymour are you related to someone called Johnny Seymour? Do you know that name? It seems strange to me that they would wish to know this.'

Out of the corner of her eye Sam noticed Dedan had reappeared and was talking to the younger group of men sitting on the stoop. But he was still listening to Sam, and when he heard what the old ones had asked he drew nearer, bobbing his head, encouraging her to answer.

'Yes – it is true,' Sam said. 'I am related to Johnny Seymour. I am his granddaughter. Why do they ask?'

The man who had asked Kamau about Johnny climbed to his feet and Sam feared she was going to be asked to leave.

Then he opened his arms and spoke in good English.

'Come here, child.'

Sam smiled falteringly, not understanding. Suddenly all the elderly people were coming towards her and she was being embraced and hugged and their voices were strong.

'*Karibu*, Sam, *karibu*.'

Welcome, Sam, welcome.

Chapter 11

Nairobi, January 1953

Many hours after leaving the Long Bar at the Stanley, Johnny and Porter were in less salubrious surroundings. Johnny hadn't checked his watch for several hours but through the bar's windows he could see a new day arriving, the sun just starting to smear its colours on the lightening sky. Porter, however, was heading in the opposite direction, sliding inexorably into deep drunkenness, his beet-red face sweating with the effort of maintaining consciousness. The dark mahogany bar was sticky with the spilling of a dozen whisky chasers. Bottles of ginger ale were carefully lined up next to an ashtray overflowing with half-smoked Dutch cheroots. It was an old drinkers' trick but even Porter had lost count. In the corner an African prostitute sat astride Benson, the American from the *Christian Science Monitor*. Her skirt had rucked up and as she gyrated her large buttocks around his lap she revealed glimpses of green knickers, their fluorescent hue perfectly matching a strange feather affair on her head that had survived the initial grapple.

Slumped at the bar, Johnny stared at the headgear which drooped over the woman's hair, brushing Benson's cheeks every time she jiggled her hips. Johnny's alcohol-soaked brain could not fathom how Benson could stand to be tickled at such a moment. He giggled foolishly, wondering if the American had paid extra for the service.

'Fuck you laughing at?' Adams demanded from the adjacent bar stool. Adams was an American too, and for a moment Johnny couldn't recall who he was or why any of them were there. Then he remembered.

'*Adams*,' he said, wagging his finger. 'The first newspaper man. Adams. That's who you are. *New York Tribune-Herald*.'

The American downed his drink and slung his linen jacket over his shoulder.

'*Herald-Tribune.* Jesus, you're as fucked up as your friend.' He pointed his thumb at Porter, who had slumped into a cocoon of his own fumes, head hanging from his shoulders like an unstrung puppet.

'You guys had better quit,' Adams said, levering himself up from the stool. 'Or you'll never get out of here.'

'Where you going?'

'Back to my hotel. Take a shower; think about how we can file some of the stuff your friend gave me. Seriously, Johnny, if we ever manage to get this past the desk there's gonna be shit all over that fan. You and friend Porter need to be a long way from me when it happens.' He pointed at Benson drowning contentedly beneath wobbling oceans of flesh. 'And from him.'

Johnny took this in with the slow logic of the drunk and understood it to be true, though for the life of him he couldn't think why. His head felt as if it was going to spin off. He shut his eyes to assemble a reply but by the time he reopened them Adams was gone. And Benson. Deep within him, an atavistic self-protection mechanism kick-started a homing beacon. Time to go.

Porter didn't want to leave, but with the help of the bartender Johnny managed to find a taxi and squeeze his companion inside. Johnny decided the driver looked like a rogue so climbed in too. He'd never been to Porter's flat but knew it was somewhere off the Burhannuddin Road. All the roads looked dangerously similar but he still found himself shouting at the driver that he wasn't going to be pissed about and driven halfway to the Ngong Hills. He had no change for the fare so wrote a chit on the back of an old receipt and threw it at the driver, yelling he was lucky he didn't report him.

It was not elegant, and when he woke on Porter's lumpy leather sofa a cloying sense of having behaved badly edged ahead of his thirst and headache.

It was already afternoon, sticky and torpid. A fan swished noisily, but when he rose to take a piss the rest of the room thankfully remained still. After he'd helped himself to a cold bacon sandwich he felt better. Porter's place was a one-bedroom bachelor flat with little in the way of soft furnishings. The living room-cum-kitchen was spartan, with only the leather sofa, a desk and a leather armchair to adorn it.

The bedroom door was open and Johnny could see a neatly made bed but no Porter. The Yorkshireman would be back in an hour or so. He'd wait. He wanted to find out what Porter had tried to ask him last night. In the bar his friend had got so drunk so quickly it had been impossible to unravel any sense. When the Americans turned up it had been Johnny's turn to drink himself into oblivion; not that fun, but better than thinking about Tansy.

There was no radio to listen to so he went to the desk, intrigued by what he might find. He suspected that, underneath it all, Porter was a cultured fellow, and he was curious to see if he was writing anything beyond press releases. Why have a writer's desk otherwise?

He flicked through a sheaf of papers. They were mostly routine, press releases with the odd newspaper clipping thrown in. A pile of cuttings held together with a treasury tag contained stories from the local press, but not any that were linked to normal Information Department work. Bizarrely, Porter seemed to have developed an interest in construction. Not culture at all. Johnny retreated to the armchair to read them. It appeared the building trade was picking up. Government contracts all over the place. Wood, cement, brick, wire. Someone was doing well. There were dozens of facts and figures. He tried to follow them but he'd never been good at numbers and inevitably the details had a soporific effect; he felt his eyelids drooping.

When Porter returned Johnny was still there, snoozing in the armchair, a pile of cuttings on the floor.

'Found anything interesting?'

Johnny woke with a jerk. He'd been dreaming about riding naked on his bike, free but exposed. There was someone behind him but every time he tried to turn his head to see who, the wind whipped it back again. Porter went to the kitchen and Johnny heard the stirrings of a kettle.

'Tea?'

'Anything stronger?'

'Didn't you get enough last night?' Porter handed his guest a mug of steaming liquid. It was barely more than yellow hot water, loose leaves swilling round; no milk.

'What the hell were we doing there?' Johnny asked, searching for a cigarette. 'I don't even remember getting there from the Stanley after Grogan and Tansy left. But I do have a memory of you talking to those Yanks for hours. Why were *they* there?'

Usually Porter looked chipper whatever the circumstances but today he seemed older, the folds under his eyes protruding and vein-cut, hair that had been so carefully combed this morning distinctly unkempt. Porter ran his hand through it, his grin as weak as the tea.

'Wanted somewhere discreet. Don't need witnesses if it kicks off.'

Johnny looked blank.

'Fuck me, Johnny – don't you remember any of it? Bloody southern lightweight.' Porter shook his head, mumbling how it was impossible to trust a man who couldn't take his ale. Then he looked up and smiled.

'But I suppose if Tansy likes you that should be good enough.'

Tansy liked him? Not any more apparently. He felt a wave of embarrassment at having hung around her like a puppy. It wasn't as if she was the first pretty face in his life.

'Pay attention, Johnny,' said Porter sternly. 'Apart from when-ever Tansy's name is mentioned, you seem to handle yourself OK. Fetching that lad Macharia from the copshop, for example. Impressive. Most people wouldn't have given a shit about an African. So I feel I can trust you. Hope I'm not wrong.'

At the word trust, a worm of alarm wriggled in Johnny's stomach. It usually meant a secret coming your way and he could do without any more of those. Porter paced the length of his small flat a dozen times.

'You must have noticed what's going on out there,' he said even-tually, gesturing towards the window and the city beyond. 'It's not just a bit of bother in the margins any more, a driver picked up here or there. It's everywhere. Just this morning I heard about an inter-rogation centre in Nyeri District where they're piling the bodies up outside. Apparently it's got a moat round it with sharpened sticks and a drawbridge ... it's fucking medieval. And everyone looks the other way. This is not what I signed up for.'

Johnny stared at him.

Porter sighed theatrically.

'All right, if you won't ask I'll tell you. Thing is, Johnny, I've been talking to those Yanks. Leaking a bit of information here and there.' He paused. 'Well, OK, quite a lot actually. In fact, over the last few weeks I've given them all the official reports I could lay my hands on, handed over every paper that makes reference to shooting, maiming, any and every torture under the sun. It's off the fucking scale, though I doubt they'll ever print anything. It's too big and the official denials are too strong.'

Johnny whistled softly.

'Even so, man! *Jesus!*'

No wonder Porter was rattled. They'd all had to sign the Official Secrets Act and you could get thirty years for breaking it. It was a real prospect too: only last month a junior official had been put away in the notorious Kamiti prison for trading secrets.

The atmosphere in the flat was oppressive and Johnny stared out of the window at the tree-lined street, wishing he could un-hear what he'd just been told.

When no reaction came, Porter threw the undrunk tea down the sink before humming fretfully, taking his time to arrange an antimacassar on the sofa.

'Look, the reason I'm telling you this is because something else is brewing,' he said finally. 'It's serious, Johnny. I wouldn't blame you for looking the other way, but the truth is I need your help. So should I go on, or do you want to make your excuses and leave?'

Johnny hesitated. Whatever Porter was doing was bound to end badly. He should walk away now, deny all knowledge. He tried to think of a joke that would soften the blow. Then, unbidden, the image of the hunter turned security man slid into his mind: Graves gliding towards prisoners squatting on the ground; his gun against their heads.

'All right then,' Johnny sighed. 'You know you'd just get pissed and tell me anyway. May as well be hung for a sheep as a lamb – isn't that what you always say?'

Porter beamed.

'Good lad, you're learning. But don't say I didn't bloody warn you.'

Opening his desk drawer, he extracted a single manila file, from which he took a cluster of papers. As he laid them out in order on the table, he continued to speak over his shoulder.

'This bollocks we're doing now – nothing to do with journalism, is it? Information Officers my arse. We're just a lying bunch of sleaze

157

hounds pouring lies into lazy ears. Far worse than anything I ever did in Fleet Street. I was a reporter for thirty years – a good one too. But when that all went tits up I didn't mind being paid handsomely for churning out bullshit in the African sun.

'But only if it doesn't hurt anybody.'

Porter moved towards the window and the sun caught his glistening hair, producing a distorted halo effect – though Johnny found it hard to imagine him as an angel.

'Listen, I don't want to give you a bloody lecture but we're talking about British people, Johnny, same as you and me. Blokes who say they like cricket and queues and *fair play*. Who ask if there's honey still for tea before they go out and slice the ears off a fucking "Kyuke". Well, we're not all like that and I'm going to do something. Try to, anyway.'

He coughed, embarrassed at his own passion, and finished laying out the documents.

'The irony is not lost on me that, at the point in my career when I've given up journalism for being a government tart, I appear to have the makings of the best story of my life. But it's not quite there yet. See what you think.'

Looking at the documents on the kitchen table, Johnny saw they were from official sources; most designated *Top Secret. Eyes Only*. All seemed to have passed through the Information Department. It was high-grade material. He picked one at random, his heart racing. A request for large numbers of new assistant press officers to assist the Rehabilitation Department. Nothing particularly damning there but he wondered how Porter had got his hands on it. This category of papers would have been under lock and key in Grogan's office.

'You a safe-cracker now?' Johnny asked.

Porter didn't smile.

'A source. A trusted source. Someone who's prepared to put themselves on the line because they believe what's going on is wrong.'

Johnny tapped the paper he'd been reading.

'A request for more staff hardly seems the sort of thing to lay yourself on the line for.'

Porter retreated to the sofa and lay down.

'Don't be so daft. Look at them all and use your nous. Put the pieces together, then tell me what you think.'

Johnny picked up another document. It didn't look that terrifying, or secret either – this one listing locations dotted around the country. Fort Hall, Embu, Meru, Nyeri, Kiambu, Rift Valley, even the coastal region.

Another was a schematic of the railway system with notes on additions and timetable alterations. A memo dealt with how to treat the press during a forthcoming operation in Nairobi. Normal procedure so far. Then Johnny frowned. In a further memo they talked about the same operation involving twenty-five thousand members of the security forces. *Twenty-five thousand!* He scanned through the rest quickly. Individually they meant little but taken together they began to add up. One of the memos echoed the newspaper clippings he'd found on Porter's desk, describing a detailed budgetary request for tens of thousands of pounds' worth of building materials.

Two words leapt out at him: *Guard Tower.* It was humid and close in the room but he felt a chill that was both premonition and remembrance. Porter was studying him hard.

'Getting there now, are you? Told you it was serious, Johnny. It bloody well frightens me.'

Johnny re-read the papers one by one, hoping for a more innocent explanation. As they came from Grogan's department the emphasis was on propaganda: how to scotch rumours; how to inflate successes; the right kind of terminology to be used. But behind the slant, the letters and memos being circulated to a handful of senior names were painting an unambiguous picture.

'*Jesus.*'

Porter paused to let it sink in.

'Trouble is, Johnny, it's not enough. On its own everything you've just seen is deniable. Scoping exercises and contingencies. What we need is proof. Hard evidence. If the bastards are serious about this we need to fight it cleverly.'

He looked at Johnny apologetically,

'The thing is – and I admit I should have warned you – I told the Yanks we'd get them some. Proof, that is. More to the point, you'd get them some.'

'*Me?*'

'Yes, lad. You.' Porter smiled broadly. 'Seems like you and me are off on our travels. Didn't Grogan tell you? He briefed me yesterday.

We'll be driving up to Nyeri District in the Information van to make some bollocks film about getting the Africans to surrender. Mattingly's been sent to Lari, poor sod, so we're on our own. Don't you see? It'll be perfect cover to have a look at what's really going on.'

Johnny smiled slowly as he worked through the implications. It might be possible to find out something if they were away from Nairobi but, much better, they'd be out of the city. Away from all the nonsense. Away from Tansy.

'It might work,' Johnny said. 'Although I don't fancy acting as your bloody chauffeur while you moan and backseat drive.'

Porter cackled.

'You won't have to. The beauty of it is that Grogan wants to get shot of Macharia as well. Seems getting your head kicked in is bad ju-ju for His Highness. So he's given him to us. You do the pictures, I do the words. Macharia drives. We'll be visiting virtually all the places named in those memos – couldn't be better.'

The Yorkshireman snorted delightedly, describing in more detail how it would work, ending up coughing and laughing.

'By day, propagandists for the evil government regime; by night, Scarlet fucking Pimpernels. We seek the truth here, we seek it over bloody there . . . '

Johnny thrust his long legs out and sat back in the armchair. It wasn't funny but Porter was grinning like a soused Cheshire cat.

But could it really be true? If the colonial government was embarking on such an ambitious plan, it would have to have had the blessing of the Cabinet at home. It wouldn't be possible that such a vast enterprise would go forward in secret.

As they often did when a crisis loomed, his thoughts moved to Grogan. Surely he would share their reservations. Might he be prevailed upon to use his seniority and experience to squash it from the inside? He was exactly the kind of progressive voice in government who could have real influence.

But when he put this to Porter the answer nearly snapped his head off.

'Don't talk to me about Grogan fucking Littleboy,' Porter said, eyes darkening. 'You don't understand the half of it, Johnny. I'm not going to explain now but trust me – we're not going near him with this until we're fireproof.'

160

Chapter 12

The air was blessedly cool against her skin and for a moment Tansy felt she was back at her parents' farm, sneaking out for an illicit after-dinner smoke. It wasn't as high here as at Glenmore but it was still nearly a thousand feet above sea level and the night temperature could drop low enough for you to see your breath. She was standing near the last lean-to, where lightly wounded patients slept on mattresses on the floor. Their cotton palliasses were lying in rows on the ground, and from her position behind one of the columns holding up the walkway roof Tansy kept a watchful eye, enjoying her last cigarette before midnight rounds.

When she'd first arrived, the mission hospital's four main wards all had free beds. Now they didn't know where to put them. The numbers had been rising ever since they'd started building out at Umua. First the vast irrigation works, giant ditches and canals hewn from the plain by thousands of spades and pick-axes. Then the camps. Although they were only five miles away from the hospital's forest compound, Tansy had never been there. No time. In fact, she realised, she hadn't been away from the hospital for one solitary day since starting. Now the camps were finished they were almost overrun with patients. What kind of work were they doing up there that resulted in dozens of injured men being ferried to hospital every week?

How different from when she'd started nursing, before she'd been persuaded to leave and sing for her supper, performing like a pouting idiot because Grogan had asked her. Before she'd learned to say no. What had she been thinking of?

Prior to the Emergency the usual types of injury at the hospital were the normal African diseases caused by animals and poverty.

161

Jiggers and yaws, snakebite and ulcers, malaria and cataracts. Now it was predominately gunshot wounds and skull injuries, flesh burned or flayed. Once a man had been brought in barely alive, his entire back a welter of stripes from a caning that had started on his calves and worked its way up to his neck. Tansy had counted them; there'd been fifty whip marks precisely. Each stripe caused by one cane stroke. On the back and ankles the blow had often cut through to the bone. When she asked the other prisoners who did this they looked away, though one dying man whispered the word *Zebra*. She didn't understand it or anything about the brutality in what was meant to be a work camp.

It had taken weeks for the poor man to be allowed to turn over, and if it had not been for Jeremy and Daniel, the Kikuyu ward assistants gently tending his wounds every day, he would certainly have died. Jeremy, so tall and gracile; Daniel the opposite, squat and angry until he smiled with a wattage that brightened the entire ward. Yet these two men, whom Dr McGregor called the living heart of the hospital, were the reason Tansy was now keeping an eye on things from behind her column.

She'd begun to notice something fishy on the day it was announced there wasn't enough food for breakfast. The early morning meal wasn't much – a bowl of ugali and a drink of milk, perhaps some fruit – but to have none at all was odd. And recently other items had failed to make an appearance, the evening bread supply or a sack of potatoes simply vanishing. More seriously, bandages were going missing and only last night a batch of penicillin. No one knew anything. Dr McGregor had questioned the local staff after morning prayers and their response had been unnerving. Usually bright, confident nurses and hospital assistants stood in a row with eyes cast down, shuffling and murmuring. It reminded Tansy of a scene in front of her old headmistress; no one allowed to leave until the culprit owned up.

The veteran Dr McGregor was not known for his docility, and although he must have been in his late seventies he'd given full, hostile vent, his thin Scottish brogue whipping over the bowed heads of the shamed assembly. He'd been with the mission at Kagamo since it began as a one-room consulting space in the early twenties and he'd never – *ever* – seen anything like this. Someone must have seen something.

162

But no one had. While most workers stared sullenly at their feet or into the air, she was sure she'd spotted Daniel giving Jeremy an anxious look, Jeremy shaking his head curtly in reply. She'd not said anything to Dr McGregor, not wanting to blame anyone on a suspicion; the world was too full of false accusations as it was. But she decided to keep an eye on the pair. Their work could not be faulted but the more she thought of it, the more she felt they weren't behaving normally. They were always giving each other meaningful looks and slipping off together. For a while Tansy thought they might be lovers; the way they worked together so seamlessly with the patients sometimes reminded her of a married couple. Tansy certainly would have had no problem with that, regarding herself as, if not entirely liberated, as her sister might have said, then certainly broad-minded. Along with most others her age, Tansy accepted that sex before marriage was definitely a possibility with the right person, although in her limited experience there was a distinct tendency for it to happen with the wrong person. And as long as homosexuality wasn't flaunted in public – it was illegal after all – it might even be rather sweet. But she was wrong. Daniel turned out to be married and a few nights ago she'd seen Jeremy in a passionate embrace with one of the pretty new female nursing assistants.

So, something else then.

From her position behind the column, Tansy could see Jeremy's shadowed form at the end of the corridor linking the hospital's outbuildings. There was a dirt path round the entire perimeter. At the front was a small car park for staff vehicles and the old Bedford that passed for an ambulance. Here at the back, however, the path gave directly onto the forest and it was there that Tansy could now make out a small group of people. She extinguished her cigarette, slowly approaching, using the columns to hide behind. It felt ridiculous spying on her own staff but if Jeremy was stealing he had to be stopped. The mission couldn't sustain these losses. Every scrap of bandage and medicine was precious.

As she crept forward Tansy had a queasy sense of the precariousness of her position. For months now stories had been circulating about how even the most loyal Kikuyus were turning on Europeans they'd worked with for years.

A patient in one of the wards started coughing and the sound instantly doused her fears, replacing them with the stirrings of a cold, righteous anger, the dangerous Tansy-Thompson-brooks-no-nonsense kind that several men from her past might have recognised. How dare they steal from the most vulnerable? It could be them next. There was no electricity on the wards and she reached into her pocket for the torch she always carried on evening rounds.

'You there,' she said firmly into the night, knowing it sounded ridiculous. 'Whatever you're doing stop it right now. Come out where I can see you. This isn't funny.'

For a moment nothing moved except the pale beam from her wavering torch. The batteries had better not go now.

'Come on. I know there's someone there.'

Come on? What an absurd phrase. Sounded like she was geeing up the horses on the farm. *Come on. Walk on.*

'Have no fear, memsahib. It is only I – Jeremy.'

Jeremy walked forward and the beam caught his aquiline profile as he turned to mutter instructions sideways into the darkness. Behind him the line of people had frozen, their bodies dimly visible in the torchlight. Not run off to hide, Tansy realised, just standing there waiting to see what she would do. She peered at them, not recognising any of them.

'Well, what's going on?' she demanded.

Jeremy turned to a man and spoke quickly in Kikuyu. Tansy couldn't catch it, something about fetching or bringing. The line moved silently into action and a few moments later a makeshift stretcher was being lifted towards her. They parked it at her feet and the man on it moaned. The torch revealed a young Kikuyu, face bleached grey beneath the beam. He was naked from the waist up, a crude bandage made from a torn shirt tied to his torso with jungle vine. There was a crusted layer on the shirt but Tansy could see fresh blood oozing out of the side. Chest wound. She knelt automatically to feel his pulse. As she counted, two more palliasses were brought forward and deposited. The pulse was so weak she feared she'd made a mistake. She counted again, professionalism taking over.

'Jeremy, tell these people to move this man to the surgical ward. Then wake up Dr McGregor and as many of the theatre nurses as you can find. When you've done that come back and we'll start preparing for surgery.'

164

'Memsahib. This cannot be done.'

'What are you waiting for? If we don't treat this man he'll die. He needs to go into surgery this minute.'

'He is a fighter from the forest, memsahib. As are the others. We cannot let anyone know they are here.'

Jeremy's voice was calm but sad, a pained teacher explaining an obvious point. This was absurd. All Tansy's experience told her she needed to act fast. The man whose wrist she held was dying.

'I know what he is,' she said tersely. 'Do you think I'm an idiot? The mission does not discriminate between who it treats. Unless we do something it'll be too late.'

Jeremy smiled.

'We do know who you are, Miss Thompson. You are certainly not an idiot. That is why we have come here to this place where you enjoy your smoking, away from the proper entrance. Dr McGregor may be a good person but he is a man of regulations and will feel obliged to report this and then these men will be dead anyway. And perhaps the ones who help them too. Please, do what you can here. Or we will have to act on our own and that will have consequences.'

Tansy was shocked by the implicit threat. Five minutes earlier she wouldn't have believed he was capable of such a thing. Gentle Jeremy, the healer. The war was standing everything on its head.

A quick glance at the two other wounded men showed they also had gunshot wounds. One to the shoulder and another in the abdomen. If she didn't help them the patients with chest and stomach wounds would die within hours. Yet what could she actually do? She was a nurse not a doctor and had neither the experience nor the equipment to do anything but patch them up pending proper surgery.

Then there was the small question of directly and overtly aiding the enemy. What on earth would Grogan make of it? Inevitably he'd say they'd brought it on themselves and report them without a qualm. But she was not Grogan. Nothing like Grogan, despite his views on Kikuyu women and other apparently progressive matters. God, what a mess. For a second an image of Johnny flitted into her mind, smiling, laughing softly. What would he say? He claimed he never wanted to get involved in anything but she'd seen how he acted when they went to get Macharia. No, she told herself firmly, no point in thinking about that – it was over. Before it had started.

165

'All right,' she said to Jeremy. 'I'll help. But you'll need to do what I say.'

As she issued instructions to move some of the existing patients to make room for the new ones, she was aware of crossing a line. Jeremy had described McGregor as a good man and that was true, but he was a man of his times. He had strong views on Mau Mau and even stronger ones on rules. A mission hospital could not run without them. And she'd just broken one. Not for the last time either, she thought.

Chapter 13

Coastal Province, April 1953

They were lost but none of them wanted to admit it.

Macharia, normally so good at directions, had crossed the river twice and was about to go back for a third time when Johnny spoke up from the back of the van.

'Please! If we're going to go round in circles at least let me consult the map.'

Porter sniffed and cleared a small patch of dust from the passenger window. Outside scrubland stretched for miles in every direction. Only the dry riverbed stood out and if it hadn't been for their tyre marks it would have been impossible to tell they'd been here before. The guidebook said this was savannah but it looked like desert to Johnny and he was tired of it.

'Macharia knows what he's doing, Johnny,' Porter snapped. 'You attend to your lenses. Last time we stopped you wasted half an hour getting the damn things clean.'

Johnny grimaced, slumping back onto the makeshift seat squeezed up against camera boxes and tents. It was uncomfortable and hot inside the Land Rover and all three of them were nearing the limits of their patience. Macharia had proved to be an excellent driver but he wasn't infallible.

Enthusiasm for the project was waning as fast as Porter's whisky supply. The film Grogan had tasked them to make about Mau Mau surrenders had been easy to do, taking less than a week to knock off. Ever since, under the guise of picking up better shots, they'd been on the road trying to film evidence of the secret camps. Based on the newspaper cuttings and official memoranda Porter had assembled, they'd devised an ambitious itinerary taking in the major building sites all the way from Lake Rudolf on the northern border with

Abyssinia to the shores of Lake Victoria in the west. The Central Highlands appeared to be the epicentre, with dozens of areas carved out as incarceration zones, but so far they hadn't managed to grab any footage. The moment they got near they'd been shooed away by vigilant guards. Down here on the plains was their last chance.

'I need to get out,' Johnny said, unable to bear another minute inside the van.

Macharia pulled up at the bottom of a ridge that looked like every other one along the arid plain. Johnny opened the back of the van and jumped out, pleased to be doing something. Porter stayed inside and smoked while Johnny stretched, then wandered to the top of the ridge, the burning winds scouring his face. The rains hadn't reached here yet and the countryside was yellow with the fine dust-sand that cloaked everything. A distant clutch of baobab trees quivered through a heat-haze while the squat bushes around it flickered, burning with invisible flames. How could anyone live among this?

'Look, Johnny.' Macharia had appeared silently by his side, pointing. 'Can you see, far over to the right? A wall of some kind?'

Johnny shaded his eyes from the sun and peered into the distance. Macharia's eyesight was significantly better than his or Porter's and again the Kenyan had spotted something first. There was something there – a splash of white. Straight lines on the horizon. Not natural. A group of buildings? Maybe the old aircraft hangers they'd been looking for.

'Might be Mackinnon Road,' said Johnny quietly. 'Worth checking out anyway. We'd better go.'

Soon after the expedition began Macharia had guessed what Porter and Johnny were looking for. At first the *wazungu* tried to pretend they were making a film about little-known tourist locations but that was so obviously a lie neither man was shameless enough to repeat it. Macharia did not mind in the least. The trip was producing better intelligence than he'd ever gathered as a driver for Grogan Littleboy. When the white men marked each camp they found on a map Macharia noted them in his head, memorising routes and natural features until their positions were fixed in his own mental constellation.

Bucking across the dry plain, the van's wheels swirled dust and sand into the air, creating a mini tornado, and Johnny feared they'd be spotted from miles away. It had happened too often already. Just as they'd pull up at a camp a klaxon would sound and guards loped towards them like hungry pi-dogs. Johnny tried not to dwell on it and went back to preparing the camera. It was difficult to do, bouncing around in the back, but the equipment took so long to set up on the ground every second gained in the van would count. As they drew nearer the three men fell silent, opening the windows to listen for the familiar whine of a camp siren.

But today there was no noise apart from the throaty diesel chug of the van.

'There,' Porter said, indicating a shallow depression where the van might remain half hidden.

Macharia was already heading for it and Johnny opened the back door in readiness. Before the vehicle came to a halt he jumped out, camera head attached to the tripod. Running to a spot he'd earmarked from the road, he put the heavy new Bolex camera on the ground, adjusting the tripod legs to ensure it was level. So far he'd reduced the time it took to get the camera operational by ten minutes, but it still took another ten to make sure everything else was functioning and dust free.

Porter came to stand next to him while Macharia turned the van round, ready for a quick exit. If anyone approached they'd established a cover story which involved Porter leaping in front of the camera declaiming about the touristic joys of Kenya.

Johnny held his handkerchief in front of the lens for a white balance. This part was always tricky and he had to focus. One of the tripod legs suddenly gave way and he swore.

'You're not paying attention to your craft,' Porter said. 'Dreaming about Tansy again? My advice: don't even think about it. She's not in your league, lad.'

Johnny tried to ignore him, dusting the lens with a fine-haired brush to remove sand grains. Fuck Porter, he didn't know everything. He was nearly ready when Macharia let out a cry.

'*Jeep coming!* Approaching fast from the south.'

Johnny whipped his head away from the lens. Less than a mile away, plumes of dust were coming rapidly in their direction.

'Hurry!' Porter said.

They had a couple of minutes at best. Finally satisfied with the light levels, Johnny squinted through the eyepiece, zooming in on the camp. In close-up he could see a mass of construction activity. Within the perimeter men were putting up hundreds of white tents, using barbed wire to divide the compound into square sections.

'Bloody hell,' he muttered, panning slowly. He let the camera roll, looking at his watch. To capture the whole camp would take at least another half an hour. He swept the lens patiently from right to left, tilting it slightly to take in the height of three tall guard towers. This was strong material. Suddenly there was an urgent hiss from Porter.

'They're here! Bastards came the last bit on foot. For fuck's sake, Johnny, stop filming!'

Porter walked up onto the ridge to stall them while Macharia slipped inside the van, waiting in the driver's seat like a good driver boy should.

A tall British officer appeared, taut-faced, holding a pistol.

'Who the bloody hell are you?' he demanded. Half a dozen askaris took up position in a semi-circle on the ridge, aiming their rifles at the men below.

The officer noticed Johnny continuing to film. 'That man by the camera – stop what you're doing at once and face me with your hands in the air.'

Johnny ignored him. He had put the finished reel containing the pictures of the camp into one of the film canisters and was in the middle of opening a fresh one to replace it on the camera itself. If he could just get the . . .

Bang!

The sound of the pistol was shocking, producing an instant effect. Johnny froze then turned slowly, new reel in a hand that went automatically into the air.

'Can't you speak English?' the officer said. 'When I say stop, I fucking mean it. The next shot does not miss. Now, you have five seconds to start explaining. Who are you?'

Porter began to give the rehearsed line about making a tourist film but the officer, a single pip denoting a lieutenant, was fidgety and nervous, not wanting to listen. He was much more interested in Johnny.

'What are you filming?'

170

'Oh, we were practising a piece to camera,' said Johnny. 'That's when the reporter speaks to . . . '

'Yes, I know what it means. But you weren't, were you? Your man here is nowhere near the camera and I clearly saw you pointing it towards the camp. So, I ask again – what are you doing and on whose authority? Why's this area of any interest to you?'

Porter jumped in, waving a docket he'd retrieved from the van. Johnny knew it was an order with Grogan's forged signature. The lieutenant was unimpressed.

'Anyone could have written that. We have information on all forces activity in this sector and nobody has said anything about you.'

He advanced on Johnny.

'Better give me that film – the one you were trying to hide.'

Johnny felt a sudden prickle of sweat on his skin as the hot wind instantly dried it. He thought about the rash of recent war films where daring English commando infiltrators got away with it by barking officiously at guards in fluent German. Then he smiled, as he realised there might be a way out after all. Barking officiously would never work with an English officer; it would only put his back up. An Englishman, a *gentleman*, required a different approach.

'Sorry? *Hiding?*' Johnny said, effortlessly sliding back into his class uniform. 'Good Lord, we're all on the same side here. Terribly sorry no one's alerted you to our presence – typical bloody head office foul-up. Look, we can sort it all out easily. Now, do you mind if I put my hands down? They're beginning to ache and I'd rather like to solve this one over a beer. We've got some in the van if you fancy it.'

Porter watched Johnny's hands come slowly down. The famous Johnny charm that Grogan had warned the office about before his protégé arrived had been in short supply lately, but Porter had seen it in action before and knew the lieutenant would be easily handled from here on in.

Even as the thought passed through Porter's mind the young officer was replacing the pistol in its holster, chatting to Johnny as if they were old schoolfriends comparing notes about mutual acquaintances in Kenya. Johnny kept his smile in place and batted names to and fro until it seemed to Porter they'd got away with it.

But as they reached the van and Johnny was fumbling in the back for the promised beer, the officer asked another question that made Porter come to an abrupt halt.

'Do you know Graves?' the officer had asked, '*Ewart* Graves? I was at Oxford with his nephew. I gather he's a bit of a legend out here.'

Johnny stiffened and rose slowly, holding two bottles.

'Yes, I've bumped into him on the circuit. Heard he's a hell of a tracker.' He looked at Porter. 'Apparently he can find anyone, anywhere.'

The officer looked pleased and the crisis was over as they clinked bottles and returned to cricket and schools, exploring the contours of a shared heritage that was as alien to Porter as it was to Macharia.

Porter realised his mistake had been to open his Yorkshire mouth in front of one of the sons of Empire. '*Poor show,*' he grinned to himself, scooping up the canister with the original film before trotting obediently behind Johnny and his new best friend.

Porter was in high celebratory mood that night and as the three men sat round the camp fire, watching it fizz and spit into the darkness, he shared the last of his Scotch, insisting on making a toast.

'To a job well done and the prospect of a comfortable bed.'

Johnny returned the toast half-heartedly. Earlier Porter had said it was time to head back to Nairobi, announcing he'd endured enough of the rough pleasures of life on the road. For Johnny the opposite was true. Out here he was living life as it should be in Kenya: in the bush, stars for a roof, lulled by the sounds of the African night.

'I like it here,' he said seriously. 'Apart from when some idiot fires a gun in your ear, it's so peaceful. Can't you feel it, Porter? There's a connection here to ... I don't know, something bigger. All I reckon is that life in the city holds little attraction compared to any of this.'

Porter drew on one of his foul-smelling cheroots. He'd seen Johnny dip into these moods before and thought he knew the cause.

'Look,' he said with equal gravity, 'I'm sorry I ribbed you about Tansy earlier. But it's obvious no good can come of it. Doesn't matter what you think or even what she thinks. It's Grogan that counts. At the moment he's on your side but he can turn. He smiles as he struts, never raises his voice, you'd think butter wouldn't melt, but he's got a nasty streak that one. He won't do you to your face but turn your back and you won't even feel the knife going in.'

172

Johnny winced at Tansy's name. Whatever spark might have been was extinguished, at least on her side, so there was little point in lacerating himself by talking about her.

'If Grogan's such a bastard,' he said, 'why do you still work for him?'

Porter grinned and tapped his cheroot towards the fire.

'Didn't they tell you?' he cackled. 'Journalists are like everyone else. Hypocritical bastards. Moved off the gold standard to the double standard years ago.'

The haul back to Nairobi would only take a couple of days. Now they weren't meandering around the countryside they could stick to the main road. At the nearest town with a proper hotel in it Porter insisted they stop for a shower and a decent night's kip. Johnny loathed these places and his despair at leaving the bush took a ratchet downwards.

After they'd checked in and dumped their bags in the rooms – dark, musty places smelling of rotten crotch and urine – Johnny went downstairs to see if he could at least scare up a cold beer. Porter was on the lobby phone, scowling.

The receptionist was busy so he went outside. One single, dusty street constituted the entire town. Along the pavement Africans had laid out their wares – bowls, shoes, bags, rugs – but no one was stopping to buy anything. A man with a patch over one eye sat in the shade sharpening a panga on a slowly revolving whetstone powered by bicycle pedals. Sparks flew into the air as the blade scraped the stone. Aware of being watched he looked up, his single eye scanning the street until it landed on Johnny. He maintained the stare until Johnny looked away.

'Right,' said Porter, shouting from inside. 'Where's that fucking beer? Bloody Grogan.'

He joined Johnny outside looking red-faced. He reached for a cheroot and swore when it wouldn't light first time.

'I tell you, Johnny, that man wants to keep you away from his beloved as long as possible.'

'She's not my beloved.'

'Well, anyway. We're going to be stuck in the bush for bloody weeks.'

'So we're not going to Nairobi?' Johnny grinned.

'No we're bloody not. His Foulness wants us to do another film.'

Porter explained that Grogan required a short documentary extolling the virtues of the 'villagisation' programme. He pulled out a tattered map from an inside pocket and stabbed his finger angrily at the centre of the country.

'That's where we're heading. Gatura, middle of Nyeri District. Means a bloody long drive back into the Highlands. Somewhere near the mission hospital where Tansy's working.'

Johnny looked up sharply but Porter was on to him immediately.

'I know what you're thinking and the answer is no.'

'But surely afterwards we can drop in on her?'

'No chance. The second we've finished I'm bloody leaving and that means no detours.'

'I don't understand why you're so pissed off,' Johnny said. 'Sounds easy enough. Might even be enjoyable.'

Porter made a noise of exasperation.

'*Jesus!* Do you know what "villagisation" is? In fact, did you ever actually go into the office?'

'Nope.'

'You idle bugger. There were endless bloody briefings about it. These New Villages are the ones I was telling the Yanks about. Our lot burn their old homes and force the poor sods at gunpoint into a virtual prison. Deny their resources to Mau Mau. They're not good places, Johnny.'

The journey took most of the day and as they climbed back up into the Aberdares the air cooled and the hues of the landscape turned from sand-brown to the deep greens and reds of the hills. But even the fresher air failed to improve Porter's mood and there was little talking.

Stuck in the back again, Johnny closed his eyes and tried to sleep. But the prospect of heading towards Tansy made it impossible. He had little doubt he'd eventually be able to persuade Porter to visit her hospital, but perhaps it was a stupid idea. It – whatever 'it' was – was over. However often he'd gone over her sudden coldness that night at the Stanley, he could never fashion anything good from it. She'd played him and that was that. So why then, Johnny asked himself, did it feel like unfinished business?

*

174

Gatura New Village lay at the bottom of a hill bordering the forest. The road ended well short so they had to park half a mile away on the other side of a slope, forcing them to lug their heavy equipment up and then down the hill. When they reached the village they saw a large ditch had been dug between it and the neighbouring tree line. Sharpened staves joined together by rolls of barbed wire pointed outwards at an angle. The village itself consisted of three rows of identical thatched rondavels: two open windows, one wicker door each. Every hut exactly the same distance away from the next, laid out in straight lines, the ground in between neatly brushed, devoid of any stones or scrub. Like a military camp, Johnny thought. Fires had not been lit and the few cattle stood forlornly in a small enclosure.

As they walked towards the centre of the settlement to begin their filming, it felt like a ghost village. Too well-groomed to be real. And hardly anyone in it. There were a few toothless old men sitting about but no one else. No dogs, no babies, no goats. Women could be seen in the distance digging a further fortification, raising great clouds of dust. Where were the men?

Johnny looked at Macharia. His face was sombre and he was muttering to himself.

'You OK?' Johnny asked.

'This is a bad place,' Macharia said. 'Let us do our work and go.'

'Just shoot a few wides and we can get the fuck out of Dodge,' Porter said. 'This I do not like one bit.'

The anxiety was catching and Johnny sped up, working fast. They finished everything in the village within half an hour. Just one more angle was needed to make sense of it – a pan of Gatura from the top of the ditch facing the forest.

Making their way out through the village gate, they were watched by Home Guard men lounging next to their post, smoking silently, scrutinising their every move. Johnny was thankful when the three of them were on the other side of the wire.

They set up on top of the mound and he'd executed a few pans of the village below when he noticed the women starting to return. It would make a great shot and he gestured to Macharia and Porter to follow him nearer the trees, where he might be able to capture a dramatic angle against the setting sun.

Porter stopped halfway. He told Johnny to be quick; he was tired and going back to the van. He'd start her up and expect to see them in less than five minutes. Sundown wasn't far off and they shouldn't be travelling in the dark.

Johnny agreed, delighted to be working alone with Macharia. In the field the Yorkshireman was a nuisance, criticising Johnny's angles and generally grunting with displeasure most of the time. Macharia was more helpful and frankly better company. They were a good team. He set off for the place he'd picked out in his mind and smiled as he saw Macharia heading straight for it too.

That's when he spotted them.

At first he couldn't understand what it might be: a rustling sound and the green of the forest edge shimmering into movement. Even when they were all finally in view they were hard to spot – the faded hues of their clothes perfectly matching the surrounding forest. From nothing to a line of men kneeling at the edge of the tree line. Staring at him.

Armed.

His mind took in the details: shotguns, pangas, a revolver. Hair matted and wild. Faces gleaming. Black. Clothes ragged. He could smell them from where he stood – sweet, dirty, retch-making. He looked behind him. Porter had gone and Macharia was stock still, staring back. The women marching back from digging had stopped too. Everyone frozen; everyone looking at everyone else.

Johnny's first thought was that it was a surrender party. Where were the British troops? He looked around again. Not a soldier in sight. Even the Home Guard men had vanished. Were they going to surrender to him, the only white man visible? His second thought was that this would make a fantastic shot. The camera was in position on the tripod and he switched it on, slowly turning the lens towards the men. In the absolute quiet of the moment it made a deafening noise, whirring and clicking as the frames whipped through the aperture. A kneeling man with a revolver stood and for a moment Johnny thought there was something recognisable about him. His profile or stance. He dismissed the idea swiftly as the men still kneeling were starting to make a noise, a kind of low howling like men in pain, or men imitating the sound of some jungle animal. The hairs on his arms rose instantly as he realised a surrender party would not make that noise. A surrender party would step forward,

176

lay their arms on the ground and squat, awaiting their turn to be frisked by a British soldier. But there were no British soldiers and the men were not laying down their arms. On the contrary, the guns were pointing at him.

Johnny had never actually been in combat. By the time he'd joined up, most of the fighting was over. The only action he'd experienced had been the horror of discovering the camps. The older soldiers had spoken of it and they'd all said the same thing. The first time you didn't know how it would take you. That initial moment when you were shot at or saw a gun pointing your way or a bomb exploded, you would either shit yourself or fight. Most wanted to run and it was only discipline and fear of letting your mates down that made you clench hard and fight back. Johnny was clenching now, an oily convulsion running through his guts. He wanted to run.

Then a voice.

'*Turn that fucking camera off.*'

Johnny froze, searching for the source. He recognised the settler twang but couldn't see where it was coming from.

'I said – *turn it off.*'

The man with the revolver took a few steps nearer and Johnny's eyes widened.

'My God, is that you? What the hell are you doing here?'

'Yeah, yeah, good to see you too. Now turn that bloody thing off.'

Johnny snapped the camera off and looked hard at the policeman. Now he was only a couple of feet from him, Graves's features came more into focus. He had blackened his face and arms, wore a stinking bushbuck-skin coat and sported a plaited wig. A double-edged Kikuyu sword dangled from his waist next to his bamboo cane.

'What are *you* doing here?' Graves demanded tightly. 'No one's supposed to know about this – let alone film us, for Christ's sake. You'd better open up the camera and expose the film. What the fuck were you thinking of?'

Johnny explained what they'd been asked to do by Grogan but made no move to open the camera. If he let the light in all the earlier footage would be lost. He looked at the men behind Graves. There were rumours about patrols like these. Pseudo gangs, or counter gangs, they called them, groups of turned former Mau Mau led by Europeans who delved deep into the forest to ambush and kill their old comrades. He'd always thought it was a story put about to scare the Africans.

Graves's hand fluttered to his bamboo stave and Johnny could see the effort it took for the policeman to contain himself. Mixed in with the forest grease was an odour he remembered from the Cunningham incident: blood and faeces. *Death.*

Graves's bloodshot eyes darted wildly and Johnny could sense the killing lust upon him. He prayed he wouldn't turn his attention to Macharia, who was looking at the ground, eyes averted, trying desperately to make himself invisible.

'Look,' said Johnny slowly, with as much calm as he could muster. 'I was only filming for a few seconds. I thought you were another surrender party. If I just rewind for a few seconds it'll destroy all the frames that might have you on them. OK?'

Graves said nothing, eyes flicking from the camera to Johnny and back. The contrast between whatever blood-soaked mission he'd been leading and now was disconcerting him. Johnny slowly moved his hand to the camera and engaged the reverse. There was a longer pause as the three men stood listening to the camera's motor whirring. After several seconds Johnny switched it off.

'There. It's done,' he said soothingly. 'Gone now. So we can all go about our business.' To Macharia he snapped: 'Take this all back to the van. Now.'

Johnny wanted it to sound normal to Graves. White orders black. It almost worked. Macharia had half dismantled the camera head when Graves seemed to notice him for the first time.

'Wait a minute. Who the fuck's the kaffir?'

Macharia had been about to take the camera off the tripod but he stopped and stood, head bowed, knowing better than to move. His heart was racing. From the moment Graves had emerged from the forest he'd known who it was. But did the white man recognise him? He doubted it; white men didn't tend to notice other men's drivers and the last time the two had met was in the police cell where Macharia had been so swollen and beaten he didn't resemble a human being, let alone himself. No normal person would be able to tell he was the same man. But the Zebra was not a normal person. Macharia felt an involuntary spasm in his stomach, forcing himself to concentrate with all his might to prevent a shameful act.

'He's no one,' Johnny said quickly. 'Servant from Nairobi. Acts as my runner. I trust him.'

Graves walked to within a few inches of Macharia. Replacing his pistol in his waistband, he removed the cane and tucked it under Macharia's chin, forcing his face up.

'Look at me, boy. I know you, don't I?'

Macharia hesitated and the stick snapped across his face so rapidly he couldn't have seen it coming. He cried out in pain and a thin line of blood appeared on his cheek. Graves spoke softly.

'I don't say things twice. When I say look, you fucking look. Now, runner boy, what's your name? What's your village?'

'My village sir, is—'

'I said I vouch for him,' Johnny broke in, finding his voice, torn between anger and the need to maintain composure. 'Just let him go.'

Without looking at Johnny, Graves shouted something in Swahili towards his men. One of the Africans came running.

'If you want to see this boy again, Seymour, you'd better shut your trap. He's witnessed things no Kyuke should and I want to know who he is. My boy here knows every Mick in the neighbourhood. He can smell the bastards.'

Graves's man was Kikuyu. To Johnny's eyes he looked similar to Macharia: tall, even elegant, were it not for the monkey-skin jacket and necklace of human ears around his neck. He walked on the balls of his feet, almost dancing as he approached. Macharia stood absolutely still, the blood from his wound spilling unevenly down his cheek, as Graves's man waltzed round him, sniffing and muttering. He circled him twice before sidling back to his boss, leaning down to whisper.

'He says you've got a Mau Mau brother who makes weapons,' snapped Graves. 'Is that true?'

Macharia looked at Johnny but Johnny stared ahead, willing him not to reply.

'Well? Answer me boy or you die right here. Understand?'

'No, *bwana*. I do not know the man you are talking about. I come from Nairobi. I have no brother, sir.'

Of all things, he would never give up his brother. *Hold on to that.* Macharia's voice was steady but sweat trickled down the side of his neck. Graves's man put his mouth to his *bwana*'s ear once more, staring at Macharia as he did so, the whispering sibilance muffled. But if the words were inaudible their message was clear.

Death sentence.

Graves nodded slowly. 'Agreed.'

His hand moved back to his waistband, towards the grip of his pistol.

Johnny was exaggeratedly aware of time, which seemed to have folded in on itself, decelerating into a state where he was able to think absurdly fast while everyone else moved in slow motion. In the second it took for Graves to touch his revolver Johnny was able to calculate how far it was to the van, how long it would take to get there, how many seconds' running he might have before they shot at him and whether Porter would have started the van's engine. He knew – could almost literally see it happening – what the sequence of events would be. The pistol in Graves's hand, the pistol against Macharia's head, the shot, the crumpling of Macharia's body.

The adrenalin which was spurting into Johnny's system demanded he run away as fast as possible, abandon Macharia and get out. This was not his fight. He had never asked to be here. Filming in Africa was only ever meant to be about wild animals and clichéd sunsets. Bad stuff always happened. You couldn't stop it. Life was an unending lava flow of shit drowning everyone who didn't move out of the way. He could move now. Should move now.

And yet.

It is rarely given to a man to recognise one of life's pivotal moments but Johnny was aware of being in one now. If he ran away, who was he? What was the point of him? Was he going to stand on the sidelines of everything? Of a man's execution? A glacial anger cut through. *Fuck it.* Fuck Graves and the rest of them.

Macharia flicked his eyes sideways and Johnny found he couldn't look away. The gaze between them lasted no more than a second but it underlined everything. It had taken some time, but Johnny finally knew what the right thing to do was.

Graves's hand was on his pistol. It had to be now.

'Come on, Graves,' Johnny said, putting every ounce of honey into his most reasonable voice. *Come on, old chum*, the sweetness said, surely this was only a minor dispute, which could be settled like gentlemen. He stepped to within touching distance of the camera. Slowly. Reasonably.

'Look, old chap, if we could only . . . '

The camera and tripod combined must have weighed over thirty pounds. It was a hefty piece of equipment. As he ducked down to grasp two legs of the tripod, Johnny prayed the camera head was screwed on tight. It was, whirling through the air like an ancient broadsword, smashing into the side of Graves's head with a satisfying, deep smack. Graves dropped immediately, no time to register surprise. His companion was rooted with shock and Johnny was astonished he was just standing there, waiting to receive his blow. Johnny punched the camera into his chest with as much force as he could muster. The air went out of the Kikuyu and he too collapsed. The camera head snapped free of the legs and landed on the ground, upside down. The activity must have turned it on again as for a second there was no sound at all save the whirring of the camera pointing into the sky above the kneeling ranks of Graves's silent watching pseudo gang.

Johnny scooped up the camera and turned towards the mound, shouting as he erupted into a sprint.

'*Run!*'

Macharia spat, taking a few steps back before darting at the unconscious form of Graves to deliver a mighty kick to the fallen man's head. He spat again, then looked triumphantly at the line of men at the forest edge before sprinting for his life.

They were halfway up the hill before the firing started.

Chapter 14

Nairobi, March 2008

The journey back to the hotel was much quicker. There were no stops to take on extra passengers and Dedan had turned the music down, allowing Kamau and Sam to hold a conversation without shouting. The *matatu* veered about the road and Sam was dismayed to see Dedan steering the van with his arms, leaving his hands free to roll tobacco. He finished and pulled out a lighter in the shape of Nelson Mandela. Flames leapt out of the President's head and Sam smelled the unmistakable sweetness of weed.

She looked at Kamau, who smiled and shrugged.

'So, Sam,' he asked, 'did you get everything you wanted today?'

The old ones' testimony had been very powerful. Several times the details were different from those they gave in their affidavits but Sam was impressed at how much they could remember. She'd gone back over individual stories and their accounts never deviated. A smart lawyer could probably find enough discrepancies to make a jury waver, but as far as she was concerned there wasn't a shred of doubt they were telling the truth.

Compared with the outward trip she felt more relaxed and it wasn't just the smell of weed, pleasant though that was. The veterans had given her a boost. As in previous cases, testimony came alive the moment she met her clients for the first time. No one could really tell the truth from a piece of paper. But a face, a human face, was the best lie detector you could have.

The way her name had acted on the group had been bizarre. Thank God it had gone the right way. When the old man with the tie had started asking about her being a Seymour she'd thought they were going to turn on her for something Johnny had done. Some of them had known him in the old days; one had even been friends with his driver in Nairobi, another was at a camp with him – which was intriguing as she hadn't realised he'd worked in the camps. They couldn't have been nicer – any granddaughter of Johnny Seymour was a friend of theirs.

She stretched her back, wriggling in her seat, covertly watching Kamau. Tapping at his phone with his long fingers, he also seemed content with the day's work. But why hadn't he asked her? She would have been bursting with questions about why the Seymour name had provoked such an effect among the elders. Was he not just the smallest bit curious? He looked up and she fancied there was a faint air of puzzlement, but then he dipped his head back to his phone without a word.

She laughed and Kamau peered at her resignedly.

'Have I done something to amuse you?'

'Not at all. I think it's good that you're not curious.'

'And what should I be curious about?'

'All right, since you ask: I'm a bit surprised you don't seem to want to know about why those veterans reacted so well when I told them my name.'

'But I do know.'

'Really? How could you?'

'Please, Sam. Many of us have heard stories from our parents of the white *mzee* who was involved in the Mau Mau struggle but I confess, until today I had no idea he might be connected to you.'

'*White mzee?* How was he involved?'

'Ah, that I do not know. My mother's family came from Nyeri District and as I recall, it was my aunt who mentioned the name when I was little. To tell the truth, I'd forgotten about it until today. Who would have thought it – now I am translating for the granddaughter of the legendary white *Mzee* Seymour. How does it feel to be famous?'

'I just hope it isn't infamous.'

He laughed and Sam allowed it to wash over her. She wondered how he'd react if she invited him in to the hotel for a drink – just to go over the translation notes.

Instead she asked, 'Will you enquire about him for me? From your family? There's so much I don't know. I'd love it if you could ask about him. And find out about his wife too – Tansy. She was my grandmother but she seems to have disappeared without trace.'

Kamau agreed he would try to discover more and for the remainder of the journey they were able to chat normally. She no longer felt the need to prod a reaction out of him, while he had lost his earlier aloofness. Kamau, it turned out, knew quite a lot about the colonial era, significantly more than she did, though she took care not to let that particular imbalance become visible. He was a history graduate studying for a PhD on land reform under British rule at the University of Nairobi. She pressed him to describe what he was covering in his research, but when he began to explain the complex kinship system of the Kikuyu tribe, on which land ownership was based, she could not follow and to her horror a yawn bubbled up, which she could only suppress by turning it into a very false-sounding cough.

Kamau stopped.

'You are right, Sam, it is not as exciting as what you are excavating now – though I will say that if the colonialists had got land reform right then Mau Mau might never have existed. But I suppose their version of restructuring and mine might be rather different. Whenever the British reformed it they seemed to reform the best of it into their own pockets.'

Kamau explained he'd only taken the translating job to pay his university costs. He was thirty-two now and the doctorate had already taken him five years as he'd had to take so much time off his studies to work. Fees were expensive and he had to live, to support his family.

'You're married then?' Sam asked, irritated the question had come out so quickly.

No, he was not married, though he did have younger brothers and a sister who required help.

'Why aren't *you* married, Samantha?' Dedan asked, joining in from the front, peering at her in the *matatu*'s mirror.

Kamau was regarding her intently and Sam felt unexpectedly embarrassed. If someone had asked her that in England she would have been straight at them. It was no one's business but her own. But she supposed she had started this.

'Never found anyone I wanted to spend that much time with, I suppose.'

'It is lucky you came here to Kenya then,' Dedan chuckled, 'where there are real men!'

Sam blushed and Kamau looked away. She stared out of the window and noticed they were already in town – had been for a while.

'Right,' she said briskly. 'I'd better tell you where we're going next. There's nothing on for a couple of days, but then we're off again. Pugh gave me the name of the village. I have no idea where it is.'

She read out the name from her notes and Dedan said he'd heard of it. As they pulled up at the hotel he reached over his shoulder with a business card.

'This has my number on it,' Dedan said. 'Night or day, Sam – ring me if you need me.'

'OK, thanks.'

He turned to face her.

'I mean it, Sam – it is what I am here for. It would not be good if you wandered off on your own now.'

Sam frowned and Kamau told her it was good advice.

'After your words at the village this afternoon you need to be careful,' he said. 'Kenya is a large country but in many ways it is like a village. Talk travels fast. And if you are on your own you need to be vigilant.'

She nodded dutifully. It had been a long day and all she wanted was to get to her room and into a hot bath. She wasn't sure if the men, especially Kamau, were mocking her or being serious. Then Kamau scribbled something down on a scrap of paper and handed it to her.

'And this is my number. The same goes for me. Night or day.'

The back of his hand brushed against hers. She took the number and grabbed her rucksack, mumbling thanks as she tried to open the *matatu*'s door. She tugged at it several times but of course it would not open. Kamau leaned across her and slid it open with ease.

'Good night, Sam Seymour.'

She stumbled out, breathing quickly and taking care not to look back.

Ridiculous.

The *matatu* waited until she was inside the hotel before roaring away, the music again on at full blast. It was blissfully cool in the lobby and Sam marched to the lifts. Just as one pinged to announce its arrival a voice came from reception.

'Miss Seymour?' The receptionist was waving at her, a piece of paper in her hand. 'You have a message, Miss Seymour.'

It was a small envelope with her name on it and Sam did not bother to open it, jumping into the lift before it could take off again. In the mirror she saw a woman who had caught the sun: windswept, hair all over the place, arms pink, cheeks over-flushed. Though that, she knew full well, was not entirely the fault of the sun.

Sam regarded herself as quite a tidy person; not as retentive as her father, but she liked her room to be welcoming and had taken to stowing her belongings away in as orderly a fashion as a hotel bedroom would allow. Which is why the sight of her clothes and things strewn everywhere robbed her of her breath.

She knew it could happen, had read all the warnings. Even Pugh had advised her to take extra care. Just because she was in a hotel where many Europeans stayed, that did not confer automatic protection. She threw down her rucksack and the message onto the bed and began to poke around. All her clothes seemed to be there. There was no money missing and she was not exactly the type of woman who travelled with a jewellery case. Some depositions had been scattered about but they all seemed to be present too. In fact, nothing appeared to have been stolen. Perhaps they'd given up when they found nothing of value. How had they got in? There was no sign of the door being damaged. She couldn't stay here – she would ask for another room; one with a bloody huge chain on it.

First she needed a drink. The minibar had not been ransacked; at least there was that to be thankful for. But when she saw it her heart started rattling. Under the minibar was the room safe. It opened with a combination number set by individual guests. It was small and metal and looked relatively heavy. But secure it was not. The door was hanging open.

'*Oh fuck.*'

She knelt down and reached in. Her passport was still there, along with a few notes of English money. And, thank God, Johnny's scrapbook was intact, all his bits and pieces stuffed safely inside.

But the envelope was gone. The papers were missing.

Mattingly's precious documents had been taken, and with them proof that the British government knew about the abuse of Kenyans. The case she'd been convinced she could win for the victims had been stolen from under her. Worse – someone knew she'd been given the papers and that someone had broken into her room. Could easily do it again.

She tore off the top of a vodka and poured it down her throat, immediately opening a second one on the way to the telephone by the side of her bed.

Reception was engaged so she opened a window and lit a cigarette. It was a no-smoking room but she wasn't going to be here much longer. She tried again; it was still busy.

Then she remembered the message.

She ripped it open to find a hotel hospitality card carefully inscribed with a message from Esther.

Sam – take care. I think they know about the present we gave you. Move out of there. And ring me. As soon as you can. We must meet. This is very urgent.

She had Esther's number on her mobile, copied from the back of the envelope Mattingly had given her. But where was her bloody phone now? Not in her pocket or handbag. The rucksack. She turned it upside down and emptied everything onto the bed, and there it was, wedged among a sheaf of papers. As she picked it up she noticed the heading on one of the pages: *Secret*. A wave of relief swept over her. The bastards hadn't got all of them – she remembered how she'd taken the first few pages to read on the bus. Looking at them, she realised she still possessed the most important ones: key minutes from the committee and the circulation list. It wasn't everything, but it was enough.

But would the people who'd stolen the envelope notice? Of course they would. And if they knew what was in the envelope they'd also know they hadn't found everything. Which meant they might be coming back.

She dialled Esther's number with trembling fingers but it rang and rang with no one picking it up up.

She was about to hang up when a man's voice answered.

'Yes?'

'*Mattingly?* Joseph, is that you? Are you—'

'Who is this?' the voice asked aggressively.

'Is he there, please? Or Esther. Can I talk to Esther?'

There was a pause and a scuffling sound as the person on the other end put his hand over the receiver. She heard muted voices then he came loudly back on the line.

'Esther Mattingly cannot speak to you. I repeat – who are you?' He was shouting. 'Tell me who you are!'

'This is . . .' Sam paused.

The voice didn't sound right. In the background she could hear odd noises, as if things were being thrown around. This was very wrong.

Click.

The line went dead.

Chapter 15

Macharia flew up the hill, his feet given wings by fear and elation. He had struck back at the enemy in the most direct way possible! The physical moment of foot kicking head surely spelled his true birth into the struggle. For the first time he was living up to the ideas of manhood fostered by *irua*, the initiation into adulthood undergone by all Kikuyu men. A kick for a kick! Gatimu would be so pleased.

As he sped over the uneven ground, zig-zagging like an impala, trying to follow Johnny Seymour's path, he felt a fierce joy. So this was the soaring euphoria of battle they talked of. He risked a look behind. At the bottom of the hill the gang's rifles burped circles of smoke into the air. It was odd to connect them with the cracks and whines passing over his head or the spurting dust around him. Although he was running away, Macharia felt unshackled. Free.

The sensation was novel and pleasing, putting even more strength into his legs as the crest of the hill finally came into touching distance. Once over it, they would be safe.

A bullet is a small thing and yet the round fired from a quarter of a mile away hit Macharia's shoulder with such force it threw the running man high into the air. He yelped, more in surprise than pain. For a moment he lay face-down on the earth, gasping for breath, the shoulder merely numb. But although it did not hurt, his body was informing him that great damage had been done; a giant had bitten him, ripping muscle and pieces of bone, spitting out blood and gristle.

Johnny was already at the top when he heard the cry. He glanced behind and saw Macharia on the ground. Ever since he'd lashed out at Graves he'd been acting on instinct. And it was instinct that now pushed Johnny back down the hill without hesitation.

When Macharia saw him sprinting back towards him he first thought the Englishman was making a charge at the enemy. Was he mad? Macharia laughed at the folly and sheer bravado of the act, and wished he could get up and join the assault. But he was so weak and everything was becoming unreal, as if he were looking at events through one of Johnny's cameras when the rains smeared the lens.

Johnny stopped at his side, sweating and screaming: *'Get up, man!'*

But Macharia could not move. Shock had set in and blood was beginning to pool, mixing with the red of the earth. Someone had cut his strings. He couldn't remember why he was here at all. Nothing that ran through his head made any sense. Johnny tugged at him, viciously yanking on his good arm, shrieking in his ear.

'Move!' If you stay here you're a dead man.'

Reality rushed in on waves of pain. He did not want to die on a hill. Forcing himself up to lean on Johnny, he somehow found the strength to limp up the slope, aware only of dragging one foot after the other, dust kicking up as bullets gouged the ground around them.

Agonising seconds later both men reached the summit, tumbling ever faster down the other side, spurred on by the blessed sight of Porter sitting in the driving seat of the van, engine idling, unconcernedly blowing smoke rings out of an open window. When the Yorkshireman saw the running, yelling, blood-spattered men, the cheroot dropped from his fingers and his mouth gaped open. Johnny bundled Macharia into the back and screamed at Porter:

'Drive, drive! Go!'

Simple commands, but Porter didn't seem to understand, his eyes swivelling from the bleeding man in the rear to Johnny.

'What the *fuck*?'

'No time,' Johnny gasped. 'For the love of God just drive. *Fast.*'

A spooked Porter accelerated away, speeding ever faster as Johnny explained through gasps what had happened. Porter listened aghast, staring ahead, while Macharia struggled up on to his good elbow to look out of the rear window to see if anything was chasing them. The movement nearly made him black out with agony. He laid his head back down on the seat, trying not to think about the hole in his shoulder or his blood flowing into the runnels of the Land Rover's floor.

Porter did everything he could to hide their tracks, driving back onto the road before veering off again into the bush, twisting and turning at random through the scrub. Eventually Johnny had to tell him to slow down or they'd crash; even the best tracker wouldn't be able to catch them for a few hours.

It was dusk when they finally stopped. Johnny jumped out to examine Macharia, lighting a Tilley lamp which he handed to Porter while he leaned over the wounded man in the back. The shock cushioning Macharia from pain was wearing off and when Johnny pulled back the cloth from what remained of Macharia's shirt the Kenyan let out a loud bellow. Johnny peered at the shoulder, wrinkling his nose in disgust. He went to his suitcase and found a towel, which he pushed directly onto the wound. Macharia didn't have the strength to cry out with any force but the hurt was so overwhelming his eyes swam and he fainted.

When he came to the white men were talking over him.

'Doesn't look good,' Johnny was saying. 'Poor bugger's in a huge amount of pain and he's losing blood. An old towel and some aspirins aren't going to cut it. He needs proper attention.'

He drew back and looked at Porter.

'How far is Tansy's hospital from here?'

Porter flinched.

'*Kagamo?* Don't be a fool, man, we can't go there now. Graves is bound to follow. We can't let him get anywhere near Tansy.'

'But she could—'

'*No!* It's far too risky. We just can't. If we leave now, we can make it to Nairobi. The native hospitals there would take him. He might make it.'

In the flickering light of the storm lamp, Johnny's face was strained.

'OK, look,' he said slowly. 'Here's the logic, and it's pretty simple. He's going to die in a few hours if we don't get him help. Right now. Tansy's place is the nearest. She may say no, in which case we piss off and see how far we get before he cops it. If she says yes, we can work out how to deal with Graves. The longer we stay here the more likely we are to be found by his trackers.'

Porter grimaced, stroking his beard which looked greasy in the half light. Listening to the exchange, it occurred to Macharia that the Yorkshireman might be a little in love with Tansy; everyone else seemed to be. As Macharia knew from his own exchange with her at the police station, Tansy Thompson was a formidable character. Porter and Johnny stared angrily at each other until Macharia could endure the pain no longer. He groaned, forcing both men to look at him.

'OK. You win,' Porter sighed. 'But if Graves and his men catch us we're dead. And if Tansy comes to any harm as a result of this I'll kill you myself.'

Johnny smiled and told Porter to throw him the keys.

'It's going to be fine,' he said. 'We're the Scarlet Pimpernels, remember? You just keep a look out and make sure I don't wrap us around a tree.'

Chapter 16

Kagamo Hospital, April 1953

If Tansy believed in premonitions she'd have said she woke up with one that morning. All day a feeling of dread welled in her stomach, a sensation that something awful was going to appear just around the corner.

In the fortnight since the Mau Mau arrived at the hospital her nerves jangled at the smallest thing. The wounded men had been stowed in the section of the nursing quarters where Daniel usually slept. He'd moved out and persuaded three other roommates to vacate as well. Bunks didn't make the best hospital beds but they were lucky to get anything. Tansy looked in whenever she could, though it was a miracle two of them weren't dead already. One of the men's wounds was beginning to suppurate and if his moans didn't raise the alarm, the rotten smell soon would. She'd done her best to persuade Daniel and Jeremy to let their comrades receive proper treatment but they were adamant. Jeremy had changed over the past few days. He brooked no argument, an officer giving orders.

Last night she'd told him no man was going to die on her watch. She would be informing Dr McGregor. Jeremy had merely drawn back the sheets of the man on the bottom bunk. Lying on the mattress like outsize, oily black slugs were two revolvers.

Tansy had been forced to back down, but she was incensed. Guns in a hospital – her bloody hospital! It was insupportable. The men would have to be moved out – but how? And where? It was hopeless. Even more so since she knew something Jeremy didn't: there was a patrol of Devonshires in the forest, bivouacked at the next village. A captain had already visited the hospital asking for supplies. No wonder she was so jumpy. The wounded men would absolutely have to go. Even a makeshift camp in the forest would be better. She was either going to have to stand up to Jeremy or enlist Daniel's support.

That evening Tansy embarked on her evening rounds with the feeling of dread still in her stomach. Earlier she'd caught McGregor peering at her in the dispensary. Normally he might have barked a cheery 'hullo' but this time he'd glanced sideways, hurrying back to writing his endless notes. What was he doing? Totting up the number of bandages that had gone missing, that she'd been forced to take without a chit?

She stamped out another cigarette – when had her smoking increased so much? – and marched to Daniel's room. Before she could knock with the prearranged signal, two short raps repeated three times, she heard tyres on the gravel at the front of the hospital. She looked at her watch. Nearly eleven. Who on earth would be arriving at this time? The hospital ambulance had been out of commission for weeks – emergency rations, all petrol reserved for the generators. It didn't sound like an army truck, more like a private vehicle. Tansy frowned and made a quick decision. No time to run, no time to alert anyone – even if she warned Jeremy and Daniel it would be too late for them to move the wounded men. She would have to front up to whoever it was.

Turning on her heel she walked briskly towards the main admin block where visitors usually arrived, praying McGregor had gone to bed. The Scotsman usually retired immediately after supper so she might have a clear run. Jeremy should have the good sense to keep away. Flicking an imaginary crease out of her skirt she held her head up, urging herself to be calm. Steady the Buffs.

'*Tansy!*'

The whispered hiss almost shot her out of her skin.

'Tansy – *over here*. Quick!'

She looked over to where the voice was coming from – somewhere behind the trees lining the path. She didn't recognise it. One of the Devonshires? What would they be doing here, at night? If she turned now and made it to the admin block she might be able to wake someone. She set off rapidly though it was impossible to run in heels, even low ones. Why the hell did regulations forbid women from wearing anything practical?

She had almost made it to the hallway when she felt a hand on her arm, pulling her round.

'*Tansy* – stop! It's me.'

In the darkness she could only make out the shape of his face. It was unmistakable, but wrong. He was miles away.

'*Johnny?* Is that you? What on earth are you doing here?'

His hands were on both arms now and he pulled her gently towards him.

'Tansy.'

He was unable to say more as she'd wrapped both arms round him, flinging her head against his shoulder.

'Johnny! Thank God. I was so worried. I thought it was ... '

'Hey, it's all right. It's OK.' He held her and for a second everything was pushed blissfully away. Tansy allowed herself to inhale his scent: peat, fire-smoke and sandalwood. She raised her eyes, looking at him properly. This was not how she'd planned it but she didn't care. He held her gaze and smiled before pulling her softly back in, kissing her gently.

'I've missed you,' he whispered.

'You're not supposed to say that.'

'I know. But it's true. More than true.'

They kissed again. This time his arms pulled her into him so strongly she felt herself literally bending before him. It was some time before she regained sufficient composure to disengage and remind herself where she was and what she'd been about to do.

'Johnny, we need to talk.'

He laughed and tugged at her arm.

'That's exactly what I was going to say, but first you need to come with me. We've got a wounded man, bleeding all over the place. He needs help.'

'Seriously? Who? What's happened?'

'Gunshot wound. I'll show you, come on.'

The van was parked a discreet distance from the hospital. Porter emerged from the passenger seat looking tired and serious. He opened his arms and squeezed Tansy in a bear hug.

'Sorry about this, love. I know it puts you in a difficult position but we'd no choice. Better have a look. It's someone you know.'

Macharia sprawled in the back. When the door opened he tried to sit up, but gasped in pain and fell back heavily. When he saw who it was he grinned weakly.

'Hello, Miss Thompson. I am sorry to be meeting you again in these circumstances.'

'Macharia! What happened to you? Where are you hit?'

Tansy felt around the wound before putting her hand on Macharia's forehead. Hot. It was too dark to see, but the way he winced when she probed round the shoulder suggested the muscle and tendons had been badly damaged. The exit wound was much larger and blood ran down his back in a sticky mat. No arteries punctured or he'd be dead by now.

She drew Porter and Johnny to one side, gently closing the van door. Her lips still tingled from the kiss. Nothing made any sense. *Concentrate*, she told herself; she was a nurse. Lives were at stake. She glanced at Johnny, who was staring intently at her.

'Look,' she said, addressing Porter, unable to look at Johnny. 'It's not good. He's already running a fever and is still losing blood. There could be shot or bits of bone still in there. You did the right thing to get him to a hospital.'

'Thought so,' Johnny said, looking sideways at Porter. 'The thing is, Tansy, we need a bit of discretion here. Can't let the Brit doctors see him. It's a long story, but we think Graves is tracking us – it was his men who did this. If you could deal with Macharia on the QT we'd be rather grateful.'

'*Graves?*'

If he arrived now it would be a disaster. The hospital was turning into a secret triage centre for the enemy and no one was better at sniffing out Mau Mau than the great hunter.

'You're going to have to tell me what's going on,' Tansy said. 'And if it involves Graves there may be a real problem. Actually, quite a few problems.' She hugged her cardigan around her.

Tansy was surprised at her voice sounding so level. She didn't know which was more unreal, Johnny emerging out of the darkness to embrace her or being pitched into some impossible adventure film, starring herself as the reluctant nurse behind enemy lines. Before tonight she'd forced herself not to think about Johnny. Then at his first touch all her barriers had tumbled. Still, it was only a kiss, she told herself. It didn't have to mean anything. But even as the thought formed she understood it wasn't just that at all. Never had been.

'OK,' she said, 'I'm afraid things are even less straightforward than you think.'

The wards and corridors were full and Tansy could only think of one place where Graves might not look – her own bedroom. It was a long shot, but in the short time she'd been courted by him she'd come to know he was painfully shy with the opposite sex. He might be someone for whom the delicacies of a lady's boudoir would present a more formidable obstacle than the best camouflage. Porter and Johnny would need somewhere to stay too; they could bunk in there together while she and Jeremy tended Macharia's wounds.

Neither Porter nor Johnny liked it but there were no other options and they were running out of time. As they manhandled Macharia onto the bed she watched Johnny surreptitiously appraising her things. Every room gave clues. What did hers say about her? A silver hairbrush she'd had since childhood; the photograph of her sister Janie in Paris; a disgracefully pristine copy of *Mrs Dalloway*. Too late she realised she should have moved another picture of herself in evening gown with a resplendent Grogan wearing a dinner jacket on the night of the Nyeri summer ball. God, that seemed a long time ago.

Porter and Johnny were whispering to Macharia when Johnny suddenly glanced at her, catching her eye. The power of the desire that lay behind it unbalanced her and she purposefully looked away, breaking the moment by throwing a couple of cushions outside onto the patio. She told the men they'd have to sleep on the floor while she'd make do with the couch in the small examination room on the other side of the corridor. She nearly giggled at what the head nurse would say if she saw the sleeping arrangements, though that was decidedly the least of their worries. She stopped mid-smirk, aware of Johnny and Porter looking at her again.

She couldn't seem to behave normally, her thoughts a tangle. She ought to be exhausted, but despite everything she wasn't tired at all. Quite the opposite. She felt elated and alive, inoculated against fatigue. Everything was turned on its head. She wasn't even sure who the enemy was any more. It wasn't Jeremy or Macharia who were threatening the people she cared for.

From the second she'd recognised Johnny's voice earlier that evening everything had changed. She'd been pushed to the edge of what was right and found to her great dismay that she liked it there. Not even a painful image of Grogan smiling sadly in the back of a car could drag her away from the precipice. Whatever reason Johnny had had for leaving Nairobi all those weeks ago no longer mattered.

What a time to find out. You are a bloody fool Tansy Thompson, her inner voice berated, and this is a bloody mess.

Get out of this one.

Chapter 17

Graves didn't slink in from the forest like a creature of nightmares. He arrived at Kagamo Hospital the following morning, politely via the front door, hat off inside, minimum weaponry on display.

Tansy woke after a fitful night, hearing the sound of engines in the forecourt. She'd taken the precaution of going to bed in her clothes, and after slipping on her shoes she was up and ready in seconds. Running to the end of Number 1 corridor, she saw Graves's men sliding silently from their trucks, dispersing across the lawns, heading into the building from different angles. Graves himself waited till last, sauntering towards the main door as if he were an ordinary hospital visitor.

She sprinted back down to her room, barging in without a knock. Porter was sitting on Macharia's bed, halfway through *Mrs Dalloway*, while Johnny lay on the patio outside, eyes closed, snoring gently.

'Wake up, Johnny – he's here!'

Johnny sat up and began to mumble good morning but she ignored him, making straight for Macharia. She'd thought about this last night and had a syringe full of morphine ready. Pushing Porter to one side, she pulled back the sheet, brusquely turned the Kenyan on his side and plunged the needle into his thigh. He moaned, opening his eyes in alarm, but within seconds he'd slipped into unconsciousness. He was still in a bad way. Although they'd extracted one bullet and several shards of bone last night, his forehead was parchment dry and hot. The morphine wouldn't help that, but at least he wouldn't be feeling any pain. More to the point, he wouldn't be crying out if Graves's men came near.

'Get up, Johnny,' Porter said. 'Graves is here. We need to hide. Get a move on, man.'

'*Graves?* Christ!' Johnny leapt to his feet.

'I'd better get out there,' Tansy said. 'Just make sure they can't see Macharia if they come in. Cover him with the blanket, but leave an air hole for his face or he'll suffocate.'

She glanced at Porter to make sure he understood before hurrying from the room. For a moment the two men stared at each other as they listened to Tansy's heels clacking swiftly away up the corridor. Johnny's mind was enveloped in a delicious haze. When Tansy had come into the room she'd been flushed and slightly out of breath, and Johnny's stomach dipped as he realised how much he wanted her.

'For the last fucking time,' Porter hissed, cutting into Johnny's thoughts, 'pull yourself together and help. Where the hell are we going to hide if . . .'

Porter froze. Footsteps and men shouting. Johnny shook his head, lurching back into the present. He sprang to close the curtains, motioning to Porter to stand against the wall behind the door. The room was dark now and might pass cursory inspection if someone glanced in. But if anyone actually entered they were finished.

For the moment there was silence. Johnny opened the door a fraction, ignoring a '*For fuck's sake*' from Porter. Through the crack he could see movement. Graves was striding into view: tall, stooping, his newly bruised face in profile talking to Tansy. It was a heated discussion. Johnny winced. He could see the cane dangling from the policeman's hand, tapping impatiently against his thigh. Tansy was holding her clipboard defensively in front of her chest, one foot behind the other as she pleaded. It was a posture of exquisite anxiety and Johnny's heart broke to see her protecting them. Protecting him.

He was about to shut the door when he became aware of motion in the part of the corridor he'd been ignoring. It was just a foreshadowing, a hint of movement rather than movement itself. Someone was definitely out there. He willed himself to look, turning his head slowly.

A man was standing three feet away on the other side of the door, eyes level with his, staring directly at him through the crack. It was one of Graves's squad, a fighter wearing old military fatigues topped by a monkey cowl. He looked puzzled, unable to see into the darkness of the room. He slowly lowered the weapon towards Johnny's midriff, finger tightening on the trigger.

Johnny forced himself to remain still, holding his breath. His stomach turned over, pushing against his bowels. He prayed Porter didn't make a sound. The African outside was so close Johnny could smell the rancid stench of the forest leaching through the crack; could see the red veins on the soldier's eyeballs, huge and nervous, flicking one way and the other.

Suddenly Graves shouted. Johnny heard a whip slicing through the air and Tansy's high-pitched yelp. The soldier on the other side of the door turned to see what his commanding officer was doing. Then more shouting from the corridor. Graves yelling in Swahili. The eyes disappeared. Feet running. The sound of a door being battered down. Cries of pain.

Johnny couldn't stand it any longer. He pushed the door open a few inches more and stuck half his head out. Tansy was crouching on the floor, head in hands, while Graves and his men piled into the room where the Mau Mau patients were hiding. Anguished noises from inside. Slaps, blows, screams. For a moment the corridor was clear, all of Graves's men inside the room. Johnny whistled softly at Tansy, waving urgently. When she looked up her eyes were so black and wild Johnny thought she'd been beaten round the face. Then he realised it was mascara running. She wiped her nose with the back of her hand and shook her head vigorously at Johnny, mouthing '*Get back! Get back!*'

Johnny closed the door quickly, his hand shaking on the handle, a terrible sensation of being trapped welling up inside him. Porter was breathing heavily and sweating.

'What's happening?' he whispered.

'Graves has discovered the Mau Mau wounded,' Johnny replied. 'Poor sods are getting it.'

'*Tansy?*'

'Don't know. She wants us to stay in here. But she's not—'

'Not what?'

Johnny chewed on his finger. He didn't want to imagine what had happened, didn't want to say. Why was she crying? What had Graves done? Johnny's insides were on fire and suddenly the old anxiety was rising in hot waves.

'I can't do this, Porter. Can't let Tansy cope with this on her own.'

Images spiralled in front of him. Prisoners in camps far away, clawing at him.

'I have to get out. Can't stay inside any longer. *Have to.*'

His whispers sounded odd, high-pitched and strangled. He could not have a fit now. Must not. But neither could he remain in here, cooped up, hemmed in, trapped. He reached for the door.

Porter moved fast, grabbing Johnny by the lapels, pushing him hard against the wall.

'Don't you fucking dare. If you go out there we're finished. You might as well shoot Macharia yourself. So bloody well calm down and see how this plays. Until they're in here pointing a gun at my face it's not over. If Tansy wants us to stay in here, we stay. Got it?'

Johnny nodded, not trusting himself to speak. He crumpled to the floor, sitting in a ball, rocking his back against the wall, unconsciously echoing the posture of the woman on the other side – the woman he could do nothing to help.

Chapter 18

Kagamo Hospital, May 1953

Macharia lay on crisp sheets in Tansy's bed, fighting the rottenness invading his wounds. By the time he recovered consciousness Graves had gone, but events were hazy, dream-like. Dizzying rounds of pain were relieved by Tansy appearing with her hypodermic. A sharp jab in his buttocks or thigh and he was surrounded by a blissful numbness again.

Fragments returned. Jeremy – or Kariuki Kihara, to give him his proper Kenyan name – coming into the room. Macharia whispering in his ear, asking the code question: where had he been circumcised? The nurse answering with the correct phrase, '*At Karimania's, with Karimania's son*', making it clear he was Mau Mau too.

The African staff had remained loyal to the last and the Zebra had been convinced. But there'd been a price. When the lorries carrying Graves's men and the wounded Mau Mau departed they also contained Jeremy and his friend Daniel, trussed like chickens on the way to market. Tansy had seen them dragged out of one of the wards, kicked and taunted all the way to captivity.

Since then he'd spent the best part of two weeks in the hospital, enduring repeated examinations and painful probing. Johnny and Porter were forced to remain hidden, confined to Tansy's room with Macharia for hours on end. They played cards, read the entire contents of the hospital's small library, ate smuggled food, quarrelled and bickered. They were nervous, acutely aware that when the Zebra found no clues of their party in the city he might retrace his footsteps. It had become a race for Macharia to get better before the hunter returned.

He did his best. He was strong, delighting Tansy by getting up out of bed after only six days. Strapped and bandaged, he struggled round the gardens after dark, trying to put strength back in his limbs. Johnny helped, distracting him from his pain by asking about plants, the names of trees or the habits of a particular night bird. Johnny's passion for Kenyan nature was unquenchable and Macharia found the act of explaining it to another helped distract him from his pain.

Johnny had his own predicament, which amused Macharia but infuriated Porter. When the Yorkshireman left the room to take a call of nature Tansy and Johnny would cling to each other, shamelessly kissing and murmuring endearments in front of Macharia, who pretended to be asleep. There were times when Macharia feared they'd turf him out of bed to use it themselves. When Porter returned they'd spring apart, looking self-conscious and flushed.

Ten days into Macharia's recuperation Tansy examined his shoulder for the umpteenth time, and instead of immediately re-dressing it announced it was beginning to heal.

'You should be up and about in a few days. Until then eat, rest and walk as much as possible.'

And pray, thought Johnny, pray that Graves does not decide to come back or that Dr McGregor doesn't make a snap inspection of the staff quarters.

In the end it was not Graves or McGregor who intruded but Grogan, calling the hospital telephone demanding to speak to Tansy, asking if she knew where Johnny and Porter were. Questions were being asked in Nairobi. Where was the film of the New Village? Had no one ever heard of a thing called a deadline? Tansy had replied with a partial truth: they'd called in but had left several days ago. She didn't know where they were now, but if she saw them again she'd pass on a message.

Tansy had the distinct feeling Grogan knew more than he let on. It was their cue to leave. Macharia was well enough to travel, and unless they ran into Graves they reckoned no one would dare stop a vehicle with two white men in the front and a white nurse transporting a patient in the back. The men waited until dark and slipped off to the van parked down a side lane a few hundred yards from the entrance.

Tansy thought of pushing a leave docket under McGregor's door to account for her absence, but knew she'd been compromised. She didn't care. A different future beckoned now. She rapidly packed a small bag and went to join the others.

They drove through the night, arriving at the outskirts of Nairobi on a grey dawn, the air heavy with rain. They were too early for the rush hour that usually clogged the city's arteries. It was only when they'd passed Githuru on the main Thika road that they encountered a problem and slowed to a crawl.

From there on the van barely advanced, stop-starting, making painfully slow progress. The constant jogging woke Macharia, who eased himself up so he could see out. Tansy was leaning forward and Johnny and Porter were silent, staring out of the window. Macharia asked that they look out for a certain shoe shop where he might be dropped off but no one replied.

At the side of the road were hundreds of army vehicles of all description. Trucks with wire mesh covering the back, trucks with benches of bored, smoking soldiers, empty trucks with the names of camps daubed on crude signs. Land Rovers, *garis*, military motorcycles, staff cars. Any vehicles going in the opposite direction, trying to leave town, were hailed down and the occupants hustled away. Luckily the Information van was travelling in the right direction and was waved through impatiently by tough-looking Military Police.

'What do you think it is?' Porter asked out of the side of his mouth.

Johnny frowned. He was reminded of the big push south on the autobahn outside Munich in '45. Soldiers everywhere, barely concealed aggression, action in the offing.

'No idea. Just keep going and don't stop.'

It was Porter's turn to drive and he had an old man's desire to piss. After sitting still at one junction for twenty minutes he plaintively insisted on taking a detour to park up and refresh. When he tried to turn off, an officious redcap shouted them down, demanding to know *what the fuck they were doing* and *where the fuck they were going*. It was only a smiling intervention from Tansy, jumping out of the back to twirl her hair and smoke a lazy cigarette, that persuaded him to let them rejoin the snails' convoy into town.

Porter drove hunched over the steering wheel, swearing under his breath.

'This is a bloody disaster. When we get into Nairobi we should

205

split up,' he said. 'I'll take the footage of the camps back to my place and Tansy should book into a hotel while you, my friend, are going to have to do the decent thing with your old pal.'

'I thought you said Grogan wouldn't help us?'

'I know, but we need him. Even if we avoid Graves for a bit he's sure to catch up with us sooner or later. We can't deal with him on our own. That means after you've given Grogan our little propaganda effort you'll have to confess what happened to Macharia and get his support.'

As they dribbled nearer to the centre of town they were aghast at the scene unfolding. Armed soldiers were tumbling out of trucks, seething onto the streets. Coils of barbed wire spread messily along the road, onto pavements. Long lines of Africans were being split into gender, manhandled, marshalled aggressively into trucks with rifle butts to the back. Shrill whistles and snarling Alsatians straining to bite, barely restrained by sour-faced handlers. Africans boarded trucks, some still smiling, others understanding, waving frantically to family.

Jeeps with loudspeakers mounted on their roofs paraded slowly along the side roads shouting a message in English and Swahili. Johnny undid the window and leaned out. He didn't understand Swahili but the English was clear enough – orders to pack one bag only with essentials and assemble. Bring medicines and a change of clothes. That was all. Failure to comply would result in instant arrest.

An elderly woman with an armful of pots dropped one. But when she stooped to pick it up the rest of her wares crashed to the ground and as she scrambled for them a British soldier kicked them away, screaming at her to get up.

The city was unpeeling, the van's windscreen offering a private viewing of public despair on an epic scale. Intimate but detached.

Outside a barber's shop a row of men waiting to see which queue they should join – one still with a sheet round his shoulders; a woman weeping, lost in grief, renting her clothes, beating her chest; two soldiers laughing. A lost child crying, running in small circles.

'It's happening,' Porter said. 'It's bloody happening.'

'What is?' asked Tansy from the back, hands to face, unable to look or look away.

'The Kikuyu – they're rounding them all up,' Johnny said. 'No wonder they needed twenty-five thousand soldiers. *Jesus.*'

'Makes sense now,' said Porter. 'All the building work we saw, the secrecy, the railways, the extra staff. That's where these poor bastards are going. The camps.'

The van came to a halt again and Johnny saw they'd been corralled into a queue of cars and trucks behind the bus station. Soldiers were going from vehicle to vehicle demanding papers, forcibly ejecting passengers.

Underneath the main bus shelter a row of desks had been laid out, staffed by British officers. A row of soldiers wielding Sten guns stood guard behind. Next to each white officer sat a hooded African, eyeholes cut in the hessian sack covering his head. A line of men shuffled forward to each of the desks. Passes were presented to an officer, who would write something down in what looked like a clerk's ledger. Occasionally the hooded Africans leaned forward to whisper in the officers' ears. When this happened the man was taken roughly to one side and made to join a growing pool of men squatting in a small space enclosed by barbed-wire coils. The pool was drained every few minutes by the arrival of a caged army truck which scooped up twenty men at a time. These were the trucks Johnny had seen earlier, each one adorned with a crude hand-painted sign. Most of them had the same name: Langata.

'Johnny, listen,' Porter said urgently. 'Those squaddies will be at the van any minute. When they look in the back Macharia's fucked. You should follow whatever truck he's put on so we know where to find him later. I'll take Tansy, install her in the hotel and get back to mine. I'll type up my notes and attach them to the footage we got of the Mackinnon Road camp and stash it somewhere while I see if those Yank reporters are as brave as they claim.'

'You can also take that reel we shot of Graves's gang coming out of the forest,' Johnny said. 'I didn't mention it at the time but rewinding a film doesn't erase anything unless you film over it, so I'm thinking we should have some interesting shots on there.'

Porter smiled.

'Excellent. You're not as daft as you look.'

Johnny accepted the compliment but didn't like the idea of leaving Tansy and said so. She was leaning over from the back, pushing her head between theirs, so close he could kiss her.

'We can meet later,' Tansy said. 'Porter's right. If you can't stop them taking Macharia we need to know where he's going – get Grogan to get him out later.'

There was a sharp rapping on the window. Two soldiers and a sergeant were outside. Porter made to slide the window back, looking at his friend. He smiled the first proper smile Johnny had seen from him in weeks.

'You're a good lad, Johnny. Sorry to have got you into this but you're doing the right thing. And remember – *fuck the lying bastards*, it's the only way!'

Porter removed a hand from the steering wheel and patted Johnny on the shoulder. It was not a gesture he'd ever made before and it caught Johnny off guard.

Before he could reply soldiers were banging on the side of the van. '*Get out!* Everyone out now!'

When the soldiers saw an African in among the whites a brief hiatus of surprise swiftly gave way to a sergeant shouting at Macharia to move away from the van and give him his *kipande*. Porter and Johnny got out at the same time.

'Leave that man alone,' yelled Porter.

'Who the fuck are you?' the sergeant snarled. 'Nobody's supposed to be driving in Nairobi.'

'No one told us anything about it,' Johnny said, trying to remain calm. Out of the corner of his eye he saw Porter beginning to move away. Macharia was standing with his head down, his arm clasped by another squaddie.

'You are joking, aren't you?' the sergeant said to Johnny. 'Can't be a white person in Africa who doesn't know about this operation. All Kyukes to be taken into custody for questioning. Been brewing for months, pal. You live on another planet?'

'No,' said Johnny tersely. 'I live on this one and I'm not used to some little prick shouting at me because he thinks a gun gives him the balls he never had. You let him go or I'll ... '

It was a useless threat and the sergeant knew it.

'Or what, mate?' he grinned, blowing his whistle. Soldiers from all around responded and Johnny found himself in the middle of a semi-circle of men pointing guns at him. An officer marched over to find out what was happening. At that moment Tansy emerged from the van. Gently she told Johnny not to be so stupid, taking the officer away by the arm to explain. Porter had not made it far and he stopped to beam at everyone with what he once told Johnny was his shit-eating grin. Anger levels dipped and they might have got away with it, but just at that moment Macharia decided to make his bid for freedom.

Sensing there might not be another opportunity he backed slowly away from the soldier, holding his *kipande*. But another soldier he hadn't noticed standing behind hit him hard in the back with a rifle butt, ordering him to stand still. The blow struck just below the shoulder, and while missing the centre of Macharia's wound it was near enough to cause significant pain and – worse – an eruption of bleeding. So much blood gushed onto the road that even the officer allowing himself to be whispered to by Tansy stopped abruptly and began to issue orders.

Macharia's shirt and bandages were ripped off, revealing an injury immediately recognisable to any infantryman as a bullet wound. More soldiers crowded round barking questions. How did he get that? Where was he from? Which Mau Mau unit did he belong to? The officer scrunched the shirt into a ball, pressing it to the wound, directing Macharia's hand up over his neck so he could staunch the blood himself.

'You're fit enough. Now get over there,' he said, pushing Macharia towards one of the lines, marching over to the senior officer in charge to have a word.

Macharia looked round carefully to see what had happened to the others but couldn't spot Porter or Tansy. Only Johnny was visible, waving his arms around in a way that was dangerous when there were so many guns around. All about him, Macharia was aware of his fellow citizens shuffling forward in different files, waiting to be told their fate by officers behind desks with men in hoods beside them.

'Who are those people?' he asked the man in the neighbouring queue, nodding at the hooded ones.

'*Gakunia*,' the man spat back.

For Macharia this one Kikuyu word described it all. 'Little sacks'. *Traitors*. Oath-breakers. Cowards who whispered in secret.

When it was his turn to stand in front of the desk he mumbled answers and pretended to be cowed and afraid. The officer handled Macharia's *kipande* with distaste, brown-gloved fingers barely holding on to the edges. Furtively Macharia watched the *gakunia* peering at him from the safety of his hood. There was something about the eyes when they blinked that he recognised. As the British began firing questions at him, the hooded creature was growing excited, the filthy sack on his head swaying from side to side like a cobra about to strike.

Macharia couldn't bear it a moment longer.

This was a Kenyan sending other Kenyans into captivity, perhaps to their deaths. He had no right to hide. Macharia let the shirt he'd been clutching slip to the ground. As he moved forwards, instead of retrieving the shirt he launched himself over the desk at the *gakunia* and, before anyone could react, ripped his hood off. It stuck on the man's chin but with his other hand Macharia managed to land a blow on his throat which made the traitor gasp for air. As he straightened his neck to draw in breath Macharia whipped the sack off.

And there he was for all to see.

Joseph Nyaga, a man who lived not three huts away from Macharia in his own village. A friend of his brother, Gatimu. Macharia had always thought he was going to join the Movement. But he'd been turned by the British and now he sat in a puddle of fear because the hessian sack covering his features had been his sanctuary. Exposed, he was a dead man.

When Macharia's fellow Kikuyu saw one of the *gakunia* naked to the world and the eyes of all men there arose a terrifying sound. It started as a low moan and rose to a full, deep-roaring howl. For a moment it looked as if there might be a mass rushing of the officers and their hooded helpers. But the British army responded swiftly, firing shots into the air, forming a cordon round their officers.

Macharia did not see what happened next. Seconds after ripping off the hood he was oblivious, bludgeoned into unconsciousness by rifle butts, his act of rebellion glorious but short-lived.

Chapter 19

Nairobi, March 2008

The *matatu* could move stealthily when it had to. The music had been turned off and Dedan extinguished the headlights as they glided into Mattingly's street. There were lights on inside the house. He killed the engine and Sam began to open the door but he insisted she wait, speaking with a seriousness she'd not heard before, no signs of any lingering effects of the ganja.

'You do not know who is in there,' he said. 'Or what. Let us wait.'

Sam wished Kamau was here but there hadn't been time for him to come back. After her alarming conversation with the mystery man at Mattingly's house she had rung him immediately, but he was on another bus, heading miles in the wrong direction. Dedan, however, had come at once and she suspected he'd been parked round the corner from the hotel.

It was nearly ten now, and although it was still cloyingly warm outside Sam found herself shivering. If Esther's message had chilled her, the voice on her phone had been worse. Why hadn't she answered? Something was very wrong. A few pedestrians strolled past the van and a dog sniffed the wheels, but otherwise there was no one about.

'It's very quiet here,' she said.

'It is a quiet neighbourhood. It means nothing.'

'How well do you know Esther?' Sam asked. 'Is she likely to be there now?'

Dedan rolled his neck.

'I do not know, Sam. I do not know either of them well.'

Sam frowned. When Dedan had first presented himself at the hotel, announcing he'd been sent by Mattingly, she'd assumed he must have been a friend. There was a tremor of wrongness about this too. But this was not the time. Besides, Kamau seemed to trust him. The thought prompted a keen sense of his absence.

A sense of how absurd this all was descended on her. She was a lawyer not a detective, sleuthing around a town. A very foreign town. But Esther had been specific. She needed to see Sam, and after everything she had been through Sam was not going to let her down.

'This is ridiculous,' she told Dedan. 'We could be here all night. I'm going in.'

'No – *Sam*—'

But Sam eased the *matatu* door open and was halfway to Mattingly's front door before he could finish the sentence.

There was a small alley leading round the side of the house, but it was dark down there and she didn't fancy it. She rapped on the front door and waited. Before there'd been noises of someone moving inside but now, when she strained to listen, there was silence. No one came. The air was textured with unfamiliar night scents, jasmine and mimosa layered with rotting fruit. She knocked again, harder.

She peered in through the window. A blind was half drawn and when she ducked her head she could make out a room that was probably Mattingly's study. A desk stood in the corner and bookshelves lined the wall. But there were no books on the shelves. Someone had thrown Mattingly's library onto the floor. Books and papers flung everywhere. A globe lay on its side and a leather chair was at a strange angle against the wall. The frame of a photograph had been broken; the glass missing and the black and white picture inside torn off its mount.

Sam knocked on the door again.

'Hello – anyone in there?'

Even as she said it, Sam was aware how foolish this might be. If there was anyone still inside who shouldn't be it was madness to advertise herself. But the sight of all the books on the floor reminded Sam of her own hotel room and the anger that had begun then, brewing underneath the shock, came seething to the surface. Who did these people think they were? She had to get inside.

But perhaps not the front door. Sam moved to the side of the house, gesturing to Dedan where she was going. He shook his head vigorously but she ignored him and took a deep breath. The alley it was.

212

Using her left hand to guide her, Sam felt her way cautiously along the passageway. It was pitch black and she stumbled almost at once. Something metal clanged and she grazed her ankle, stifling a cry before walking on, picking up her feet with exaggerated care. Her fingers brushed against something fluttery and wet and she let out a small gasp as it slithered away. After twenty paces there was a dim light. Poking her head round the corner, she found herself behind the wall of the courtyard where Mattingly and Esther had served her coffee.

The double doors to the courtyard were open and she saw movement: someone walking quickly through the room. Not Esther or Mattingly.

Sam stretched her leg up and over the wall, stepping onto the pulpy softness of the gardenia bed. Passing the courtyard table, she slipped inside the house, cocking her head to listen. There were voices. One of them coming from upstairs. She tiptoed down the hallway connecting the garden room with the rest of the house. The voices were louder now. African voices. Male. What had she been expecting? Someone speaking English, inviting her in for a cup of tea? Sam became coldly aware of her position. How would she explain what she was doing there?

A noise of pans clanging was coming from a room a few paces up the hallway, off to the left. Sam thought she remembered it as the kitchen. She crept nearer, imagining it might be Esther's relatives helping in the aftermath of the break-in. But, she realised, that could never be the case. Esther didn't have any relatives.

Edging into the kitchen, Sam didn't spot the source of the noise at first. Then she noticed a man squatting down, going through the lower cupboards, urgently shaking jars, turning saucepans upside down. She watched silently, dithering with indecision. Should she announce herself or leave the way she'd come? Esther clearly wasn't here.

And then she saw something that forced her to bite her lip to prevent herself crying out. There *was* someone else in the kitchen. Lying on the floor, torso hidden by a central island, was a pair of legs – a man's legs by the look of the trousers. *No.* Sam walked slowly away, not daring to breathe. She had reached the door when another man's voice cascaded down the stairs.

She froze, then tip-toed backwards, feeling behind for the door, slowly turning into the hall. A little further and she'd be in the garden room, just feet away from the courtyard. One hop over the wall and she'd be down the alley and in the safety of the *matatu*.

'*Hey – you!*'

The man from upstairs was descending fast towards her, yelling in Swahili and English, ordering her to stop. For a nanosecond she considered running. The shouter was big and sweaty, his white shirt damp and untucked, flannel trousers slung low on fat hips.

She could outpace him.

She was mid-turn when she felt her arm being grabbed. Hard. Fingers pinching into upper-arm flesh. It was the other man, the one she'd seen rummaging in the kitchen. He was not big but he was wiry and strong, and Sam knew there was not a chance she could outrun him.

The big man approached and said something to his companion, and Sam found herself being hauled into the garden room.

'Hey, stop that. Let me go,' Sam shouted, tugging back. 'Who the hell are you anyway? Where's Esther?'

The man stopped dragging her but maintained his grip. Sam moved her free arm and swung down with all her might, thankful for all those cold evenings in self-defence classes. *Never show fright. Take control.* The move worked and the man pulled back his hand as if he'd been stung. He shrugged, making a pacifying gesture, saying 'OK, OK.' But on the last syllable he launched forward and pushed fiercely. It was just one blow but it was hard, more like a karate hit, his palm punching into her chest. It caught her at the top of her left breast and she tottered backwards, arms flailing, tumbling back onto a small sofa.

The big man advanced and looked down at her. He was seriously sweating now, great drips smearing his upper lip.

'Who are you? What are you doing here?' he said in broad-accented English.

'I asked you the same question,' she said, with more defiance than she felt.

'Be quiet! Who are you?' he shouted. 'Tell me your name immediately.'

Sam didn't answer and the man looked to his companion, speaking fast in Swahili. At least she thought it was Swahili. It could have been Kikuyu or any African language at all, she really had no idea.

The kitchen man looked unhappy at whatever suggestion had been made but said 'OK' and left.

The front door closed and she was alone with her African interrogator. Or was she? What about the man lying in the kitchen? Then she remembered something about him and felt a peculiar sensation. It reminded her of when she'd had her tonsils out, the anaesthetic icily racing up her body into her head just before she lost consciousness.

The legs. They'd been covered in blue cotton trousers. *Blue cotton.*

They were Mattingly's. He'd been wearing them the last time she'd been here. Oh Jesus, what had they done to him?

Where was Esther?

The man reached slowly behind his back. Into his back pocket. Sam jumped to her feet, not thinking. Acting.

She caught him by surprise, emulating his companion's earlier action, slamming the heel of her hand with as much force as she could muster into his chest. She felt something click in her wrist and a spasm of pain but she was scarcely aware of it, sidestepping the African, ducking under his arm, bolting for the terrace doors.

Legs pumping as if she'd injected a triple espresso directly into her veins, she cleared the wall by miles, zipping through the alley and into the street, screaming for Dedan before she'd drawn three breaths.

'Got to go,' Sam shouted. 'Now – come on!'

She knew he drove fast, but they were off the street and out of the neighbourhood in seconds, an alarmed Dedan driving with his head half-swivelled round to see what they were fleeing.

As the adrenalin slowly subsided Sam found it difficult to stop her teeth chattering. She kept thinking about the legs she'd seen, lying there so still. And the man digging around as if they didn't exist. If Esther was in the house she was probably dead too. It amazed Sam she could think so coolly. The episode felt oddly unreal. Her wrist ached and her arm stung. She wished she'd smashed him in the face. There were deep red finger marks imprinted on her skin, the flesh around them turning blue. They really were a perfect impression of someone's fingers. Perhaps she should show them to the authorities for identification.

Sam began to gabble a description of what she'd seen inside the house. Dedan was patient, telling her to take her time, to breathe in between the words. 'So,' she concluded, 'we should go to the police, report this quickly before they can move the body – or bodies.'

Dedan looked at her seriously.

'That would not be a good idea.'

'Of course the police must be told. How are they going to catch who did it if they don't know there was a crime in the first place?'

'It is not so simple,' he said. 'That man, the big guy I saw coming out of the house, running after you. I recognised him. Did he not identify himself?'

'No he bloody didn't. Who is he?'

'His name is Githaiga. A CID man. Bad guy to get on the wrong side of.'

It was hard to breathe again, the air refusing to stay in her lungs.

'But Dedan, how could they be police? They didn't say anything. Why were they throwing everything around, searching the place?'

Sam stopped, cursing herself. She was an idiot! They could easily have been police. Mattingly dead; called to the house. Find the body – search the house. And then a European woman lumbers into the house from the back. Of course they'd want to speak to her. And of course they'd be suspicious when she tried to run. But why hadn't they identified themselves? And why hadn't they opened the front door when she knocked?

First the hotel break-in, now this. She breathed deeply through her nose, urging herself to calm down. Again, she thought about Kamau and wondered what he'd be saying now. He'd left a message on her phone, telling her he'd be at the hotel first thing. But she needed to leave there as soon as possible. Perhaps she could ask him to find her somewhere to stay. She looked at Dedan. He seemed relaxed, the epitome of cool. Given what he'd just been told, perhaps too relaxed. He was a laid-back guy, she understood that. But this level of tranquillity in the face of Mattingly's death was unnatural.

'You seem very calm, Dedan. Mattingly is dead, maybe murdered. His wife missing – possibly killed as well. Aren't you just a bit worried? Didn't those two ask you to be my driver?'

Dedan coughed and concentrated on the road ahead.

'That is so. Mattingly did ask me. I have told you no untruths, Samantha. But it is also the case that, as I told you earlier, I do not – did not – know him very well. He was a friend of a friend. I believe he was acting on that friend's behalf.'

'You're saying Mattingly was acting as an intermediary for some *other* friend? Who wants you to be my driver but couldn't ask himself?'

'Yes. That is so.'

'*And?*'

'And I am afraid I can tell you no more.'

'*What* – for fuck's sake, Dedan. None of this makes sense.'

Dedan fed the steering wheel through his large hands and his eyes narrowed as if he were concentrating. To Sam it looked more like he was in pain.

'Look,' he said, still staring ahead. 'I would tell you if I could. But I cannot. When the time is right I am sure you will find out. For the moment please accept my apologies. After what has happened to Mattingly this has become a very serious matter and I will never let you walk into another house alone. My job was to protect you as well as drive you and I have failed. I will not do so again.'

Sam shook her head. It didn't sound right but she was in no mood to argue or probe further. She would ask Kamau about it tomorrow. Dedan pulled in to the hotel's dropping-off point and a night porter arrived from nowhere to hold the doors open. It was just past midnight. She was amazed to see she'd only been gone a couple of hours.

Dedan looked at her remorsefully, saying he'd return at dawn. And please, she was not to go anywhere without him. Kamau was coming tomorrow as well and she would be safe. In the meantime she was not to open her door to anyone.

'Fine,' Sam said. 'And in this meantime you can go and ask your friend – or friend of a friend, or whoever the bloody hell he is – and tell them I want to know who they are. Deal?'

Dedan beamed, transforming into his old self.

'It is a deal, Samantha Seymour. Go safely.'

The bar was still open.

Sleep was an impossibility; she was too wired, the events of the evening pinballing round her head, tilting and jolting in lurid flashback. A joint might have been useful, though any ensuing paranoia would not have been funny. Alcohol was the only option.

217

There were a few drinkers still going, clustered round tables in the sticky neon shadows of the Palm Cocktail Lounge. Sam ignored them and sat on a barstool downing whisky sours, feeling very much on her own and not a little sorry for herself. Her wrist hurt, her arm hurt and unless she drank another couple as fast as the previous three, her brain would no doubt continue to hurt too. Sitting alone in a sleazy late-night bar was not her thing, although an evening when she'd been robbed, attacked and discovered a dead body might constitute extenuating circumstances. What a lovely coupling. Robbed and attacked. She was not in Kansas any more, M'toto.

'Hello, Sam. What brings you out on this fair night?'

Pugh's tie was undone and his usually immaculate cuffs scrunched up. The light was gloomy but she could still make out the flush on his face. She slurped another mouthful through her straw.

'Is it a fair night? I hadn't noticed.'

'Why don't you come over and join us?' he asked, pointing to a table where three others were sitting. Jules was among them. He caught Sam's eye and gave a cheery wave.

'No thanks. Been a long day. Long night too. Are you celebrating something?'

'God, no. It's been a nightmare. I don't know how many villages we trekked out to today. No one ever seems to be there. It seems word's got out that we are not to be trusted. How's it going with you, Sam? We haven't seen you for a while. Everything OK?'

Sam crunched an ice cube and thought about how much she should tell him. *Could* tell him.

'I had a break-in to my room earlier. Hotel thieves. Apparently it's very common. The strange thing was, they didn't seem to want any of my money. Left it all there. Odd, isn't it?'

'Oh no, Sam – I am sorry.' Pugh looked it too, radiating concern as he allowed his hand to stroke her shoulder in comfort. 'Did they take anything? Passport? Anything at all?'

She considered it. But there could only be one answer to Pugh.

'No. Nothing.'

She gave up on the straw and knocked back the rest of her whisky, gesturing to the bartender she was ready to sign.

'Sure I can't tempt you to another?'

'Why was there no one at your villages, Pugh? Why is it exactly that Kenyans don't trust you?'

'Don't you mean "us" – trust *us*? You're still part of this mission, Sam.' He laughed. 'You haven't gone native on us?'

Sam signed her tab and stood up, annoyed at slipping immediately on a floor that seemed to be sloping, coming up too fast. More annoyed still at Pugh's hand shooting out to steady her elbow, holding on for just that second too long. Fuck he was fast.

'You all right, Sam?'

'I'm fine, thank you,' she said, trying to smile through it. 'Shouldn't you join the others?'

'I thought we were getting on just fine here, the two of us.' Pugh leaned in, placing one arm on the bar in front of her, penning her in.

Sam stopped smiling. Was he really doing what she thought he was doing? How fucking tedious. She pushed past his arm. Told herself not to say anything. Made it to the end of the bar. Couldn't quite hold it in.

She turned unsteadily.

'You know why they don't trust you? *Us.* Whatever.'

'Who, sorry?'

'The villagers who run away every time they see the mission turning up. They know we're here to trip them up. And they're right, aren't they? Don't tell me Her Majesty's Government will ever in a million years pay these people a penny. However many of them have been beaten and assaulted. Raped. Your villagers might have run away, Pugh, but I've managed to speak to plenty of men and women. And guess what? Their stories tally. A few mistakes here and there – why wouldn't there be after more than fifty years? But mostly they were spot on. On the money. Except there won't be any bloody money, will there?'

She hadn't realised her voice was so loud. Every head in the room had turned in her direction. Jules was making an 'oh dear' face, but when Pugh wasn't looking he was also dragging his finger across his throat in a 'you are so dead' gesture.

'Ah, I see,' Pugh said and Sam noticed his shirt sleeves had miraculously moved, re-arranged neatly down the length of his arms as if they had never been rolled up at all. Not a crease on them. How had he done that?

'Do I detect just the hint of an opinion there, Sam? A dash of pash to lighten our dreary lives? How *limitlessly* thrilling. I do hope it won't interfere with your brief. You know, the one that says you swear to be impartial and go about Her Maj's business without fear . . . or favour, Sam. Favour – that's the key here, I believe. And I do think there might be the teeniest drop of favour in there. Do tell me there isn't.'

To Sam it seemed as if his words were aimed at the others listening. She might have had too many but she was certainly not going to reveal her hand now. Then she saw his eye move and realised he'd just winked at her. He'd actually fucking winked at her.

'Whatever, Pugh. I'm tired and I'm going to bed.'

'Is that an invitation?' he asked quietly.

Sam almost laughed again. There was not a conceivable parallel dimension in which what she'd just said could possibly, *in a lifetime of lifetimes,* have constituted an invitation of any kind. But from bitter experience she knew better than to dare to laugh when a man's pride was at stake.

So instead of calling him out or just kneeing him in the balls, she said:

'No. It is absolutely not an invitation. Good night, Pugh.'

Suddenly very sober, she marched out of the bar. A quick look over her shoulder showed she'd been the only woman in the room and that Pugh, the fucking creep, was following.

She pressed the button for one of the lifts and Pugh loitered by reception, flicking through tomorrow's lunch menu. The lift was refusing to come. She tried the other one. The light showed both were stuck on the fifth floor. She thought about taking the stairs but the stairwell was dark and her room was on the seventh floor.

He kept looking over at her, sidling nearer, ostensibly engaging the night porter in some chat about the weather. But she was certain he was waiting for the lift to arrive so he could get in it with her. This could not be happening to her. After everything. She couldn't cope with that. She pulled her phone out and dialled Kamau's number. Please answer. *Please.*

'Hello – is that you, Sam?' His voice was thick with sleep.

'Yes it is.' She turned her back on Pugh and lowered her voice. 'Sorry for calling so late but I need you. There's a man. I'm worried he might . . . He's—'

Kamau was instantly awake, cutting in.

'Are you all right?'

'No, I'm not. *I'm scared.*'

'Where are you?'

'In the hotel.'

'Good. I will be with you in one minute. Stay there.'

'But, I thought . . . Where *are* you?'

'In Dedan's *matatu.*'

'How did you get there?'

Click.

Braver for hearing Kamau's voice, she turned back to face Pugh. He looked so innocent – *pleasant* – she had a pang, thinking she might have misread him. He was peering through the large plate-glass windows at the front of the hotel. He made a signal to a car outside that he was coming. Pugh hadn't been loitering; he was waiting for someone. My God, she *had* misread him. He walked towards the exit and as he passed he looked directly at her, his lips moving silently, mouthing 'next time', and she knew she hadn't.

The porter let him out, ushering him into the back of his car. Kamau was bounding up the steps, but instead of looking at him her eyes were fixed in horror on Pugh's vehicle.

As the car began to pull away the driver wound down his window to stare at her. There was something about the face. Out of context, it didn't come at once. But when it did it hit so hard Sam gasped.

The man from Mattingly's house.

The one who had dug his fingers into her arm.

Chapter 20

Nairobi, May 1953

Johnny was beginning to sweat.

He sat in a near-empty office, papers and manila folders stacked neatly in packing cases on the floor. Grogan's large teak desk was shining, clear of impediment. The door to the press office was closed but a dozen typewriters could be heard clacking frantically as the Information Department wrapped its tendrils round the day's events. The Nairobi operation was big news, and although it was already past curfew by the time Johnny extricated himself from the Military Police, the office was still going at full tilt.

He'd seen a few of the draft releases awaiting printing in the Information Officers' out-tray. *Government Operation Hammers Mau Mau. Thousands of Terror Suspects Rounded Up. Army Deals Body Blow to Mau Mau. Go Home or Go To Gaol – Terror Tribe Told To Quit Capital.*

Grogan produced a yellow handkerchief from the pocket of his shorts, meticulously wiping away imaginary specks of dust from his glasses. Johnny pulled a cigarette out but his boss told him to put it away. Hadn't he heard? Grogan didn't live here any more, and his successor hated the smell.

'Promotion,' he explained. 'Not my office now. Just clearing out a few last things. Going to Rehab: pointy end of hearts and minds. In the camps. End the war a lot quicker than all this lot put together.'

It had taken several hours to track down Grogan, yet the memory of Macharia being beaten unconscious and hefted onto a lorry like an animal carcass was vividly fresh. Johnny had been detained almost immediately after Macharia was on the truck so hadn't been able to see where he was being taken. The Military Police questioned Johnny for hours and it was only repeated mention of Grogan's name that prevented him from being carted off as well. Instead, he'd been ordered to report to MP HQ where a file had been opened on him. *A file.* Another way of saying he was being investigated. Compared to Graves, that was the least of it.

Johnny told Grogan as much as he could, describing what had happened since meeting Graves and his patrol on the forest edge, skirting over events beforehand. As far as Grogan was aware, Johnny and Porter had simply been acquitting their duties making the propaganda films. But even as he relayed it, Johnny realised the story made him appear impulsive to the point of recklessness.

Grogan's brow twitched a beat between incredulity and anger. With the door closed it was stiflingly hot in the office and Johnny was aware of sweat rings around his armpits. Grogan paced before rounding on him.

'Are you seriously telling me you clubbed a fellow officer with a camera and helped a possible Mau Mau suspect escape? And then here in Nairobi your driver assaults one of our informants? And yet you seek to defend him? It's almost unbelievable, Johnny – whose bloody side are you on?'

Johnny flailed about for a justification. How could he explain the instinct that had prompted him to save Macharia? Truth was, he hadn't thought about it for a moment; he'd just done it. Grogan would never be able to comprehend something so divorced from rationality.

'I'm not on anyone's side,' Johnny said. 'I acted on the spur of the moment. Even you might have done something if your driver was about to be shot.'

'*Be quiet,*' Grogan snapped. 'Let's deal with the facts. Are you certain that after the episode in the hospital Graves is still after you?'

'Yes.'

'Where's Porter?'

'Don't know. Home, I think.'

'And Tansy?'

'I don't know.'

'*Don't know?*'

Johnny wasn't going to confess. If things needed to be said they should be said by Tansy or both of them together. It was cowardly, he knew, but he didn't want to complicate matters. For the moment it was important only to get Grogan's protection. Without it they were all at risk. Tansy included.

'Look,' Johnny said, 'Tansy and Porter left while I was being questioned. Porter promised me he'd make sure he got her to a hotel.'

He realised the mistake as soon as he'd said it.

'Promised *you*? Why would Porter make *you* a promise about Tansy? I'm afraid I don't understand, Johnny. In fact, I don't understand why you were within a thousand miles of Tansy.'

'We've all become close, Grogan.'

'*Close?*'

Johnny wanted a cigarette badly. He waved his hand in an approximation of annoyance. He was not good at this.

'Yes, the three of us. We've all been through it. Look, I'm aware we were selfish. We shouldn't have put Tansy in danger. I know that. But the hospital was the only place to go. Macharia was bleeding to death, for God's sake. We felt responsible for him. Sorry.'

Grogan's mouth made a moue of disbelief. He found the yellow handkerchief and returned to wiping his glasses. Johnny glanced through the interior window at the toiling Information Officers. Apart from Mattingly, none of them had looked up to greet him when he came in. He'd never belonged here.

'OK,' Grogan said finally, holding his spectacles up to the light for a last inspection. 'Let me get this straight. You and Porter suddenly find a hidden sympathy for the underdog, a sympathy that wells up inside you to such an extent that when a policeman wants to question a Mau Mau suspect – in case you'd forgotten, they're the ones we're fighting – you knock him unconscious and flee the scene.'

'It wasn't like that.'

'*No*,' Grogan said, letting his anger show. 'I have the floor, I think. You flee the scene and not to just anywhere, but to the hospital where my fiancée works.'

Johnny stiffened.

'Yes, Johnny, fiancée. She didn't tell you? We are to be married – *married*. Tansy has consented to be my wife. Yet in the hospital you suborn her to shelter a fugitive. When the police arrive, legitimately looking for said fugitive, they discover a nest of Mau Mau. Your man remains at liberty while the others are arrested. Result? Tansy is put at great risk in the middle of a fucking shitstorm!'

Tansy engaged? What was he talking about? She would have told him. Grogan was lying. Johnny began to protest but stopped, realising this was not the right time. Grogan had placed the spectacles on his nose and was peering over them.

'If this was another century,' Grogan intoned, 'I'd be horsewhipping you for traducing my fiancée. You're a bloody fool, Johnny. Becoming a dangerous one too. Christ, man – you were just meant to keep your head down and take some pictures. Was that so hard?'

Johnny dipped his head and soothed his temple with his fingers. All he could think of was ringing Porter to find out where Tansy was and heading there immediately. The staccato hammering of next door's typewriters was the only sound in the room. Grogan remained mute, staring into the middle distance.

'Do you still have those photographs of Graves at the Cunningham place?' he asked abruptly.

Johnny couldn't hide his surprise.

'What photographs?'

'Oh for God's sake. Not again.'

Grogan marched to the interior window and gazed out at the typing press officers, hands behind his back.

'This office, these people,' he said, continuing to look out. 'My life's work for the whole of this past year has been directed to one purpose. Winning the propaganda war. Why? For fun?'

Grogan whipped round to face Johnny.

'No, I do it because it will shorten the conflict, because in the long term fewer people will suffer. Towards that purpose I have said and done things which in a normal context would be regarded as deceitful or outright lying. I am, do you see, a professional dissembler. *Professional*. Means I'm very good at it. Means I know a truth from a lie when I see one. So don't fucking lie to me, John Seymour, I can smell it like a wronged wife smells another woman, and at the moment you reek.'

For a second Johnny thought Grogan was referring to him and Tansy, but if he was the message was subliminal for he left the subject immediately, returning to his desk to busy himself with a notebook plucked from his breast pocket. He turned the pages until he found what he wanted.

'Right, I've found his number. So – I will help you, Johnny. Not because I owe you; your actions have discharged that debt forever.' Grogan's voice barely concealed his disdain. 'As for any affection I

225

might've had, that disappeared the moment you set out your stall for Tansy.'

Johnny stared at Grogan. Perhaps this really was nothing to do with hitting Graves or helping the so-called enemy. Johnny had seen it before around the office. Cold and sharp. Effective.

'I'm going to help,' Grogan continued, 'because not to would put the woman I love in danger. But also because I may have need of you in my new job. If and when that becomes the case, you will come running, Johnny. Do you understand?'

'You've got this entirely wrong, Grogan.'

'*No!* Be quiet and listen. This is how it's going to work. You are going to return to your hotel room, pick up both the pictures and negatives of Graves and give them to me. When I've received them I'm going to ring him to say I have those pictures. I will inform him in very clear language that unless he leaves you and Tansy alone, and even Porter, though God knows why I should help that drunken fool, then I will release the pictures to the relevant authorities.'

Johnny thought quickly. Porter had wanted Grogan's support and here it was.

'Fine, I'll give them to you. But you have to promise you'll find Macharia and try and get him out. Failing that, make sure he's unharmed. He's an innocent party in all this.'

'Innocent?' Grogan looked astonished. 'You think there's a single innocent Kikuyu? Macharia's got Mau Mau stamped all over him. You're more naïve than I thought.'

'Maybe,' Johnny replied. 'But the pictures could be damaging to you too, Grogan. Imagine the reaction if one of your Information Officers announced that you suppressed photographs of a war crime. That there was proof in pictorial form.'

Grogan's lips twitched around his small mouth.

'That is an exceedingly stupid thing to say. Besides which, there would be no proof.'

'Wouldn't there? Negatives can be copied.'

Grogan's eyes iced over and Johnny realised he'd gone too far. But it was too late to back down now.

'Be very careful, Johnny, you've just crossed the line.'

Grogan smiled thinly.

'Dangerous place on the other side; no guarantees there.'

Chapter 21

Central Province, May 1953

When Macharia came to he was rattling around the bottom of a truck, eyes level with the feet of twenty fellow prisoners crammed inside the vehicle's cage. It was still daylight, and he felt cold and sick. His wound ached but at least it hadn't reopened. As he struggled to raise himself up, an old man moved to one side of the bench so he could sit properly. Another saw Macharia was shivering and offered his jacket. It didn't fit but he accepted gratefully. He asked the Mau Mau code question of a few of the men but their answers showed they were not in the Movement. Their only crime was being Kikuyu.

The old man squashed up against him smiled at Macharia, revealing gap teeth.

'We saw what you did to that *gakunia*,' he said. 'Since I've now become the "enemy" it was good to see the face of my foe! You are already famous, my friend.'

Macharia mumbled thanks, pleased his actions were recognised.

Langata camp was huge. A barbed-wire fence twenty feet high and interspersed with wooden guard posts disappeared far into the distance. They drove through the gates to a small enclosure bound by bundles of razor wire on each side. A zone was marked out for turning, and lorries were shedding their human cargo at great speed before heading back to Nairobi to pick up more.

Macharia was mildly impressed at the efficiency, but the feeling evaporated when two guards leapt onto the lorry's side plates.

'*Out! Out!*' they screamed, lashing with their staves at anyone who paused for even a second. Macharia took a glancing blow to the side of the head but it did not cut the skin. On the ground they were ordered to squat in lines of five until they formed long columns,

227

sitting next to similar columns of other new arrivals. A white officer, also carrying a stick, marched up and down counting heads before ordering them forward to another checkpoint. If anyone moved he would be struck hard. Those sitting on the outside rows received more blows and Macharia soon understood why there was considerable competition for the middle positions.

There were still some who held on to bags or parcels. One old man carried a cooking pot tied up with string. Other metal implements clanged around inside it. At the checkpoint each man was searched by two tribal policemen, patting them down, ordering them to empty all pockets. After a few anxious moments Macharia passed through, the guards relieving him only of his watch.

The elderly man with the cooking pot fared badly. The lid of his pot was ripped off and the items inside tipped onto the ground, revealing themselves as nothing more sinister than a fork, a spoon and a small drinking cup. Their loss enraged the man. When he saw his belongings joining the growing heap of discarded goods he threw himself at the guards with a terrible creaking fury. Macharia watched, sickened as the warders batted him off easily, making short work of breaking his bones with their staves.

Most turned their eyes away but Macharia forced himself to look. He owed it to the courageous old man to bear witness to his final moments. It did not take long for him to die, though the beating continued longer and the sound of hard wood on wet flesh would stay with Macharia for ever.

Next they were herded through more reception pens before being allocated tents. There were hundreds of the canvas lean-tos, stretching in row after row. Twenty prisoners to a tent, no bed, just a small space on the ground. In the corner was a hole in the ground. The place stank of shit and fear.

Macharia was given no food that night or the whole of the next day. There were stand-pipes, but water was limited to two cups a day. By the end of the second night, men were collapsing. To complain was to invite a beating. Three men from Macharia's tent were carted away after these assaults, not to be seen again. Their absence meant a little more space under the canvas but added to a terrible feeling among the rest that it might be their turn next.

On the third day, after their first meal of inedible porridge, prisoners were ordered to squat in their columns. A white officer spoke through a megaphone, telling them that if they cooperated they would soon be freed. If not, they would be despatched to more specialised camps.

'The purpose of your visit with us,' the officer shouted, 'is to discover your level of commitment to the terrorist group known as Mau Mau. Those of you who have nothing to do with it will be free to return to the native reserves, while the rest will be questioned further at your next camp.'

Macharia's first interrogation was brief.

Inside one of the huts near the perimeter sat two white men in plain clothes, while half a dozen Tribal Police stood behind. Macharia found they already knew his name as he'd been identified as the one who'd attacked the *gakunia*. He was forced to his knees and ordered to clasp his hands above his head. One white man had his *kipande* and some other documents in front of him, while the other wrote notes. The first question came without either of them looking up.

'You are Muraya Macharia, aged twenty-six, from Nyeri District?'

'Yes, *bwana*.'

'How long have you been a member of the illegal terrorist organisation Mau Mau?'

'It is not my privilege to belong to that organisation, *bwana*.'

The reply at least forced the interrogator to look at his prisoner.

'*Not my privilege?* Been to school, have you, boy?'

'Yes, sir.'

'Teach you to be a cheeky bastard did they?'

'Cheeky? No, sir. Not at all, sir, I—'

The blow came from behind with a shattering force. Some blunt instrument knocking the side of Macharia's head so hard he was driven headlong into the dirt floor of the hut.

'Sit up, boy.'

He tried to do so, and could barely hear the next few questions for the ringing in his ears.

'I repeat: how long have you been in Mau Mau? Where did you take your oath?'

'I am not—'

Bang. Again, another blow.

229

'Who administered your oath?'

'Nobody, *bwana*. I do not belong to Mau Mau.'

Another blow, and another.

The questions came in such a lazy way, giving little time to respond. Macharia suspected all that was required from this beating was the formality, the first application of white force upon the black man's oath. All knew it was only the beginning, a prelude to the next camp.

'Black,' the leading white interrogator pronounced, delivering his verdict. 'Mark him down black and make a note that he's a nasty little trouble-maker.'

An hour later Macharia was on a train, compressed against dozens of other trembling men in a cattle truck heading, rumour said, for Coastal Province. Glimpses of the countryside rolling past were framed by barbed coils covering the small windows.

A suitable picture, he thought, of a once free land strangled by wire.

Chapter 22

Tansy sat at the vanity table in her hotel room, brushing her hair. There were still a couple of hours until Johnny arrived and using the old silver hairbrush was a comfort, a reminder of a home and a life that seemed a long way away. The brush and a few old photographs were all she'd had room to pack when she left the hospital and she wondered whether she'd ever end up in her own home, surrounded by her own things – her own family.

A few minutes later she heard a knock at the door. She smiled. Impatient boy. How delicious. When Johnny had phoned that morning she'd said he wasn't to come before six. She hurried to the bed, gathering clothes, unceremoniously sticking them in the cupboard. With a last glance at the mirror she took a deep breath and opened the door.

'Tansy – ravishing as always. Hope I'm not intruding. May I come in? I won't stay long.'

Grogan smiled wolfishly, pushing past Tansy's arm, which had not moved from the door.

'Come and sit down, my dear,' he said. 'We need to talk.'

Grogan perched on the side of the bed so Tansy retreated to the chair at the vanity table, pulling it back as far away from him as possible.

'To what do I owe the pleasure, Grogan?' she asked, reaching for a cigarette.

Grogan had the stillness of a man at ease with himself and the world. He waited for her to settle before steepling his fingers in front of his mouth like a headmaster delivering a homily – more in sorrow than anger.

'Tansy,' he said, exhaling her name. 'I feel it's only fair to let you know that Johnny came to see me.'

'Oh?'

'He was trying to get me to look for your new black chum – my old driver Macharia, who seems to have got himself into another fracas with security. As I suspected, he is not all that he appears. Seems to be making a habit of assaulting people.'

Tansy's shoulders, which had been tightly hunched since Grogan had walked in, slackened. So, not about Johnny.

'Have you found him yet?'

'No,' Grogan said, springing to his feet. There was little space for him to roam but his paces were smaller than most and he managed six or seven before reaching the bathroom wall and pivoting, as if on parade.

'Thing is, Tansy, I've got a new job. I'm heading to one of those camps. Been handed a tricky one. Got to convince the inmates their best interests lie in coming across to us. They're not exactly persuaded at the moment so it might be tough. Anyway, I'm en route there now, which is why I thought it would be wise to have a chat. Better than the phone, don't you think?'

'You're going? Leaving Nairobi?' Tansy tried hard not to let her excitement show. 'Grogan, you will take care out there, won't you? I know Johnny and Porter had a few scrapes when they were in the bush.'

'Thank you, Tansy, your concern is touching. Believe it or not, I do know what's going on "out there". Actually, I'm glad you mentioned Johnny. It's him I wanted to talk to you about.'

Grogan twiddled with one of the curtain tie-backs, pushing at the tassel, a cat pawing at a ball.

'There's no good way to say this,' he said, still facing the curtain. He turned his head slightly without fully looking at her. 'So I'll jump straight in. Johnny suggested something might have happened between you two at Kagamo.'

'No, Grogan, absolutely not. Nothing happened at all. Why would you say that?'

'Please, Tansy, I know all about your little infatuation. It shames me to say, but it was noticed by others at the hospital too.'

'Who? McGregor? Interfering little Presbyterian. He's never liked me. He's always finding fault.'

'*Tansy!*'

Grogan swatted the tassel with a hard blow, swivelling round to confront her head on. His glasses had slipped down his nose and he held his head back to keep her in focus.

'This does not dignify you. The point is that whatever took place cannot be allowed to happen again. My feelings for you have not lessened, so on this occasion I am minded to overlook it.'

'What are you talking about? We never—'

'*On this occasion* I will overlook it. Even I understand how passions can be *heightened* in the heat of the tropics, not to mention all that danger with Graves looking for you. Yes, I know about that too. Terribly exciting, I'm sure. Point is, Johnny put you in an intolerable position and I intend to make sure it was for the last time.

'You see, I'm willing to do the decent thing and put down this *foible* of yours to pre-match nerves – but only if you promise never to see him again. He's no good for you, Tansy.'

During Grogan's speech Tansy watched him with incredulity, the cigarette between her fingers unsmoked, its ash lengthening in a downward curve that matched the angle of her mouth. He hadn't finished.

'If you keep to that – never see him again and never speak of this matter to a living soul – I am prepared not to punish Johnny and to let our engagement continue.'

It was Tansy's turn to stand, savagely grinding out the dead cigarette in the ashtray.

'*Punish?* What the bloody hell are you saying? What engagement? There's never been an engagement. In the car when you asked I said—'

'You said "yes, but not yet". That was an acceptance. That was an engagement.'

Tansy opened her hands in front of her as she might on beginning a song. But the hands were tighter, not an overture to any melody.

'I said no such thing! Were you listening to my words or to what you wanted to hear? Good God, Grogan, you're deluded.'

'I know what I heard, Tansy.'

'I said I'd *wait* – that's not the same as *yes*. And who are you to start talking about *punishing* anyone? And for what? If I wanted to kiss Johnny – or marry him, or anything else – it's of no bloody concern to you.'

'Johnny has been involved in a serious assault on a member of the security services. And I believe my fiancée is of legitimate concern to me.'

Tansy clutched her hands to her face.

'Can you hear yourself? Can't you get it into your thick skull: *I do not love you.* I never bloody loved you ... I thought we could be friends – Christ, I thought we *were* friends. I even admired what I thought was ... But now I can see I was mistaken. How *dare* you fucking threaten people?'

For a moment Grogan did not stir, only the eyes narrowing behind his owlish glasses hinting at the fact he had heard.

'Have you quite finished?'

Tansy yanked the door open and gestured towards the corridor.

'Yes – I'd like you to go now, please.'

Instead of moving towards the exit, Grogan abruptly pushed his face into hers, so near she could see herself reflected in his thick lenses. Because she wasn't wearing shoes they were almost the same height, and she was forced to lean backwards. His face darted still nearer and the malevolent intent radiating from him was so powerful she feared he was about to hit her.

'You've no idea have you?' he said quietly. 'If you can keep silent for two seconds I will explain where matters really stand. When Johnny came to see me he vouchsafed he had something that could keep Graves at bay. You didn't know about the pictures? Well, he's going to give them to me. I understand they're really quite powerful in their way and the possibility of them having a wider audience will certainly keep Graves off your collective backs.'

Tansy did know about the pictures. Johnny had told her all about them while they were hiding in the hospital. But she wasn't going to talk to Grogan about it, would never talk to him about anything to do with Johnny for the rest of her life.

'I will use them against Graves if he ever shows signs of wanting to do you or your little friend Johnny any harm. But, and this is the important part, Tansy, those pictures could go missing at any stage. They could, in a sense, be *revoked*. D'you see?'

Grogan laughed harshly.

'Graves is a difficult beast to keep on a leash at the best of times. A hound of war who'd slip his surly bonds as soon as I lifted my little finger. Is that what you want?'

234

Grogan stared at her, waiting for an answer. But Tansy said nothing, trembling as she pushed the door even wider.

'Fine,' he continued. 'I'm a reasonable man. I don't expect an answer immediately. But decide by lunch tomorrow. I'm leaving for Coastal Province in the afternoon, travelling directly to Manyani, some godforsaken camp out towards Mombasa. Shouldn't be there too long. After that I expect to be posted to Umua – perhaps you've heard the name? It's only a few miles from the mission hospital. When I arrive I look forward to discussing the details of our wedding. Ring me with your answer – I'll be at the club.'

Grogan attempted a smile, his expression fluttering disconcertingly between warm and chilled, but Tansy would not meet his eye, staring fixedly at the floor.

'Believe it or not, I'm doing this for your benefit,' he said. 'I'm not a vindictive man.'

'Just get out!' she spat. 'Get out this bloody moment or I'll call security.'

Grogan rapped his fingers on the side of his shorts, but whatever he was planning to say, he reined it in, nodding to himself before marching towards the door. Halfway through he looked over his shoulder.

'You will remember what I've said, won't you? Oh, and Tansy, I'm a liberal man in many respects but I never want to hear my fiancée swear in private or in public again. See to it, please.'

Tansy slammed the door with such ferocity that the room boy in the corridor, waiting attentively on the *bwana* and his memsahib, ran to find screwdrivers to mend it. Tansy didn't notice. She paced and swore, shouting a sequence of curses viler than she knew were in her. When that didn't work she threw the hotel Bible at the wall, cursed God, cursed Grogan, cursed herself for becoming involved and threw herself on the bed. She cried for hours, and no sooner had she stopped than she started again.

She picked up the phone from where she'd cast it on the floor and demanded a bottle of whisky from room service. When it arrived she fetched a glass from the bathroom and filled it half full, drinking it in one go, not even coughing before pouring herself another. Johnny would be coming to the hotel soon and she needed to think, required the numbness from the whisky to dull the white pain in her heart.

She knew what she had to do. The ugly rationality that Grogan used to value so much, and which she now loathed with any passion she had left, had resurfaced. For in the face of a threat that no amount of wriggling or evasion could diminish, what other path was there?

However he twisted it around, Johnny hadn't been able to find any alternative to producing the photographs for Grogan. Giving up his last card exposed him even more, but at least Macharia would be getting some help inside whatever camp he'd landed in. And Grogan would never be sure he hadn't kept copies somewhere.

When he returned to the Information Department to surrender the pictures, Grogan had disappeared. His boss's former secretary had instructions to lock the photographs in his old safe but she had no idea where he could be contacted. Grogan Littleboy was *hors de combat*, below radar.

Johnny, relieved at not having to see Grogan, used the office phone to try Porter again. Yet again nothing. The Yorkshireman's absence was starting to worry him. During the last two days he'd made every effort to contact him, ringing constantly, slipping a note under his door, even sending an expensive telegram. Johnny decided he must have gone on a bender. He'd turn up when he was sober.

Meanwhile, it was time to visit Tansy at the Stanley. Of course he was missing her, but more than that he needed to discover whether Grogan was lying about their engagement. However impossible it was, the mere idea of them being together chafed at him and he couldn't stop torturing himself with it.

The hotel receptionist was happy to phone the room but after a short conversation put the receiver down, embarrassed.

'Miss Thompson is busy and asks you to wait or to return another day.'

'What's her room number?' he asked. 'I'd like to talk to her myself.'

'I'm terribly sorry, sir, but Miss Thompson was very clear. On no account are you to go to her room. If you wait she will come down.'

He was baffled. Had he done something wrong? Had something happened to her? Should he go up anyway? Knock on every door until he found her? A sensible voice urged caution. These were early days. His claim on her was fragile. Besides, she'd been through the mill, looking after wounded Mau Mau, harbouring fugitives, nearly getting arrested. Anyone would have been rattled by that. Calm down, Johnny. Play the long game.

He went to the bar and waited.

It had become dark and he was on his third drink when she finally descended. She was drained and pale. Her make-up applied too thickly. She looked older, like someone's once-glamorous aunt – over-powdered, whisky fumes spiking through the perfume. She allowed Johnny a glancing peck on her cheek but pulled away when he tried to hold her hand.

'Are you all right, Tansy? What's the matter?'

Tansy shook her head vigorously in small, sharp movements, mouthing *nothing*. Nothing was the matter, nothing to explain.

'Looks like you need a drink – what can I get you?' he asked.

'Nothing, thanks.'

'Sure?'

Again, the sharp head shake. Apparently she had no words for him.

As they sat opposite each other at a window table Johnny had the impression he was meeting the wrong woman. The real Tansy of a few days ago would never have behaved like this. He tried a few more openings but she sat upright in her chair, hands clasped tightly on her lap, hardly looking at him. The only person she was concerned about was Macharia, expressing relief that Grogan was looking for him. But on the subject of Grogan, she flatly refused to talk about it at all.

After ten minutes Tansy pleaded tiredness, announcing she was going back to her room. The idea of her engaged to anyone else, let alone Grogan, was making Johnny feel sick. And the more she deflected his questions the more he doubted everything she said. She rose to go but before she could walk away, he clasped her arm.

'*Tansy*, wait. This is not right. What have I done? Is there something wrong?'

She withdrew her arm sharply.

'Wrong?'

'I've obviously done something to offend you. You suddenly seem—'

'Yes? What do I suddenly seem, Johnny? Older? Wiser? Less able to take in the fact that we've been sheltering an enemy? That we've been close to being killed – by our own side? That our lives have been turned upside down, that we're still in bloody danger?'

'But we're not. I talked to Grogan.'

'Yes, I know. He told me you'd seen him. Explained he was dealing with it. But it's never over with a man like Graves. *Never, Johnny.*'

Tansy shivered and it was all he could do to stop himself putting his arms round her. But he feared she'd just shake him off and he couldn't have borne that. Instead he stepped back a pace, literally trying for a new perspective. She was behaving so oddly he needed some detachment. A terrible anger at the unfairness of it was mounting inside him.

'Listen, Tansy,' he said, 'I don't know what the hell's going on but you owe it to me to speak to me.'

'Owe it to you? Do I? Do I really?'

'Please, Tansy – I haven't come here to fight. What did you and Grogan talk about? Did you tell him about us? *Anything?*'

Tansy sighed and walked over to one of the lobby side-booths, avoiding other guests waiting for the lift. 'Last cigarette?'

He offered her one and lit another for himself.

'Well,' he said. 'Did you?'

Tansy exhaled, her eyes flicking away from his, roaming the lobby.

Johnny could hold back no longer.

'Grogan told me something, by the way,' he said tightly. 'Claimed you were engaged. That you'd "consented to be his wife". I said it wasn't true. Couldn't possibly be true because you would have told me. Was I right, Tansy?'

'Gosh, what a lot of talking about me you and Grogan have been doing,' she said, finally meeting his eyes, anger sparking. 'With all that locking of horns I wonder how you found time to discuss Graves or Macharia or any other of the no doubt far less important but nonetheless *life-threatening* things going on.'

Her sudden display of temper didn't seem genuine in the least. Johnny pressed on. His anger easily matched hers, rose above it by a long way.

'*Tansy. S*top avoiding this. Are you his bloody fiancée or not?'

Tansy paused and stubbed out her cigarette half smoked, the prop no longer required.

'Yes.'

Johnny waited for more but there was nothing.

'That's it – just "yes"?'

A wave of anguish washed over Tansy's face.

'*Yes*. Look, Johnny, grown-up things are always more difficult. If you don't understand that then I can't explain. Can't . . . '

As her words trailed off Johnny felt the pain of a cold knife stabbing at his soul, scouring out everything that was good.

'*Grown-up things?* I see. Just a bit of fun. A lark before you leave and settle down with . . . with . . . '

He couldn't bring himself to say the name. It was revolting and he felt marked by it, a tawdry sense of being used.

For a moment Tansy wavered, forcing herself to bite back the words she wanted to say, clamping her arms to her side as they began to rise towards him of their own accord.

'Oh Johnny, I'm so sorry.'

She crumpled, face in her hands.

But Johnny was already walking away and he saw nothing of that, only betrayal and a vast emptiness beckoning.

Three days later and Tansy was still snapped in two, neither side of herself allowing the other any forgiveness. Johnny's furrowed face tormented her. Every second of every day since that awful evening she'd regretted what she'd said. All she'd really wanted was to bury her face in his neck and let him take her upstairs. She'd never known such longing; it invaded her whole body, obsessed her thoughts, violated her dreams.

Yet if she loved him there had never been a choice. And she did love him beyond measure. But no amount of rationalising or reasoning provided any hint of balm.

She was desperate to speak to Porter. He was the only person left who might possibly understand. Of all people, he would appreciate why she'd been forced to act in that way. Knowing him, he might even come up with a way round it.

She took a taxi, no idea if the Yorkshireman would even be at home. There'd been no answer from the phone and none of her messages to his house or club received a reply. She climbed the dozen stairs to the first floor without much hope.

The first few knocks resulted in nothing. She tried the handle but the door was locked. The only thing to do was keep knocking until he answered. For ten minutes Tansy did just that, hammering on the door, shouting his name until she was hoarse. Even someone in a drunken stupor would have heard. But there was nothing. Nothing except for an elderly Asian woman who emerged silently onto the shared landing to find out the source of the racket.

'Are you a neighbour of Mr Porter?' Tansy asked.

The woman scrutinised her before nodding.

'Have you seen him at all?'

The woman shook her head and gathered up her sari, preparing to disappear back into the flat opposite.

'Just a moment,' Tansy insisted. 'I'm a friend of his. No one's heard from him for several days. I'm a bit worried. Could you tell me when you last saw him?'

The woman looked as if she might not have understood, opening her own front door, head bowed. But just before she closed it behind her, her head popped out.

'Please, madam, we are only trying to mind our own business. We want no part of this. But you are right to be worried. Last week some men came and—'

The door suddenly slammed shut and Tansy heard a man's voice shouting. *Right to be worried?* She knocked on the woman's door but she didn't answer. A curtain drew back and a male hand made the unmistakable gesture of shooing her away.

What men? Tansy was alarmed. *It couldn't be.* A malignant wave swelled through her stomach. She should go. It wasn't safe. But she needed to find out. And that required getting into the flat. Retreating downstairs she walked along Porter's tree-lined road until she found what she wanted, stamping on it to bring it to a manageable size.

Armed with the branch she returned to the flat. As was common in the Asian workers' apartments that Porter preferred to the more substantial bungalows of the European quarter, the bottom half of the door was made of wood. But the top was glass. If anyone asked she could say she was the district nurse on an emergency visit.

240

She swung the branch like a golf club but it bounced off pathetically. The next time she took a half-run, half-skip and smashed it with all her might. To her satisfaction, the glass shattered into a thousand small squares. Ignoring movement in the window of the Indian flat behind her, she used the branch to clear the remaining shards from the door and put her hand inside, fiddling with the lock until the Chubb clicked open.

The moment she entered the small hallway she recoiled at the stench.

Putting her hand over her nose, she stepped cautiously into the flat. The main room was strewn with debris. Papers, books, broken glass and kitchen utensils thrown onto the floor. A desk looked as if someone had axed it for firewood. A leather armchair lay cut open on its side, stuffing everywhere, springs uncoiled.

Porter had just made it to his bedroom. He lay half on the bed, face beaten almost beyond recognition, body twisted, one hand by his throat, a leg bent underneath him at a dreadful angle, one shoe off. Tansy approached, holding her breath against the sickly perfume of decaying flesh.

She put her hand to his neck, a reflex to find a pulse. But any rhythms of life had been beaten out of Porter long ago. Tansy had witnessed death in many forms but never seen anything like this. Porter's mouth was open in a soundless scream, congealed blood forming a dry crust on his beard. His shirt was ripped open, trousers and pants round his thighs. His groin and chest looked purple-red, every exposed piece of flesh stripped of skin. The weals were so close together they'd merged to form one huge open wound. Tansy could feel herself breathing too quickly, knew she was hyperventilating, nearing shock. But years of experience dealing with trauma made her aware she could function if she pushed herself. She must not collapse, must not weaken.

She walked backwards out of the bedroom, snagging her stockings on the armchair springs. She looked round wildly. What to do, what to do? Call the police, get help? No – run. Run now. As far and as fast as possible before they came back. Before *he* came back. *Oh God, poor Porter.*

Her legs began to tremble violently. *He was her friend.* He'd made her laugh; once said he loved her. Like a daughter. She'd never talked

241

to him enough. What would his family in England say? She didn't even know if he had a family. The nurse inside Tansy understood her own collapse was moments away. No one could be expected to take in what she had just seen.

There was a phone on the floor and when she put the receiver on the cradle it crackled, suggesting it might work. She repeatedly hit the switches with her fingers until an operator's voice came into her ear.

'May I connect you?'

'Police,' Tansy said. 'Police. *Now.*'

Her voice was surprisingly calm. Only a matter of time.

'Putting you through—'

'No. I've changed my mind.'

'Are you sure? I can easily—'

'No! Connect me with the Muthaiga Country Club. Immediately, please.'

'Thank you. Putting you through.'

The receptionist at the club wasn't sure if he was there but they could send out a boy with a message. If madam could wait?

She nearly put the phone down a dozen times as the minutes ticked by. By the time another voice came on her eyes were pressed shut to stop the tears and she was pushing the receiver against her ear so tightly it hurt.

'Hello, Seymour here. Can I help you?'

'Johnny? Oh God, Johnny, something awful's happened. You have to come. It's Porter.'

Then the tears came and she could say no more.

Chapter 23

Nairobi, March 2008

Sam sipped her coffee and grimaced at the bitter strength. She'd forgotten to put sugar in and tittered uncharacteristically, noticing her hand shaking as she replaced the cup on the saucer. Fearing someone might be staring at her, she glanced furtively round the hotel lobby. Two European teenagers at the nearest table were deep in their mobile devices, cut off from the world by white earbuds and dark aviators. A party of businessmen argued loudly over an agenda while an elegant African woman sat to one side, reading the *Financial Times*. No one was looking at Sam. Why would they? How could they possibly tell that she'd been subjected to the most momentous night of her life?

She felt at her side for the suitcase. That wasn't going to be stolen as well. She scanned the bill again. It seemed an awful lot for a fortnight's stay. Perhaps she'd still be able to claim it on expenses. Pugh had assured them the Foreign Office would pick up the tab at the end of the mission, although he'd said nothing about the protocol of leaving early. Bollocks to them; she wouldn't be lingering a moment longer and if they dared complain she'd slap a harassment suit on them.

Kamau was outside, talking to Dedan. Together they'd find her somewhere to stay, she was sure of it. Life had just become considerably more complicated but she wouldn't remain in Kenya any longer than necessary. Though she did want to find Esther before she went. She was so worried about her. There were too many questions: what was going on with Pugh's driver and the policeman? How did Mattingly die? More to the point, why?

Thank God for Kamau. When she'd explained it all in her hotel bedroom last night he'd looked very grave, put the stupid chain lock on – as if that could keep anything serious out – and started writing things down. But then she'd begun to cry, silently at first then embarrassingly louder, with great nose-smeared sobs as everything crashed in on her – the awful story from Esther, that sad, sad mass grave, the sight of Mattingly's dead legs on the kitchen floor while that horrible man searched around him. Her hotel room ransacked and the precious documents stolen. Then the bloody creep Pugh and his oily, predatory games.

Mid-cry was when the complexity really began.

Kamau had put long arms round her, holding her tightly against his chest. She'd been afraid of making his shirt wet and then that hadn't seemed to matter because somehow his face was pressed against hers and it was hot and he was kissing the tears and she'd turned her head and he was kissing her lips and she was kissing him back with a strength and open-mouthed passion that had propelled them both onto the floor.

From there it got a little hazy. No wonder her hands were still trembling this morning. Underneath Kamau's gentle exterior had lain a surprising strength. Of mind too, because he had pulled away, holding her at arm's length, shaking his head as he tried to find his will.

'No, Sam, it cannot be like this – here.'

Sam hadn't understood, had thought he was joking.

'Look around us,' he said. 'This is not how two people should begin their journey. You are upset and it cannot be right to start like this.'

'But I want you. Don't you want me?'

'*Of course I do*, Samantha Seymour. From the very start. I have thought of nothing else. I was amazed I could translate anything, my head was so full of *you*. All I wanted to do was hold you. If you had heard what I was saying sometimes: those old *mzees* were laughing at the rubbish I was coming out with, forgetting immediately what you'd just said. Gazing at you like a . . . '

He laughed then and Sam had laughed too, and the moment shifted as she accepted the rightness of it. Apart from a party long ago when she'd made a stupid move on a boy wearing eyeliner, no man had ever in her entire romantic life said no, at least not at the stage when mutual interest and arousal was assured. And now, when she desired it most, it had happened. Be careful what you wish for, Sam Seymour.

So instead they'd moved onto the bed and held each other and talked. Cocooned in Kamau's arms she felt completely safe and her past flowed out as she told him about her parents, why she hated and loved the law, the strange quest Magnus had set her on, her revulsion at the depositions and her determination to do something – any-thing – to try to make amends. And then Sam had turned to the present, purging herself of all the bad things she'd experienced since setting foot on Kenyan soil.

Kamau listened seriously before gently kissing her again. And that had been so much better than words or sympathy that it had proved impossible to lie in his arms and do nothing. So she got up and walked around and drank water.

Passing the mirror she paused to look at their reflection: a flushed white woman and a calm, handsome young black man sitting propped on the bed, clothes askew. Until that moment she could honestly say that the colour of her desire had not entered her mind. For her Kamau was a man, a man who had gorgeous dark skin, not a 'black man', although naturally he was that as well, just as she was a 'white woman'.

None of that seemed to matter, but whether it was because the snapshot in the mirror made her see it too starkly or whether she was just beyond tired, Sam was immediately confronted by a collage of images from history, of white people doing terrible things to black people. The colonial horror stories she'd read and heard had always provoked a profound, intellectual rage but the picture of herself and Kamau in the mirror smashed it home. This had become close; intensely personal. It was entirely possible they'd discover that one set of relatives had tortured another. She'd felt dizzy at the foulness of it.

She lay beside Kamau then and quietly told him of her fears; about the gulf that the past had forced upon them and the barriers they might have to overcome. Even as her words emerged she was aware of how fast she was moving, and in the silence that followed she feared Kamau thought so too.

But after a pause he rested his chin on the top of her hair and answered with the gravity that was never far away.

'You may be right about the nineteen-fifties, but I don't think it is as bad now. Economically perhaps, sometimes, but not on the personal level. Though it is certainly true our generation – in your country and mine– are both contaminated by the fallout of colonialisation. Which means that you, Samantha Seymour, are just as much a victim – or a possible victor – in all of this as I am. Which is which we are yet to discover.

'But important as deconstructing post-colonialism is,' he said, suddenly smiling, 'I fear that further discussion must wait.'

He had kissed her then, with increasing intent, and Sam found it quite easy to forget about the past. However, some minutes later Kamau pulled back once more, even though she'd managed to unbuckle his belt this time. He sat with his arms folded, amusing Sam by looking so frustrated. She kissed him on the cheek and went to the kettle, thinking that if they couldn't make love they would at least make tea. How very English. She was sure Magnus would have approved.

Armed with a brew lightened by fake hotel-room milk, it had been her turn to listen as he described his own life, growing up in the suburbs of Nairobi with his two younger brothers and younger sister; how he wanted to follow in the footsteps of his parents, both teachers. A college somewhere, if not Nairobi, perhaps Mombasa. The more he learned of history, the more he yearned to tell others about it and show how the past stalked the present, reminding it, goading it, changing it. For several hours, as night ticked into morning, it had all sounded so blissfully normal she'd been able to forget she was lying in a bedroom surrounded by the detritus of a break-in perpetrated by men who had robbed her and quite possibly killed someone else.

Sam pushed her coffee to one side and looked out of the window to see if Kamau and Dedan had finished their negotiations. They'd decided last night it would be tricky to stay with Kamau's overly traditional parents – that apparently required a lot more diplomacy than they had time for – so they were leaving it to Dedan to come up with somewhere. He'd been phoning people for hours.

At last Dedan put his mobile away, forced to address a smartly dressed man who'd turned up with a clipboard. Kamau left them to it and swept effortlessly up the hotel's outer stairs towards her. He really was good-looking, she decided. Such a stillness about him, hardly moving his head as he took the steps three at a time.

She exchanged glances with the pretty receptionist who was also watching him and felt a stir of pride. He was hers. For the moment, anyway. She felt like a teenager again and giggled. As he drew nearer, she saw Kamau was wearing his serious look.

'Hello there,' she said, unable to stop the joy she'd felt since last night escaping onto her face. 'Do we have a plan?'

'Well, we might have found you somewhere to stay but there's a complication – you'd better come and see. Hey, let me take that suitcase.'

Outside Dedan was leaning back against his *matatu*, surveying the world through impenetrable wrap-around lenses and doing his best to ignore the clipboard-wielding African in front of him.

'This guy says he comes from Grogan Littleboy,' Kamau said. 'He wants to be your driver for the day. I told him you already had one but he is refusing to go away.'

'Grogan?'

'Yes,' said the man, handing Sam an envelope. 'Colonel Littleboy would like you to read this. I am either to give you instructions on how to find us or to drive you.' He waved at a large white 4x4 parked next to the *matatu*. 'And it would be very comfortable.'

Sam read quickly, remembering how Grogan had said she must visit him. He had to attend a conference in a week's time so, if it were convenient, she might do him the courtesy of coming today. He hoped she could make it for there was something important he wished to show her that might shed light on 'matters you are examining – indeed, matters that might be of personal interest too'.

She looked at Kamau, who'd joined Dedan in a staring contest with the driver. The new arrival clearly had put their backs up. She rather liked the idea of Kamau protecting her. How very old-fashioned! She felt a surge of desire. A vast part of her just wanted to escape somewhere with him. After last night her horizons had changed, the present for once competing on equal terms with the past.

But there was too much unresolved business. *Family* business. If anyone could throw light on matters from the past it would surely be Grogan. She'd warmed to the twinkling old charmer, and what he might be offering was enticing. He had known both Johnny and Tansy after all. Although the picture of the three of them at the ball

247

did suggest not all might have been well between them, Johnny's face declaring how little he wanted to be there. What *had* happened to Tansy? Sam had a wave of nostalgic longing. She wished she'd met them, just once. How funny to have such a yearning for something she'd never experienced. She wondered if there was a word for it. Doubtless the Germans had one.

The thought of her grandparents involved in some love triangle was deliciously intriguing and Sam laughed at the outrageousness of it as she tugged Kamau back into the hotel lobby. She moved to an alcove out of sight of reception and after sneaking a covert kiss, asked what he thought. And, crucially, whether he would go with her.

'No,' he said. 'You should definitely go but I'm afraid I've got some other things to attend to.'

Sam frowned.

'But why can't the two of us visit the old bugger?'

'I'm afraid the timing's wrong. Later, Sam, we can be together. Dedan and I have been talking. There's a place we might go. It sounds wonderful – somewhere special that I'm sure you will love. Out in the country. But first I need to do something, actually quite a few things, so it would be good if you did go to this Littleboy man. Dedan can take you there – I don't trust that other snake of a driver – and then afterwards you can both come and join me.'

'Why – where are you going?'

'It is best I do not yet say.'

'And you are the best judge of that because . . . ? What is all this mystery suddenly? I don't get it.'

Kamau looked intently into Sam's eyes, both hands moving to hold her forearms. Sam felt a terrible sense of foreboding. She wanted to speak but her throat felt constricted by a great weight. But then Kamau's face slowly creased into a smile and Sam again felt a tug of longing mixed with an overwhelming sense of relief. Bloody hell. Be careful, she told herself, be very careful.

'Listen, Sam. I don't understand yet what is happening between us but you must know that I care for you.' His thumbs gently caressed the inside of her arms. 'Very much. So, please trust me on this. If I manage to accomplish what I want, then it will be to your benefit – mine too, I hope.'

Sam was both relieved and terrified. Her world was shifting, accelerating with perilous speed away from everything that had come before. He pulled her to him and the heat of his skin drew her lips to his neck. She kissed him lightly there and for a suspended instant they stayed that way before he disengaged, drawing his hands away.

'I don't want you to go,' she said.

'Sam,' he smiled. 'We can certainly do this small thing. Everything is dancing before us now. Do you not feel it? We will meet up again in a few short days. And when we do I may have something very special for you. I hope you will like it. If you do not, then at least you will know it was done with the best intentions.'

He drew in for one more kiss, a lingering one that caught the corner of her mouth before sliding perfectly over her lips.

'OK,' he murmured, 'perhaps not all the best intentions.'

Grogan's house lay more than a dusty mile along a private road, three hours north-west of Nairobi. From the outside it looked vast, colonial meeting Scandinavia, red roof and sharp concrete angles, plates of dark blue glass. And in front of that his very own guardhouse with two beret-wearing men in pretend uniforms. Khaki and guns. Sam knew little about weaponry but recognised the familiar shape of an AK47 from a thousand and one movies. Dedan peered forward.

'*Whoa* – what is this?' he said quietly. 'Stay in here, Sam. Make no sudden movements.'

He wound the windows down slowly and removed his sunglasses, issuing a wide grin before saying something in Swahili. The tone was mellifluous and soothing. She heard her name and '*Bwana* Grogan'. One of the guards kept his distance, with his gun pointed at Dedan. The other went into the guardhouse, where Sam watched him talking on the phone. He emerged a minute later, barking at his colleague, who lowered the gun. He walked round to the passenger side and peered closely in at Sam.

'You are Samantha Seymour? We thought you were coming with our driver. We were not expecting *him*.' He jabbed a finger at Dedan. 'You can follow me but he must stay.'

Sam looked at Dedan.

'I don't like this,' he said out of the corner of his mouth while

249

maintaining his grin for the guards. 'I do not think you should go in there on your own.'

Sam thought quickly. This really was absurd. She had not come all this way just to drive back again. She got out of the *matatu*.

'Let me use that phone to call the Colonel,' she said. 'I'm not sure he would be pleased about you pointing guns at his guests.'

The man stood his ground but Sam pushed past him imperiously, going into the guardhouse. The phone mouthpiece glistened with spittle and she held it away from her mouth.

'How do you get this thing to work?' she shouted at the guard. 'Come here at once and help.' Her heart was racing but the adrenalin had lifted her to a place where it felt rather enjoyable to play the memsahib. She was glad Kamau couldn't see her; she feared it might be coming a mite too naturally.

But the guard did not move and when Dedan began to open his door his companion raised his gun again. For a few tense seconds no one moved: Sam at the guardhouse, Dedan halfway out of the door, the guards halfway to wanting to shoot someone.

Suddenly a window opened in the main building and a recognisable voice trumpeted out instructions loudly and rapidly in Swahili. The guards reacted as if they'd been struck, standing immediately to attention.

'My sincere apologies,' Grogan said, his head appearing through the window. 'Buggers don't know friend from foe. We've had a lot of problems with gangs here. Poachers, thieves. Armed to the teeth, so my men are very nervous about strangers. Still, it's no excuse. Just walk through the door both of you – it's open.'

Grogan was already downstairs to greet them when they came into a stone-flagged hallway. The first thing Sam noticed was the cool, then a tinkling sound of running water. An interior fishpond had a small fountain in the middle and Sam had the impression of entering a sumptuous Arabian caravan from the dry of the desert. Grogan had summoned a tall African man with a scarred oval face, who completed the picture by offering them steaming hot towels.

Introductions made, Grogan asked if Dedan would like to peel off and have a beer in the bar area.

'I believe there's some kind of football match on the television,' he said.

250

Dedan looked enquiringly at Sam and she nodded. As far as she could see, there was little to be concerned about, though she was pleased Dedan was being so solicitous.

'I will be here if you need me,' he told her.

Grogan led Sam past the pond, through another courtyard into a large drawing room. It was airy and bright light shone through slatted shutters. Sam found it surprisingly serene. Two large cream sofas were adorned with pretty scatter cushions and there were fresh white flowers in a vase on the mantelpiece. If it hadn't been for a giant water buffalo head mounted above the fireplace and the crossed spears and shields on the wall, Sam might have suspected the presence of a woman.

'I like that man of yours,' Grogan said. 'Fine specimen. Is he Luo? Chap I worked with years ago swore by them. Wouldn't hire anyone else. Said that, in loyalty, they were second only to the Masai. How'd you find him?'

'Oh, he's a friend of a friend. I sort of picked him up on the way.'

'Excellent. That was quick work. Well, if you need a Masai, Jordan will advise. He's the tall one who let you in. My major-domo. Man of many parts. He's illiterate, but keen as mustard if the going gets rough. Ruthless bugger, actually. Once saw him hamstring a man with a dagger he keeps in his pantaloons. Good fellow to have at your back.'

The way he'd talked about Jordan unpleasantly reminded her of how farmers in Lincolnshire spoke of their hunting dogs. Noting how fast the conversation had turned to servants, she couldn't work out why Grogan still needed a man at his back, let alone one good with daggers. She asked whether he minded if she smoked.

'Good heavens no. Love the smell. Waft it my way. Everyone used to smoke in the old days. Couldn't see one end of the office from the other.' He put his hand on his stomach and looked at Sam coyly. 'Had to give up, though, after my . . . accident.'

'Oh? What happened?'

'Nothing really. A bit of trouble towards the end of the Emergency. Now please – sit yourself down.'

Sam chose one end of a sofa while Grogan elected to sit on a small cane chair, pushing it in front of the fireplace so they were only a few feet apart. Standing, Grogan appeared as small as she

251

remembered, but sitting, the proportions of the chair enhanced him and both his shoes touched the ground comfortably. He beamed at her while drinks were fetched; too early for alcohol, so fresh lemonade for both.

'Well, Sam, I'm delighted you're here. Once again I have to comment on how much you resemble your dear grandmother. Quite takes my breath away. I must say it *is* lovely to have another Seymour under my roof again. I wasn't sure if you'd come. I wondered if . . . '

Grogan's words ran out and as he stared from beneath his absurd glasses Sam wondered if he was looking for something new or reminding himself of the past. Despite his conviviality, he had an air of reticence. She'd expected Grogan on his home ground to be more effusive. But there was something about him. He was definitely holding back. Perhaps it was seeing a woman invading his quarters. She wondered if he'd ever married. She remembered feeling flattered by his attention at the High Commission party, imagining that if he was like that now he might well have been rather attractive in his prime.

'Would you like a tour of the estate, Sam?' he asked. 'Late afternoon is a wonderful time for game. There's a watering hole near the orphanage that might even have baby elephants there. What do you say?'

Sam vacillated. The idea of seeing animals would ordinarily have been appealing but she didn't want to allow more time for his hesitancy to grow. She sensed she should strike now while her presence was still new to him.

'It does sound fun, Grogan, but do you mind if we pass on that? It was a long journey up here and I'm afraid I'm a little tired after all the work on this Mau Mau business. Perhaps we can just go straight to that chat you promised about Johnny and Tansy.'

Grogan sprang to his feet and held his palms up in contrition.

'My dear, I'm so sorry. Not used to having guests up here these days. I wanted to show you everything all at once. You must have a rest before dinner; we can talk much more about your grandparents then. And afterwards I've unearthed something rather amusing to show you. Come with me, I'll take you to your room. I've given you the Huxley suite – the views from the balcony are wonderful.'

Leading Sam up the stairs, Grogan asked how her work was going.

'Oh fine, thanks,' she said, non-committal. She wasn't going to tell Grogan what she'd really discovered. There remained the possibility he might have been involved in some of it. Though watching him usher her into a spacious bedroom, enthusiastically pointing out the view, she didn't think so.

'Well, I'll leave you to it,' he said. 'See you downstairs when you're ready? Drinks on the veranda at – shall we say six? No need to dress up.'

He moved to close the door but popped his head back in at the last moment.

'Oh, I meant to say – did you hear? There's been some rather bad news from Nairobi. My old colleague Mattingly's died. He was the bearded wonder in his cups at the Commission – do you remember, the one who mistook you for Tansy? I think he was a bit in love with her. We all were, I suppose.'

Sam tried not to let her surprise show as she scrutinised Grogan. But he smiled warmly, so if there was meaning there it was well hidden. He couldn't have known she'd been at Esther's house anyhow. Instinct told her it might be better to keep it that way.

'Mattingly? Of course I remember him. I'm very sorry. How did he die? What happened?'

'Don't think anything happened as such. Old age. Booze. Poor bugger had a heart attack at home. He and Esther had a nice place out towards Karen. Did you ever go there?'

'Their home?' Sam blinked rapidly. 'No – I just met him at the party. Why do you ask?'

Grogan beamed jovially.

'No reason at all. You have a jolly good kip. See you later.'

After a shower and a rest Sam felt fortified. She rang Dedan on the mobile to see if he was all right and of course he was. He'd got bored of watching TV and was in the middle of a dice game with the guards. She was not to worry about him, but if she needed him all she had to do was phone or text and he'd be inside the house in seconds. And if it was all right with her he'd be spending the night in the *matatu*.

'The air is better outside, cleaner.'

Dinner was pleasant but turned out to be a formal affair after all

253

and Sam was glad she'd made an effort. There'd been hardly any-thing to wear that wasn't dirty or lying scrunched up at the bottom of her suitcase, but she'd hung her one and only party dress on a hanger and fixed it to a hook in the *matatu*. By the time they arrived the worst of the wrinkles had fallen out. Grogan wouldn't remem-ber she'd already worn it. With a bit of eyeliner and her over-bright airport lipstick, she thought she scrubbed up well enough. It helped that her skin had calmed down from the day in the sun with Esther, settling into the nice olive complexion she strived so hard for on holidays.

The dinner preparations were magnificent, the table heaving with candles and silver. The wine was a gorgeous South African red and she'd barely sat down before servants flourished platters of fish and game, followed by a roasted haunch that Grogan described as deer, though not one she'd heard of. He was certainly trying to convey the right impression.

Finally, when all the small talk had gone and they were left with only the polite hum of the house's sleek air conditioning system, he got to it. Pushing away his plate containing the last of their dessert, a sickly milk-pudding confection, he waved an arm.

'Come on then. I can see you're catting to ask. Though I'm not really sure what I can tell you about your grandparents that you don't already know.'

'What were they like?' Sam enquired eagerly, relieved they were finally getting to it. 'Apart from poor old Mattingly, I haven't met anyone yet who knew them both and is prepared to speak about them.'

'Has your family not told you anything, then?' Grogan asked.

'Not really. It was all a bit of a taboo in our house,' Sam explained. 'For reasons I don't exactly understand, my father refused to talk about Kenya at all. So you see, Grogan, you are my only link to that time.'

'I do see. Your very own time capsule. Well, I'll happily tell you what I know, but it's not likely to be much, I'm afraid. It seems like a different world back then and of course they're both sadly long dead now. So I can't pretend I'll remember all of it.'

Grogan rang a small bell to summon a servant.

'You can take the plates away now,' he said. 'And can you make

254

sure everything is ready and prepared in the drawing room? Tell Jordan we'll be going through shortly.'

He turned to Sam.

'Right. Let's see. Tricky thing, memory.'

He began confidently enough with Germany, where he had first commanded a very young and very green Lieutenant Seymour. As he moved on to Kenya the fluency continued and it seemed to Sam that Grogan actually had excellent recall.

'Your grandfather was really quite a shy man,' he said. 'Got on much better with wildlife than people.'

Grogan's eyes widened beneath his thick spectacle lenses as a recollection struck him.

'I've suddenly remembered his enthusiasm for the African forest. Thought it a bit odd myself, but he loved to go into the bush, disappear for days into his beloved woods. Always going on about the healing power of this and the beauty of that.

'Yes, in many ways he was a gentle man. Looking back I rather regret asking for his help in some things. But towards the end it was all hands to the pump and I had to get his assistance in the camps. He couldn't really cope with that.'

'Camps? But I thought you all worked in propaganda?'

'We did, Sam. But a lot of that effort was directed towards getting Mau Mau pushed through and out of the camps so some of us had to move in there. The hard-core buggers were insisting on martyring themselves by staying behind the wire. We were desperate to let them out and get on with the peace process.

'Anyway, it became a central part of our mission to persuade the hard core to get out. Trouble was, they'd all taken a Mau Mau oath, binding them to fight to the last man, never give up – that sort of thing. Believed their heads would fall off – other parts of their body too, for that matter – if they gave up their oath. So it became rather important to all sections of HMG's forces to persuade them to let the oaths go.'

Sam was rapt by Grogan's words. It was as if she'd been studying some historical battle and one of the generals had emerged from the trenches to tell her all about it. Even so, she couldn't let his comments pass without scrutiny.

'Many of the people I've interviewed,' she said, 'claim the worst treatment they endured was when the authorities were compelling them to give up these oaths.'

Grogan stood up and fetched a candle snuffer from a sideboard. Leaning in to extinguish the flames, the lights flickered under his chin, giving him a vaguely demonic air. The impression wasn't helped when he issued a half-laugh, chuckling as if she'd suggested burning a church together.

'They would say that, wouldn't they? I'd bloody say it if I thought I could earn a decent bob in my old age.'

'Not true then?'

'Gracious no. If we'd done half the things we're being accused of there wouldn't be any Kikuyu left. We weren't saints but then no one was: black, white or in between. It's true there was a bit of rough stuff round the edges, regrettable in retrospect, but really no worse than anything that goes on in the rugby fields on any given Saturday afternoon in England.

'No – given the provocation, the reality is we acted with commendable restraint. The camps were full of educational activities. Kikuyus would arrive "black" and with a strong dose of muscular Christianity they'd be rehabilitated, passed out "white", ready for society. It was called the Pipeline. Dirty water in one end, fresh out the other. We just did what we could to make the water flow smoothly, as it were.

'Trouble was, your Johnny wasn't up to it. After what he'd seen in Germany, there was no way I should have made him go to another camp. He couldn't take it. Blame myself. Ah well. Twenty-twenty hindsight is a wonderful thing.'

Grogan looked at his watch.

'Do you mind if we carry on this conversation later? Should be plenty of time tomorrow. You are staying, aren't you? I fear I'll have to go to bed shortly and I do want to show you what I promised. Shall we go through?'

The drawing room was almost in darkness, only one lamp on. At the far end furniture had been cleared away and a couple of dining-room chairs brought in to face the wall. An old-fashioned projector had been set up a few feet away with an elderly African servant sitting next to it. He had a leg in plaster, which he stretched out in front of him.

Grogan motioned for her to sit.

'How's the leg, Samson?' he asked, addressing the servant.

'Much better, sir, thank you, sir.'

He turned to Sam.

'Poor old Samson here took a bit of a tumble. Fell down an ant bear hole while feeding the chickens. Weren't looking where you were going, were you, Samson?'

'Just old, sir. My eyes are not so good.'

'Well, we're all old but we don't all break at the first stumble. Anyway, have you loaded the film?'

'No, sir. No film here.'

'What? Where's Jordan?'

'I do not know, sir,' Samson said, looking pained. 'I believe he has gone into town.'

'Hell's bells. He must have returned it. I distinctly told him to keep it out, not *put it back*.'

'I could fetch it down, sir. It's probably back in the loft.'

'Don't be ridiculous. How on earth are you going to get up a ladder with that bloody thing in plaster? It's hard enough for me—'

'Couldn't I get it?' Sam interrupted. 'I could easily fetch it from your loft place.'

Grogan thought for a moment.

'No, Sam, most kind but I can't have my guests running up and down ladders.'

Sam was already on her feet.

'Don't be silly. Of course I will. You were looking forward to this and you've got me rather excited at the prospect. I love films.' She smiled sweetly. 'Especially old ones.'

Grogan led Sam along a couple of corridors into a small annexe which was being used for storage. Using a pole he found in the corner, Grogan reached up and undid a latch that released a articulated ladder down into the room.

'As you go up, there's a light switch on the right – at floor level. Turn it on and you should see the canister. A silver, chrome thing. About half the size again of a large dinner plate.'

Sam did as she was told while Grogan stood respectfully back from the ladder, though when she looked down she saw him gazing at her legs. Probably reminded him of Tansy, she thought. Randy old bugger.

The loft was a large space, dusty and smelling of mice and sweet decay. A series of wooden beams lay along its length, on top of which were boxes and trunks and suitcases of all sizes. She could just stand if she bowed her head and she shuffled along looking for the canister.

'Can't see anything, Grogan,' she shouted. 'What was it kept in?'

'Should be on its own. If not, Jordan probably put it back in the case. Look for an old suitcase. Near the front; he won't have stacked it far away.'

There were so many suitcases Sam wasn't sure where to start. She looked into a dozen of them and the odd trunk, but they were either empty or full of clothes and household ornaments. Then, pushed back behind one of the eaves, she saw two suitcases, side by side. Sitting on top of one was a single chrome canister. They had to be the right cases. There were initials on the lid: JLS. She remembered something from Johnny's scrapbook, right at the start. Hadn't his middle name begun with an L? Interesting. Popping the clasp on the top case, she saw it was full of canisters. She quickly opened the other one. Equally full. It was like a film archive up here. Carefully closing the cases again, she took the loose film canister and made her way back to the trapdoor, waving it at Grogan.

'Is this the one? Honestly, Grogan, you should get these old films seen by someone. They look as if they belong in a national collection.'

'One day perhaps. Never seem to have the time to sort them out. Need categorising and copying before I hand them over. Now, come on down.'

Once Sam was settled in her seat in the drawing room Grogan took charge of the operation, dismissing Samson and putting the film in himself.

'Right,' he said, 'prepare to be transported. Pun intended. I only remembered this existed the other day. Your presence in Kenya must have reminded me. There's no sound but the film quality's surprisingly good. Ought to be – it was shot by an expert. Should answer a few of your questions about the detention system as well. Ready?'

The film flickered into life.

They were in a camp. Smart barracks, guard towers manned by

smiling warders. The black and white film was grainy but the focus was sharp enough to see everything with perfect clarity. The camera panned along a row of prisoners jogging round the perimeter. None of them looked at the lens and as they went past they seemed no more dejected or downtrodden than any group of men made to go on a run. The scene shifted to a classroom. Africans sitting in orderly rows watching a white woman at a blackboard. The angle switched to look at the detainees from the teacher's point of view. All were staring intently into the middle distance and Sam again noticed that none of them looked directly into the camera. They were either well trained in documentary-making, or scared. Beneath closely cropped scalps they seemed flat and sullen, doing what they had to do without any joy. The camera lingered on them but never once did any of the men smile. And yet, as she had swiftly learned, no one smiled more often or more warmly than Kenyans. Combined with the lack of sound there was an uncomfortable unreality to the images. Men walked, ran, sat without a word; all with angry indifference.

The shot left the classroom to view it from the outside. The camera moved in on a partially open window so Sam could see the sitting men inside listening to the teacher. And there, reflected in the window, she could just make out the smaller image of something happening behind the camera. A man on the ground, two men over him.

Suddenly a hand came into shot and the picture jiggled and waved as someone took the camera off its tripod. The image wobbled about as the shot tracked in and out like an accordion before settling on a white man making a 'give it back' gesture.

The man, obviously the real cameraman, was tall and terribly thin. His shirt was untucked and he looked defeated.

Sam leaned forward. *My God.*

Underneath hair standing on its end like a rooster's crown, the man's face was hollow, desperate. He stared into the lens with almost no expression, just his eyes burning with a dark rage. Johnny Seymour looked as if he could commit murder.

Chapter 24

Mombasa, March 1954

Johnny stood quietly on the balcony and looked into the bedroom. He was sweating freely after his run on the beach. Although the sun had barely risen, it was already hot and sunlight was beginning to edge onto the mattress. Through the mosquito net her form was opaque, dark hair shading the white linen. He moved next to the bed, pushing the netting to one side. Her body came into focus as if he'd removed a distorting lens. She was lying on her side, the sheet tangled beneath her, and he could see a long brown leg leading sensuously to the curve of her buttocks.

The sight stirred him and for the thousandth time he uttered silent thanks to whatever gods were out there for granting him this beauty. He moved inside the net and knelt slowly on the mattress, bending until his face was next to hers. She turned and drowsily slid a hand round his neck, drawing him in to kiss her. She smelled of morning and warm skin and promise. Yet again just her presence, the simple fact of her, aroused him. He moved the sheet to one side, slipped off his shorts and lay behind her, pressing himself against her naked back. She felt him and wriggled her buttocks before taking his hand and guiding it between her legs.

'I love you,' he whispered into her ear, the saying of it out loud sending a pulse through both of them. She sighed softly and pushed against him, so wet he slipped inside her effortlessly. They moved together. Slowly at first, then harder, his arms wrapping her tight into him, the palms of his hands cupping her breasts. Every time they made love he marvelled anew at the eternal wonder of love and sex combining, reinforcing one another, fusing into perfection, more arousing and more satisfying than anything he could have dreamed of.

Never sated, Johnny thought. I can never do this enough; I always want her more.

They lay entwined, content in the silence, breathing returning to normal. Tansy drifted off to sleep but Johnny lay still, savouring the start of another day. He loved this time of the morning. The radio banished. No distractions of stories of human frailty. The phone happily downstairs out of earshot; no post. Nothing to do except watch the blue sky, listen to the yellow songbirds in the palms, bask in the luck that delivered him to this place.

An hour later and the positions were reversed. Johnny had fallen asleep, waking to find Tansy sitting on the wicker chair wearing one of his white shirts, her bare feet up on the balcony edge, sipping coffee, watching him. A mug of cooling coffee lay next to him on the upturned tea chest that formed their bedside table. He reached for it and drank appreciatively.

'That's good,' he murmured. 'Thank you.'

Tansy smiled.

'We're running out, by the way. I couldn't get any more from the *kahawa* man. Couldn't find any change. We owe him quite a lot – it's getting embarrassing.'

'We'll manage,' he said. 'It'll be fine.' Tansy flicked her eyebrows up.

'But it's true,' he protested.

'Darling, we've been here nearly a year. It's been wonderful, but we can't stay here for the rest of our lives.'

Johnny got up from the bed and stood behind the chair, moving her hair to one side to nuzzle the nape of her neck. He loved the scent of her there and he wrapped his arms round her, covering her breasts, aroused once more.

'OK, perhaps we can,' she laughed, folding herself to his contours.

But even as he was embracing her Johnny understood that her words – even in jest – pointed to a problem that couldn't be ignored for much longer. Something had to give. It wasn't just the money. Tansy was restless. She swore she never regretted calling him after discovering Porter's body, but reason had flown out of the window for both of them that day. When he'd seen the tortured corpse of his friend he'd known only one thing: they both had to run as fast and as far as possible. If they hid, they might be safe. If they stayed they

261

would be the Zebra's next victims, no matter how hard Grogan tried to protect them.

They'd spent the night at Johnny's flat, driving towards the coast early next morning. Tansy had not bothered to check out of her hotel, pausing only to get money from the bank. The side pannier on the Triumph barely had room for his camera and a change of clothes. He'd enjoyed the feeling. Travelling light, unencumbered, embarking on a fresh start.

They found a beach house sitting at the head of its own private bay. A settler family once kept it as a summer retreat but they'd left Kenya and now no one seemed to want it. Nominally the nearest village owned the land and a few shillings a month to its headman guaranteed they wouldn't be bothered by unwanted paperwork. Joshua, a local boy, was employed to fetch their water and provide them with fruit.

Johnny and Tansy slept in the house at night and spent most of the day on the beach. One morning he'd discovered an old Arab dhow washed up in the neighbouring bay. No one claimed it so he felt free to mend it and make it theirs. Look, he'd said proudly on the day of her maiden voyage, fish for supper and we can sail wherever we want.

Tanned golden by the sun, making love, discovering each other and themselves. As far as he was concerned, there was no place he'd rather be. They could survive on next to nothing. They were together; didn't need anyone else.

'We're free, Tansy,' he'd said.

And in those first few weeks they were. But looking down at Tansy now from behind the wicker chair, Johnny seriously questioned how they were going to manage. Escape was one thing: survival was another.

Shoes, thought Tansy as she wiggled her toes in the sand, shoes would be one of the things she hated most about returning. Here she was barefoot all the time, revelling in the elements brushing against her skin. The notion of forcing herself into those dreadful pumps was appalling. The idea of any part of returning was appalling. Except seeing her parents again, she conceded. And Janey too, if her sister ever came back from Paris.

Tansy stretched out her long legs, satisfied to note they'd acquired a deep brown hue. The red of her painted toenails winked up through the white sand like bright coral. Brown and red, she thought, the colours of her freedom. An image of Macharia in detention popped into her mind and she sat up, embarrassed by her own triteness, reaching in her bag for cigarettes. It didn't matter how long she lay in the sun, she could never quite push away the reality of what lay out there. Johnny could. It was astonishing how he buried himself in the present. Not the future; certainly not the past. Johnny had told her a little of what happened to him during the war, whispered one night after making love, the words emerging haltingly into her ear as he lay curved in a tight ball. No one should have seen what he had, particularly no nineteen-year-old, not much more than a child. And Grogan of course had been the one to preside over it all, not caring about the effects of his crusade to record everything in those camps. No one could fault his motivation, but why had he pushed Johnny out there – so young – while he sat in his tent beyond the wire directing events? *I'm a means-ends man, Tansy.* How often had he said that? Mean to the end of your days, she'd wanted to say. Instead she'd always smiled and nodded encouragement. Though he'd never needed any bloody encouragement. She knew that now.

She found a cigarette packet in the bottom of her bag but it was empty. She crumpled the pack, just stopping herself from hurling it in the sand. The bay was perfect and nothing should change it. Tansy forced herself to her feet and stood blinking against the glare, watching the waves caressing the sand at the water's edge. Later on towards evening the currents would produce giant breakers but for now it was serenely peaceful. It was a wrench to go back inside but she wanted to finish her letter to Janey. She recognised that the act of writing, putting everything down on paper, helped make sense of what had happened.

She would nip into town and post it after lunch. Johnny was out on the boat and wouldn't be back till late. She'd take the bike. Johnny didn't like her travelling by herself, but if he could spend the day alone, skimming about on the Indian Ocean, she could take a short trip into town. It hadn't taken long to learn how to ride the Triumph and she enjoyed the sense of liberty it gave as she zipped along the dusty lanes.

Inside, she poured herself a drink of cold water and headed for the stairs. The balcony was where she liked to write; she could keep her head in the shade while still enjoying a full view of the palms and the ocean. She was halfway up when she heard the noise, a scraping sound followed by footsteps outside, retreating from the house.

'Joshua?' she called. 'Is that you?'

There was no answer from the houseboy, and Tansy went back down the stairs.

'*Joshua!*'

The front door led onto a small dirt lane. If the houseboy had come in and gone again he would only be a few yards away. But there was no one outside.

It was only when she was closing the door that she noticed the envelope stuck under the frame.

It was warm downstairs, the heat of the day only just kept at bay by thick whitewashed walls, but Tansy felt a chill. They did not get letters here. Especially pristine white ones with the words *Tansy Thompson: personal and confidential* written in ink on the front. She picked it up, holding it at arm's length as if its very existence oozed poison.

The handwriting was elegant, belonging to someone well used to wielding a pen. She knew immediately who it was. She sat on the leather pouf they'd bought at the market in Mombasa and bit a nail, feeling sick. Not again. Please no. How could he have known? And why hadn't he come in?

She ripped it open. A single sheet contained just one sentence and a telephone number.

Call me. It's important. Grogan.

With trembling hands Tansy folded the note into small squares and tucked it into her pocket. She needed a cigarette now more than ever. Why was she always running out? 'Because you've got no bloody money,' she muttered out loud. She would finish the letter and go and buy some at the same time as posting it to Janey.

And she would ring him.

There was no avoiding it. If he knew where they were he could swoop in and pick them up whenever he liked. From the moment the letter had scraped its way under the door there'd been no choice. There was never any bloody choice.

At Mombasa's central post office there was a bank of telephone booths where you could book a call. Sitting waiting her turn, Tansy flicked through an old *Vogue*, unable to concentrate. Finally her name was called. She put the magazine down on a side table and out of the corner of her eye she could have sworn she recognised someone over by the door. It was just for a second, but when she looked directly at the man he'd already melted onto the street. For the briefest moment she feared she'd seen a cane tapping against a thigh.

Grogan's voice down the line was tinny but ebullient.

'My dear, how are you? Thank you so much for ringing. Enjoying Mombasa?'

'What do you want, Grogan? How did you find me?'

'There are certain resources available to me that make hiding a fairly foolish thing to do. Really, Tansy, did you actually think you and Johnny could bury yourselves away for ever?'

'Johnny isn't with me. I'm alone.'

A silence, followed by a distant laugh.

'Seriously, Tansy. You have to grow up. I know exactly what's going on – have done almost from the start.'

Tansy felt as if her lungs were being squeezed and her breaths came in short, ragged bursts. She pinched her arm to stop herself crying.

'What are you doing, Grogan? Why are you tormenting me? What have I done to deserve it?'

'You sound upset, my dear. You must calm yourself. I'm afraid this Emergency hasn't given me as much time for personal matters as I would have liked, so I have decided to leave you be – *for the moment.*'

'How dare you—'

'Please – allow me to finish. If I know the phone system in Mombasa this line is not likely to last long. You obviously require more time to consider, but you need to know my offer is still firmly on the table. Meanwhile, I cannot see you starve so I have arranged a wire transfer of cash in your name which you can – and must – pick up at *Poste Restante* Mombasa.'

'*Money?* Are you mad? Do you really think I'd accept your bloody money? I will not take a single solitary penny – do you understand?'

'But that's where you are wrong, my dear,' Grogan said. 'I've been laissez faire for too long, my mind on other disagreeable matters. But from now on you will do exactly what I say. Graves is still out there and has not forgotten what Johnny did. If I can find you, don't you think he might too? It would be a shame to see the protection I have been affording withdrawn.

'For the moment you are free to return to your paramour, but at some point soon I'll be in contact again and on that date I will expect your prompt return. And please, don't think about telling Johnny any of this. If you do or if you try and run off again all bets are off. Permanently. I'm really not joking about this, Tansy. I do hope you—'

The Mombasa exchange was as bad as Grogan predicted.

The line snapped dead.

Chapter 25

Coastal Province, June 1954

It took most of the day for the train to reach Manyani depot. Macharia stood all the way, wedged tightly against a group of men slippery with fear, taking it in turns to face the door and relieve themselves. There was no water and several men passed out, their unconscious bodies lolling against their neighbours, held up by a crush of humanity. Macharia felt he was being squeezed to death, the men on either side helplessly squashed into his rib cage. For long periods he could do no more than fight for breath, sucking in short pants of stale air whenever the pressure on his body eased. Then, blessed relief, it was his turn to face the door. His piss had dried out but his lungs could expand. He sucked in air and grew giddy with the prospect of surviving.

They had grown used to the train lurching to a stop, standing motionless in the heat of the day, no air coming through the vents, and when it halted this time Macharia barely noticed. But there was a difference. Soon he could hear men shouting and the sound of banging and scraping from up and down the train. Suddenly the noise was coming from in front of him; it was almost unbearable, as if he were inside a giant drum as someone beat on the skin. More shouting, much closer now, and the next instant the doors were wrenched open.

For a second all was still, motion suspended, sound muted. Macharia blinked, holding his hand up to protect his eyes against an intense brightness. Then – a terrifying roar of yelling and barking. Chaos. Alsatians snarling and throttling themselves on their leashes, jumping up onto the carriage in a drooling attack frenzy; batons reaching in, poking and stabbing, levering prisoners out like black sardines from a rotting tin. Behind him Macharia heard a great wailing and the beginning of a panicked push for the light. The next moment he was on the ground being dragged and shoved. All around him men were dropping, kicked by guards, trampled by fellow detainees.

In front of him two lines of guards formed a funnel. The first wave of prisoners was already being beaten through by guards lashing at them with long staves. As Macharia was herded towards the funnel he felt a clarifying sense of detachment, the blows striking but not hurting, as if they were being administered to someone else. The prisoners at the front were running as fast as they could but there were so many others still emerging from the train that a lump of men had formed. Macharia found himself in the middle of it, watching as others closer to the guards were smacked on the face and shoulders.

Suddenly the knot of men around him eased and Macharia was in the funnel, running for all he was worth, ducking and swerving but seldom avoiding a clip from a baton. Other men received worse – a crack to the back of the legs, a blow on the shoulder, a cruel bite at the elbow. A sweating guard wearing a fez seemed vaguely recognisable and it was only when Macharia saw him again that he realised the guards must have been doubling up, running round to the front when the last prisoner had passed.

In front of him a man dropped and the mood of the guards changed. Scenting weakness, they packed around the fallen man like jackals tearing at a corpse. At last the running stopped and Macharia collapsed with the other men in a vast compound. As they caught their breath, more warders emerged from a hut, sauntering towards them. A white officer in a peaked cap walked to the front. A whistle blew and the guards screamed for silence. Slowly the men quietened, the only sound the rasping of their breath.

'Listen to me now,' the officer said. 'This is Manyani.' He repeated it, drawing it out, speaking slowly and loudly. '*Man-ya-ni.*'

'You are here because you are members of an illegal organisation. If you obey the rules you will be treated fairly. You will receive one meal a day – eight ounces of flour and beans – and unlimited water. When a guard gives an order you will obey *immediately* or there will be painful consequences.

'From here you will go to the delousing centre. Monies and

268

valuables are to be handed in straight away. Failure to do so will result in permanent confiscation and further punishment.'

He paused and prisoners began muttering and coughing again.

'*Silence!*' he shouted. 'You will not like it here, but that is our intention. The sooner you see the error of your ways, the sooner you can leave.

'When that is, is up to you. It is *all* up to you. Clear?'

Called through thirty at a time, the men were instructed to strip naked and place their belongings in different piles. Clothes in one, shoes another, personal items in a third. Macharia watched with growing apprehension as the group in front of him ran through a water-filled trench, guards on either side spraying them with powerful hoses. While still wet and naked they were ordered to run past orderlies squeezing what looked like balloons filled with white dust at their hair and faces. Covered with insecticide powder, the men were then ordered to jump up and down with their hands in the air. A few coins and bits of paper fell from their groins, but long after the last hidden item had been discovered some men were forced to continue dancing while guards laughed and pointed at the men's wobbling genitals. The rest of the prisoners looked down, refusing to participate in the painful humiliation, but Macharia forced himself to watch.

'Remember,' he told himself through clenched teeth. 'Remember it all.'

When Macharia was transferred to Manyani from Langata he'd been designated YY. Everyone at Manyani was in the 'black' category but there were further gradations within that. One Y denoted simply 'black' while two meant he was blacker than black. The next and ultimate designation of blackness was the final letter of all – Z – and Macharia was sure he'd get there soon enough.

Today he was squatting outside in the shade of his accommodation block, reflecting on how amusing it was to be informed as to the nature of his own blackness by the *wazungu*. A short laugh escaped his cracked lips. It was not a mirthful sound. Last night he'd lost two more teeth after a guard clubbed him in the mouth. Now he sounded more like a hissing snake than a man.

He needed to commit that guard to memory, a smooth-faced

Dutchman named Schapps. Macharia was trying to remember everything in the camp. As long as some of his wits remained unclubbed, he could contribute to the Movement by providing an account of what happened inside the wire. If the world learned what was being done by the British in places like this it would be a valuable propaganda coup.

To assist his memory Macharia had stolen a sheaf of the old newspapers tossed to prisoners to wipe their arses. He wrote at night with a smuggled pencil, scribbling tiny notes of the week's events: the small acts of resistance, the beatings, the reasons for the beatings, deaths, names. He hid them under a stone at the corner of the latrine – a stinking ditch at the rear of the camp.

The question of how he might get his notes out of the camp vexed him. He couldn't give them to departing prisoners because those who left Manyani either went to an even more secure camp or were released following the recanting of their oaths – and oath-breakers were beyond trust. Macharia concluded that all he could do for now was hoard his pile and make sure no one discovered it. He was confident no one would. He still had a reputation as the man who exposed a *gakunia*, and his new comrades were serious men who would ensure compliance with his wishes.

If the notes were discovered and traced to him, he was a dead man. But it was a risk worth taking. It was vital that a prisoner's record of these camps should one day form part of the history of the liberation war. As the saying went, the vanquished were the first to learn what history had in store, but he was determined to change that.

From his time as a driver he'd seen how Europeans revered memoranda and paperwork. If his account was written down it would acquire gravity, might even have seriousness for future *wazungu* historians. He knew those pale men who pored over archives enjoyed a good document, according it weight over the spoken word even if it was merely spoken words transcribed on a page. Europeans had lost their oral tradition. For them the act of writing had become transformative, fetishised. Displayed in ink or hammered through a typewriter ribbon, the written word took on iconic strength, acquiring the lustre of truth.

The British would be hard at work writing their own version.

270

Macharia could not allow their reverse image to become the dominant truth. Already he had heard how *wazungu* guards referred to activities in the camps. The process of torturing prisoners to recant their oaths was termed rehabilitation. How sanctifying that sounded. Language was truly part of the struggle.

When Macharia first wrote about these screenings it also forced him to think about the importance the British attached to Mau Mau oaths. It seemed to have become the very crucible of the war. If sufficient numbers were forced to recant, the oath would lose its power and Mau Mau would lose its backbone.

Before he was captured Macharia had read European press accounts of oathing ceremonies that had little to do with reality. According to these papers, they were depraved orgies where men were forced to copulate with goats; drink semen and menstrual blood while being flagellated, naked. The British, he understood, liked to be frightened with tales of witchcraft and sorcery. Making out their enemies were not men but savage demons encouraged the belief that their foes weren't human. And if they weren't human they didn't have to be treated with any humanity. A member of Mau Mau became a thing to be destroyed. And how could it be wrong to do harm to a mere thing? Was it torture when a rock was cast into a lake? Did it cause pain to cut down a tree for firewood?

One matter white propagandists had got right about the oathing ceremony was its power. Macharia recalled the night long ago when his brother Gatimu took him from his uncle's sickbed to the secret hut to speak the words so many thousands of Kikuyu had done before him. He'd felt such a unity with his people it was as if someone had turned on an electricity switch, linking all the connections in his brain and heart with a dazzling light, illuminating the true path.

Given the power of it, perhaps it was no wonder the *wazungu* were frightened of the oath and wanted to beat it out, screaming at them to recant.

Chapter 26

Mombasa, September 1954

Johnny tended his fire pit on the beach. The embers were smouldering nicely and the snapper wrapped in banana leaves could go on soon. He salivated at the thought of the cooked fish and took a short swig from his bottle, wanting to eke it out. It was the last beer but it had been a good day, so why not. They were still alive, still together. It was an achievement; worth celebrating. He'd spent the day sailing and fishing, losing hours watching the hooked bait skip and dance hypnotically through the wave-tops – an ideal way to help push away still further the terrifying period in Nairobi.

It was almost possible to believe that Porter's murder, the camps and the Zebra did not exist, so perfect was this haven.

And yet.

The banana leaves sizzled as he laid the fish on the hot ashes. Tansy was sitting across the fire from him with her knees up, staring out to sea, her form shimmering through the heat. He wondered what she was seeing. She wasn't interested in birds or fish yet could study the ocean for hours. This evening she seemed wrapped in a melancholy that not even the rich smoky smells from the fire pit could penetrate. He didn't know how she could do it. The aroma was driving him crazy.

She turned his way and he was shocked at how sad she looked, so at odds with how he felt.

'Penny for them?' he asked.

She was on to him immediately, as if she'd been waiting for him to say something disagreeable.

'*Penny?* We haven't got a farthing.'

'Hey, we'll be fine.'

'*Fine?* You always say that. But sometimes it's not fine, Johnny. Not everything is always as it seems. Sometimes . . .'

She absent-mindedly scooped some sand, letting it trickle out through her fingers.

'What?'

'Doesn't matter,' she sighed. 'As long as we're together – isn't that what you also say? Have you considered there may be other things in life? Doesn't there have to be a . . . I'm not sure . . . a *balance*?'

Tansy threw a pebble with some violence towards the sea.

'With what?' Johnny asked.

'Oh, I don't know – medicine, parents, other people, money. *Children.* All sorts of things really.'

Money. They'd managed not to talk about it but it was getting harder to ignore. His savings, such as they were, were running out. While he'd managed to sell a couple of wildlife photographs to an Italian magazine it hadn't led to any more commissions as he'd been obliged to conceal where they'd been taken – they were meant to be in hiding, after all. Tansy had emptied her bank account in Nairobi before they left, and while it had seemed an enormous amount then it was almost gone now. It was a miracle they'd eked it out this far. He was sure she was borrowing from her sister. For a while now, every time she came back from town she brought extra treats they couldn't afford: macadamias, beer, a spare roll of film.

'I think we need we need a proper drink,' Tansy said. 'There's one bottle of wine left. I'll fetch it.' On the way she gave him a hug, her tone softening.

'I'm sorry, Johnny – I *am* fine. I always will be. Here with you. You know that.'

Watching her pick her way across the cooling sands, Johnny kicked himself for being so selfish – soaked in love, brain addled with pleasure. Tansy concealed it well but the guilt of living a life of ease while the country burned around her was becoming too much. She was trained to heal, not idle her life away on the beach. Of course she'd never say any of that, but as he was beginning to understand, what Tansy didn't say was often more important than what she did.

For too long he'd clung to the hope the Emergency would somehow claim Graves, that the bastard might solve their problems by dying in action. It had never been much of a plan and last week, on a rare visit to the barber's, he'd seen an old newspaper story that reported how a 'courageous police superintendent' had ambushed a gang of Mau Mau, shooting three dead. Johnny hadn't read it, wanted to know nothing about the Emergency, but the picture jumped out from the newsprint, the thin face immediately recognisable. Graves would never die.

Tansy rose quietly without disturbing Johnny. By the time he came downstairs she'd had breakfast and was putting her boots on.

'What are you doing up at this hour?' he asked sleepily, wrapping his arms round her.

She shrugged them away and walked to the sink, throwing the remains of her coffee down the drain with so much force it splashed onto the floor.

Johnny frowned.

'What's wrong?'

'Nothing's wrong. Why do you have to assume that unless I'm cooing over you there's something wrong?'

She stalked off and he pretended to concentrate on boiling water. While he stirred in the coffee from their dwindling supply he came to a decision that couldn't be avoided any longer. He let the grounds settle and went to look for her but she was already wheeling the Triumph out from its shelter.

'I hesitate to ask,' Johnny said. 'But just what are you going to do in town?'

She flashed her eyes at him.

'I told you last night.'

'I don't think so.'

'The doctor's?' Tansy said. 'In the old town?'

He had forgotten, and he frowned trying to recall what she'd said. He certainly didn't remember anything about her being unwell.

'Are you ill?'

'If you're a woman you don't have to be ill to see a doctor, Johnny,' she snapped.

Johnny nodded gravely, secretly relieved. She heaved the bike back onto its legs, flicked the starter pedal sideways and kicked at it as she opened the throttle. The bike roared into life as if she'd been doing it all her life. He knew she was perfectly competent but he could never quite relax when she drove it on her own.

274

'You will drive safely?'

'Don't I always?'

Tansy pulled his head down for a kiss and for a moment they held each other.

'See you later,' she said, clambering astride the motorcycle. She was wearing trousers, and with a helmet on she could fool most of the locals into thinking she was a man. Many of the Africans who lived between the beach house and Mombasa were Muslim and would certainly disapprove of women driving a motorbike. Even for a memsahib that was shameful.

The helmet lay on the seat in front of her and she fiddled with the leather straps, annoyed at having been too lazy to undo them last time. Her face creased with concentration and to Johnny she seemed horribly vulnerable. He stood astride the front wheel of the bike, holding the handlebars.

'What is it?' she asked.

He shrugged.

'Don't know. Just a feeling.'

She put her head to one side.

'*Darling.* I really will be fine. The first sign of anything wrong and I'll race back here. Then we can set off into the sunset like we did last time.'

Johnny didn't smile.

'Keeping one step ahead of the baddies,' she said, trying to gee him up. 'It's very romantic.'

'I know you hate all this hiding, Tansy. But things will change, you'll see. I promise it won't be for ever.'

The brown eyes that had been sparkling with teasing hardened.

'Nothing lasts for ever, Johnny.'

Tansy shook out her hair before placing the helmet over it. The sun had given it a reddish tinge and to Johnny she was the most extravagantly beautiful person he'd ever seen. They weren't even parted, yet he ached for her, a disproportionate sense of loss already haunting him.

Tansy grinned at him from beneath the helmet and gave a thumbs-up.

'Now wish me *bon voyage*. The sooner I leave, the sooner I'll be back.'

She's like a lioness, he thought. Braver than me by far.

275

Chapter 27

Manyani Camp, September 1954

Macharia's new home was hut number eighty-six. He spent almost all of his time lying on the crowded floor, avoiding guards, avoiding the harsh sun, emerging only at mealtimes. Apart from unwanted missionaries, no visitors came. The food was scarce and foul, and many prisoners had succumbed to typhoid or dysentery. Macharia witnessed the men around him turning bitter and shrivelled, malevolent fruit unable to ripen.

Casual violence was a part of daily life. Detainees were beaten to hurry, beaten to slow down, beaten for punishment and beaten for sport. Not everyone was beaten every day but the opportunity was there for all – all of the time. While official chastisement meant whipping or caning – and, ultimately, hanging – unofficial punishments involved anything the guards could devise, with some of the warders taking obvious pleasure in their work. Macharia took care to note the names of these men on his hidden scraps of paper.

For these sadists, certain punishments and methods to obtain a confession grew in vogue, particularly mutilation of the sexual organs. Prisoners' genitals were beaten, crushed, flailed, burned, cut. Instruments were inserted, orifices filled and ripped. He knew of one old *mzee* forced to stand on his hands – upside down! – with his legs against the wall while the guards did their worst.

Apart from physical pain, there was clearly an intention to cause mental harm. There was a coursing shame in having another man strike your manhood or insert dreadful things into your anus. There was also the terrible realisation for those being beaten that they might never be able to have children, might never be able to function as real men again.

Was there a sexual nature to this torture? How could there not have been? Macharia had seen how it had been present from the start, in the way the guards made prisoners jump naked in front of them at the delousing centre. The fact the groin and buttocks were attacked so often was not coincidence. These punishments glinted darkly in the corner, making any call to the guards' post more awful for the prospect.

It was worse for the women.

They were gaoled in a separate location, and while Macharia hadn't witnessed what they endured word often filtered back and it was obvious the sexual nature of the attacks on women was even starker. Macharia was angered and ashamed to hear how many women were dragged inside guard posts for the gratification of the male guards. Outside the camps too, in the new wire villages, there were terrible stories of rape and intimate assaults on women of all ages by British forces with bottles and other instruments.

It was torture with a vile twist. A perverted power ran through these attackers' pathetic loins and Macharia marked the assailants' names down in his notes with a small x at the side. However he could arrange it, he was determined to ensure these men would be hunted down and executed.

Macharia knew his real screenings were yet to come. They would be harder than anything he had endured so far. Yet amid the defeat of imprisonment there were victories to be had, and maintaining the sacred oath would be the most important. The idea of resisting sustained him, giving him something to cling to as the day of his own reckoning grew nearer.

But when Macharia discovered the identity of his new interrogator, he was filled with despair.

He'd seen him long before he met him. He was impossible to miss. In the mornings he liked to issue a bright 'good morning' to all he passed, whether prisoner or guard. Later in the day he barked 'good afternoon' with the same cheeriness. If prisoners didn't answer he would shout 'STOP THERE!' and write down their prison number in his black leather pocketbook. Each evening those so numbered received a visit from the guards. It was an effective method to ensure a reply and it was always a curious thing to hear the sullen congregation of prisoners responding with such alacrity. If Macharia closed his eyes he could sometimes follow his progress round the camp by tracking the fretful greetings.

The new white officer was soon renowned throughout Manyani as *Mapiga*. There were several white officers in the camp system who'd achieved this accolade, but the *mapiga* at Manyani swiftly earned the tribute of being chief of all. *Mapiga* meant 'beater'.

The men used to mock his short stature, imitating him behind his back as he rubbed his glasses with an oversized yellow cloth. He had lost some more of his hair since Macharia drove for him but he was still always correct on parade, sporting short trousers and long socks with impressive rectitude. On his feet, sandals had been replaced by stout boots, laced tightly to just above the ankle.

When officers wanted to see prisoners they would send guards to haul them out. When Grogan Littleboy wanted Macharia, however, he came himself, as if making a house call, one neighbour to another.

'Hello,' he said, putting his head inside the hut. 'Macharia, isn't it? Thought I recognised you. Small world! How are you doing here? Not much of a place is it really? How's the food? Getting at least one square a day? Good, good. Don't suppose you do much driving ... *ha ha*. Wondered if you'd care to pop along to my office and have a chat? More private.'

Grogan's office was the end building of a row of bungalows where the white officers had their quarters. The room Macharia was ushered into was plain. Two chairs, a desk. Desk lamp. Strip lighting. Fan, turned off. The floor was concrete, and although dry, smelled of damp. Another odour – freshly sprayed insect repellent – clung to the air, masking earthier notes that made Macharia shiver. A picture of Queen Elizabeth hung on the wall, Mona Windsor smile in place.

'Sit down.'

It was the first chair he'd sat on for months. *Mapiga* took his time to flick through a brown file in front of him, occasionally shooting glances over the top of his glasses, muttering 'Good, good.'

'All right then,' he said, pushing the file to one side. 'Where shall we begin? Perhaps you have some questions for me?'

Macharia had a hundred but knew he should keep his counsel. In his new guise, Grogan frightened him. Of the dozen or so men *Mapiga* had entertained before Macharia, not a single one of them had remained in the camp. All had recanted the oath. Some prisoners believed he had an unseen accomplice, a phantom with a whip who would do the dirty work; others thought he performed it himself.

'Very well,' Grogan said jovially. 'You are naturally cautious. I understand that. Let's start with something more *neutral*. Tell me, Macharia, do you think you are going to win?'

Win? Macharia was not expecting that but he saw no mileage in a reply.

'Come along, there's no one else here. I'm not recording you and I give you my word you will not be punished for anything you say.'

In the face of Macharia's continued silence Grogan blew out his cheeks and took off his glasses, his features a picture of regret, reminding Macharia of Mission teachers before they caned you. It was a '*this is hurting me more than you*' face, and Macharia wanted nothing more than to strike it.

'Come on, Macharia, I've got all day – literally – and you have a lot longer than that. So why don't we make ourselves comfortable?'

He put his boots up on the table.

Macharia glanced at the Queen, who was still smiling benevolently. The crown looked light upon her head. What was she thinking about? She'd been in Kenya when her father died. It was said she loved the country, though Macharia knew that for many whites this really meant that they loved African wildlife – shooting it with rifle and camera. Several prisoners had written directly to her, believing she might intervene personally with her African subjects. He was not aware of her having done so. One day news had filtered into the camp that some of the comrades had burned the hotel she'd been staying at – Treetops, it was called. Would they have burned it if she had been inside? Macharia hoped so.

'I said,' *Mapiga* continued after a few minutes, the words emerging slowly, following one another with great emphasis. 'Do – you – think – Mau Mau will win the day?'

However hard he tried, Macharia could see no trap.

'That depends on what you mean by win,' he replied.

Mapiga removed his feet from the table and tucked them under the desk, banging his fist on the table-top in joy.

'You see! That wasn't too difficult. And you want to know the

279

terms of engagement – what do I mean by win? You've cut right to the heart of the matter. Excellent.'

He began polishing his glasses with the yellow cloth but stopped suddenly, replacing them on his nose.

'Yes, I think I like you very much. I can certainly see why Seymour liked you. He tried to help, you know. Wanted me to find you – and I did! And I now discover you are an educated man. I can't tell you what it means to finally be having a conversation with an African thinker. We should have chatted more when you worked for me!

'Anyway, back to business. So how might one define winning in this context – a military victory?'

With some difficulty Macharia kept the words from coming out. Once he began to talk, he might find it hard to stop.

'No? OK, let's examine that for a moment. Do you think the few hundred armed men still at large in the forest are capable of winning a military victory against the British army, not to mention the Kikuyu Home Guard? And the Kenya Regiment? The combined forces of the British and colonial police? Seriously?'

Macharia recognised the strength to this argument. Many comrades believed a purely military victory was never going to be achievable. At the start, there might have been a chance, if the whole nation had risen up, perhaps. But even then the British Empire would have regrouped and retaliated harder. No, the victory they'd always sought was political. But he wasn't talking to the *wazungu* about strategy.

'No,' Macharia said.

'Exactly!' *Mapiga's* face beamed in agreement. He sensed they were getting somewhere. 'So, if not military, what? How will you win? Not going to answer? Fine, let me try and guess.

'Perhaps you believe there are progressive forces at work in London or elsewhere that will eventually prevail and make the colonists give up their grip. But if that were the case, would they not have made a move earlier? Have we even heard from these people? You might notice the Labour opposition howling occasionally at some perceived outrage or other, but they're not seriously contesting the game.

'So, maybe you think there are secret negotiations going on with your friend Kenyatta. He's more than up for it, we know; he's a pragmatic fellow, never really believed in your Mau Mau nonsense. But do you seriously think we would for a moment consider engaging properly with anyone on your side while your men are running around the hills trying to kill us?

'Of course not. So where does that leave us? Where does it all go from here?'

Mapiga got up off his chair and perched at the front of the desk, his short legs dangling. He stared hawkishly down at his charge and Macharia noticed his socks were in perfect alignment, neither one an inch higher or lower than the other.

'Do we want to talk to your chaps?' Grogan continued. 'Naturally. It may surprise you to learn, Macharia, there are many of us on this side of the fence – myself included – who would like nothing better than to be rid of the whole rotten enterprise and give you back your country ...'

He was in full flow but he stopped when he saw Macharia raising an eyebrow.

'That surprises you? My word, an intelligent fellow like you really shouldn't conflate the interests of colony with wider British concerns. Change is afoot! No modern government wants to hang on to expensive colonies, especially where the natives are restless.'

He saw Macharia was not laughing and put up his hands in mock appeasement.

'Sorry, would you like some water? Gets terribly hot in here and I can't get the fan to work for the life of me.'

Always polite, *Mapiga*. Macharia hadn't noticed a side table behind him with a carafe and two glasses. It was a strange thing to find in a room like this. It took some time to pull the stopper out of the carafe. It was a thin, baton-like affair made of hardwood that reached about six inches down into the neck of the crystal. Grogan replaced it after pouring them each a glass, handing one to Macharia who accepted it and drank slowly.

'America,' *Mapiga* said, pacing the small room. 'If you want to understand why we can't hold on to Kenya you have to understand our new relationship with America. They're the masters now. Being former members of the colony club themselves, they don't really like to see it anywhere else. Morality, you see. Morality in foreign policy, despite the fact they've not been entirely inactive in their own backyard. Drives the French mad – they thought they'd cornered the market in hypocrisy!

'You see, Macharia, I wanted to explain all of this to you because you have to know why I want *you* publicly, of your own free will, to recant this wretched piece of superstition you call an oath.'

Now they were coming to it. Macharia put the glass back on the table.

'Firstly, you can't win.' Grogan counted the points on his fingers. 'Secondly, we want to give back your damn country and, thirdly, in order to do that we have to talk to you. But, and this is the big one, we can't negotiate with a gun to our heads. We believe the boys in the forest are only continuing because you die-hards in here are holding out. All very honourable I'm sure, but the time for that's over. Realpolitik now, Macharia.'

Grogan came back to the desk, placed both hands on the table, knuckles down, and peered at his prisoner. One of his eyes matched the yellow of his cloth. Jaundice, perhaps.

'You see,' he said, every ounce of his voice soothing and compelling. 'Once you fellows behind the wire give up the oath, your comrades in the forest can hand in their arms and talks can start. Independent Kenya here we come! Everyone happy, all friends, sheltering from the new American world order in the jolly embrace of the Commonwealth. God save Jomo, God save the Queen. God save us all.

'Well? What d'you think? Isn't it time to give up this . . . *unpleasantness?*'

It was a good speech. Some of it was even true. Perhaps more than some. But none of that mattered to Macharia. What would this kind of independence mean? After so much suffering it could not be given – it had to be taken. Mau Mau had fought for it so now the British would have to concede it.

Besides, thought Macharia, why should he trust this man whose class had tormented his people for years? Raped, stolen and burned what was not theirs? Killed in vast profusion, as though on a game shoot, heedless of wiping out entire species? Did past behaviour count for nothing? Could the white man do as he pleased, then when his days were numbered ease his burden by arguing his way out of his crimes? How could the torturers who perpetrated this be forgiven?

As *Mapiga* continued with his self-justification, all Macharia could

282

think of was the sickening sight of him polishing his glasses in sorrow while he went about the camp 'visiting' detainees, his face a picture of false remorse. The picture of everything that needed to be obliterated for ever.

'Not going to answer? Nothing to say?'

'No.'

'Is that a final no?'

Macharia spat.

'You will never win, *Mapiga*. You cannot beat a people into submission.'

'Really? Is that your last word? I expected better. Pity.'

The kindly smile leached out of his eyes. He reached for the carafe, a heavy affair that had seen better times in a more appropriate place. He slid the long stopper out and held it in one hand, the carafe in the other.

'Would you like some more water?'

Macharia reached for his glass, and that was his mistake.

He was slightly off balance when the carafe connected with his skull and he fell to the floor. It was a hard blow and he must have been temporarily on the edge of consciousness for he didn't remember guards coming in, hauling him to his feet and ripping off his clothes before strapping him naked to the chair. The restraints on his ankles and wrists were thoroughly tested before the men were dismissed, leaving him alone with his interrogator.

Macharia shook his head to try to clear his vision. It remained stubbornly unfocused, but not so badly he could not see *Mapiga* open the drawer of his desk to remove several implements, laying them all out on the yellow handkerchief, an occasional clink identifying them as metal.

When he saw the pliers he began to retch in terror.

The last thing Macharia remembered clearly was *Mapiga* advancing slowly towards him, whistling a hymn he dimly recognised. Grogan had removed his spectacles and his perspiring face jutted out before him as if he were peering into the darkness. In his hand was an item it took some seconds to identify. The stopper from the carafe, long, wooden, metal-tipped. It was blunt but *Mapiga* must have used it before, for he began to employ it skilfully.

Even as Macharia began to scream Grogan's sorrowful expression told him he thought he was doing him a favour.

Chapter 28

Grogan's house, March 2008

She was being hunted.

Down a dark passage, through shadow rooms, the pursuer approaching ever nearer. Panicked running, flinging open doors – a burst into light, slipping on a wet floor. Wet with blood. White dress, red spatter; sliding on her arse in blood. Shoes and legs drenched; a snarling buffalo's head vomiting pink foam, viscous liquid flowing upwards, enveloping her torso, her mouth. She couldn't breathe, tried to cry out. Suffocating—

Sam came to in a running sweat, her mouth buried in her pillow, dream screams mutating into a waking mewling. She sat up, looking around wildly, senses scrambled. A large gulp of water from her bedside glass and the room came into focus. Still in Grogan's house.

Under the door, a note. She pushed back the drenched sheet, wide awake now but an aerosol of disquiet clung to her, refusing to disperse. Something was edging into the side of her brain, sharp and uncomfortable. She couldn't place it. She fetched the message and opened it, the roof of her mouth sticky-dry.

The note was brief. Grogan thanked her for her company last night, hoped she'd slept well and apologised for having to depart early to visit his orphanage. He'd be back for a late lunch, which he sincerely hoped she'd stay for. In the meantime she was to make herself at home and ask Jordan for anything she required.

Sam went to the window to draw back the curtains, feeling vaguely disappointed. After last night she had the strongest feeling Grogan wasn't revealing everything. She opened the window. The air was warm and she inhaled deeply, allowing the scents of the day to chase out memories of the night. Arid scrubland stretched out far ahead of her on every side and she tasted mopani and dry grass, baobab and the fainter notes of wood smoke.

It was only under the shower that the last of the night fears washed out and she emerged invigorated, drying herself roughly with a large towel embroidered with a zebra. Walking down the wide staircase she passed a series of wall-mounted glass cabinets, each containing a stuffed tableau of dead animals. A freckled pi-dog's beady eyes followed her, and what she'd thought of as a collection of sand and stones turned out, on closer inspection, to be a coiled snake, its little black tongue sticking out from a mouth concealed by shiny yellow scales.

She paused at the bottom. On the wall were two photographs, one in black and white. She'd noticed them yesterday but hadn't stopped to look closer. In the first, a young Grogan wearing military gear, gun in hand, posed in front of a burning village. Mau Mau prisoners were squatting, shackled and desolate, at his feet. The other, a contemporary full-colour picture, revealed an older Grogan at an orphanage, standing beside happy, smiling African children.

She peered closely at his face in the black and white photo. He was smiling, looking over his glasses at the photographer. He appeared happy, almost triumphant. Yet at his feet were three African men whose expressions displayed agonising distress. The distinction from the orphanage shot could not have been greater. How could one man transform into the other? Was this Grogan making amends?

The question that had been lurking ever since she woke pulled into sharp focus. When Grogan had moved into the camps could he have been involved in more than mere propaganda? She stood back, scraping at her thumb flesh with a nail, a tendril of anxiety from the night reawakening as the consequences fought to make themselves understood. It made little sense. Everything she knew about Grogan suggested it was unlikely. He was a civilised man. She had eaten at his table. He went to government cocktail parties; a man of substance and standing. He had been friends with her grandparents. A family friend.

She pursed her lips, soiled at the train of thought because she recognised the refrain. *A family friend.* She'd once prosecuted a case on it; saw again the parents learning the identity of their child's abuser for the first time. Couldn't be, they'd said. Everyone knew him. They trusted him. Known him for years. A civilised man. *A family friend.*

Sam did not know what to think, suddenly cold as if ghosts from the picture had reached out to touch her. She hugged herself and wished she'd put on a sweater, hurrying into the drawing room, where she'd watched the film last night. The projector was still there, facing the wall, though the chairs had been put away. There were fresh flowers in the vase, red ones this time; Sam had no idea what kind, but felt an unreasonable anger towards them.

Five minutes ago she'd been hungry, looking forward to acting the memsahib again and getting the strange manservant to find her something to eat. Now the idea of breakfast made her feel faintly sick. Because there was something else as well. If it was possible Grogan had been involved, then why not Johnny?

Looking at the projector, she remembered Johnny's face in the footage from Grogan's little film show. Haunted and hollow, voided by what he'd seen. A forced witness of an awful camp system. That's what she'd thought last night. But what if he hadn't been just a spectator? What had he really been doing? Surely he couldn't have been involved in any of the same things as Grogan. He'd been a lowly propagandist in the Information Department.

And yet.

Propaganda had moved to the camps, Grogan had said, and with it the personnel. All hands to the pump, helping the flow of water along the Pipeline. Muscular Christianity. Practical measures for the greater good. Nothing more than a bit of rough and tumble. Like a rugby game.

But that was not what the depositions and the witnesses said. They had been very clear. Torture was not a game.

Sam perched on the edge of the sofa and thought about the film. In the loft there had been at least two cases with Johnny's initials on them. And inside them had been many more films, so he must have been at the camps for weeks. She remembered the reflection of the warders in the window glass, bending over someone. What else might he have captured? Did Johnny appear in any more of it?

She glanced at the projector. It couldn't be that hard to work. She examined it more closely. It was plugged in and so it would just be a question of fitting the reel, turning it on and focusing. She looked about. No sign of Grogan returning, or of anyone else.

She saw the bell that Grogan had used last night to summon the poor man with the broken leg. She rang it; the tinkling seemed very loud but no one responded, and after she'd rung it again and waited a minute Sam felt at liberty to put her plan into action. She'd tried, but if they wouldn't come to help that wasn't her fault. Grogan had said to make herself at home. So she would. He probably wouldn't mind and besides, it might be far better to look at the footage without his running commentary. If she did find anything incriminating she wasn't sure she wanted Grogan to know.

What she needed to do was get into the storage room with the ladder up into the loft. Preferably without anyone seeing her. She wondered if she should try to let Dedan know what she was up to. But her phone was upstairs and going outside might alert the household. Now that she'd settled on her plan she realised it would certainly be best to avoid the silent, morose servant – Jordan, the one who apparently liked to cut people's hamstrings with his knife. She had to act now, before anyone returned.

Retracing her steps from last night, she located the room and at once found the long pole required to release the ladder. But attaching the head to undo the latch in the ceiling was much harder. Grogan had wielded the pole with ease and she realised that despite his age he must have retained much of his strength. Sam couldn't stop the tip waving this way and that. It was like trying to push in a drawing pin with a billiard cue.

Then *snap*, she hit the target and the latch popped, letting the stairs unwind smoothly. Perhaps she would only take one of the reels, which she could hide down the back of her jeans in case she bumped into Jordan or Samson. She raced up the ladder, pausing halfway up, thinking she'd heard footsteps outside. She listened for a minute, her heart hammering in her ears. Nothing. She needed to get on with it. Where was the bloody light switch? She felt about on the floor but couldn't find it. It couldn't have moved.

There. She flicked it on and light bathed the loft, illuminating all the suitcases and trunks, just where they'd been yesterday, thank God. There were four steps of the ladder to climb.

She was on the third when she felt her ankle gripped hard. Sam let out a half-scream. Looking down she saw the hostile face of Jordan.

'Hi there,' she said. But Jordan said nothing. She wriggled her leg but he wouldn't release her.

'Do you mind letting me go?'

Jordan tightened his grasp. This was absurd. Should she kick down? If she did it hard enough she might be able to shake free. As if he'd read her mind, he squeezed even harder and, worse, his free hand wrapped round Sam's other foot.

'Hey, that hurts. Could you just let me go, please?'

'You need to come down, Miss Samantha. At once.'

'I'm just having a look. I was up here last night you know. With Grogan. Your *master* . . . hey, *ow!*'

Jordan had dug his fingers into both her ankles at once and the pain stabbed up through her leg with such force she almost lost her hold on the ladder.

'Come down now,' he said. 'You are in a private place. The Colonel would not be happy to see you here.'

Sam knew he wouldn't let go so there was nothing to do but descend. Jordan's hands remained on her ankles all the way down until they were level with his head, at which stage he shifted his grip to her waist. He hoisted her off the ladder, squeezing her rib cage with force. When she reached the ground he did not release her.

'Look, will you let me go?' Sam said over her shoulder. 'I've bloody come down, haven't I?'

Jordan tugged suddenly and Sam found herself tripping backwards towards him. She turned the movement to her advantage and swivelled round. Facing him, she could smell his breath: milky and hot, a hint of peppermint. He was tall, towering over her. His blouson had come loose at the top and his chest glistened with a sheen of sweat. The last time she'd seen gleaming skin she'd been filled with desire. Now she was frightened. Why wouldn't he let her go? He leant in closer and she pulled her head away and back from him as far as possible. But leaning backwards had the effect of pushing out her stomach, which connected with his groin. He grinned and pushed back.

This could not be happening.

'Look, Jordan, you'd better let me go right now or I'll tell Grogan you assaulted me.'

Jordan smiled, revealing uneven teeth.

'I do not think you will tell Grogan anything,' he said, pressing himself against her.

'What the fuck are you doing? Get off me!'

The sickening fear from seconds ago was evaporating, replaced by a fury surging to the surface, directed at the man in front of her penning her in, hurting her, wanting to do God knows what. Who the bloody hell did he think he was? More to the point, who did he think she was that she'd put up with this shit?

Jordan lifted one of his hands from her waist and in that smallest of moments Sam saw her chance. Launching herself forwards and up, shifting her neck back as far as it would go, she delivered a powerful head-butt. Because the blow came from below it didn't quite hit his nose head on, but there was a satisfying pop and she felt warmth ooze onto her forehead.

Jordan wheeled backwards clutching his face, grunting in pain.

Sam ran.

Past the fishpond, past the front door, past an empty guardhouse, straight to the *matatu*. Dedan was sitting at the driver's seat, tapping his steering wheel to the beat of music she couldn't hear. When he saw Sam flying towards him he jumped out of the van and raised his hands in question.

'What's the matter, Sam?' he began to ask, stopping when he saw Jordan running towards them. He pushed Sam gently behind him, took a step forward and folded his large arms.

'We need to leave,' Sam said. 'But I have to go back and get my things. I've left them all in my room. But that bastard ... he ...'

'Do not worry, Sam,' Dedan said quietly. 'Get into the van and lock the door. I will deal with this Masai dog.'

Dedan drove west for a shade under two hours, hitting the main road at Gilgil before turning north.

'Where *are* we going?' Sam asked.

Dedan smiled enigmatically. Except it wasn't enigmatic at all, more bubblingly superior. Like a big kid with a secret. He'd refused to say all journey. Sam didn't mind. The more time she spent with Dedan, the more she liked him. It was impossible not to trust him, whoever his real employers were. He presented such a tough and fierce demeanour but she suspected it was really only concern. After Sam had calmed down sufficiently to explain what Jordan had done he'd hardly been able to drive and was all for turning round and sorting out Jordan again.

'But what did you say to him?' Sam asked. 'How on earth did you make him pack my bag?'

Dedan laughed and slapped his steering wheel.

'It was nothing. Just some old words for an old enemy.'

Sam couldn't get any more out of him but she'd been astonished at how Dedan had managed to get Jordan to do his bidding. When the servant had approached, Dedan had moved with viperish speed, darting his hand inside the servant's billowing folds and grasping him somewhere so that Jordan had bent double, puffing with pain. Dedan had moved his head beside Jordan's and spoken quietly and the two of them had trotted off without fuss.

They'd reappeared five minutes later with all of Sam's clothes in her bag and – she checked – Johnny's scrapbook. She wasn't sorry about lashing out at that hideous servant and was more than happy to be out of the house, but she recognised Grogan was still useful. He could add to the Johnny story and she reflected it might have been better to have waited to say goodbye in person. The regret was only tactical: the longer she'd been at his house the more she'd felt something about Grogan was wrong. She couldn't get rid of the image of those Mau Mau prisoners sitting at his feet, the look of triumph on his face. Nor all those dead animals locked away in glass cabinets, their dry carcasses bleached symbols of decay and death.

In truth, she was mightily relieved to be out of there, careering along country roads with Dedan, listening to his crazed music and thinking of Kamau. They'd been apart for less than two days but she was ridiculously excited at the prospect of seeing him again.

But she was also, she admitted as yet more featureless African scrub zipped past the window, just a little bit fed up with not knowing where they were going. When she asked Dedan about their destination he just shook his head.

'I am so sorry. This is a hard time for you,' he said. 'Sorry too that I have not been able to tell you everything. It's difficult for me to remain silent, but hopefully when you see why you will forgive me. It is going to get better – that much I can say.'

Then he said a surprising thing.

'I have been looking into your new friend, Kamau. And it is good news, Sam. He is a fine man, from a fine family.'

Sam wasn't sure whether to be amused or annoyed. Was she not able to do anything on her own here?

'What do you mean, looking into him?'

Dedan chuckled. '*Ah* ... come on now, Sam. You don't think we could let you venture among Kenya's manhood without a little oversight? Suffice to say your instinct is sound. And I hate to say this about a man who has obviously stolen the heart of the most beautiful woman in Kenya – apart from my wife, of course – but I like him. *We* like him. Yes indeed.'

'Married? I'm afraid I don't believe you, Dedan. And the "we" in this case is who, precisely?'

He shook his head.

'No, Sam,' he laughed. 'This is where I become mysterious again. What do you say – good things come to those who wait. Perhaps even better ones to those who are patient while they do so!'

They turned off the main road at a sign to Lake Nakuru National Park. She'd not heard of it but when they dipped through green hills to glimpse the lake from the ridge it looked stolen out of a guidebook, a teeming expanse of water flocked with a mass of birds, most of them pink. *Flamingos!* She'd always loved flamingos and there were hundreds of them, if not thousands, adorning the water with a pinkish hue. They drove along the lakeside and Dedan pointed out the different species. Storks, Herons, Hammerkops, Ibis. Even he had never seen so many all in one place.

After about a mile they headed away from the water and up into the hills. They passed a couple of sleek game lodges and Sam wondered if Kamau had reserved a place at one of them. They did look inviting. But as the road became dustier and more pot-holed, the lodges ran out and they bumped through yet more scrub. The further they went, the more eager she became to see Kamau again, especially out here. This was the Kenya she'd always dreamed of, the African heartland that had fired her childhood imagination. She wondered if she would glimpse hippos, the Monarchs of River and Marsh, or hear their bassoon notes. Winding up through the hills, she felt folded into this beautiful place and understood what Johnny must have felt when he was out in the bush, far away from the horrors of the city and the camps.

Finally they turned a bend and there it lay, a wood-framed house set into the hillside with large windows and a sweeping teak-decked balcony. Dedan sounded his horn and Sam jumped out. The air was cooler up here – but the view! Through a gap in the acacia trees most of the lake was magnificently on show, the rim of a giant ancient volcano etched into the valley. With the backdrop of the hills and the warmth of the sun and the pink-flamingo water Sam felt her eyes prickle at the immensity of it. She was blinking it away when she heard Kamau's voice behind her.

'Don't you like what you see, Sam?'

She spun round and there he was, tall and inviting, hesitant at Sam's reaction to the big surprise. She had planned to be cool about it but couldn't stop herself, wrapping her arms round him, holding him as tightly as possible.

'I've missed you,' she whispered.

Still holding her, he gently drew his head back to look at her properly.

'I too, Samantha.'

They kissed and Sam happily surrendered to an embrace that could never have lasted long enough. It was only when the *matatu*'s horn blasted that they pulled apart, sheepishly remembering they weren't alone. Dedan had started the engine and was turning his van round to face down the hill. He waved from the window, leaning out to shout:

'Goodbye, Sam. I shall see you in a week. Be good!'

Sam caught herself blushing. She waved back.

And then, finally, they were alone.

Kamau led her up the terrace. Logs were burning in a fire pit but she shivered slightly.

'Look at all this. It's amazing,' she said. 'You're so clever to have found it.'

'Not that clever really,' he replied. 'I had a little help. But I am truly happy that you like this place. It's called Ngare Lodge – Kikuyu for leopard. There are plenty of them about, by the way, so don't go wandering off alone. Anyway, welcome to the family property.'

He stood with his arms round her as they watched the *matatu* weave back down onto the lake road, occasional snatches of music floating up as Dedan resumed full volume.

'He just told me what happened back there,' Kamau said quietly. 'It sounds vile. You must have been so worried. I am very sorry.'

'Don't be,' she joked, not wanting to spoil the atmosphere. 'It got me here faster.'

One of his arms was round her waist and he draped the other over her shoulder, down across her chest. She placed her hand on it, absently stroking his forearm. At last. She was safe here. They could do what they wanted.

Chapter 29

Mombasa, September 1954

With Tansy away at the doctor's, the atmosphere at the beach house changed.

The place *looked* the same. Johnny could see physical evidence of her in her things: a discarded paperback, her hairbrush, a lip-sticked coffee mug. But devoid of her presence, the house was hollow. Even the view was different. The sea that morning was at its most impressive, heavy rollers pounding the water into rainbow mist. But without someone to share it with, it became distanced, distorted behind a gauze of unreality. As he stood alone on the balcony, Johnny understood a great truth: Tansy was the eye through which he wanted to perceive his life; sharing it with her was the only way it could be assimilated or understood. Without her, he was half blind.

He couldn't shake a dull but constant apprehension. Why was she really going to the doctor? She looked well enough. In fact, as she'd admitted only the other day, she was feeling better than she'd ever done in her life. He didn't really believe the smoke and mirrors nonsense about 'women's things'. He should have pressed her, but then Tansy was never going to tell him anything she didn't want to. A solitary day stretched ahead of him. It wasn't just Tansy being away for a few hours that provoked this Sunday-afternoon feeling, it was the reality she'd made him acknowledge. She was right: they couldn't hide here for much longer. He needed to plan their next escape.

Fresh air was required. He thought more clearly when he was outdoors. He could lose himself for hours walking in the bush, taking pictures, thinking. Planning.

There were a number of trails leading off the beach and Johnny took the farthest one, about a mile from the house, leading up the slope to the forest. He hadn't been that way for weeks and the houseboy Joshua had told him excitedly that a troop of Sykes' monkeys had taken up residence there. As Johnny moved away from the continuous artillery of waves crashing on the beach it grew quieter, easier to reflect amid the calm of the steepling cedars and spreading acacias.

He remembered again the names of the trees: sausage trees and pigeonwood; white stinkwood and buffalo thorn. One night he'd amazed Tansy by reciting them all. His party piece. He breathed deeply; nature as always putting everything, if not to rights then at least in perspective. He paused to take a few shots of a hoopoe, sitting wisely on its perch, refusing to move for this insignificant human. Creatures like it had inhabited this forest for thousands of years. This part of Kenya, at least, hadn't changed for millennia.

Then he remembered Tansy's odd comment: *nothing lasts for ever.* A shiver ran through him and he couldn't stop an image of Grogan invading his thoughts. How Johnny hated him now. Previously he'd thought of Grogan as, what, an uncle? Elder brother? Something between the two. Now he was his enemy just as surely as Graves.

Fuck Grogan.

Johnny smiled, realising that running the syllables together made it sound like one of the tree names. *Fugragan.* He looked at the thick trunks, wrapped in their tangle of strangler-fig vines and whispered the list of names again, letting his tongue roll over the syllables, caressing the old colloquial terms. *Blood lily. Screw pine. Fugragan.*

Fuck Grogan.

He suddenly saw it: they had to return and deal with Grogan before he dealt with them. There were powers higher in the land even than Grogan. Simple, really. Johnny turned to go back, happy that nature had once again helped him come to a decision. Tansy would be pleased.

But as he walked along the same paths back down towards the beach he knew something was wrong. Not with the plan but here, at this moment. Well-attuned now to the ways of the bush, he could sense something following in the undergrowth. His spine prickled as his ears and nose strained to make out what his eyes could not. A crack of a twig, the deadening of bird song, a faint whiff of metal or grease. He was not alone.

He didn't run, instinct suggesting that would be more dangerous. If he could only get to the beach, he might swim out beyond the rollers and bide his time, sneak back to the house later.

But these were professionals.

They waited until he was almost out of the forest. One second the trail was empty, the next three men appeared on it, a dozen paces away, pointing guns. They wore forest garb, Mau Mau cowls, filthy trousers, matted locks. It was the rifles that gave them away. Lee Enfield bolt-action .303s. Standard British army issue. They might have been stolen by forest fighters, but the fact that Johnny was still alive and wondering made him certain these were Graves's men. Real Mau Mau would have left him for dead by now.

A voice made him look round. Five more men had taken up positions to the rear, cutting off any prospect of escaping back along the trail.

'Hands on head.'

The command was given by a man carrying a Sten gun, the fancy firearm denoting leadership. Johnny did as he was told, raising his hands slowly.

'What do you want?'

'Walk, please. Walk ahead. Back to the house.'

'Why?'

'No questions, please. Just walking. Be very careful, sir, we are ordered to shoot to kill if you try and run. Do not do that please, sir, my men are very fast. Very accurate.'

The man was being polite, which told Johnny they were not planning to kill him yet. It didn't help much. If these were Graves's men, Graves was bound to be nearby. He prayed Tansy was still with the doctor in Mombasa. He walked as quickly as his nerves would allow, reasoning the sooner he got this finished, the less chance Tansy would walk in on them.

As the odd shooting party approached the house, Joshua was sitting in his usual secret place underneath the veranda, watching with growing alarm the armed men guarding his *bwana*. Joshua was smart but could not be expected to know the difference between a Mau Mau rifle made from stolen piping and a regular .303, and so could only believe his master was in the clutches of the guerrillas from the forest. He did not know how to help when he saw them ushering Mr Johnny up the stairs above his head at gunpoint, nor was he aware there was someone inside already. He could not be blamed for this as the visitor was probably the best in the business at not being detected.

Joshua only saw him when he stuck his eye to the knot hole he'd bored in the wall for when he wanted to catch a glimpse of the beautiful white woman. Now he witnessed a terrible series of events. Lounging in the room's only armchair was a thin *muzungu*, leg hanging over the arm, cane tapping against the matt brown leather of his boot. When Johnny, hands still on his head, was pushed in front of him, the thin man leapt to his feet, immediately striking Johnny on the neck with his cane. It was a diagonal blow, coming with so much force that Joshua heard the bamboo swishing through the air before it hit. During the next few minutes Joshua remained as still as he could, even though he wanted to shout 'Stop!' many times when he saw what the thin man was doing. Johnny had fallen to his knees and Joshua was proud of his master for not crying out. The man doing the whipping must have been very angry because he was muttering as he went about his work, the strokes falling venomously quickly.

The phone rang then and the beating stopped. Joshua heard the man snarl at Johnny.

'Answer it then. It's for you.'

Joshua did not wait to see what happened next. Slipping out from his hiding place, he ran for his life.

Inside, Johnny staggered through to the hall, praying it wasn't Tansy. As he put the receiver to his ear he realised Graves had spared his face. The cane had hit him everywhere else. Two special blows reserved for his neck, one on either side – 'That's for fucking hitting me' ... *crack* ... 'And that's for fucking running away.'

The voice on the other end was calm, even jovial.

'*Johnny!* At last. How have you been?'

Of course, it had to be him. Graves had lit a cigarette and was leaning across the doorway.

'Grogan. What do you want?'

'I assume you've met up with Graves?'

Johnny didn't trust what he might say, his hand shaking.

'I take it from your silence the answer is in the affirmative. Good. Now listen carefully, Johnny. Your life depends on it, d'you see?'

'How did you find me?'

'The colonial police force is not entirely stupid, though it does try its hardest to appear so. Anyway, remember when I told you I'd want something in return for using those little photographs of yours? Well, that moment is now, Johnny. Graves is going to escort you to me. You're going to come willingly and you will not make a fuss. If you do Graves has carte blanche to do what he's wanted to do for a very long time. Got it so far?'

Johnny wanted to be certain Tansy was kept out of it.

'I understand. Where's here?'

'Come to that in a moment. But first, Johnny, I have to know you're taking this seriously. Unfortunately chaps like you, wandering around the bush, are simple prey for Mau Mau terrorists. Don't want to see your name on the casualty list. Are we clear on this?'

'Fuck you, Grogan,' Johnny said. 'Get on with it.'

'Careful, Johnny, I'd just listen if I were you. Point is, there's some filming to be done. Need someone I know will do as I ask. This will be no great shakes for someone of your talent. We've got all the gear. All you have to do is point and shoot at what I tell you. You do that and I continue to keep Graves off your back – in perpetuity. All right? Sound like a deal?'

Blood was trickling down his neck onto his chest. He looked over at Graves. What choice did he have? Every second he spent arguing on the phone brought the possibility that Tansy might walk in on them.

'OK. I'll do it. But you have to leave Tansy alone. None of this is her fault. This is between you and me.'

'*Tansy*. How touching.' Grogan dropped the false bonhomie. 'I was going to talk about this later, but since you mention it: she's not in your little beach house, is she? Where do you think she is? Well, I'll tell you. After she popped into the doctor – she's fine, by the way – she took the train to Nairobi. She wants to go abroad, I believe. Paris, I think she said. Too much pressure on the poor girl.'

Johnny felt as if he'd been stabbed.

'*Paris?* What are you talking about? And how the hell do you know about the doctor?'

Grogan laughed thinly.

'Because she told me. Because she's finally realised your time is up.'

Johnny was pushing the phone against his head so hard it was almost ripping his ear off. This was not possible.

'*No!* You're lying. How can she have told you? No one knew where we were—'

'Really? Come on, Johnny, do you seriously think a European couple can just disappear? From me? God, you're still so naïve.'

'I don't bloody believe you.'

'OK, so how do you think you've been surviving down there? Your money ran out weeks ago. How was Tansy able to afford all those little extras when she went to town?'

'*You?*'

'Yes, Johnny, me. I'm not the type to abandon a cause, you know that. Tansy showed me in Nairobi she won't be rushed and I wanted to make sure she was all right while she made her mind up. Not going to have someone I care about starve.'

Johnny thought quickly, racing through the permutations. Grogan was a manipulator; that's what he did. He *had* to be lying. He'd said he'd known where they were for months, so why hadn't he done anything before now? Tansy would have said if she'd been in contact. But where *had* the money come from? He'd thought it was the sister, loving letters and the odd cheque from – oh God, Paris.

'Why now?' Johnny shouted. 'Why has she gone now?'

Grogan laughed.

'Ours not to reason, old thing. I suppose she wants to put a bit of distance between her and all these dark doings in the dark continent. Told me she not only needs time to think things through, but space. Time and space – from you and me. Very modern.'

The notion that Tansy had unburdened herself to Grogan was impossible; that she'd left, even more so. She loved him, Johnny knew she did. Graves waved his cane, signalling he should get off the phone.

'Anyway, Johnny, you'd best be on your way.' Grogan's voice was crackling through the ether, taking on a higher pitch. 'Terrible business, war, isn't it? Love should never get mixed up with it. Still, let the best man win I say, or perhaps that should be the last man standing.

'*Do take care.*'

Chapter 30

Mombasa, September 1954

Tansy was so excited at coming home she didn't put the bike up properly and it toppled against the side wall of the beach house. She left it there, in a hurry to tell Johnny. She would have been back hours ago except for that bloody road block; stupid policemen taking ages to question everyone passing through, particularly Europeans, for some reason.

On the ride back she'd told herself she'd be cool; allow the news to emerge over the bottle of wine she'd bought. Johnny must be getting suspicious of how she could afford to buy anything but it didn't matter. Nothing mattered now except the news she had for him.

'*Johnny* – where are you darling?'

There was no reply and she went upstairs, expecting to find him still enjoying a siesta. He wasn't in the bedroom. Damn, he had to be out on the boat again. She returned to the kitchen to open the wine. Probably just as well he wasn't here yet. He pretended to be terribly modern with all his technological expertise with cameras and motorbikes, but underneath it he was surprisingly old-fashioned and she wouldn't have been surprised if he'd tried to stop her having a drink.

But the doctor in Mombasa had said she didn't have to give up anything. Smoke, drink, sex – everything could be done in moderation. Just relax and try to enjoy it, he'd advised. Women had been doing this since the beginning of time and the body knew how to cope. Eat well and take an ordinary amount of exercise – though he didn't advise riding. And when she reached her final trimester she should try to get as much rest as possible.

Tansy leaned on the balcony rail. You clever thing, she thought, before toasting Johnny, acknowledging he might have had something to do with it too. She lit a cigarette and enjoyed another sip. They would have to leave the country, she saw that now. The thought of taking the boat to England was rather thrilling. *London.* Her sister could come over from Paris to see them. Janey would be an auntie!

Where *was* Johnny? She put her cigarette out and collected the wine. She'd better get on, preparing his steak like a dutiful wife. Although of course she wasn't his wife. Would he mind having a child out of wedlock? They might have to get married. Couldn't ships' captains perform the ceremony? God, there was a thought. How utterly conventional. Rather nice, though. In the living room she noticed Johnny's shirts lying on the sofa. Strange. He must have been sorting them out.

The steak took no time to prepare and she moved the chair outside to the front of the house to enjoy the sunset. A sea breeze kept the mosquitoes away and she refreshed her glass, listening contentedly to the breakers.

An hour later and Tansy was tempted to throw the steak in the dustbin, cursing Johnny for an ungrateful swine. Where the hell was he? He was never usually this late. Typical that he should choose tonight to extend his fishing into the evening.

There was a sound from the back of the house. She ran to the door and wrenched it open.

'Johnny? Is that you?'

A noise of footsteps rustled in the bushes on the other side of the road but there was no one to be seen. They'd never had any hint of trouble here. They were Mijikenda round here, not Kikuyu. But she was alone.

She slammed the door shut, drawing the bolt before searching for another cigarette. Through the window a shadow sped across the sand. Johnny did not move like that. Now she was scared. In the kitchen, she picked up a carving knife.

She was walking towards the stairs when the phone rang. The sound was unnaturally loud and she jumped like a scalded cat, adrenalin squirting through her system in gushing spasms. She marched to the phone. If it was Johnny he'd better have a good explanation.

'Where the hell have you been?' she shouted. 'Why aren't you . . . ?'

'Hello, Tansy.'

Grogan's voice sounded much nearer than last time.

'What do you want?' Tansy had to contain herself to keep from shouting again. Where'd he got the number? He had to get off the line. Johnny might be trying to ring.

'Tansy, calm down. I need to talk to you about Johnny.'

'What is it? Is he OK? Where is he?'

'He's gone, Tansy—'

'*Gone?* What do you mean, gone?'

'OK – deep breath and hear me out.'

Tansy listened, her emotions vaulting from anger to rage. Grogan's emollient tones hid the talons of a rotten Mephistopheles, clawing at her, gouging out his bargain.

Johnny knew everything. Grogan was sorry, but he'd been patient long enough. He had told him all about the money he'd given Tansy. Johnny hadn't believed it at first, needed some persuasion. Grogan knowing the exact dates of her visits to Mombasa had proved it. He'd taken it badly. Shouted and cursed, said he was sick of the pair of them and was going back to Europe.

'The part he really didn't like was you keeping it from him. Swore rather a lot at that juncture – I see where you get it from. Wanted to get out of the country as soon as possible. Didn't trust himself around you, I'm afraid. But this is what happens when people don't follow their true instincts, Tansy.'

But Tansy was not to worry: Grogan had managed to persuade Johnny not to leave Kenya. He'd offered him a job upcountry, surrounded by the nature he was so keen on. Unfortunately it was located at Lodwar, towards the Abyssinian border.

'It's a long way away from you,' Grogan said. 'But Tansy, this is the important part – it's really not that far for a determined man like Graves. Particularly if he knows where to look. You do understand, don't you?'

Tansy stared unblinkingly at the phone cradle, her face pale.

'You still there?' Grogan asked. 'I don't like seeing you left in the lurch like this so I'm sending a car. Should be with you first thing in the morning. Give you time to pack. And you're not to worry about being alone in the house; I've got some good men watching so you will be perfectly safe. Oh and by the way, I've talked to McGregor and your old job at the hospital's still open.'

302

'How could you . . . ' was all Tansy could manage, each sentence uttered by Grogan a steel trap around everything she wanted, everything she loved.

'Come on, Tansy, you've had a good run. Now it's time to act like a grown-up. No tantrums, please.'

When the phone went mercifully dead she could barely bring herself to go upstairs. At the time she needed him most, Johnny was gone. The gulf between what she'd believed of him and how he'd acted was so vast, so incomprehensible, she couldn't take it in. How could he have done this? To leave without a single word. It was beyond callous, cruel, so . . . *final*.

But she hadn't told him the truth either, and the really hideous part was knowing that if it had been the other way round, if she'd discovered he'd been secretly communing with Grogan in return for money, she'd have done exactly the same.

Chapter 31

Lake Nakuru, April 2008

The days flowed away with impossible speed and Sam mourned their passing with hollow dismay. Ordinarily she might have placed caveats on the fire that consumed her, but this was no ordinary moment. There was magic in this place of leopards and though she understood time was limited, even this added stimulus. Life on the edge of a razor, much the sweeter for being sharper.

The lodge was elegant but comfortable. Everything from the two sketches of Mount Kirinyaga above the mantelpiece to the bookshelves lined with worn editions of Conrad, Achebe and Lessing made her feel at home. It wasn't an English home, but strangely for somewhere so obviously African it had a patina of Englishness. The familiarity tempered the new, producing a sensation of freedom for Sam, as if the very walls were giving her permission to act as she pleased.

And so she did.

In the short time she'd been here it seemed she'd experienced every desire, quenched every longing: making love, wandering the hills, watching kudu strut past the house, viewing flamingos on the lake, building the fire, lying under the stars, listening to the leopards growl at night, talking, sleeping and making more love. That was all, and for a time it was everything; certainly it was enough.

The inevitable questions came towards the end of the fifth day. They were sitting with blankets around them, their backs to the house, looking up at the night sky. They were snacking on chilli peanuts and passing a bottle of beer between them. Sam was impressed with Kamau's foraging skills, but even more that he'd thought to stock the house with drinks and chocolate, and even put some flowers in a vase.

'This is all so clever of you,' she said. 'When did you have time to arrange this and buy all these provisions?'

'I didn't,' he replied. 'But I'm glad you appreciate them.'

'I do. I love them. So did you have some help then?' Sam asked lazily, not expecting any real reaction. But Kamau sat up, dropping the blanket from his shoulders.

'Yes, well. No, not really. The place was pretty well stocked so I just got the main things – the beef we ate last night and the fruit and vegetables. The owners said we could take what we wanted.'

'Owners? I thought Ngare Lodge belonged to your family?'

'Not exactly.'

Sam sat up too, not alarmed; still playing a game.

'Either it does or it doesn't. I really don't mind, Kamau. It's lovely whether it's yours or not. I don't even care if you stole it. I've always wanted to be a squatter. It's rather romantic.'

Kamau laughed sadly, not looking at her.

'No, it's all above board, I can assure you.'

'So whose is it then?'

Kamau reached for Sam's hand, which he held gently between both of his.

'Look, Sam. I feel I am bursting with many things at the moment. My feelings for you. My desire ...' He paused. 'But also another matter – an important one. I want to tell you something, but I have been forbidden.'

Sam withdrew her hand sharply.

'You sound like Dedan! What possible reason could there be for not telling me who this house belongs to?'

She hated being corralled, kept out of the loop. The sooner he understood that the better. Ever since arriving in Kenya she'd seemed to be operating in the dark. A bit of it was her fault due to her own ignorance, but some of it was down to deliberate obfuscation by others; others who were meant to be – who claimed to be – on her side. Whatever that meant now.

She stood up and threw the blanket on the ground. She hadn't had a cigarette since she'd got to the lodge but she badly wanted one now.

'In fact, Kamau, I think it's time you explained what's going on. Do you know who Dedan is working for? Are you working for them too? Just what the fuck am I being lined up for here?'

Kamau stood too, uncoiling long limbs, an athlete preparing for the contest.

'Hey, come on now, Sam. This is not a bad thing. You are not being kept out of anything. Well – not for ever. I know it must be a little strange but—'

'But what?'

Instead of answering, Kamau moved to the railing at the end of the decking. Putting his hands to his mouth, he let out an exasperated howl. Sam was unimpressed.

'Is that your answer – speaking in animal tongues? Some kind of African-style communing with the spirits? I'm not buying it, Kamau.

'All of this,' she said, pointing to the fire and the house. 'None of it means anything if you can't be honest with me. If it's all just a game for you I don't want to play any more.'

Kamau rounded on her, the flames from the fire pit reflected in his eyes. He looked so fierce Sam felt a little frightened. So this was the mighty Kikuyu warrior. Well, he'd better not come near now.

'Sam, listen to me. In two days – just two days – count them. One, two. Everything will be revealed. Don't you understand? I love you, Samantha Seymour. I have never felt anything like it. The more I am with you, the more I want to be with you. I cannot see a future without you. I think you feel the same. When I say I can't tell you now it is because *I cannot*. Not because I don't want to, not because I'm seeking to control you. But because I cannot. I have given my word to others. And I give it to you now. I promise that you will know everything soon enough.'

As he spoke, Kamau padded around the deck, his eyes never leaving Sam's. If someone had claimed shape-shifting was real at that moment she would have believed them. He was not a warrior at all. He was a leopard.

'If that is not enough for you then I am sorry. I will call Dedan. He can be here within the hour and take you wherever you want to go. But before you decide, you must understand. This is absolutely not a game. My feelings are not a game; the work you do is not play. There is much at stake here. It is not just about you. Or me. This is serious, Sam Seymour, perhaps the most serious moment in your life.

'Choose well.'

He pulled open the sliding glass door to the house and went

inside, leaving Sam alone with a sputtering fire and stars that had lost their sparkle.

It was past midnight when she crept into the bedroom. Kamau was lying on his back, and though his eyes were closed she knew he was awake. She leant over him and examined his face: the cheekbones so fine they were almost pretty; his full mouth, so serious when he wasn't laughing. Tenderly she ran a crooked finger down the side of his face. He *was* beautiful. Sam felt the tears that had flowed on the deck come again. He was the real thing. Inside and out. When she thought how close she'd just come to walking away, losing him for ever, she felt sick. She didn't like the mystery, hated thinking she was being toyed with, and if it had been anyone else she would have gone.

But it wasn't anyone else. It was Kamau. She trusted him. Believed him. Did he know the power he had?

She brushed her lips over his.

His arms came round her and without opening his eyes he kissed her. The breath went out of her and she felt her body open to him. His lips crushed hers with a serious desire. But it spoke of wider truths too: of love, of kindness. Of the future.

God help her, if he wasn't being true she would never be able to trust again.

The last days at Ngare were as ardent as the first but there was structure now. Sam had her own work to do. Kamau's words had been correct, her work was not play. Far from it. There was much to accomplish and she needed to take stock.

Despite everything that had happened in Kenya, there was actually very little she could add to the family story. Her father might be interested to know what Grogan had said about Johnny or what Mattingly thought, but none of that added much flesh to the bones. If she could locate her, Esther might throw much more light on what Johnny was really like – better to have it from a friend's perspective than Grogan's. Sam rather regretted not having taken her chance, although there had been more important matters to attend to. Poor Esther, how she would be grieving for her husband. Sam had come to the conclusion that she must still be alive because when Grogan mentioned Mattingly's death he hadn't said anything about his wife.

But Sam had no idea how she would ever find her again. When she'd asked Kamau he'd seemed uninterested, saying merely that if someone wanted to get lost in Kenya they tended to stay lost until they chose to be discovered.

In a notebook she jotted down some thoughts, a list. She was good at lists.

So, item one – find Esther. Make sure she was all right; ask about Johnny. Did Esther know what Johnny had really been doing in the camps? The image from the film at Grogan's house still haunted Sam: her grandfather's face had been like the pictures of young soldiers in battle, the empty, thousand-yard stares, scarred by what they'd seen. *What they'd done?*

Also, Esther must have some knowledge about the documents her husband had given Sam. Might Mattingly even have attended the secret committee meetings as an Information Officer? If she could get a statement from Esther it would be useful. Not primary testimony, but still good supporting material. And what about Esther's story itself? Sam didn't know if she dared ask her to go over it again but if she could manage to record any of it, it would be so powerful. Rape testimony from a woman who wasn't claiming reparations. Authoritative in itself, but also crucial as back-up evidence for the other women's statements.

Which brought her to item two. What to do with the testimony from other survivors? Clearly Sam was no longer part of the government mission, thank God. But there was so much in them that she could use if she moved across to the opposition. There were a handful of law firms who specialised in this kind of human-rights work. One in particular was interested in Kenya, had in fact been garnering statements in partnership with the Kenya Human Rights Commission. They had an excellent reputation and if she could get alongside them it might open up all kinds of possibilities.

Enthused, Sam put her laptop on the table, pushing aside some nature photography books by someone rejoicing in the name of Roy Muse, and began to hammer out a plan of what she knew and what she still needed to get. She wondered whether Pugh and the others were still in the country. Her mobile was stuffed with messages from him, demanding she got in touch. She'd deliberately avoided replying. What was there to say? It must be evident she was off the case.

And then there was the matter of what the hell his driver was doing at Mattingly's house. In truth, she hoped Pugh had buggered off back to England. The only time she wanted to see him again was in court, as an opposing counsel. With what she was concocting now, she'd wipe the floor with him.

Happily typing, she was unaware of Kamau coming into the living room. He must have been watching for some time before she glanced up and saw him standing by the doorway, a bundle of papers under his arm.

'You look very busy,' he said.

Sam yawned and stretched.

'Actually nearly finished. I started out with visions of a grand list but there are only a few things on it of any importance.'

'Do you have enough to interest the English law firms you were talking about?'

'Not sure. Probably. With so little contemporary written material it all comes down to the strength of the personal testimony. And it is incredibly strong. Trouble is, it's all a bit similar so it might lose its power in front of a judge. He may well think it's rehearsed.'

Kamau dropped a sheaf of papers onto the table next to Sam's laptop.

'Will these help?'

Sam picked them up. They were an assortment of government documents from the Emergency era.

'Where on earth did you get these?'

Kamau sat opposite her and grinned.

'Government Records in Nairobi. As a PhD student I'm meant to know my way around the archives, so I spent two very profitable days there while you were swanning round the Littleboy estate pretending to be a memsahib.'

She flicked through them. There were five bundles separated from each other with paper clips. The first four related to various colonial edicts and orders. No testimony or supporting evidence of crimes that Sam could see, but fascinating. She put them down to hug him.

'You clever thing. Thank you so much. They'll be invaluable in building a picture.'

Kamau heard the disappointment in her tone. He pointed to the table.

'Thank you. But there's one you missed. Have a look. I don't know what it's referring to, but given who it's from, it could be of some interest.'

The reason she'd missed the document was because it was only on one piece of paper, a confidential letter to a senior police officer. But it was from Grogan! The date showed that it was written near the start of the Emergency. She scanned it and felt a quickening pulse of excitement tinged with dread.

Her mind sped back to something Mattingly had said. About how Johnny had changed when he'd had to take photographs of the aftermath of that murder at the Cunningham place. It was the same incident she'd read about in the newspaper cutting kept by Johnny in his scrapbook, she was sure of it. She would check later but she was certain the reporter had described a scene of barbarity, and mentioned 'dark horror' too upsetting to repeat.

She read the letter again more slowly as the implications sank in. But there was still too much she didn't understand. Who was this man Graves? And was Johnny a willing accomplice or had he been forced into it? And what about Grogan? What the hell was he doing, talking about 'dealing with corpses'? A young corpse, too. Who was that referring to? Then Sam remembered another line from the article. The young victim at the Cunningham house would have been their baby.

Chapter 32

To: Superintendent Charles Cameron, Fort Hall
Police Command.
From: Colonel Grogan Littleboy, Information
Department, Staff HQ, Nairobi.
Date: 29th October, 1952

Dear Charles,

It was good to meet. We must do it more often. These
are difficult times and, as you said, men of purpose ought
to stick together.

I regret this missive cannot touch on lighter matters.
Please allow me to present formally my commiserations on
losing such a fine and able officer as Cedric Cunningham.
Ghastly business, his wife and child too.

I know your chaps will want to be all over it and
rightly so. But as I mentioned last night, thanks to your
early warning there may be an opportunity to turn this
unpleasantness to our advantage. As I understand it, at
present only a very small number of people know what has
happened there and they are all good men who can keep a
rein on their mouths. If you can delay your detectives
for two more days I will have made my dispositions.

I have taken your recommendation and seen the man
Graves. He was known to me in another capacity and
I would not say we were friendly. However, he is a
first-class officer and not squeamish. He has undertaken
to perform the sensitive work we discussed. He simply
needs 48 hours to get up there and make sure it is done.
Therefore I would be grateful if you did not make the

311

murders public until Sunday. As it happens, Graves and I will both be attending social functions in Nyeri that weekend so he can go straight there, do what has to be done, scarper and return to the scene within hours once it becomes public.

I am aware of your reservations about dealing with the corpses in the way we discussed but the plain truth is that the dead feel no pain, however young they may be, and the manner of their departure can be made to help immeasurably in preventing any more killings. If we could fight and win this struggle by keeping our hands clean I would be the first in line at the sink. As it is, we may find we have to do what is necessary more often than we would like.

I will secure the services of a professional photographer. I have one in mind whom I can trust.

Best wishes,

Grogan

Chapter 33

Manyani Camp, February 1955

Macharia had stopped thinking of Grogan as Grogan. He'd become fully the *Mapiga* the rest of the camp knew him as. He could have beaten Macharia to death at any one of their dozen sessions yet he stopped short. There were no witnesses in the damp concrete-smelling room, but that was not what prevented him. It was, Macharia understood, much worse than that. For *Mapiga* this had turned into a personal affair, a measure of his own success or failure.

Earlier that day, when Macharia had been writhing naked on the chair, begging to die, *Mapiga* had chuckled politely, shaking his head as he meticulously used a nail to remove a piece of skin from his pliers.

'No, my friend,' he said, cleaning his thumb on the yellow cloth, 'I'm afraid this only ends when you stand freely before your so-called comrades declaring loudly and happily that you have forsaken your oath.'

Macharia spat out a mouthful of blood and flecks of gum.

'If you are torturing me,' he wheezed, 'then it cannot be said to be freely.'

Mapiga bent to straighten a sock, rising with a smile.

'Ah, very good. Admire a man who keeps a sense of humour. By the way, this will be our last meeting here.'

Macharia looked up warily. He was used to these games.

'Don't believe me? Can't say I blame you, but it happens to be true. Your name's on the transfer list. Put it there myself. You need a change of scene. Might provoke a change of attitude. We're sending you to a new camp called Umua. Reserved for hard nuts. Rather a lively regime.'

Mapiga laughed again.

'But it's very near your own neck of the woods, not far from that hospital you were in. Perhaps the smell of the forest or the chatter of the monkeys will tempt you into wanting to return to the outside world. We'll see.'

Macharia spat again, refusing to answer. Underneath, his heart soared. *Umua!* He hadn't realised there was a camp there but he knew the village, had passed through it every day on the walk to college. He was going home! Finally leaving this filthy, hot dust-bowl for the cool of the forest.

And he had kept faith with his oath.

Mapiga had lost.

Grogan was as good as his word. The next day Macharia found himself among a batch of prisoners marched at double-quick time to Manyani rail depot. Knowing he was on the list had helped him prepare, allowing just enough time to scoop up his notes and secrete them in his underwear. After being locked up for so long, with no access to the outside world, guards no longer did personal searches and Macharia thought it unlikely any would take place on the train.

The carriage was packed, but as they crept back across the dust plains of Coastal Province Macharia knew he would happily have endured worse because this time they were heading in the right direction.

There was just space to sit and Macharia dozed, waking at one point thinking they'd arrived, but when the doors opened it was only to push in another thirty men from another camp in the system. It became uncomfortable, standing room only. But at least the heat was diminishing as they climbed into the cool of the Highlands, and Macharia was reminded of when he'd made this journey by road, driving Porter and Johnny. Since his own travails he'd given them little thought but now he wondered where they'd got to. It was unsettling to think of them as belonging to the same white tribe as *Mapiga*. Then he chided himself – the three of them had endured much together. There would always be room in his heart for them.

There had never been a railway at Umua so the British must have built one especially for the Pipeline that ferried prisoners between the camps. When Macharia finally heard the locomotive squealing to a halt, he braced himself for the kind of assault he'd endured at Manyani.

At the siding four lorries were parked up, each containing a guard of ten warders, an NCO and two prisoner trusties. In the end there was little need for force; the prisoners emerging from the train were exhausted and clambered aboard with scant protest.

Macharia thought about the nature of the place they were coming to. If *Mapiga* believed it was a lively regime, it would surely be awful. The lorries left at fifteen-minute intervals, and when it was his turn Macharia was struck by an eerie quietness as they neared the camp gates. Then he saw why. At Umua there was not a funnel of guards but a small army, easily double the number of prisoners. The reception committee was menacingly silent. For the first time since leaving, Macharia felt alarmed.

Some of those waiting to greet them were prisoners, sporting new shorts and a kind of sailor's blouse. The uniform of the turned. In among them were several whites. Macharia's small group was again divided up and made to squat in the camp square in batches of ten men.

Scores of white guards and native police surrounded them and Macharia saw how well organised this was, presaging something truly bad. The silence was maintained as detainees and their new captors surveyed each other, the arrivals in filthy rags and matted hair, the warders and trusties in smartly pressed traitors' garments. Some of them held shears. He had heard about head-shaving – was this to be their fate here? The enemy were armed with nightsticks and cudgels. It was about to become intimate, and in a curious way Macharia was pleased.

Now, thought Macharia, now we will see what the other is made of. Let it come. Then amid the row of white officers nearest him Macharia saw a face he thought he'd left behind.

'*No!*' he cried out softly.

Mapiga was smiling again, sorrowful face gone, replaced with a countenance burning with zealous certainty. This was a face that knew something; that had a plan.

Macharia's old foe was well-prepared for the encounter, efficiency and decorum personified. The very model of a model colonial general. Shirt crisp, white, ironed; shorts creased and pressed for action;

315

long socks neatly suspended by elasticated garters. Metal toe caps on boots, polished and spotless. In his hand a long baton, which he tapped against his palm.

When he saw Macharia he smiled, before removing his glasses, thrusting out a face beaded with anticipation. He was ready to play.

The game was on.

Chapter 34

Umua Camp, March 1955

The detainees sat in ordered rows. Sixty prisoners, Johnny counted. Warders patrolled the back of the room, batons at the ready. The lecturer at the front was doing his best but it must have been hard to address a group of people who employed absolute silence as a weapon – the only one they had. Today it was unnervingly quiet. Apart from the drone of the lecturer listing the crimes of pre-colonial tribes, Johnny heard only the whirr of his camera and an old man who clicked every time he breathed in.

A small lizard darted among the rows, scampering around bony buttocks. Not a man looked down. A prisoner, still staring ahead, flicked his hand out. In one movement the lizard was swept into a giant black fist, the head pincered between thumb and forefinger before the still-twitching body was secreted in a pocket. All the while, the shaven heads faced forward. Discipline maintained, silent hatred projected at the white man at the front.

Johnny had seen what happened when a warder perceived any threat to that discipline. Instant retribution. At least three men to a prisoner – batons and fists cudgelling the victim into the ground; like vipers guarding a hole, sticking their fangs into anyone who came near.

In the month he'd been at Umua Johnny had seen so many terrible things he feared he might be becoming immune to the violence. There were certainly no signs of any of the panic attacks that used to assail him. He wasn't sure whether he should be pleased or worried. At least panic meant he was alive and reacting.

After he'd been introduced to the prison staff he'd become invisible, free to roam with his camera wherever he liked. Occasionally a guard would think it funny to grab the camera and pretend to film, but otherwise they didn't seem to notice him, or if they did, took no heed, administering beatings in front of him whenever they wanted.

Compelling force, Grogan had said. Nothing for liberal knickers to get into a twist about. Rough and tumble, that was all. Johnny needed to understand these men were hard-core. They'd dished it out in their time, so there was no need to feel sorry for them. They were ugly customers who could stop the treatment whenever they desired by confessing their crimes and recanting their oath. Thousands had already done it and the quicker these remnants did so as well, the sooner the Emergency could come to an end. Grogan recognised it might sound odd to outsiders, but the harder they beat them the better off they'd be in the long run. It was genuinely for their own good.

Johnny panned the camera across the backs of the sitting men, twisting the focus to move in for a close-up of a prisoner's head. He could just about see him in profile, eyes narrowed in false concentration. Fresh scabs on the back of his recently shorn head suggested he must be a new arrival. The man turned, aware of the scrutiny. There was no expression on his face but Johnny sensed the burning resentment.

His filming wouldn't be allowed to reflect that – or any of the daily acts of brutality that scarred the camp. The brief from Grogan was clear. A twenty-minute piece on the wonders of rehabilitation. He could go anywhere within the perimeter – never out of it – and film anything. Anything, that was, as long as it showed men learning to be new model citizens. Everything else would be left on the cutting-room floor, Grogan to see the final cut and no funny business. Graves was still around; could be summoned via the field telephone at any time. Johnny shouldn't even think of leaving because the master tracker would be only too pleased to hunt him down. Stay put, do the right thing and he could depart once the film was finished. If he didn't . . .

There'd been no need to finish that piece of advice. Johnny had learned his lesson. The news that Tansy was in Paris had destroyed any faith he had for anything, let alone courting danger on someone else's behalf. What was the point? At any time in his life when Johnny had felt inclined to engage with the world, the world had

318

reached back and hit him. All he wanted was to get this bullshit out of the way so he could wash himself clean of Umua, leaving Kenya and the memory of Tansy behind.

Tansy.

There were times when he wanted to kill her. And that was not a figure of speech. Anger welled up in him so strongly he sometimes imagined shooting her. Had she been acting the whole time? Everything pointed to it. He hadn't believed Grogan at the start – he'd say anything to separate them. But it had to be true: how could Grogan have possibly known about the money? The doctor? And then there was the odd way she'd behaved when she'd left for Mombasa. Her phrase haunted him. *'Nothing lasts for ever.'*

Apparently not. But it still didn't make sense. No matter how many times he went over their time together in Mombasa, he couldn't find any clues. Had he been too possessive? Too relaxed? Too what? *'Nothing lasts for ever.'* And yet she'd said she loved him. Maybe she had – at the time. Maybe not. His brain told him that what Grogan said must be true, but his heart pleaded to allow the possibility it might be otherwise.

He missed Porter. The Yorkshireman would have chided him for being a fool, told him to pull himself together. But he would have understood. When he thought of Porter it was the nearest he got to wanting to re-enter the world and if someone had presented him with a way of killing Graves he would have taken it. *Killing.* There he went again. Christ, he was becoming infected by this place.

Johnny moved outside and made his way to the hut where one of the Christian women from Moral Re-armament was addressing another group. Another series of lies for a film of lies. He didn't know what the subject was this time – abstinence, probably. Prim hypocrites loved the thrill of standing in front of a bunch of hard-faced prisoners, talking about sex. It was all a bloody sham. The reason Grogan wanted him to produce this particular piece of propaganda – *Rehabilitating the Peace* – was because a visit from the International Red Cross was due within the next fortnight. The need to have a film had been prompted by the fact that some prisoners' letters had successfully been smuggled out, provoking rumours among the international community of something rotten in the State of Kenya.

The visitors wouldn't be able to see everything in a single day so a short film displaying the finer points of rehab might swing it. Johnny wondered if watching the arrival of a new batch of prisoners would be on their agenda. Shaving heads, stripping inmates, shoving mud into their mouths until they passed out and beating mercilessly was not a poster for the British way of rehabilitation. There was only one other place it could possibly remind anyone of, a parallel so obvious it might even penetrate the apathy of the British public.

But out here neither the African warders nor any of the European officers appeared to believe a single thing they did was wrong. Johnny knew all about obeying orders, but the enthusiasm here ran much deeper than complying with someone else's direction. There was real belief in the project. When Johnny had arrived at Umua, warders were buzzing with pride at the fact the colonial authorities had seen what they were doing and approved. A whole squad of Colonial Office worthies from Nairobi, including the Attorney General and the Director of Prisons, had descended on the camp. According to gossip, they'd lined up to watch a batch of new arrivals getting it, and apart from one sensitive type who'd turned green and vomited, the visitors had broken out in a smattering of applause when the last man was dragged off. The Attorney General had praised Grogan and the senior staff. 'Well played.'

The game was on, Johnny kept hearing. *The game.* What kind of fucking game was it that shaved men's heads and kicked them into oblivion?

Johnny walked past his own quarters towards the shower block, nodding at the old trusty assigned to clean his rooms, and more importantly the man who polished and guarded the Triumph. Astonishingly Grogan had fetched the motorbike from Mombasa. 'Do this film for me and you can ride off into the sunset and put all this behind you.' Stick, stick, carrot, stick. Fucking bastard. Johnny might be numb to the violence but it didn't mean he couldn't hate.

It was noon, the hottest part of the day, and a group of prisoners were lined up for the camera, getting ready for a wash in preparation for the Red Cross visit. Normally the showers were reserved for staff, natives one side, whites the other. Now the signs had been removed and a line of men stood with towels, grinning in disbelief.

320

'Soap!' he heard one man say. 'Perhaps they want us to wash our skin white.'

A passing white officer heard too.

'Who said that? Who fucking said that?'

The line stopped shuffling forward and no one spoke. The officer walked up and down shoving his peaked cap into the prisoners' faces as he bellowed.

'Come on, out with it! Which parasitical abortion said that? If the man doesn't come forward in the next ten fucking seconds this whole line is on field punishment.'

The line kept a frigid silence. Johnny wanted to walk away but a small part of him still thought that if he was present the punishment wouldn't be as bad.

'Right. *Ten!* Nine, eight, *seven . . .* '

The count continued and there was not a sound. As the numbers fell Johnny saw the men straighten their backs and in that second he admired them, wishing he had their resolve.

'*Three*, two . . . '

Just before the officer could finish, the line rustled and a man stepped forward. Like many others he was recently shaved, with grey stubble emerging from his scalp. He limped forward slowly, one shoulder lower than the other.

He threw the soap on the ground.

'Now I can stay black,' he said in surprisingly good English, his voice calm and well-modulated.

The officer's face flushed.

'You little *cunt*. Who the fuck do *you* think you are?'

The man grinned and Johnny almost dropped the camera. There were several teeth missing, one eye was swollen and partially closed and his cheeks were sunken with malnutrition. The face could have belonged to any one of the prisoners here, but the grin was unmistakable.

Before he fell under the flailing fists and boots of the warders Johnny was certain the familiar lips were mouthing his name.

Chapter 35

Umua Camp, March 1955

It was hard to write now, his hands swollen and cracked. The knuckle on his middle finger had been dislocated months ago and stood askew from his fist like a broken tower. But Macharia was not broken. He was still alive! And now, after all the punishments, there was finally hope. The notes might find a way to the outside world despite everything. He should keep them short. His strength was fading. Cruel irony. Just when he needed it most, his body was faltering.

Johnny Seymour! He'd known him from the second he clapped eyes on the hunched *muzungu* behind the camera. The sight of him had been so extraordinary that at first Macharia thought he was seeing things. But the shock of white hair that still crowed into the air ensured it could only be one man.

But as Macharia had watched him, his joy turned to suspicion. What was he doing here? Any white man inside the camp gates was guilty unless proved otherwise and nothing Johnny was doing, traipsing round with his camera, offered any such proof. He could only be there by permission. The filming he did was surely part of some propaganda exercise.

In the following days Macharia had trailed him. The Johnny he'd known would not have been making propaganda. And sure enough, if you knew what to look for – and Macharia did – you could see that Johnny's lens did not always aim at the scene in front of him. He was listless, pointing the camera with no conviction, not even adjusting the focus. This was not film-making, but someone who wanted others to think it was film-making. His old friend's features were blank, as if someone had rubbed them off.

Macharia's heart soared. He had found his old friend and, more importantly, a possible ally in getting his material out. Not before time. The numbers in the camps were diminishing. God only knew what *Mapiga* had in store for those remaining.

Choosing his moment to make contact, Macharia had walked in front of him and attempted a smile. But Johnny had looked through him. The white man did not know him. Had Macharia truly become so different? He'd hurried back to his hut to borrow a mirror. What he saw shocked him. His hair was going white! His mouth was puckered and empty of teeth, his eyes sunken and hollow, the lines across his forehead more numerous than all the strands of barbed wire in the camp. No wonder Johnny didn't recognise him.

The scene outside the shower block had been painful and Macharia knew his body could not endure many more beatings of that severity. But it had been worth it to see Johnny's face.

Macharia had fashioned a similar hiding place for his notes in his new camp, and after he'd finished writing he secreted them in the latrines before making his way back to his hut. The other detainees were all attending one of the lectures in the hope of looking up a white missionary woman's skirt. He might lie down for a while out of the sun and rest his weary bones.

'*Macharia* – it *is* you!'

Johnny had been hiding behind the door and Macharia gasped when he saw the white man towering over him.

'Johnny Seymour. How are you, my friend?'

Johnny's face crumpled.

'My God, Macharia, how are *you* – what have they done to you?'

'Calm yourself, Johnny. We must be careful. There is great danger if you are discovered here.'

'But you need a doctor.'

'*Please*, Johnny. We must be careful. Guards are everywhere. Now we have found one another we must not lose each other. There is much to say and discuss. We can find out about each other's journey to this hateful place later. First there is something important that you can do for me. I need to tell you immediately, in case . . .'

Macharia left the sentence hanging, motioning for Johnny to be silent. Two warders were talking outside the hut. He reached for Johnny's shirt and pulled him gently down to his level to whisper in his ear. In short, rasping sentences he explained how he had been keeping an account of what was going on in the camps.

'The notes must get out, Johnny, and you're going to help.'

'Of course I will,' Johnny whispered, scarcely believing the beaten husk in front of him could be the same man. 'But you need to get out too. *Now.* You won't last much longer in this place. These people are fucking animals. Look, I can help you break out. I was thinking of how I'd escape if I were a prisoner, and I'm sure there's a way to get out on the death truck. If you hid in one of the compartments we could smuggle you out.'

'No, Johnny.'

'But there would not be too much risk. I've had a look at the seat compartments and seen how one of them might be hollowed out to fit a man inside.'

'*Johnny* – you must understand me now. I know you are trying to help and I appreciate it. But you have to recognise that my part in the struggle lies here – inside the wire. My true liberty will only come when I am released as a free man. Or go out on the death truck as part of its real cargo. Anything else, including escape, is a victory for Grogan.'

'Grogan? You've seen him then?'

Macharia spat.

'Oh yes. I've seen him.' He pointed to his face. 'He was responsible for this ... and for many other things you cannot see.'

'*He* did that? Why? My God, he's out of control. Out of his fucking mind.'

'Oh no, he knows precisely what he is doing. But Johnny, it is so good to see you I do not want to waste time talking of him.'

Macharia smiled, gathering his strength.

'Now listen, these notes are *important*. They are at the heart of it. It is vital you understand how crucial it is to tell the world what the British are really doing here.'

Johnny nodded.

'There is one more thing,' Macharia said.

'When you go round the camp filming, could you not also record what really goes on in here? Secretly film the reality? A reel of brutality stolen from under Grogan's nose! How sweet that would be. Think of it, Johnny – a continuation of our work. Getting footage of this place would be the best proof of all. We can be a team again. Imagine what Tansy and Porter will say when you tell them what you have achieved.'

Johnny winced.

'Porter is dead. And as for Tansy . . . ' His voice caught, and in the silence that followed Macharia feared Johnny was going to weep. Johnny cleared his throat and told Macharia how Tansy had found Porter's body whipped to death by Graves.

Macharia took the news calmly, nodding slowly. When he spoke his voice was hard.

'The Zebra will be dealt with in due course. Truly I am sorry about Porter. He was a good man and he died fighting for a righteous cause. But what are you saying about Tansy? She cannot have perished.'

'Tansy isn't dead, though she may as well be,' Johnny said. 'She ran away, Macharia. Just when it was becoming good between us, she fled. The minute she . . . '

Again Johnny choked but this time Macharia was mystified.

'*Run away?* I think she did not run very far. Everyone here knows the beautiful Tansy is at Kagamo hospital – we detainees are sent there. Grogan wants the last of us kept alive so we can recant before we die. Better value that way.'

Johnny looked at his friend as if he'd lost his senses.

'Did you say Tansy? *Near here?* You must be mistaken. She's living in Paris now.'

'No, I am very sure, Johnny. She has been tending the wounded from Umua these past months. After my beating at the shower block I am due there myself. Many of us have her to thank for our survival.'

Johnny said nothing, frozen in confusion. It could not be. And yet Macharia was smiling. Then as understanding slowly thawed, he began to pace the hut. *Grogan.*

'That fucking, *fucking* bastard. I'll kill him. The sack of lying, cowardly filth. I'll bloody cut his evil bloody throat.'

Macharia grinned at seeing the life rush back into his friend, flooding his features on a tide of profane rage. Then Johnny's features shifted as he began to grasp the immensity of it, hopping and whooping and clasping Macharia in joy.

'Be silent, my friend,' Macharia said urgently, lowering his voice. 'We must not be caught, now when there is hope.'

Johnny calmed down and the two men grinned at each other.

'Come,' Macharia said. 'Can we not sit? As you said – I am weak, but we have much to plan and I see no reason not to be comfortable.'

Chapter 36

Lake Nakuru, April 2008

Sam hated leaving anywhere, but particularly now.

The week at Ngare Lodge had been the happiest of her life. Not just because of what had happened within its walls – and not even because of its enchanted location. Something less definable. There was an air here, a spirit that imbued a sense of belonging. It might be foolish to think she belonged anywhere, let alone a lodge in the middle of the bush, but everything about the house had been just right: the watercolours on the wall, the old English books by the fire, the ancient knick-knacks stuffed away in cupboards – even a Scrabble board, her favourite game.

The lodge had been a blissful retreat from the world where she could draw breath and plan a future. And thanks to Kamau and the work she'd done on the witness statements, there was a genuine prospect of some kind of future. Whatever Dedan had up his sleeve, whatever surprise Africa would throw up next, she felt prepared. And she needed to be, for when she stepped away from here she'd be plunged back into a struggle that had become intensely personal.

The journey seemed to take longer than the two hours promised. Yet again they were heading to some mystery destination. She should have been angrier but the calm of the lodge was still with her, and they'd promised this was the last secret. It had better be.

Kamau wanted to sit in the back to catch up on some reading and an uncharacteristically perfunctory Dedan was keeping a stern eye on the road. If she didn't know better she would have described them as nervous. She stopped making an effort to talk, concentrating instead on the passing scenery. It was beautiful enough, but as the *matatu* hurtled further away from the lake she found it harder to appreciate, a fluttering fear of never returning that increased with every mile.

She turned her mind to the prospect of flying home to England. She'd talked it over with Kamau and they'd agreed that while it would be painful, a pause might be beneficial. Some distance was required, if not to reflect then to cool a little. If it got any hotter they would combust. And when she returned it would be on an equal footing. She needed a job, money – a status more than that of appendage. Hopefully that money would come from working for another type of legal mission altogether, one that genuinely had the interests of the reparation claimants at heart.

Home. That didn't seem like Lincolnshire any more, if it ever had. It would be so alien going back. It was after Easter, yet the ground there would still be hard, the trees scratch-brown and lifeless. As she gazed at an entire palette of jungle green collaging past the *matatu* window, she wondered how she could ever leave this behind. She understood now how old colonialists never thrived back in the motherland, shrivelling and dying of cold and sensory deprivation in their ugly Eastbourne bungalows. Once experienced, Africa didn't leave lightly.

Her thoughts drifted to what it must have been like here in the old days. There had to be more traffic now: the main artery they were driving on was busy, motorbikes laden with clinging passengers, open trucks with waving gangs of labourers overtaking on corners. But some things hadn't changed at all. At the roadside, bands of schoolgirls swayed and sang while women – never men, Sam noted – balanced firewood on their heads or lugged heavy plastic water containers. She wondered whether this timelessness was why she felt so comfortable in Kenya, hoping she wasn't succumbing to some kind of colonial nostalgia. The era when the white man's burden encompassed so much of the globe seemed to have acquired a romance, swathing the age in a sepia glow. Sam could never feel that. Her view of the past was drenched in what she'd read in the wretched testimony of so many Kenyans. For her this country was about much more. History, of course, personal family history too, but also the prospect of a future, one that had only come into focus when she met Kamau.

Dedan turned the *matatu* off the main road, heaving and bouncing down a rutted lane.

328

'Not long now,' Kamau said from the back, his head jiggling as he clung on to the strap. 'How are you feeling?'

'Fine,' said Sam. 'Although it would be altogether more grown up if for once you told me where we were going.'

The constant bouncing and jolting was wearing away the feeling of calm engendered by the lodge, and Sam had reached her limit with these childish games. Unless Kamau or Dedan showed her whatever they'd been concocting pretty bloody soon she'd make them turn round and drive straight to Nairobi. But she forced herself to keep her composure. It would be a shame to spoil the memories of such an idyllic week.

Finally, at the end of a particularly pitted road, the *matatu* stopped.

It was just another village, scattered houses, some with grass roofs, others with corrugated iron. Chickens and a dog, children with plaited hair or shaved heads. Corn and sisal. Then she noticed a well and, beyond the houses, a solar panel tower rearing over the banana trees. Electricity was rare in the countryside.

Sam was intrigued.

Dedan honked his horn and as always in Africa, the children responded first, crowding round the *matatu*, giggling and pressing their noses against the window.

All three of them got out of the van and stood stretching their backs and, in Dedan's case, shaking his cramped limbs one by one – much to the joy of the children, who took this as the start of a dance and pranced around clapping and singing.

'Well?' said Sam.

The '*Is this it?*' was unspoken, but heard well enough by the two men. Kamau looked anxious but Dedan simply laughed and picked up one of the noisier children who'd been singing.

'They are pleased to see you, Sam. They are chanting a welcome song. Welcoming you to the family.'

Kamau had gone on ahead, walking past the first huts to a larger one, whitewashed with a proper roof, that Sam hadn't noticed before. It stood slightly to one side, with a neat front garden where, instead of the usual maize, flowers grew in careful rows. He knocked before entering. Sam didn't know what she should do. The children had formed a ring around her, holding hands and singing. Ordinarily she might have joined in, but she had a sense of imminence so strong

329

she barely noticed them. Kamau emerged within seconds, carrying two chairs, which he placed in front of the house, arranging them so both were in the shade.

A figure moved in the doorway. A child, it looked like. Because the sun was shining directly in her eyes, Sam had to squint and she couldn't be sure. Kamau was pointing towards her, then he waved and she heard his voice shouting.

'Come, Sam, over here!'

The child figure next to Kamau moved to sit in the nearest chair, shading its eyes to watch her approach.

Sam gasped. It was not a child at all.

'Welcome, my friend,' Esther said. 'It is very good to see you again.'

Esther was carrying the grief for her dead husband well. Outwardly the African woman seemed happy enough, but she was not the vibrant, open woman Sam had previously met. There was a tightness about her mouth that made her smiles shorter and contracted her sentences.

Dedan and Kamau had made themselves scarce after fetching a small table on which some women from the village had placed a pot of tea and some biscuits – Huntley & Palmers, Sam noticed, very English. Where did they find those nowadays?

Sam had a thousand questions but she sipped the milky tea first, knowing it would be rude to plunge straight in. Esther was content to sit back and watch Sam nibble at the biscuits. By rights Sam ought to have been hungry – it was well past lunch – but instead of joyfully relaxing into the revelation Kamau had prepared for her she felt tense, a vague threat of something waiting for her in the margins.

When she put her tea down, half drunk, Esther clucked and shook her head.

'So – here we are, Sam. What do you think of this place?'

Sam was surprised, imagining Esther would be focusing on weightier matters.

'Well, it's very nice,' Sam said. 'It's very . . . homely?'

'Is it?'

'Well yes, I suppose so. I'm not sure I know it well enough to venture an opinion. What do you think?'

'I think,' Esther said, sweeping the village with her eyes, 'I think

330

it is a good place to die. There are fine people here. The soil is good. There are children who will grow and remember.'

'Is this where your husband is to be buried?'

'Joseph? No, dear me no. The poor soul is buried in Langata. We were lucky to get him in – it's nearly full, you know. No, I was thinking of someone else.'

'I didn't realise you'd already had the funeral.' Sam said. 'Wasn't there a post-mortem, then?'

'Good heavens no. Why do you ask that, child?'

Sam explained what she'd seen on the night of Esther's phone call. Watching the house being ransacked, the policeman trying to stop her; how his companion had turned out to be Pugh's driver; how she'd then run away, scared for her life but most of all fearing for Esther. As Sam described events from her perspective Esther became more animated, moving to the edge of her chair, her hands flying to her face when Sam came to the part about Mattingly's legs lying on the kitchen floor.

'Ah, my poor Sam – I did not realise you were there. I should have phoned you again. My call was to warn you that some of the authorities were going to be searching for those papers Joseph gave you.'

'But you also said you wanted to meet?'

'Yes I did – I remember now. That was before certain matters were resolved.'

'I'm afraid I'm rather lost. I thought you were in danger.'

'Well I was. So were you. I'd better explain.' Esther looked at her watch. 'We have about an hour, so I can try and fill you in on what I know.'

'That would be helpful,' Sam said, disappointed Esther had to leave so soon.

'What you have to understand,' Esther said, 'is that the divisions in my country which were sown during the fight for our independence have never truly gone away. And now, with the reparations claims, some of it is resurfacing. There are men and women who will benefit from the claims and others, particularly the ones who took the British side during the war, who may lose out. Although it is to a lesser extent and rarely visible, there is a struggle continuing among the current generation in many sections of society – including the police.

331

'Luckily for us, in this instance the policemen who are favourable to our position, the sons and grandsons of the uprising, have prevailed. The ones who are sympathetic with the current British regime have been marginalised; others have taken their place.'

Esther described how before the internal power battle had been won, some 'police elements' friendly to the British had been tipped off about the papers Joseph had given to Sam. They had obviously searched Sam's room first, and when they realised there were still papers missing they'd gone back to the source. Esther had returned from town to find men going through her things. Until Sam mentioned it she'd believed they were both policemen, but in light of what Sam said it made sense that one of them had been Pugh's man. Joseph was many things – courageous, loyal – but discreet he was not, particularly when he'd returned to the bottle. He must have let something slip at the High Commission, which would have explained the presence of Pugh's driver at the house.

'When I arrived Joseph was furious, shouting at them to get out. But he'd also been drinking. There was a terrible scene in the kitchen. It was awful, Sam. He was so angry. To be fair, they tried to calm him, but he kept trying to push them out of the house. That's when the big man pushed back. Joseph clutched his chest and fell down. He died immediately – the life just went out of him. One second burning angrily, the next – nothing. He was gone. But I wouldn't believe it and ran for his heart pills upstairs. I couldn't find them – the men had thrown everything everywhere. That's when I thought they might be coming for you next so I rang you but they caught me. They took my phone and locked me in my room while they continued their search. I was up there for hours. It was an awful time, knowing Joseph was lying downstairs, that he was . . . They wouldn't let me out, Sam. I must have been up there when you came in – I heard them speaking to someone but I didn't know it was you!'

Esther's voice caught and she dabbed her eyes.

'Oh Sam, he was a good man.'

'I'm so sorry,' Sam said. 'He was such a brave man too.'

Esther smiled.

'Yes, he was. He was very ill, you know. He didn't have long as it was. His heart was so bad towards the end the doctors told him he had only a few weeks at best, so perhaps it was a good way to go – fighting for a cause he believed in.'

Sam felt immeasurably sad. All the good ones dead. And what was her generation doing about it? Most of them didn't even know about this, or any other struggle for that matter. And if they did know they didn't care, or worse, were encouraged by men like Pugh to suppress it. She repeated the thought out loud.

'*All the good ones dead.*'

Esther dried her eyes and looked at Sam in surprise.

'That is not quite true though, is it, Sam?'

'I'm afraid it is.'

'They really did not tell you then? I wondered why you were not mentioning it.'

'Mention what? Who was meant to tell me?'

'Your lovely friends – Kamau and Dedan. He is a fine boy, by the way, your Kamau. You have chosen well.'

'Thank you,' Sam said, slightly put out that Kamau had already told Esther. It seemed as if they'd all been in constant, secret touch since they'd left Nairobi.

Esther stood and breathed deeply through her nose.

'They have kept their word too. They would have made good soldiers in the time of the oaths. But your wait has been long enough. I can see it is taking its toll. Stay here, Sam – just two minutes more and you will have all the answers you have ever wanted.'

Sam was puzzled. What more was there to explain? She watched Esther walk quietly into the house, closing the door behind her.

Kamau was with Dedan at the *matatu*, and when he saw Sam was alone he jogged over.

'How is it going?' he asked quickly, strangely on edge.

'Don't worry, it's fine,' Sam said, kissing him on the cheek. 'It's wonderful to see Esther's OK. It was fantastic of you to have found her for me. Thank you so much. How did you find her?'

'But I did no such thing,' Kamau said, frowning. 'It was she who found you – who sent Dedan. While you were at Grogan's I was here.'

'*Sorry?*'

'*Ah*, no, she hasn't told you then?'

'Told me what?' Sam felt a pressure inside her temples. Kamau had taken a step back.

'What's going on?' Sam could hear her voice rising in panic. 'I can't bear it. Kamau, just tell me. *Please!*'

Kamau was hovering on the edge of a decision, a small boy not knowing if he should tell tales.

'*Well?*'

Kamau looked over Sam's shoulder at the house, his eyes sick with apprehension.

Sam turned and saw Esther standing in the doorway, supporting a man who was limping slowly forward leaning heavily on a walking stick, his other arm linked through Esther's. He blinked as he came into the light. His face was tanned deep mahogany but it was a white man's face. It was lined and creased, his skin mottled and the hair wispy and thin. Old.

But not the eyes.

The eyes were blue, royal blue, fierce.

Alive.

They scoured Sam's face like a bladed tool, carving hidden truths. Sam felt her knees buckling; only Kamau's arm round her waist kept her upright.

My God. It couldn't be.

Ghosts.

But this one alive.

'Sam,' he said, the voice quiet but familiar, 'I've been waiting so long for this moment.'

Johnny Seymour smiled at his granddaughter.

Chapter 37

Kagamo Hospital, April 1955

Tansy knew she shouldn't be spending so much time on one patient. The volunteer nurses from Nairobi who now staffed the hospital were a different breed: young and ultra-loyal to McGregor, they were in it for the cause and wouldn't hesitate to report her. Quite what that cause was, Tansy couldn't work out. Perhaps working in a field hospital on the front line against Mau Mau seemed glamorous to the generation who'd missed the last war. It was a poor comparison. There were no fair-haired boys here to nurse back to health or flirt with, only prisoners from Umua, battered and broken. And as soon as they mended them, more arrived.

Two lorries came almost every day now. One with the dead, one with the barely alive. The wounded prisoners were offloaded and replaced with corpses from the hospital mortuary. She'd never given any thought to where the death trucks went next until a driver had cosied up to her during a cigarette break. There was a spot, he said, about five miles into the bush, where the bodies were dumped. Dozens, perhaps hundreds, of corpses were left there. A work gang from the camp was driven out to dig vast pits. Bodies all over the place. She should see the flies. Hyenas and pi-dogs everywhere. It was all they could do to keep the bastards away from the trucks. And the smell! Pardon his French but it was bloody awful.

When she saw him among the wounded with his parcel paper-thin skin and closed eyes she thought he should have been on the other truck. She certainly hadn't recognised him, couldn't associate the grey-skulled cadaver with the fit young man she'd known. It was only when he opened one eye, the familiar lighthouse smile beaming from him, that she knew.

'*Macharia!* It's you!'

'*Shhhh.*' He'd put a finger to his lips, a bruised eyelid slowly closing and opening again in a painful wink.

From that moment on Tansy devoted as much time to her new patient as possible. Ignoring mistrustful glances from the nurses, she did everything in her power to tend him back to health, knowing she was only meant to keep patients for a fortnight. Prisoners were then transferred back to Umua, repaired or not. It was cruel and Tansy hated it.

In the first days few words passed between them. Macharia was too weak and there were too many suspicious eyes. It was highly unusual for a European nurse to spend much time with an individual African patient but Tansy paid no heed to protocol, squeezing in a few minutes with him every day, checking what the orderlies had done for him, sometimes substituting an ineffective antibiotic or fungicide with the more expensive ones reserved for Europeans. She also smuggled in morsels of food. Prisoners in the hospital received one meal a day but Tansy ensured Macharia always had extra fruit and some buttered bread, stashed away from her own breakfast.

A week later she was gratified to see he was, if not sitting up, then at least taking notice. His wounds were grievous and so numerous it was a miracle he hadn't died months ago. His mouth was a mess – teeth had been pulled and the gums were pulpy and infected; there were whip marks and welts all over his back and stomach; blue and purple bruises on his lower back and buttocks. When she examined them he never complained, but he refused to let her tend his groin. Tansy knew that like so many of the prisoners he had sustained terrible injuries there, but she did not want to humiliate him. Instead she slipped him a barbiturate one night and ordered the male nurse orderlies to patch him up.

When he came to the next day, he smiled ruefully.

'Thank you,' he said. 'I know what you have done and what you have not done, and I appreciate it.'

'I don't need thanks. That's what I'm here to do.'

'But why exactly are you here?' Macharia asked, unable to stop a sly smile. 'In your state.'

'What do you mean – my state?'

Macharia laughed quietly.

'Have you been tending us men for so long you do not know what a woman with child looks like?'

Tansy blushed. Even with her nurse's whites on the swelling of her belly was obvious, pressing against the starched fabric. Everyone at the hospital knew she was pregnant. True to English form no one said anything, although she could see McGregor gearing himself up. She'd let him think it was Grogan's to keep him off her back. But it was only a matter of time before her situation became indelicate and the doctor would be obliged to step in.

'Is it that obvious?' she asked.

'Yes, and you look magnificent. Johnny will be very happy.'

Tansy stiffened.

'*Johnny?*'

She was trying very hard not to think about him, going mad with the unfairness of it. She had never, not for one single moment, stopped loving him. She looked at Macharia. He seemed so cheery at the mention of Johnny's name. But then he couldn't have known the circumstances of their parting.

'Yes,' Macharia said, pointing his finger at her. '*Johnny.* Your special friend, I believe. In Mombasa?'

Tansy was bent over the bed, plumping a pillow behind Macharia's head. She stopped, jerking her head sideways.

'Mombasa! How did you know we were there? We didn't tell anyone. Only Grogan and Graves knew. How on earth did you find out?'

'Johnny told me. He believed you were in France. I don't know where you think he is, but he's at Umua, Tansy.'

'You've seen Johnny? Not at Lodwar? He's here?'

'Very much so. And when I told him you were at the hospital he was just as surprised as you.'

Tansy sat down quickly on the side of the bed, her head whirring. Had he really not known where she was? There were a thousand questions and dozens came to mind at once. She turned to Macharia and began to list them, one after the other.

'Hey,' he said softly, 'you are worse than the interrogators. At least they give you a chance to answer.'

She laughed and wiped her eyes, squeezing Macharia's hand so hard he winced.

'I'm sorry,' she said. 'But you don't know what that means to me. Now please – you have to tell me everything.'

Tansy was determined to extract every last bit of information. How long had Johnny been at the camp? What he was doing there? How was Grogan treating him? How did he look? Was he eating, was he thin? And if he knew she was here why hadn't he visited? Was it that bloody difficult?

Macharia answered as best he could and as his words swirled through Tansy's brain she felt the deep heat of shame, not bearing to imagine what Johnny must have thought when he'd seen she was gone. Now she had to see him. He was so near. But how? Grogan would never allow it.

More tears pricked at her eyes and she felt Macharia's bony hand on her forearm.

'Please, Tansy, do not worry. Johnny wants to see you.'

'He does? He really does?'

'Yes, of course he does.' He gestured to her swollen belly. 'And I'm sure it will be even more now.'

Tansy blew her nose, laughing and crying at the same time.

'Now listen, this is serious,' Macharia said. 'Johnny and I have given the matter much thought. And it all revolves around the abomination Graves. Once that piece is removed from the board it will make everyone's life better. Not just you and Johnny. He is a constant visitor to the camp with his whip, performing Grogan's dirty work – not that Grogan is above that himself, as I know too well. The truth is that neither of them deserves to live. But Grogan is too well protected.'

Tansy looked at him sharply. Yet she felt nothing. Only a ferocious desire to be with Johnny again. Macharia paused, disturbed by her expression, misreading it.

'I'm sorry, but these things have to be said. You do understand what we are talking about here? More importantly, that you are going to have to help? We have a plan we cannot execute without your assistance. You need to understand this with great clarity. We cannot proceed without it.'

Tansy didn't care. She ought to, but she did not. She had nursed so many from the camps bearing Graves's marks that she thought of him as a kind of disease. And diseases needed to be eradicated. She looked Macharia in the eye for long seconds before nodding assent. Any qualms had died the moment she realised Grogan had lied to drag her away from Johnny and back to the hospital.

'Good. Now listen: you must find a way to go to Nairobi. There is a man who works in a shoe shop. Tell him you have seen me.' Macharia handed Tansy a tiny slip of paper. 'Give him my message and it will happen. Word will reach you informing you what to do next. This is the address. Do you have a pencil? Good, now, dry your eyes and write it down.'

When Tansy had finished she fetched a separate piece of paper, scribbling quickly on both sides.

'This is for Johnny,' she said. 'It's important. Please see that he reads it. There are things he still doesn't know about how – and why – I had to leave him. He must understand before he agrees to go any further.'

Macharia took the note and folded it small.

'I will make sure he gets it,' he said, smiling sadly. 'But Tansy, surely you must understand that whatever the circumstances of what passed between you, or whatever Grogan made you both believe, the essentials have always been true.

'And even if they weren't, the life you carry changes everything.'

Tansy hung her head. The rebuke was just and it increased her shame.

She should have known; should have been braver by far.

Chapter 38

Nairobi, May 1955

The shoe shop looked like all the other stalls along Whitehouse Road, a busy bustle of boxes and baskets bursting with goods. Its street shelves, though apparently untended, were being watched through sleepy eyes by a turbaned man hidden inside the shade of the whitewashed brick building behind. Although there was a profusion of evidence as to what the shop sold, leather slippers and sandals poking out from every nook, Tansy must have walked past a dozen times, failing to spot the sign that said *Boots and Shoe Maker: India Bazaar. Proprietor: Vee-jay Singh.*

Ordinarily Tansy would have been delighted at the prospect of spending a day at the Indian Bazaar, shopping and tasting spices. Today she longed for this meeting to be over so she could catch the mission bus straight back to the hospital. Ever since she'd heard Johnny was at Umua she'd been in a funk, a mixture of excitement at the prospect of seeing him again and fear that something else awful was going to prevent it. But Macharia had been firm. They would only be able to meet after she'd been to Nairobi to see Singh. She was not to try to contact him beforehand. Johnny was a virtual prisoner at the camp and any move by her to visit would be certain to alert Grogan.

Tansy was afraid. The capital city was overflowing with military and police. The war was all but over, but still the Emergency ploughed on. She couldn't rid herself of the feeling that if she was aware that Vee-jay Singh, proprietor, was a Mau Mau spy then every uniformed white man in Nairobi doffing his cap or raking her with his eyes must have known as well.

Opposite the shoe shop, Tansy played for time, rummaging in her bag as if looking for something. No one suspicious had walked along the street for the last five minutes. It was now or never. She took out an old bus ticket and pretended to read it for the benefit of anyone who might be watching. Just an ordinary woman out shopping, consulting a list. She crossed the road and stood toying with a bundle of sandals. The man sitting in the shade made no move to help and she took a pair of shoes over to him.

Was he Mr Singh? No response. She repeated the question and the man's drowsy eyes flicked briefly to life.

'No, sorry, memsahib. Not here. Wrong shop.'

'But I was given the name by a friend. He was very certain that Mr Singh would want to see me.'

The Sikh's expression did not change but he rose slowly, looking up and down the street. Without a word he began to gather up shoes, shouting something at a boy sitting playing with a stick on the pavement. The boy leapt to his feet and started carrying the merchandise inside.

'Sorry, Mrs. Closing now. Wrong place, wrong man.'

'But I was sent by Macharia. You must know him. I've come a very long way to see him.'

The man's face hardened.

'You go now. Wrong place. Never heard of your friend. *Go.*'

Tansy looked in her bag.

'Look!' she said, producing a crumpled piece of paper. 'Here: it says Vee-jay Singh. It is the right place. Please, you have to help.'

But it was too late. The man had scuttled into the depths of the building and she heard doors slamming and locks turning. Where a few seconds ago a busy stall spilled onto the street, now there was a neat empty space. Not a shoe remained.

For a moment she contemplated going after him but was aware of other stall-holders looking at her. A white woman running after a shopkeeper. It was not the place to make a fuss.

Angrily she threw the paper with the address on it into the gutter and began to retrace her steps back towards the centre of town. Turning past the *mandazi* sellers on Jan Smuts Avenue, heading towards the Law Courts, she had never felt so low. For days she'd been preparing herself for the encounter, certain it would be the first step towards a reunion with Johnny. Now this. What should she do? Go back again this evening? No, surely that would be too dangerous.

341

No one came to this part of town at night, certainly not a white woman on her own.

Tansy felt tears prickling. God, what a failure. A black Ford Pilot glided past and she was conscious of a passenger staring out at her. She dabbed at her eyes with a handkerchief and marched determinedly on. She couldn't bear it if some well-wisher stopped to ask if she was all right. She would probably break down there and then. The Ford halted at the junction and she had the impression that the people inside were wondering whether to come back and see if she was OK.

She'd made it to Government Road when she felt a tug on her sleeve. She jerked her arm away, worried someone was trying to pick her pocket, and turned to confront the assailant. It was the young boy she'd seen packing up Singh's shop.

The boy walked past, quickly looking over his shoulder, beckoning her to follow.

'This way please, Mrs. Quickly please. Following me now.'

Tansy's heart leapt. Of course! Vee-jay Singh had known what she wanted after all. It *was* the right place. The boy was leading her to somewhere more private. She was almost running as he guided her through the bus station and out the other side, past Reata Road.

She was concentrating so hard on following the boy, weaving in and out of the pedestrians, that she didn't notice the same Ford Pilot's long chassis keeping pace, fifty feet or so behind, never stopping, never accelerating. Had Tansy looked behind even once she might have seen a man with his trilby pushed back from his forehead, leaning out of the window pointing a camera at her, one a surveillance expert would immediately have recognised as a state-of-the-art long-lensed Canon Rangefinder.

Chapter 39

Memorandum

Status: Secret. Eyes Only
To: Grogan Littleboy, Assistant Head of Rehabilitation,
Umua Camp.
From: D. Elstein, Superintendent, Special Branch, Nairobi.
Subject: <u>Anastasia Thompson</u>
Date: May 22nd 1955

We have been made aware of your interest in the subject
ANASTASIA 'TANSY' THOMPSON and requested to provide you
with full cooperation.

The subject came to our attention during a surveillance
operation at WHITEHOUSE ROAD, NAIROBI. The premises,
ostensibly a shoe shop owned by a VEE-JAY SINGH, is
a 'post-office' for Mau Mau operatives. We have been
intercepting 'mail' and other covert communications for
the past seven months and operating a full surveillance
unit for the last five.

Anyone who enters the premises has been subject to
routine further surveillance, whether known to us or not.
The subject whom we subsequently identified as THOMPSON
was seen at 4.27pm on May 21st speaking with the man
known as SINGH. SINGH closed his shop immediately and
THOMPSON set off towards the Law Courts. THOMPSON threw
a piece of paper onto the street. When retrieved later,
the paper gave the name of SINGH and the address of the
shop. There was no further writing on the paper but the
content indicates clearly the subject did not arrive at
the premises by accident.

AANAND SINGH, son of VEE-JAY SINGH, thought to be aged 12, apprehended THOMPSON and led her to another premises at the LATEMA ROAD end of BHORA ROAD. These premises, a domestic dwelling, were unknown to us. VEE-JAY SINGH was observed entering the premises by a back entrance some 23 minutes later.

THOMPSON stayed at the premises for 44 minutes in total. On exiting she returned to the BUS STATION where she waited 34 minutes before boarding a mission bus towards UMUA.

We enclose copies of contemporaneous surveillance photographs which shows THOMPSON speaking to SINGH, being escorted to the BHORA ROAD premises, entering the premises, leaving the premises, waiting at the BUS STATION and boarding the bus.

Contact ceased at 7.02pm.

We understand that THOMPSON works as a nurse at the KAGAMO MISSION HOSPITAL, UMUA. A surveillance unit has already been despatched to the hospital and will continue a watching brief on THOMPSON.

In light of the request to grant you access to the inquiry, we are happy to share whatever intelligence ensues and would request a reciprocal exchange on anything that may help in our enquiries.

Chapter 40

Umua Camp, June 1955

A message from Nairobi central command arrived at Macharia's door via a circuitous and not always safe route. A comrade from the capital passed it to the hawker outside the mission hospital who sold fruit to the nurses. A certain melon marked with a tiny ochre cross concealed a small section of banana leaf wrapping the note containing the instructions. Once inside the hospital, the line of communication ran from Nurse Orderly Wambui, who ate the melon and read the instructions, to her cousin Kamenyi, who emptied the bins and was friendly with Warder Muraya Makundi. He accompanied the lorries to and from the camp and appreciated the cash he received when he delivered the final verbal message to Macharia after evening roll call.

Johnny had no idea of this secret postal service, did not need to know, but when he picked up a signal from Macharia via the upturned stone at the corner of the latrines, that Nairobi had decided the time had come, he did pause to marvel at the apparent efficiency of Mau Mau and wonder at the breath-taking arrogance of the British who believed they could suppress an entire country with only a few thousand troops and collaborators.

It was dangerous for Macharia and Johnny to speak openly, so when the stones indicated something needed to be said they met at night behind Macharia's hut. Long ago a tunnel had been dug from the sleeping quarters into the small sliver of space between the hut and the first of the three barbed-wire fences. If the two men crouched, their silhouettes were hidden, and it was far enough away from the guard tower for their whispers not to be heard. To be found outside a hut at night was a caning offence and Macharia was so weak he doubted he would survive a handful of blows, let alone the statutory twelve. For that reason Johnny sometimes dealt with an intermediary, but tonight Macharia had crawled out of the hole himself.

'I see you, Johnny.'

'I see you, Macharia.'

In the half-light, Johnny was still shocked at how much his friend had deteriorated despite his visit to the hospital. He was so thin, the flesh a translucent brown membrane stretched tautly over his face. Macharia too felt much older. It took longer to coax his limbs into a sitting position, every movement causing a grimace of pain. He saw Johnny watching him.

'Do not concern yourself about me. I have chosen this path and the fact I am still alive and talking means it is working – for now at least.' He attempted a smile, revealing the missing teeth and bruised lips.

'Let us hurry and talk about your journey,' Macharia said. 'We do not have much time.'

The plan was to stow Johnny underneath the exterior seat on one of the Bedford lorries tonight. The death truck had had its seats ripped out to make space for corpses, but the other vehicle, ferrying wounded detainees to the hospital, still had one left. It was a crude affair, not more than an oblong metal box welded to the rear floor of the Bedford, big enough to seat four men and just large enough to store a small man inside. Johnny was not small, but if he lay in the foetal position he should be OK. Air holes had been bored and a couple of blankets folded on the floor would provide some padding. The warder who rode in the back of the truck had been bribed to look the other way. There were occasional inspections of vehicles leaving Umua, and if one took place when Johnny was aboard they were in serious trouble. Once free of the camp it would be easier.

The journey would be uncomfortable, but it only took half an hour. At least they'd managed to change the route. Usually the trucks visited the hospital first, to offload the wounded before going on to the grave site, but the transport officer had been persuaded that some of the corpses were in such a state of disintegration they needed to be buried as soon as possible. Accordingly, no wounded would be on this trip, just a couple of guards and a work gang to bury the dead.

Johnny couldn't have cared less. As long as it got him to see Tansy, he didn't mind if he travelled in a cement mixer full of faeces. After Macharia brought back Tansy's letter he'd been so excited he hadn't slept properly for days. *Pregnant*. She was going to have a baby. A child. He was going to be a father! He had to keep saying it to believe it.

Who cared that she'd taken some pocket money off Grogan in Mombasa. Learning how Grogan had lied and threatened her changed everything. She'd acted to protect him. Grogan was a professional dissembler and they'd both fallen for it, though it was true that the danger from Graves was real enough. Which is why they had to take this next step.

Tentatively, but with increasing excitement, Johnny allowed himself to think about what their future might hold. They'd have to be ultra-cautious. Just when the prize was at its nearest the danger would be at its worst. After meeting Tansy his shackles to Umua would be broken, but he'd reluctantly concluded he'd need to return to the camp one last time. If he disappeared it would cause panic among the authorities and the first place Grogan would look for him would be the hospital. Tansy had to be gone by then and they could not rely on hitching lifts. They would need their own transport and he had just the vehicle in mind. If he was obliged to go back to Umua at all, logic dictated he may as well stay an extra day so he could do the right thing and alert the Red Cross to the real nature of the camps. Whatever Macharia's misgivings, Johnny felt he had to go through the correct channels at least once.

That hadn't stopped him preparing for his final escape, surreptitiously siphoning petrol from the trucks while they were undergoing maintenance at the camp's makeshift garage. The Triumph was now full and he was confident it could outrun any vehicle in Kenya. Once he'd fetched Tansy they would travel by night. Mombasa was less than five hours away. They'd get to the beach house by dawn, stopping there to rest for a couple of hours before continuing on to Tanganyika. They stood a better chance of getting out of Africa via another country and in Dar-es-Salaam they could pick up the Union-Castle round-Africa mail steamer, which would take them all the way to Cape Town. From there they could lie low before getting another ship to Southampton. Home before Christmas, and as

347

Tansy had reminded him, didn't a ship's captain have the power to marry? He couldn't wait to see his own parents' faces when he turned up with a bride in the family way.

He felt Macharia tugging at his sleeve.

'Hey, Johnny. Please concentrate. We need to go over the details once more. I am not strong and there may not be many further opportunities to talk.'

'Sorry, I was miles away.'

Macharia's voice was barely a whisper and Johnny saw the strain on him. He suddenly felt guilty. Planning the escape had been a huge effort and the Kenyan needed all his strength just to stay alive.

After another twenty minutes of discussing every aspect of the plan, Macharia finally eased his back with a stretch, stifling a small groan.

'Very well,' he said. 'Now you know the theory, let us hope the practice is as easy. It is late and you'd better get going. I wish you every luck, my friend. Remember to give Tansy my best wishes and tell her she had better teach your child the real history of this land or I will come back and haunt you all.'

Johnny smiled sadly and looked at his watch. The glowing hands showed twenty past three. Departure was at five. He extended his hand to shake Macharia's but the other man was tottering uncertainly to his feet and the gesture turned into a helping hand. Macharia grasped it as he steadied himself and the two men looked at each other in the darkness, neither sure of their survival beyond the next twenty-four hours, neither willing to show they knew.

Chapter 41

Umua Camp, June 1955

There was no dawn inspection and the two lorries pulled out of Umua without mishap.

The only unusual aspect was that the light in Grogan Littleboy's hut was on, and if someone had looked his way they might have spotted him standing at his window watching the lorries leave. Johnny was unaware, more concerned with his own discomfort. Within five minutes of setting off he was squirming with incipient cramp and claustrophobia. His knees were bunched up by his chest and his hip had found a gap in the blankets, jarring painfully against the metal floor every time the Bedford bumped over a rut. It wasn't made any easier by a rod of metal prodding into his back. He'd stolen the pistol from the guards' room. He didn't know if he'd need it or if he'd ever be able to use it if he did, but with Tansy pregnant everything had changed.

The Bedford finally stopped and from inside his metal tomb he could hear guards lead the work gang off, then heading to unload the corpses from the other lorry. He waited for five minutes before unscrewing the bolts that shut him in. He stretched out cramped limbs and eased himself upright. It was still early but the sun shone brightly, making him blink rapidly. They were in a field, trees surrounding them on two sides. The other lorry had parked near the forest edge, about five hundred yards away to his right. The gang's voices could be heard in the distance but otherwise there was no one else about. He grinned. According to the plan, Tansy should have arrived before him.

Keeping out of sight of the prisoners, Johnny headed for the trees opposite, squatting at the base of a palm. If an army patrol came by it would be impossible to explain what he was doing there.

The sun rose higher and an hour passed. The workers were singing, using the rhythms to help dig. It was unbearable. She should be here by now. Where was she? Unable to stay in one spot any longer he crept towards the work gang. From a safe distance he watched the men, crude cloth masks tied to their faces, unloading the corpses. Four men to a body, one on each limb, they manhandled them off the back of the truck and dumped them at the edge of a giant ditch. The bodies were bloated and discoloured, and when they landed there was a flat noise of bursting. One corpse landed on its stomach and the belly was so distended it looked as if it were on all fours. Occasionally a foul waft would come Johnny's way and he had to bite the inside of his cheek not to gag. When all the cadavers were stacked messily alongside the hole, the men picked up wooden poles and began levering them in, chanting as they did so. He breathed through his mouth, counting twenty-three bodies. He wished he had his camera with him.

The corpses landed in the ditch with a squelching thud, arms and legs at impossible angles. He wanted to look away but remembered Macharia's words and forced himself to bear witness. The last time he'd seen a pile of dead bodies, in a different camp, he'd gone to pieces. That wouldn't happen now. Must not.

Sickened, he crept back to his old position. Tansy was still nowhere to be seen. What if she had the wrong day? What if she'd been captured? Johnny was drenched with anxiety and fear. Then he heard it, a noise from the forest. Someone was coming. More than one person. He stood quickly and cocked an ear. He couldn't decide whether to hide or make himself more visible. A hint of panic stirred in his stomach, the old vulnerability still lurking. For God's sake. He made up his mind. There was little point in concealing himself at this stage.

'Tansy?'

Nothing. He repeated it, louder: *'Tansy!'*

'Joh—'

Johnny took the revolver out of his pocket, peering into the darkness between the trees.

'Tansy! Is that you?'

Still nothing.

'Tansy!' he shouted. 'Where are you? Answer me. *Tansy!'*

There was a rustle of leaves and suddenly, out of the forest stepped Tansy.

She was not alone.

He raised his pistol.

Behind her was a man with one hand across her mouth, the other holding a panga, its point jutting into the side of her distended stomach. Tansy's eyes were wide with alarm and she was shaking her head from side to side. A moan escaped from between the man's fingers and he yanked her head backwards.

'Shut your mouth. Any more and I'll cut your fucking tongue out.'

Until that point Johnny hadn't been sure.

Graves.

'Listen. This is how it's going to work,' the Zebra said, still holding Tansy tightly against him, the blade not moving an inch from her stomach. 'It's you I want, not your bitch, so I want you to walk over here nice and quietly and we'll settle this sensibly. Give the gun to my man, handle first, and start walking. Any trouble and I'll ...'

He jabbed the blade, making Tansy squeal with pain. A small patch of blood stained the side of her shirt.

Johnny took half a step forward but stopped. He *had* to control the venomous rage rising; lethal to make the wrong move now.

'OK, OK,' he said. 'I'll come. Just let her go.'

'Do I look fucking stupid? Just hand over the weapon and come here. Right now. You're not in a position to bargain.'

There was a movement to one side of Graves and from behind him emerged one of his soldiers, a reeking, matted counter-gang boy. As he walked forward, shotgun aimed at Johnny, the rest of the gang stepped forward, perhaps ten more of them swaggering into the sunlight. Johnny and Tansy didn't have a chance. The adrenalin surge melted into nothing. Johnny was crushed, helpless. No hope.

He turned the revolver grip first and slowly gave it to the man. Graves took his hand away from Tansy's mouth and pushed her away, lowering the panga to receive the pistol.

Tansy rushed to Johnny's side and he held her tight, whispering stupidly it would be OK, that everything would be OK. If they were going to die, he thought, at least they would be together. It was strangely consoling and the tension and anger leached away, the moment elongating and slowing as if they were drowning, the imminence of death granting a brief final respite. Tansy hugged him fiercely, her head on his chest, eyes closed, inhaling his scent for the last time.

Having done his duty by transferring the pistol, the soldier turned back towards the couple, raising his shotgun. The barrel had been sawn off three-quarters of the way up the length. At this short distance, Johnny estimated, one shell would put them both down, a second would finish them off. It would be quick. He stared into the bloodshot eyes of the soldier, holding Tansy tight against him.

The soldier's face cracked into a lopsided grin.

Then he winked.

And Johnny had to blink several times to take it in because he thought he was hallucinating. But it was true: he had winked. He knew that because the man then winked at him again.

Simultaneously, the fake Mau Mau soldier swivelled round so fast his locks flew into an arc behind him. The shotgun detonated with two ear-splitting explosions, one after the other as if two bombs had burst.

At point-blank range the damage was massive. Graves's body was blown violently back against a tree. Half his head disappeared in a pink mist while the second blast ripped open his chest. Smoke from the shotgun curled from the empty barrels and the sourness of burnt cordite snagged the air. Tansy sagged in Johnny's arms and he laid her gently on the ground. The soldier was casually refilling his shotgun. He looked up at Johnny and grinned.

'Please send my greetings to Macharia and tell him the job was done quickly and well.'

Johnny had thought he was beyond further shock.

'*Macharia?* I don't understand – he knew?'

The man laughed, hefting the shotgun onto his shoulder.

'Of course, my friend. A great lion needs more than one goat to be lured. Macharia said you would be surprised! He told me to inform you that not everything is black and white. What is turned can turn again. Yes, I like that.'

He pivoted to his men, issuing curt commands. Two of them sprang forward and began dragging Graves by the heels towards the ditch where the dead from the camp were being buried.

'Make sure your woman is ready in twenty minutes. My men will escort her back to the hospital. Say what you need to her quickly. When you get back to Umua tell Macharia the debt is paid. He will understand. Go well, Johnny Seymour.'

He made a gesture to the other soldiers and with a nod to Johnny turned towards the forest. As one, the band melted into the trees, just a faint rustle and a trail of blood to show they'd been there at all.

Tansy was sitting propped against a tree trunk, her face in her hands.

Johnny quickly examined her cut, breathing hard. But as far as he could tell, the wound was superficial.

'Come on,' he said. 'Let's get back to the road. Your lift back to the hospital will be here in a minute.'

She rose slowly, but when she was on her feet she threw off his arm, marching quickly away, crying. She let the tears run down her face without bothering to wipe them away, hands protectively on her belly.

'Did you know, Johnny?' she shouted. 'Goats – you heard him. *We were tethered bloody animals!*'

Johnny raised his hands, palms up.

'Of course I didn't know.'

'What kind of a start is this? It's wrong, Johnny. *Wrong.* I know Macharia wanted him killed. But we lured him to his death. Don't you see? It's founded on blood. *Blood!* We'll be cursed. Our baby is ...'

Johnny put his arms round her, stroking her face, kissing the tears away, murmuring in her ear.

'Hey, *hey*, it's over now. You're safe.' He put his hand shyly on her stomach. 'We're all safe. Darling, I love you so much.'

And finally they held each other.

'Johnny, I'm so sorry. I was just ...' She pulled back to look at him properly. 'I wanted you to be so proud of what you've created and I was so worried for the baby, when he held that panga against me I thought he was going to cut me open. Oh God.'

The tears threatened to return but Johnny put his arms around her, kissing her gently.

'I am proud,' he said. 'And it *is* all OK now. We're going to be together and I will never allow anything to happen to you. Or the baby. I swear, darling, I swear.'

And at that moment Johnny believed it with all his heart, unable to conceive of a world in which the two promises might be mutually incompatible.

Chapter 42

Johnny was alive.

Sitting in front of her, a blanket over his knees even though it was hot. Talking. Not on flickering celluloid or staring out at her from an old photo, but alive and breathing and talking. To her.

Sam couldn't take it in. She heard words coming from his mouth but didn't know what he was saying. A chair must have been brought and she sat opposite him. Dedan and Kamau were somewhere behind, silent. Esther was crying; several other African women were crying.

Sam was not crying; could not. She studied him as if he had landed from another planet. The specimen was very old. He breathed slowly, moved slowly. A turtle. They lived for ever too. This one had no shell. His skin was thin, cracked parchment, barely able to stretch over a head that seemed massive and skeletal. Ear lobes dangled pinkly from his scalp, the only exterior part of him that was not a yellowy-brown, apart from the shocking white of his remaining hair, the Seymour coxcomb lifelessly drooping over a scabbed dome. But the eyes were not old. Surrounded by a dead sea of wrinkles and liver spots, hooded by eyelids requiring constant blinking to keep them open, they still managed to shine out with blue brilliance, devouring his granddaughter's face.

She had not guessed. Not in a lifetime would she have known. She'd wondered for a while why no one ever mentioned a funeral or where the grave might be. Grogan had been so convincing. Had he known his old adversary was still alive too? All the strings being pulled, leading her here.

'Do I call you Sam or Samantha?' the voice was asking.

It was not an old man's voice. An octave higher than she might have imagined but still a man's voice, whole and rounded, not yet reedy or bubbling with air despite a cough that shook him between sentences. A smoker's cough, she thought, for some reason pleased. She'd never had a grandparent; her mother's parents had died long before Sam was born. But she knew that grandparents were meant to read stories, be cosy and warm. They didn't sit in an African village, hacking and hawking after a lifetime of smoking. And God knows what else.

'Sam,' she said. 'Call me Sam. Everyone does. Unless they're cross with me.'

'Does that happen often?'

'Yes. I rather think it does.'

Johnny laughed. It was an attractive sound, making him younger. Like Magnus, but warmer.

'My father used to call me John when he was angry. It was only when I went into the army that I earned the "Johnny". I think you should call me that; we've probably skipped the grandparent-granddaughter phase.'

He gestured for her to come closer.

'I want to see you properly. My eyes are not so good nowadays.'

Sam shuffled her chair forward until her knees met his, bony and sharp beneath the blanket. His hand came up and touched her face. It was like a claw, bent in on itself with arthritis, once-long fingers clamped half shut. His touch was surprisingly delicate, tracing the lines of her cheek from ear to chin.

'You know,' he said, 'you look nothing like Robert. I remember your father having light hair like mine, springing up like a bloody cockatoo. He hated it, always trying to damp it down. But you, Sam' – he moved his hand to stroke her dark hair and Sam found herself bowing slightly as if taking a blessing from a priest – 'you take after your grandmother.'

He sighed. 'How old are you, Sam?'

'Twenty-eight.' She was oddly surprised he did not know. 'And you are?'

'God, me? Old as Methuselah. Eighty if I'm a day. I know I look older. That's what drink does. You know I was an alcoholic? Nearly died of it.'

'No, I did not. How could I? I thought you were dead.'

Johnny laughed again. Sam liked the sound but not so much as before. The shock was fading; she was coming down.

'Yes, it must be a hell of a surprise. I'm sorry. We couldn't be sure you'd appreciate it. Weren't certain if you'd want to meet if you did know. That's why I got Esther to send Dedan. He could look after you at the same time. He's a nephew, great-nephew I suppose, of an old friend of mine. We had to be sure, you see. Things weren't exactly left well with Robert. I thought you all preferred not to hear from me again. My brother was pretty unequivocal about that. Is he alive, Magnus?'

Sam stood up, pushing her chair back with some force. Too much coming at her at once. The strings that had drawn her here, manipulated by invisible puppeteers, were now tightening round her neck. She couldn't breathe.

'What do you want from me, Johnny? Why have you summoned me here?'

'Summoned? No one's summoned you, Sam. I thought you were looking for answers. When Mattingly told me my own granddaughter was in Kenya I was so excited I didn't sleep for days. Then when I heard you were with the government side, that you had made friends with Grogan, I nearly did die. We had to be sure, Sam. I'm so sorry; I should have contacted you much earlier. But I haven't been very well.'

Sam glanced at Esther and the other Africans gathered round, then stared hard at Kamau and Dedan. Enough. It was enough. A hot rush of anger accelerated through her body.

'You all knew! How *dare* you not tell me ... What did you think I'd do? Run to the police? I don't care what you did, Johnny – I would never have turned you in. You're my family, for Christ's sake. How could you ever believe that I'd betray you?'

The tears came then, heaving, can't-breathe sobs. She turned and ran back to the *matatu*, thankful there was no one there. She sat inside for long minutes and wept. For herself, for the husk of a man she'd imagined so much about, for her own father, for Magnus. For a fucking war criminal she was related to.

The door slid opened and Sam turned away, pushing her face into her hands.

'Go away.'

Esther pushed into the seat beside her, small arms wrapping around Sam's shoulders, pulling the younger woman to her chest.

'Hey, hey, little Sam. This is more than strange for you but it is not so bad.'

Sam let herself be hugged, crying into the softness, choking out half-sentences.

'But he thought I would turn against him! How could he? Doesn't he realise I don't care what he did at that bloody camp. Well, I do care, but I don't ... Oh Esther, this is so weird. It's such a mess, it's like a ghost come to life but it's not the one I thought it would be.'

Esther held her, not saying anything. Only when the crying subsided did she offer a handkerchief and say very gently:

'But Sam, you have it wrong. Johnny never did anything bad at the camps. Why do you think he did?'

Sam blew her nose.

'Because it's obvious. Pugh told me right at the start that Johnny had been wanted for some terrible crime. My parents have always made it plain that he did something dreadful out here. Then I discovered he was involved in some bloody awful thing with a dead baby, taking pictures. And why didn't he contact me straight away? When he heard I was here? Because he was worried I'd report him to the bloody mission. That's what he said – you heard him!'

'No, that is not what he said. Yes, he was concerned about you being with Grogan. But it was because he knows what that man is capable of. It was nothing else.'

'Then why did he have to wait until now?'

Esther stroked Sam's forehead.

'Because when he says he is unwell he is not exaggerating. He has been bedridden for weeks now. He only got up today because he knew you were coming. He could not have seen you earlier.'

Sam sat up properly and used the handkerchief to dry her eyes.

'*Ill?* What's the matter with him?'

'It is cancer, Sam, and the doctor who was here yesterday says it could be weeks – maybe less. You have some precious days ahead of you. Do not let these false suspicions stop you from enjoying a man who has loved you from afar, ever since the day he heard you existed.'

Sam felt like a small girl again, ashamed. How could she have got it so wrong?

357

'But now he'll think I don't want to see him.'

'Nonsense. There is so much for you both to catch up on. Be strong, Sam. For him as well as for yourself. You will need to be. Over the years your grandfather has been very depressed. He feels burdened by the past. Guilty for not doing the right thing.'

So there *was* something. Sam didn't know which way up was any more.

'What was it? What did he do that was so wrong?'

'Ah, that is for him to tell you himself – if he wants to. Do not push him too hard, Sam. He is weaker than he seems.'

Johnny had retreated inside the house. Kamau was waiting by the chairs. He walked quickly to her and embraced her. Sam melted in gratefully, determined not to cry again. He was whispering in her ear.

'Sam, my darling, I'm so, so sorry. I wanted to tell you, to warn you, but they asked me not to. They made me swear an oath. I should have disobeyed. I will never do that again. Are you all right? Do you want to go – we can leave here now. No one will stop us.'

Sam pulled back.

'Leave? No way. I want to talk to him properly. I've behaved like a child – it's me who should be apologising.'

'Well, he's gone to lie down. I didn't know he was so ill. Dedan was telling me he was given six months to live some years ago. Your grandfather is a powerful man.'

'He's ready for you, Sam!' Esther was standing by the house, beckoning her inside.

'Will you come with me?' Sam asked Kamau.

'No, I've already spent some time with him. It's better for you to be alone. I'll be here if you need me. There are some amazing veterans in this village. I thought I might hear their stories while you get to know each other. We've been given a hut over there, by the way. Not quite the lodge but it is fine. See you later.'

The interior was larger than it looked, a fresh living room leading through open double doors to another garden secluded by a small thicket of bamboo. Johnny's bed was in the middle of the room and he lay propped up on colourful cushions.

He smiled and patted the bed.

'Come and sit down. I'm still a bit weak so it's probably better to be in here. Esther says I was just showing off by getting up.'

He turned to the African woman by his side and spoke to her in Swahili. She nodded gravely and looked at Sam. She was tall with a solemn face, impossible to tell her age – anywhere between fifty and seventy.

'This is Veronica,' Johnny said. 'She's been terribly kind to me these last few years.'

Sam shook her hand.

'Hello,' Veronica said shyly. 'Johnny asks if you would like a drink. He is suggesting gin but we have many soft drinks too.'

'Of course she'll have a gin. She's a Seymour!'

'I'd love one,' Sam said. 'A strong one, thank you.'

'That's my girl,' Johnny beamed. His face was greyer inside, the skin more stretched still. Sam had the impression of a sky lantern, thin with a burning light inside, ready to float away.

Veronica left to fetch the drinks and Esther told them she would be back in half an hour. Sam was not to tire him out.

'They're always fussing over me. I should be grateful, I suppose.'

'Is Veronica your . . .' Sam didn't know what to call her. Girlfriend? Lover?

'Not really,' Johnny said. 'Though I suppose she's become more than a friend over the years. She's very patient. After Tansy died, I rather went to pieces. Later she looked after me. Lost her own husband. Hope you can get to know her after I . . .'

He left the sentence hanging. Sam wasn't sure what to say. She certainly wasn't going to judge him for finding love again. But she thought Tansy had been his life. How long had he been without her? Johnny waved her closer.

'Don't get me wrong,' he whispered loudly, 'Veronica's a wonderful girl but she is not Tansy. Not in a million years. I don't love Veronica, never have. Never told her I did either. After Tansy died I could never do that.'

'I see,' said Sam, embarrassed at his candour. She wondered if Johnny had had a stroke. Stroke victims sometimes lost their inhibitions, saying anything that was on their mind.

'Anyway,' Johnny continued, more brightly. 'Let's not talk about death. Tell me, what do you think of young Dedan?'

'Dedan? Well, he's a fine driver. Helped me out a lot. He likes music. I can't say I know him very well. Why do you ask?'

'Do you know his second name?'

Sam coloured; no, she never had asked. He was just Dedan, the mysterious driver with the crazy shades.

'It's Macharia,' Johnny said. 'He's the grandson of Gatimu – the old Mau Mau armourer himself. Gatimu was the brother of an old friend of mine, Muraya Macharia. But unlike poor old Muraya, Gatimu managed to survive the Emergency. Dead now, but his family all live here – it's why I came. Feel at home, no need to go into any city, mix with any Europeans. Tansy loved it here too. At first, anyway.'

Sam was pleased by the news about Dedan. It made the invisible threads she'd reacted so violently against seem less constricting. But there was so much more she wanted to find out.

'Talking of Tansy,' she said, 'what happened to her? And what occurred with my father? Robert was your son. I hope you don't mind me asking, but why on earth did you get rid of him?'

'Get rid of him? Good God, it was nothing like that.'

Sam looked at him. He seemed genuinely shocked. Veronica drifted silently back into the room and presented Sam with the largest gin and tonic she'd ever seen before withdrawing once more. Johnny grimaced at having to make do with water.

'Why would you say that, Sam?'

Sam sipped her drink, gasping at its strength. She put it down, vowing to take it slowly. Johnny was peering at her, waiting for an answer.

'Well,' she said, 'to begin with just about everyone I know – your family, the government, your contemporaries – all believe you did something awful.'

Johnny's expression did not waver and Sam ploughed on, explaining how the behaviour and sheer bloody oddness of her own father, the family taboo on Africa, the rumours of something terrible, the glimpse of violence on the footage had all led her to believe Johnny had done something so bad he'd had to give up his only son.

When she'd finished Johnny sighed deeply, provoking a rumbling, mucus-filled echo from his chest. He took a mouthful of water and propped himself up on his elbow, staring at Sam hard.

360

'It didn't happen like that.'

'So what about those photographs you took? At the Cunningham place? Something pretty weird happened up there didn't it?'

Johnny slammed his glass down so hard on the bedside table that water spilled onto the floor. It jolted Sam.

'How do you know about that?' he snapped.

'I saw the newspaper cutting in your scrapbook and then later—'

'What scrapbook?'

'Those bits and pieces from your past you collected in that notebook covered with animal skin. All those old bills and press releases and photographs. There were some pictures of you and Tansy. Don't you remember? One of them was of the two of you with Grogan Littleboy.'

'I know the picture you're talking about. Nyeri, 1952. That stupid ball. My first and last. Mattingly insisted on lining us up. You say I put it in a scrapbook?' ·

'Yes.'

Johnny looked past Sam, his mind travelling through time, trying to unravel the sequence. His eyes sparked as he remembered.

'Yes, of course. I do recall something like it now you mention it. Christ, I thought I'd lost it years ago. How did you come across it?'

'Magnus must have given it to my dad.'

'Robert saw it? Good. Magnus must have taken it when he left here. Come to think of it, maybe I gave it to him. I can't remember properly, Sam. I was not in a good way when my brother visited me. But anyway, tell me more about these photographs.'

'OK,' Sam continued, 'well, I've seen a letter from Grogan to some policeman that basically said you and a man called Graves—'

'*Graves?*'

'Yes, whoever he is. You and he apparently arranged the corpses in some macabre fashion. For propaganda photographs. Sounds horrible. Was that the kind of thing you used to do?'

Johnny didn't reply. He took another large sip from his water and Sam could see he yearned for something stronger. His hand travelled over his scalp, patting the lone strands of the Seymour coxcomb back in place.

'All right, Sam. I will tell you about this,' he rasped. 'I do understand your need to know about Robert, and Tansy – she was your grandmother, after all.'

He sat up, arranging the cushions behind his back.

'But as far as Grogan and Graves are concerned you have to know they are evil men who did terrible things. This letter you speak of from Grogan – about the pictures. I've not come across it before but it explains a lot. I never really believed Mau Mau would do that. Many other things, perhaps, but defiling bodies after death, cutting a child's head off and sticking it on a bamboo pole, was not their style.'

'They did what? My God.' Sam frowned. 'Why? Why would anyone do that – I don't get it.'

Johnny reached for more water but stopped, considering whether to press on. He rubbed his eyes and sighed.

'Black propaganda. Trouble is, Sam, you can't really understand any of this unless you know the context. And it's a big one. I could tell you, but you need to be sure you want to hear it. It's not exactly pleasant. Do you?'

'Of course I do. Meeting you like this, when I thought you were dead – I can't explain how wonderful it is. Now I want to know everything. I can't think of anything I want more. *Please, Johnny.*'

Johnny smiled.

'All right then, I'll give it a go. You're very persuasive. Promise to stop me when you've had enough.'

Sam nodded and eased back in her seat, putting her feet up on the other chair. She drank some more gin and grinned to herself. But within a few short minutes her pleasure at the prospect of a final unravelling had dissipated and she found herself sitting up, rigid, the remainder of her gin undrunk on the table.

In precise, clipped tones, Johnny told her the truth about Grogan. Ranging over his own life in Kenya, he explained how Grogan had tricked and lied throughout, manipulating both him and Tansy. And when he described how Grogan had tortured his good friend Macharia Sam flinched, appalled at her own naivety.

She just hadn't seen it. Grogan had totally blindsided her. He had been the guilty one all along. And they'd sat at his table chatting about the old days as if reminiscing about school. Jesus, it would be like going to Argentina and having dinner with Adolf fucking

Eichmann. The story Johnny was telling was a tale of treachery and betrayal beyond anything she could have imagined and her heart filled with sorrow that he'd been subjected to so much pain.

Johnny carried on, describing how he and Tansy had been wrenched from their lives, thrown back into Grogan's orbit, each believing the other had abandoned them. It was hard listening and Sam leant in towards the bed, totally engrossed in the scenes her grandfather was painting. As Johnny laid bare the foulness, she had no notion of time passing, but when he began to cough more between sentences she became aware his voice was growing weaker. He paused at the point in his story where he and Tansy had just witnessed the death of the policeman they called the Zebra.

Sam sneaked a look at her phone and was astonished to see nearly two hours had passed. His face was grey with the effort and Sam knew it was enough for one day.

'Shall we stop there, Johnny? I don't want you to exhaust yourself. We can always carry on later.'

Johnny was staring out through the doors into his garden. A profusion of flowers grew there and Sam wondered if they were a legacy of Tansy's. Eventually he looked back at her. His eyes had hooded over almost completely and the brightness of the blue had faded.

'I'm sorry, Sam. I haven't talked about Tansy for years yet I think of her all the time. Not a day goes past when I don't regret what happened.'

Sam took hold of his hand, the leathery palm smooth in hers.

'It's OK, Johnny. You don't have to explain. I understand. I really do.'

He stopped and closed his eyes, trying to compose himself, but he began to cough again and this time it lasted longer, leaving him wheezing and gasping for breath.

'I know you do,' he smiled. 'Just like Tansy. And you look so like her too. She would have been very proud of you.'

Sam felt tears welling. But she was determined not to cry if Johnny didn't.

'You're right, Sam,' he said. 'I'm afraid I don't think I can do more now. Perhaps this afternoon? Could we carry on then? After raking it all up I think I need a little rest.'

'Of course,' Sam said. 'You must sleep. I'll tell Veronica we're finished for the morning. I'll come back after lunch. We've got plenty of time.'

Johnny flashed open his eyes.

'No, Sam, I'm afraid that's one thing we really don't have.'

Sam left it as late as she could before returning to Johnny's house. She ate lunch with Kamau, Dedan and Esther, but after what she'd heard she wasn't in the mood to chat, picking mechanically through a salad, her mind on the life Johnny and Tansy had led.

Many of the questions she'd had concerning the nature of Johnny's experience during the Emergency had been answered. He had clearly done nothing to be ashamed of, but if Esther was correct, there was still the mystery of why he felt so weighted by his past. Sam was puzzled. Because there *was* something, and nothing she'd heard so far could explain why he might feel guilt. Remorse and loss, certainly, both burdens in themselves; she understood that. But anything else? She couldn't quite put her finger on it but something in the way Johnny had unfolded his story felt more like protection than unburdening. There was still a secret hidden at the heart of him. Whether he had missed out anything in the telling so far or whether it lurked in the future of his story, she could not tell. She would have to tread carefully.

Veronica was waiting for her when she returned to Johnny's house at teatime. She drew her to one side.

'Please, Sam. Do not let him talk for as long this time. He gets tired so quickly these days. I know it pleases him to tell you his story but we also have to manage the life that remains to him now.'

Chastened, Sam stepped into the living room. Johnny was up again, sitting at a table, a blanket round his shoulders.

'Hello again!' he said brightly. 'Returned for your afternoon session? Sit yourself down. Want a cup of tea?'

'No thanks.'

She took a chair and pulled it nearer to her grandfather so he wouldn't have to raise his voice. He looked frail enough that a breath of wind might carry him away.

'Are you sure you feel strong enough to do this now, Johnny? We could wait until tomorrow if you like.'

364

'Strong's not a word you really use at my stage in life,' he sighed, 'but, yes, I'm ready. Now or never really.'

His skin had a waxy pallor and the flame at the centre of him was flickering. She smiled encouragingly but he was not looking at her, his eyes fixed on a point somewhere above her head. Sam could almost see his mind leave the room, winging back to the camps.

'So where was I? On the way back to Umua as I recall, after seeing Tansy safe onto her transport back to the hospital. God, I was so confident then. I just couldn't see how anything more could go wrong. But then I have always been a foolish man.'

He tugged at the blanket, wrapping it tightly round his shoulders before beginning to speak, his voice flat, already far away.

Chapter 43

Umua Camp, June 1955

Johnny went to see Macharia as soon as it grew dark. He was sitting in the usual place between the wire and the hut, watching his friend carefully. The Englishman should have been pleased to be reunited with his woman but he could barely conceal the anger.

'Why didn't you tell me Graves was going to be there?' Johnny asked. 'Christ man, you put us all in so much danger. Tansy could have been killed! We didn't need to be there.'

Macharia was unmoved.

'You knew he had to be dealt with. The Zebra was aware the mark had been put upon him. He would not have been lured out unless there was the chance of a double victory and, as you see, you would never have allowed yourself to go if you had known. Sometimes we are forced to do what is necessary before we can do what we like.'

Johnny shook his head. The daylight had faded so Macharia could only imagine the turmoil on his friend's face as he wrestled with the realities of the struggle.

'Cheer up, my friend,' Macharia said. 'The end of my time at Umua is drawing near and before I leave I would like to remember you in a happier state.'

'Leave – what do you mean?'

'I have received orders. Tomorrow I am to be sent to another camp. They call it Hola. I know little about it except that it is connected to an irrigation system and has been "modified" to deal with prisoners like me.'

'But I thought you'd be staying here until the end?'

'The end?' Macharia chuckled. 'I think the end is not far away.'

'Don't say that! You've survived all this time; you can survive one

366

more camp. This war won't last for much longer – it can't. Look how few of you are left here.'

Macharia put his hand on Johnny's arm.

'Thank you, my friend, but there will be no getting out for me. I cannot give up my oath now. *Will not.* And until I do they won't let me go. They are as bound by the rules of this game, as they call it, as I am. So that means only one thing. And if I can face it, Johnny, you can. *Please.*'

Johnny was glad the darkness of the night prevented Macharia from seeing him now. He blinked but couldn't prevent the wetness in his eyes. He grasped Macharia's hand. It was bony and dry, and felt as if it might crumble if he applied pressure. He held it gently.

'I'm so sorry. I just can't quite believe it ... don't want to ... You must understand how proud I am to have known you. You have helped me so much. And Tansy. We will always speak of you when I, when we ...'

'Come now,' said Macharia softly. 'And I am glad to have known you, Johnny Seymour. You are a true friend and a true man. And now you are helping me. It is an important task – unless people learn of what went on here it will be forgotten for ever. Your country will be doomed to repeat its mistakes while mine will continue to make need-less sacrifices.'

His voice hardened.

'So you must promise me again you will do everything in your power to make sure this is known. *Everything.* Make an oath to me that you will take your films and my notes and turn them into something good. Do it now. Swear to me.'

Johnny did, solemnly swearing he would not let his friend down. He'd already collected the reels of secret film and the bundles of dirty paper on which Macharia had recorded life in the camps, placing them all in two small suitcases – film reels in one, Macharia's notes in some empty film canisters in the other. Both bags were locked in a cupboard in his room and only Johnny had the key. When the time came he would carry the cases on the back of the motorbike. No clothes, no belongings – just the evidence, filmed and written.

Macharia smiled and asked how Johnny had managed to capture the footage.

It was surprising how many ways there were to film clandestinely,

Johnny explained. The notion that the camera might work without him peering into it had not occurred to the guards or even Grogan, who often watched him at work, fascinated by the power of what he claimed would be propaganda's greatest weapon of the future. If Johnny stood by the camera having a smoke, it didn't look as if he were filming at all. A nudge or two with a shoulder on the handle and he could obtain an effective, if jerky, pan and a similar tactic got a full tilt on the guard towers. Stationing himself at all points throughout the camp, he had captured everything he could – the wire, the dust, the warders, the white officers, detainees forced to run with buckets of sand or urine on their head, detainees made to crawl on sharp stones until the flesh peeled off their bones, detainees being pummelled by warders, detainees being dragged off into the interrogation huts.

It was just a pity the Red Cross had shown no interest in hearing anything that deviated from Grogan's glowing account of camp life. Johnny had managed a private word with one of their party but he'd kept looking at his watch, suggesting any complaint be put into a formal letter.

Johnny and Macharia sat quietly for long minutes until the African shifted position, breaking the silence with a small wheezing laugh.

'I've heard that in Hola they intend to make us work by digging. If they put a spade in my hand it would fall out on its own! I believe I once possessed some strength but these days I stumble about, hunched and cracked like an old man. It seems I have lived my life at double speed.

'Ah Johnny, it is good to smile – well, it would be if my lips did not split! Now, let us go over your escape plans one more time. Tansy knows what is expected of her?'

Fifteen minutes later Johnny moved to leave, recognising the other man was tiring. He reached through the darkness to hold Macharia's hand. The men grasped each other but the shake was brief, business-like. They had said what needed to be said.

'Goodbye, my friend,' Macharia said quietly. 'I shall think of you. Perhaps you could pray for me.'

The lorry pulled out of Umua in silence. Normally men leaving the camp sang or chanted Mau Mau slogans. Today it was eerily quiet, not a voice raised, every cough stifled, men standing motionless. Even the white guards said nothing, watching warily.

Macharia stood in the back of the truck, facing the camp. It should have been the final humiliation, the lonely figure heading not to freedom but to more detention. Hola, the last camp. The end of the Pipeline. There was not a man present who didn't think that death for this bent, prematurely aged *mzee* was days, if not hours, away.

The other prisoners in the lorry sat, deferring to their uncrowned leader, and as the vehicle rattled through the gates Macharia raised a clenched first.

'*Uhuru!*'

His voice was surprisingly steady, cutting through the compound with every bit as much force as the whips that beat them.

The answering roar was explosive.

'*Uhuru, Uhuru, Uhuru!*'

He repeated it twice more, each time underlining the word with a jab of his fist in the air. *Uhuru*. Freedom. The guards in the back of the lorry looked nervous but made no move to stop him.

The chanting continued as long as the lorry was in view, quietening only when it turned the corner to join the main Mombasa road. Some men were silently weeping while others beat their breasts in anguish. Then a whistle blew and guards appeared, staves at the ready.

Johnny blew his nose brusquely. He could not afford to be sentimental. It was done. Macharia was the best of friends but he was gone. What was important now was delivering for him. And Tansy. He needed to be practical.

Practical. Like Grogan, Johnny thought. He'd become like him, seeking utility even from the brink.

There was nothing for Johnny to do now but keep his head down and wait until evening. He was standing by the edge of the shower block, keeping an eye on his bike, mind racing over the plans a final time. The night lorry carrying the day's waste left just before sundown. It was the last time the gates were lifted before morning and Johnny intended to be right behind it. The bike was ready and primed, and he'd taken to riding it inside the compound in the evenings to get the guards used to it being around. So there should be nothing unusual about him starting her up just as the truck was leaving. He was counting on the fact that the guards would be slow to react as he drove past the truck and accelerated hard for the main road.

Johnny estimated his back would be exposed to the guards for less than a minute. They would take precious seconds to come to terms with having to shoot a *muzungu*, even though he knew they were under strict orders to do so if he ever left the compound without permission. By then he might be at the furthest range of their rifles. If he weaved he would present a difficult target.

But if he got stuck behind the truck, if anything came the other way, if he broke down, if a guard got lucky . . . It was all guesswork, a gamble. But after meeting Tansy again and seeing, touching, the life she carried he would have taken much worse odds.

Johnny consulted his watch. Five past five. The truck usually left just before six. Fifty minutes. Compared to what he'd been through it was nothing. He could do it. Relax; breathe. Soon he planned to start the motor and ride a little. He'd dismount and keep the engine running so that when he remounted at precisely the time the gate was being raised for the truck any suspicious guard would think he was returning it to the lock-up.

He lit a cigarette and looked around the compound, with its towers beginning to form long shadows over the huts and tents. Twenty minutes. He smoked fast, grinding out the cigarette with his shoe before heading for his room. He wasn't going to take anything that wouldn't fit into his pocket and he'd left a small pile by his bed: dark glasses, toothbrush, small screwdriver, money. And the key to his cupboard; he'd put that out as well. All he'd have to do was scoop up his things, unlock the cupboard, take out the suitcases with the evidence and go. It would take seconds.

Time to leave.

Rounding the corner, he saw lights in his room. He had not left them on. He opened his door and smelled him before he saw him. Lavender, very faint; an odd odour for a man.

'Ah, Johnny. Wondered when you'd be back. Enjoying an evening stroll?'

Grogan was sitting ramrod-straight in the room's only chair. He bent to pull up his right sock. Satisfied it was in alignment he stood, unsmiling. He had a whistle in his hand.

'Glad I caught you. Wanted to have a little chat,' Grogan said. 'Mind coming along to my office?'

Johnny couldn't stop his eyes flitting to the window. The shadows were barely noticeable now; the murk of dusk settling uniformly over the camp. He had five minutes at most. His toothbrush, the screwdriver and money sat on his bedside table undisturbed. He could leave them if necessary but he needed the key. Where was it? It wasn't with the rest of his things.

'Actually, Grogan, sorry. Just popped back for my lighter. Need the Heads. Rather urgent actually, so if you don't mind, perhaps we can do this later.'

'It will have to wait, Johnny. What I have to say is urgent too. You need to come with me.'

'No, really. No can do right now. It'll have to wait a few minutes.'

'Probably didn't make myself clear,' Grogan said, straightening his back. 'Wasn't a request. You need to come – *now.*'

Johnny looked at the door and back at Grogan. If he ran he might make it.

Grogan held up the whistle.

'No funny business, Johnny. If I blow this, the guards come running and the game's up. Prefer it if we talked man to man without any of that nonsense.'

Chapter 44

Nyeri District, June 1955

Tansy was at the side of the Mombasa road, literally hopping from one foot to the other, urging herself to calm down. It was jet black, barely possible to see a hand in front of her face. She should have brought a larger torch. Would have, but Johnny had been so strict. She was to take nothing but the clothes she stood up in and anything light that fitted into her pockets. The bush jacket was a bit of a cheat – when the sun rose it would be redundant – but it did have some extra pockets, where she'd stowed underwear, some make-up and her hairbrush.

Luckily her watch was a military-style one with modern luminous dials. Nearly six. If it all went to plan, Johnny would be here in less than a quarter of an hour.

If.

There was so much that could go wrong. She shivered at the image of Johnny bent over the handlebars, being shot at. If anything happened to him she didn't know what she'd do. She looked down at her stomach. How would she look after him? She was sure it was a him, too. An old African orderly at the hospital claimed he had special sight and was boasting the baby would grow into a great man and true friend of the Kikuyu people.

'You'll manage,' Tansy told herself. 'You always do.'

But in truth, she didn't want to manage without Johnny.

He'd been clear: if he wasn't there by half past she was to walk back to the hospital. It would take hours, but if she kept to the track she should be all right. He'd contact her again. Somehow. She wasn't to worry; it was going to be fine.

She smiled at the memory. Johnny always said that even though it usually wasn't. Was he really such an optimist? Or did he just say it to reassure her? Or himself? There were aspects of Johnny Seymour she didn't know at all. She looked forward to finding out at leisure.

England was where they'd go at first, until all this blew over. She knew that – it was one of the few things they'd managed to discuss. Johnny had it all planned. One of the small weekly magazines popular with the New Left was interested in Macharia's notes and he had an American friend in the film business who might be able to help with the footage. They didn't want to stay in England long. Hopefully they'd return to Africa. Tansy loved the idea of living in Kenya when it became free, Johnny taking his son for walks in the forest, fishing together, sailing. The boy could learn Swahili from the village children, find medicines from the trees, help her at the clinic she would set up.

Quarter past. She strained her ears, listening. All that came back were the hoots and screeches of the night. Time for one last cigarette. She knew she ought to cut down, but to hell with it. If these weren't special circumstances, what were?

Shouldn't he be here by now?

The thought gnawed at her.

Where *was* he?

What could Grogan possibly want to discuss?

Johnny had a split-second to make up his mind. There was no time to follow Grogan anywhere. He needed to be on that bike in less than two minutes. There wouldn't be another chance to leave tonight and with Macharia gone he couldn't get a message to Tansy. Johnny couldn't even contemplate it. Grogan was a liar and a manipulator. He'd made both their lives intolerable. And now when they had it in their grasp to escape for ever he was threatening them yet again.

'What do you want, Grogan? Can't this wait?'

'You look as if you're going somewhere,' Grogan said. 'Don't even consider it. I mean it – I *will* blow this whistle. There are guards who can be here in seconds. For the first time in your life I urge you to be sensible. If not for me then for Tansy.'

Tansy? The mention of her name confirmed it. There really was no choice. Johnny steeled himself. He had never thought it would come to this. But if it had to – so be it. The game was not up. Not yet. Grogan could not be allowed to stop them now.

No choice.

'OK,' Johnny said. 'If you insist. Just a sec—'

The screwdriver wasn't a long one. It was a handy five-incher he'd put out in case he had to remove the panniers from the bike or tinker with the fuel gauge. But even two inches could pierce the heart.

No choice.

Johnny smiled as he took the few steps over to his bedside table. Grogan didn't react as he swept up the money and grabbed the screwdriver. Hardly responded at all when Johnny turned suddenly to plunge in the shaft, just a quiet 'oh' as he dropped the whistle and slumped back onto the chair, his fingers curled round the handle of the screwdriver jutting from his stomach.

In the violence of the moment Johnny had dropped most of the money. And he still couldn't find the key. He was scrabbling on the floor when Grogan spoke.

'Shouldn't have done that, Johnny,' he said, panting ragged breaths. 'Ruined it.'

Johnny looked up, aghast.

'Ruined it? You're the one who ruined everything.'

He stood, stuffing the money into his pockets. He didn't bother with any of the other things he'd laid out. No time. But he still hadn't found the key. He searched desperately on the bed, under it. Nothing. He had to have it. Without the key he couldn't unlock the cupboard to get to the suitcases. He couldn't leave without them. He'd promised Macharia. Made a promise to a dying man. Without the film and Macharia's own notes, there would be nothing. *Where the fuck was it?*

Grogan remained in his chair, fluttering and pinned. Suddenly Johnny knew.

'Grogan – where's the bloody key? Give it to me now.'

Grogan laughed weakly.

'No dice, Johnny. Do you think I'd let you leave with that?'

'Tell me! Tell me now or I'll—'

'What? Torture me? I'm sure you'd love to. And you could, too. Require you to become a means-end man, though. Finally you'll see how things have to be done.'

Johnny punched him hard, just below the ear.

'Give it to me now, Grogan. I mean it.'

Grogan shook his head and spat blood.

'Your choice. Guards here at any moment. Prearranged. Whistle or no. You might just make it if you go now. Or you could risk everything for the key. Is it that important to you to have those films? Not sure I understand: what's in them, Johnny? Have you been a naughty boy? Filmed something you shouldn't?'

Johnny grabbed Grogan by the throat, squeezing hard. Grogan's eyes bulged. Blood dribbled from his lips. Out of the window Johnny could see guards. One looked at his watch and glanced over at the hut. Grogan was right. They were coming. And the lorry was leaving.

Time stopped, freeze-framed in a moment of decision that Johnny knew would affect his whole life. To leave now and ensure he reached Tansy, or take the biggest gamble of his life and literally squeeze the key out of Grogan? To keep a promise or keep a love.

There was no real choice.

He began to edge out of the room but before he reached the door he turned back, unable to stop himself.

'Can't you see what you've become?' he shouted. 'How can you justify any of this? *Any of it?* How could you do this after what we saw in Germany? It's OK if they're Africans? Because their skins are black? Is that it?'

'No, no ... not the same.' Grogan clutched the handle of the screwdriver, covering it so that apart from a growing stain of red on his shirt he might have been a parson, holding his hands over his belly after a large lunch.

'For God's sake, don't exaggerate. Roughhousing, that's all.' Grogan's words emerged on a crest of gasps. 'Everything for practical reasons. Pragmatic. How many more would have died if we hadn't grasped the nettle? Johnny, you've hurt me – I need help. I'm dying. *Please.*'

'*Please? Help?* Is that what the prisoners said when you were grasping the nettle – pulling their fucking teeth out?'

Grogan flapped his arms and struggled to get up but Johnny marched over and pushed him down.

'You're not dying, Grogan. I wish you were. You're like a cockroach: your type always survive.'

Grogan was pale, the screwdriver still sticking obscenely out of his Aertex shirt. Johnny could hear the night truck's engine revving.

'*Wait.* You have to know something,' Grogan said, forcing the words out. Johnny's fingers were wrapped round the door handle. 'I know about you and Tansy. Can't let it happen, Johnny. Wanted to show you the file. In my office.'

'*File?*'

'Special Branch,' Grogan gasped. 'Been following Tansy ever since she met the Mau Mau contact in Nairobi. Pictures. They have photographs, Johnny. Of then and now. Know all about the killing of Graves.'

Johnny felt the blood leave his face. How could they know?

'If they knew why haven't they done something about it? You're fucking bluffing, Grogan. That's all you ever do.'

'No, you're wrong. I stopped them. Said it was a counter-operation. Tansy working for us. But Johnny—' Grogan halted, trying to sit up, his breathing increasingly ragged. 'Know this – if you leave with her tonight a memo I've prepared will tell them the truth and she'll be arrested. Go to gaol. Kamiti's not a good place for pregnant women, Johnny. Yes, I know that too. Did you really think I was such a fool? And being a traitor to your country still carries the death penalty. No statute of limitations for treason. We'd find you. You know we would. Do you really want a life on the run? If you don't care about yourself, think about Tansy, man.'

He dabbed his yellow handkerchief to his lips, puzzled as it turned orange with blood.

'You threaten her?' Johnny shouted. 'A woman you wanted to marry? Hang a pregnant woman from a rope? *Someone you loved?* You're a fucking monster.'

'But don't you see? It's *because* I love her. Need to save her from . . . ' Grogan's breath gurgled as he saw Johnny swing the door open. 'Wait – *think, man!* I can look after her, make sure the child has a home. Safety. She'll be safe. It's the only rational way. What can you offer?'

'You're insane. How can you give her anything when she doesn't love you? She loves me, Grogan – *me*. Not you. Don't you get it?'

'Not true, not true. Can't be . . . '

Johnny slammed the door and ran for the bike. He had thirty

seconds. The truck was already heading to the gate. Behind him he heard Grogan's voice, stronger now.

'Stop that man,' he bellowed. 'Traitor! *Traitor!*'

In front of Johnny a startled guard scrabbled with his pistol holster but Johnny barged him to the ground, sprinting for the Triumph, praying it would start.

He jumped on and kicked the starter pedal.

Nothing.

He kicked desperately again. *Still nothing.*

And again.

Behind him the man he'd knocked over was getting to his feet. A whistle was blowing. More men running out of a hut. *Please God. Start.*

Nothing.

Johnny leapt off and started pushing. The bike was heavy but there was the smallest of slopes. Still it was slow. So slow. Sweat was pouring off him and he was oblivious to the sounds of men shouting. The truck ahead was almost through the guard post. He could see an askari with his hands on the long timber-pole barrier, ready to push it down. Johnny jumped back on the seat, pulled in the clutch so the bike was coasting and let it glide. He had to pick up speed or a jump start would never work. *Just a second more.* A whining noise as a bullet zipped past his ear. Come on. Just a bit faster. *Please.*

No more time. He kicked it into gear, eased the clutch lever with his left hand and held his breath.

The bike bucked and coughed and finally the engine caught. Johnny opened the throttle as far as it could go and the front wheel leapt off the ground so suddenly he feared he'd lose balance. But he hung on and when the wheel reconnected with the earth the Triumph took off with a mighty roar, spitting mud and dust and stones in its wake. The barrier was almost down and he had to duck to avoid it. A sentry leapt out and caught Johnny a glancing blow on the head, which made the bike wobble. But he accelerated through it, leaping into the darkness beyond the gate.

Johnny switched on his headlights as he caught up with the truck. As he drew alongside he could see the startled face of the driver inside. Johnny changed down a gear and the Triumph responded instantly, effortlessly overhauling the truck, launching into the night.

A couple of seconds later the camp klaxon whined violently into life and Johnny looked back. The camp was a mass of running men. A red muzzle-flash from the guard tower as the sentry opened up with the machine gun.

The road was bumpy but straight. If they were going to get him it was now. At the point where the forest began, the road curved round to the right and if he could get there he knew he'd be safe.

He looked behind for a last sight of the camp.

There were other lights on the road.

Not the truck but something else – travelling a lot faster. Following him at speed. The bike bumped and swerved and he forced his eyes back to the road ahead. A couple of hundred yards later he risked another look. It was a jeep, one of the special guard vehicles with a light machine gun mounted on the back. He'd always thought a motorbike would be quicker than any other vehicle but he'd reckoned without the dips and ruts of the African road. Four wheels could negotiate them faster than two.

He tried to accelerate but straight away hit a pothole. The bike veered violently and he wrestled the handlebars to keep the Triumph upright. He couldn't go any faster; had to slow down or crash.

The jeep was gaining on him.

Tansy would be waiting for him at the spot they'd chosen on the Mombasa road, just down the hill from the crossroads. At current speeds he estimated the jeep would be within shooting range just at the moment he would stop to pick her up.

It was not going to work. He couldn't let them anywhere near her.

Johnny knew he was in the end game, and though he squirmed on his seat and writhed through the permutations, nothing came. This was it. No way out.

All the exhilarating hope and optimism released when he'd accelerated away from the camp suddenly left him in a deep sigh of exhaled breath and flat horror. Standing with his hands round Grogan's throat he had made a choice. His own life with Tansy over an oath to a friend and a vow to the thousands of unseen, unmet victims.

Now he had neither.

He slumped on his seat, bent forward over the handlebars until he was almost lying down. He had no strength. How far would he get before they closed in? It didn't matter. Nothing mattered now except to lead them as far away from Tansy as possible. So near, and now this.

He reached the crossroads and slowed to an idle, grimly determined to make sure the guards in the jeep saw which road he was taking. Peering through the gloom he tried to make out if Tansy was down the hill. One last glimpse.

But it was too late; too dark.

Chapter 45

Tansy stamped the cigarette out, the embers under her heel the last vestige of light as night fully closed in. *Twenty-five past.* Now she was really worried.

Come *on*, Johnny, where are you?

Although it was impossible to make out the road in the dark, she'd travelled along it often enough by day to know its contours pretty well. She was standing a few feet away from the junction of the track which led back to the hospital. Johnny bloody well better make it; she didn't fancy walking down there among the snakes and God knows what else. He *would* make it. She would see the lights from the bike at the brow of the hill, five hundred yards up to her right. There was a fork in the road there. One led all the way to Nairobi while the other would take them towards the coast and Mombasa.

Five hours with stops, Johnny reckoned – and that's if they didn't hit anything. Giant black mambas liked to lie across the road at night, sucking up the heat from the tarmac before sliding back into the bush at dawn. She hated snakes.

Six thirty-two.

She knew what she was meant to do if he didn't come, but it was impossible to start back now. Another five minutes, even ten. Surely it would make no difference.

Please, let nothing have happened to him. She felt an urgent signal from her bladder. The pressure on her belly was making her want to go all the time and nerves made it even worse. A quick pee then. Perhaps one last cigarette. That would take about ten minutes.

Tansy was just standing up, patting her pocket for the cigarette packet, when she heard it.

At first she thought it was a creature growling, but as the distant hum drew nearer she recognised the deep purr of the Triumph. Lovely, wonderful *Johnny*. He'd made it! She felt sick with suppressed anxiety. Talk about cutting it fine.

Draping the bush jacket over her shoulders, she walked into the middle of the road. She screwed up her eyes, peering through the dark towards the junction where the headlights would first appear. He'd be shooting past the Nairobi turning just about now, before coming down the hill towards her.

The sound of the motorcycle ripped through the night, silencing the chatter of the forest. Tansy was thrilled by it, couldn't wait to be on the back, whisked on her magic carpet to safety with her love.

Her love. She was pleased that it sounded so right.

But it was not right.

To begin with, there were two sounds. She recognised the throb of the Triumph but not the other. A car or a lorry. And the sounds were fading, not getting nearer. Suddenly the beam from his bike winked through the trees on the other side of the hill. Then, a minute later, the twin lights of a car on the same road. Not the Mombasa road. What was going on? A terrible feeling of alarm spread through her. She stood, mouth agape. Listening, praying. *Oh God.* He knew this road backwards, had even drawn it for her, told her he had gone over it in his sleep. Could do it blindfolded.

'Johnny,' she croaked, trying to yell, her mouth sucked dry by apprehension. '*Johnny* – over here!'

But even as she shouted she knew it would do no good. Her voice was feeble and not even the loudest scream would have reached his ears. He was far away.

Johnny Seymour had taken the Nairobi road.

He had driven past.

Chapter 46

Nyeri District, June 1955

Johnny felt like a ghost. Was this what it was like to be dead? To be invisible and glide through the blackness, swooping down from the night like a shade?

He felt slightly unhinged, as if the darkness cloaking him was keeping reality at bay. He wanted to scream or laugh like a ghoul, but reined it in. Silence was still required and he had to concentrate more than ever. Without power, the wheels of the Triumph were heavy, sluggish to respond. On the gentle gradient down the Mombasa road the bike could barely muster twenty miles an hour, but even so the potholes felt massive and jarring.

He did not care. Had no single care except to carry on until he saw her. And he would be doing that any second, as he prayed she'd disobeyed his instructions and waited longer.

In the end, throwing off the jeep had been easy. All he'd needed to do was think clearly, then everything seemed absurdly simple. Waiting until there was a bend in the road, he'd driven off the tarmac, cut the engine, turned the lights off and positioned the bike behind some bushes. When the jeep had raced past a few seconds later he took the bike out and pushed it silently back up the hill in the direction he'd come, towards the crossroads. Keeping an eye out for signs of the jeep returning, he'd used every ounce of strength to push-run the motorcycle up the slope.

He knew he had to be fast. Not only might the guards come back but it was possible Tansy might have left the road to take the short-cut back to the hospital. Johnny had no idea where that was and if she started back to the hospital before he found her it was game over; Grogan would have phoned McGregor immediately. But the jeep had not returned and when finally he arrived, exhausted, at the top of the hill, Johnny mounted the bike to let gravity do the work.

Now he was coasting silently down the Mombasa road like a wheeled wraith, mosquitoes and night insects batting off his sweat-drenched face.

Tansy did not bother with her torch. Did not want to see anything, didn't want to walk anywhere, her mind a deadening panic of confusion and horror. She couldn't begin to fathom why Johnny had gone, why he had deserted her.

But he had. And now she was empty, hating every heavy footstep leading back to a life she'd stood on the brink of leaving for ever. She found the beginning of the path. Within seconds she'd be swallowed up by the forest.

Then there was a noise.

It was a noise like no other. A creeping, rolling, whooshing sound that did not belong in the African bush. She turned but there was nothing to see. She reached for her torch, fumbling to switch it on.

And there under the weak beam was a sight she would never forget, a phantom astride a motorbike, silently rolling toward her, gathering pace in the gloom.

'*Tansy!*'

Johnny leaped off the bike and picked her up, lifting her effortlessly, crushing her against him.

'Oh God, I thought you'd gone,' Tansy cried. 'Thought you'd . . .'

'I'm here,' he said gently. 'I got away. They're gone. Halfway to Nairobi by now.'

Tansy tried to speak but couldn't find the words. The enormity of it was hitting her and she began to shake. Johnny held her tighter but after a moment he disengaged and gestured to the pillion.

'We must go. There's not much time,' he whispered. 'They could be back at any second.'

She sat and put her arms around him, and he began pushing the bike down the slope, only putting both feet up when they were in motion.

'Tansy,' he said, turning, 'do you realise? We've made it! It's going to be fine.'

And despite everything, Johnny believed it. Regardless of Grogan's threats and of leaving the evidence behind, he had done the only thing he was capable of. He uttered a silent apology to Macharia, understanding there would never be a single moment for the rest of his days when he wouldn't feel the burden of that broken promise. One day, if it was possible, he would do what he could. For now he had a new life to think about. Two new lives.

Tansy heard the happiness in his voice and smiled in the darkness, pushing her face into his warm neck.

It's all going to be fine. For the first time in her life she believed it might just be true.

Chapter 47

Nyeri District, April 2008

Sam rose early, leaving Kamau sleeping. There was a faint mist in the fields and the air was cool and clean. The village was coming awake. An aroma of cooking was mixed in with wood smoke. A dog stretched sleepily before scratching on the door of a hut while chickens clucked around the yard, pecking hopefully at the red earth. Otherwise no one else was up. She was hungry. Yesterday after Johnny had completed his story Veronica had invited her to come for breakfast. Johnny apparently only slept in snatches so she'd be welcome at any time. For her part Sam had slept well despite staying up half the night replaying the details of Johnny's extraordinary end game.

She was so relieved. He had got away – with Tansy. After stabbing Grogan! And if that was his crime it wasn't really a crime at all. He'd been so brave. Sam felt a warm rush of affection towards him. Pride too. This was her grandfather! What an amazing amount he'd achieved. Why would Esther say he still felt burdened?

Johnny was sitting at the table reading, old-fashioned half-moon spectacles perched on his nose. He looked stronger today. In profile he resembled his brother and Sam reminded herself that she needed to phone home today. She might have done it last night but after meeting a man she thought was dead and then hearing his momentous story, speaking to England had seemed trivial. Instead she'd curled up with Kamau and talked it through, trying to process the astonishing events. Her grandfather alive. Even now, looking directly at him, it had an unreal quality.

He hadn't heard her come in so she stayed quiet and watched him. There was a pile of books on the edge of the table and she was amused to see at least two of them were big coffee-table books by the author with the funny name that she'd seen at the lodge. The paperback in his hand was a collection of poetry and she almost gave a start when she realised it was an edition of Tennyson. Like son, like father.

The whole thing was odd. It was still scarcely possible to believe that he existed; that for the whole of her life he'd been hiding out in this small African village, living happily ever afterwards without ever once being in contact with his English family. Except that, apparently, it had not been happy at all.

She knew the narrative of his life now, but only up to escaping from the camps. As Esther had said, there was so much more to catch up on. She also wanted to discuss the legal case. After what she'd heard yesterday she knew he'd make a great witness. If he was strong enough, perhaps she could record him. A key player from the time who'd known what it was like first-hand; who'd actually been in the camps. Who'd filmed it, for God's sake. *Filmed.* An idea began to percolate into her head. If there was unfinished business here there might just be a way to close it.

'Are you going to come in or are you going to stand there watching your old grandfather all morning?'

Johnny's voice was sturdier. There was an amused edge to it, playing uncertainly with the concept of grandfather. Sam drew up a chair and sat next to him. The more she stared, the younger he appeared. After that first burst of shock at how old he'd looked yesterday, familiarity was breeding the opposite of contempt. He really did seem to have fewer wrinkles. Perhaps this was how old people survived with each other, she thought. Instead of waking up next to a desiccated drudge, they saw only the essence.

'You look better this morning,' Sam said.

'Kind of you, but if I do, it's only temporary. I'm at my best at this time. But you actually do look stunning, Sam. Does everyone tell you how beautiful you are? I bet you're bored of it.'

'No, it's fine,' she laughed. 'You can say it as often as you like.'

He laughed too.

'After you left last night I kept wondering whether I had hallucinated the whole thing. But here you are. I can't tell you what it means.'

He reached out an arm and patted her shoulder. It was ponderous and Sam thought it was how he might have patted a dog. He doesn't know how to deal with this, she thought. But then nor did she.

Sam wandered into the small galley kitchen. Next to a kettle and a thoughtfully placed box of tea bags, there were a couple of hard-boiled eggs, some bread and a plate of cold meats. She could eat the lot; she was ravenous. While she waited for the kettle to boil she surveyed the room. Nothing of interest in it at all. No pictures, no knick-knacks, no magnets on the fridge. Functionality ruled supreme. Perhaps that was what a bachelor pad looked like.

'Have you always lived here?' she asked over her shoulder.

'Mostly,' Johnny said. 'At the start we needed to be somewhere safe and nowhere was safer than here. People have been terribly good to us. After I got out of the camps I was a wanted man. But no one would have dared come here and stir it all up again – not even Grogan. Everyone wanted to leave the war behind, negotiate with the Brits to leave so they could start their lives again. But we did have another place we'd go to if village life got on top of us.'

Sam carried two cups back and gave one to Johnny, returning to the kitchen to select a plate of food for herself.

'Oh?' she asked 'Where was that?'

Johnny smiled. He'd taken off his glasses and was fiddling around in a drawer in the table.

'Ah, now that,' he said, 'was one of the things I wanted to talk to you about. Good, here it is.'

He'd found a bunch of keys fastened to a large ring with a small wooden leopard attached, and pushed it over to Sam so it lay next to her teacup.

'I want you to have this, Sam. I'm not a wealthy man. In fact,' he laughed, 'I am an exceedingly poor man. In Western terms anyway. Except for this.'

'What is it?'

'They are keys to a house. It used to belong to Tansy's parents but they bequeathed it to us so we had somewhere proper to take Robert. It's a lovely place and we had many happy times there. I hope you do too. I gather you've already christened it well! It's yours now, Sam – Dedan is getting someone to do the paperwork, but from this moment on you own Ngare Lodge. You will always have somewhere to live when you come back here. And I know you will.'

Sam was overwhelmed. The lodge. No wonder it had felt so right. It was part of Johnny's history. *Hers.* My God. How could she ever repay him?

'Do you really mean it?' Her voice caught. 'This is so generous, I don't know what to say.' She rose and put her arms round him, feeling the bony shoulders as she hugged him tight. 'Thank you, thank you,' she whispered.

Johnny looked embarrassed.

'Yes, well. Not at all, not at all. You should eat your breakfast.'

Sam took a sip of coffee and began on her eggs. She was aware of him watching and between mouthfuls she looked up and they smiled at each other, neither quite believing the other was real. Finishing quickly, Sam pushed her plate away feeling a surge of energy. She wanted to learn everything about him. Yesterday's story about escaping from the camp had begun to fill in the gaps of his life but he had stopped short of explaining how he'd reached the village and, crucially, what had happened to her father. Now, she thought, finally we can get to it.

But when she mentioned Robert's name Johnny's chin sagged to his chest and he waved a hand in front of his face.

'Do we really have to go through all that?' he sighed. 'It's not something I've ever wanted to talk about.'

Again he resembled the old man of last night, his eyelids suddenly more pronounced, closing, age descending like a damp sack, muting his strength. Sam pressed. He wasn't allowed to be regretful. It was far too late for that.

'If you've never talked about it,' she said, 'this might help.'

'What are you, a priest?'

The tone was sharp. Sam sat back.

'No, Johnny, I'm just family. *Your* family. Perhaps you owe it to us to explain.'

'Do I? I'm not sure I owe you anything, Sam.'

'I see. Fine. Well, I'm sorry, I should never have asked.'

Johnny rested his elbows on the table and rubbed his face, pummelling his eyes.

'No – it's me. I'm sorry. I know I should talk. Ever since you arrived here I've known I'd have to explain. You deserve to know the rest. But it's very hard.'

He stared deliberately out of the window, his gaze fastened on the middle distance. When they emerged, the words were fluent enough but there was little emphasis, more a declamation of facts ground out in short sentences, foul things to be got rid of.

Following the escape from camp Johnny and Tansy stayed in Mombasa. After what Johnny had done to Grogan there'd been no point in thinking about taking a ship anywhere. The borders were on high alert. Their place on the beach was too much of a risk. They stayed only a couple of nights before Joshua, their old houseboy, helped find somewhere else nearby.

They were difficult days but at least they were together. The birth had been premature, nearly a month early. They named him Robert, after Tansy's grandfather. During those first months the security services were everywhere, searching, questioning. It would have been safer to hide upcountry but at that stage there was nowhere to go. Still, it was folly to remain anywhere near Mombasa. If the message hadn't come they would certainly have been discovered.

The contact was from Macharia – from beyond the grave, a life-saver. He'd given instructions for the Movement to keep an eye on Johnny. The old campaigner had known events rarely went to plan. Sitting behind the wire, awaiting his death, Macharia had foreseen even that. Yet another thing Johnny owed his friend. He and Tansy and the baby were spirited away back to the Highlands. Macharia had asked his own family to find a place for them in his home village.

'I nearly didn't go,' Johnny said. 'I did not deserve to be helped by that man. He was my friend and I had let him down – I had no right ... but we went. Tansy insisted because of the baby. She was correct, of course, but for me that marked the beginning.'

'Of what? I don't understand. You had a perfect right. He was helping you – just as you'd helped him. Of course you'd go.'

Johnny turned his head sharply to look at Sam. He pulled at the corner of his thumb nail, tugging at a small piece of skin, blood smearing onto his fingers.

'But I didn't help him did I? I let him down, Sam, *let him down*. He asked me to do one thing. Made me promise. You heard me last night – I told it to you just as it happened. I made an oath, remember! You know what that signified to Macharia. But when it came to it I couldn't do it. Couldn't go through with it. Don't you see? Then afterwards, when Tansy died, it made sense. It was like a curse: I wasn't allowed to have one without the other.'

Johnny's voice grew softer.

'I couldn't have Tansy; it was my fault.'

Sam shook her head.

'You don't believe that, do you? You can't.'

Johnny resumed his stare ahead; his next sentences were equally flat, a dry recitation. Sam was perplexed. Was this the source of his guilt? It made no sense.

The first years had been an idyllic time with Tansy and the boy. The Emergency was over and they kept a low profile, living in the bush. It was a fine place for a child to grow up. Johnny gave up his government pension in case anyone used it to trace him. They didn't need much money anyway. Their life was simple. And when they did need funds he started taking photographs again. Even landed a publishing deal for some wildlife books, using a pen name, an ana-gram – Roy Muse. Tansy was happy. She'd set up a basic nursing clinic, just as she'd promised. On the surface it could not have been better. Robert loved it. Had so many friends among the villagers. Ran free. Care free.

'Living was a privilege. And living like that should have been the summit. The absolute best. I regret a lot of things, Sam, but most of all I wish that I hadn't messed that up. It should have been a golden period but I couldn't shake it, you see. The debt. The unpaid debt. When people die and you don't deliver, it's different. It rubs you raw. Infects everything. If you don't know it, you can't describe it. I tried to explain but even Tansy, who understood everything, could not understand that.

'So in order to keep those feelings away, in order to pretend to my wife and son that it was fine, I drank. I'd always drunk, everyone did then. But this was different. I drank on my own. Secretly. In the afternoon. In the morning. The middle of the night when I couldn't sleep. And that was most nights. I was a drunk. I could take photo-graphs, do normal things. Function. But I was a drunk. I couldn't get Macharia out of my head. I couldn't . . .

'Tansy tried to get me away. We went on trips. She took me to Ngare. Once even into Nairobi. Travelled to see her parents, though not often as they died soon after the end of Emergency. Mary first,

390

then Paddy – he couldn't live without her, died of a broken heart. I know that feeling but I never had the courage to die.

'So, poor Tansy. There was just me. And Robert. When she couldn't help me she took him and went to the clinic, working for others.

'Mosquitoes are everywhere in Africa but the bad ones are on the coast. She must have been bitten when she took me back to the beach house. A final attempt to jolt me out of it by reliving the happy days we'd spent there.'

Johnny stopped, his breaths becoming shallower.

Worried, Sam put out an arm, stroking his shoulder.

'Hey – it's OK, Johnny. This is too distressing, there's no need to go on. You should stop. I understand.'

'*No!*' he shouted. 'You were right. I have to do this.'

Sam reached for Johnny's hand.

He smiled.

'That's what Tansy would have done. Forced me to talk about it and then held my hand when I couldn't. *Ah Sam.* You should have met her.'

Anyway, he continued, the trouble with Africa then as now was that it was poor and poor people had no medicine. Not for malaria. When Tansy fell ill there was nothing to give her. The nurse who'd tended so many couldn't be looked after by anyone. When she was slipping away Johnny got a message home to his brother. Instinct, really.

'Magnus turned up one day. Not sure when – I was too far gone, couldn't even remember that I'd written to him. Don't know what I was expecting anyhow. But as it happens he was too late. Tansy was already dead.'

Magnus had seen what he had to. His brother a drunk. In no fit state to look after himself. Let alone an eight-year-old boy. He said that Robert was being neglected – though Johnny didn't think so, certainly not by the villagers who had folded him into their lives. Magnus promised to help, send him to school in England. Said an African mud hut was no place to bring up a child. And because Johnny was weak and drunk he'd said yes when actually Africa, this part of Africa with these people, was probably the best place in the world for anyone to be brought up. So Robert went back with his

Uncle Magnus. His son hadn't wanted to go. Cried and fought and bit but his father was drunk again and Magnus was kind and firm.

And that was it. Tansy dead. Robert gone. Promises broken. Life over.

He heard from Robert for a while. Stilted letters from a cold boarding school. But after a couple of years when even they stopped coming, the shock of losing any contact with his only son finally roused him from self-pity. Veronica had come into his life then and Johnny sobered up. He wrote to Robert often but never received any reply. Johnny clung to the thought that when Robert became a man, when he could make his own choices, he would come back to the country he had loved so much as a child. His mother country.

Then one day a letter from Magnus. Robert had achieved his majority and decided not to return to Africa. He didn't wish to continue any relations with a father he believed had abandoned him. It was too painful. Johnny would be performing a kindness not to pursue the matter. In return, Magnus would provide for Robert during university and make sure he got a start in the family law firm.

'What else could I do? I'd failed Tansy, failed Macharia, failed my friends. I'd made a choice, don't you see? I didn't deserve him; couldn't stand in the way of my only son's welfare. It all stems from the choice on the day of that damned escape. I shouldn't have made it but I did.'

Johnny crumpled, sitting low in his seat, silent tears on his cheeks. His voice became very quiet.

'I see them, Sam. Hear them. Every day. The camps. The beatings. Whips. The cries of men. The cries of my friend . . . and I did nothing.'

Sam rose to go to him but Veronica had appeared, immediately taking Johnny's head in her arms, stroking and soothing him with musical Kikuyu words until he quietened.

'What did you do?' Veronica hissed. 'Yesterday was bad enough. He is so weak now. Why do you make him speak of the past? What happened to him is better left there. You must go now. He is too weak. You should not have done this.'

Sam blinked into the sunshine in a daze. She wanted to weep for him. For Tansy. Even for her father. It didn't explain everything

392

but at last she saw what Africa was to Robert, why it could never be discussed. What a burden his childhood must have been. What a burden Johnny suffered from. White men's burdens.

Sam turned his logic over in her head. But however she dissected it, there was never any way that Johnny could have made good his promise without losing Tansy. How would he have felt then? Perhaps Sam could get some of the veterans to talk to him, to explain it was not his fault. That now with the reparations campaign there was finally a real chance of this getting into the public domain.

The campaign—

The idea that had been brewing lanced into her head, powerful and fully formed, and she realised there might be a way after all.

My God, if she could pull it off!

Dedan and Kamau were standing outside, knocking a deflated football around with some of the children.

'Hey there – good morning, Sam,' Kamau said breezily. But when she got nearer the expression on her face made him instantly anxious. 'What's the matter? Is it Johnny? Is your grandfather all right? Are you OK?'

'Yes, don't worry,' she said. 'I really am fine.'

She could see the shape of it now. The idea germinating spores of action. History and the present were colliding; her personal world and the job she still had to do combining. It was not guaranteed to work; might even be dangerous. But if she could take the weight from Johnny's shoulders even a fraction.

'I think I've found the way to make Johnny fine too,' she said, putting her arms round Kamau's waist. 'But the thing is, you're going to have to help me.'

Kamau put his head sideways but before the question came, Sam was spinning away, looking at her phone. She needed to make two calls.

'Where's the best place to get a signal?'

She stopped about twenty yards away and began to dial. Kamau approached but she put her hand up to forestall him.

'Hello? Grogan? It's Sam, Sam Seymour. Sorry I had to leave in such a rush, but I have something I think you need to see.'

Chapter 48

Nyeri District, April 2008

'Hello? Mummy? It's me, Sam.'

'Hello? Yes? Is that you, Sam?'

'Hi, Mum. Can you hear me?'

'Speak up, darling, I can hardly hear you. Where are you? Have you come back?'

'Is that better? Sorry, signal's awful. I'm still out here. In Kenya. I've got some news.'

'Are you all right? Everything OK?'

'Yes, yes, I'm fine. Never better. How are you all? Is Daddy in?'

'We're fine, thanks. It's been raining a lot. Your father's some-where – reading, I think. Isn't this costing you a lot of money, Sam? I thought mobiles were hideously expensive. When are you coming home?'

'Not sure yet. Don't worry about the cost. But listen, Mummy – I've got some amazing news. About Johnny. He's . . .'

'You're fading again. Perhaps you can try later when there's a better signal. Hello?'

'Did you hear that? Isn't it extraordinary? What will Daddy think? I could hardly believe it. But he's alive . . .'

'What's that? Five? I can't really hear. *Robert – it's Sam. Your daughter, you foolish man . . . do you want to speak to her?*'

'Is Daddy there? He'll want to know.'

'Sam, darling, if you can hear me – I'm hanging up now. You're fading in and out. Too frustrating. Call me later. Bye, darling. Lots of love. Bye . . . bye.'

'Hello? Hello? Mummy? Are you there? Hello? Don't hang up . . . *fuck.*'

Chapter 49

Nyeri District, April 2008

When Sam emerged from Johnny's house she'd been dazed at the immensity of it all, shocked at the load her grandfather had been carrying. But already she sensed it was becoming lighter, even if Johnny didn't know it yet. There was a remedy. The idea that had struck her would work – she was sure of it. She knew it was arrogant and tempted fate and everything else that ought to make one tremble before destiny, but the plan was achievable and it really might ease his burden. After phoning Grogan to force the meeting she'd been so excited she couldn't restrain herself from dancing. It was not a good look – Sam was aware of her limitations in that department – but she whirled and twirled in front of Kamau anyway, exuberant at the prospect of helping Johnny. If it hadn't been for the rather terrifying Veronica, she would have waltzed straight back inside to tell Johnny there and then. She was desperate for him to understand that he needn't worry any more. For now she knew the exact location of the suitcases containing the films and Macharia's notes.

It might be late in the day, almost fifty years late, but at last there was a way he could fulfil his oath. And the timing was excellent. Already Sam could see how a legal team might use them, imagining the flourish with which a good barrister would produce the notes, picturing the darkening of the court as the jury were transported back to the fifties via the flickering black and white images.

She'd tried to see him again, sticking her head round the door to Johnny's house an hour later, but the lights were off and she felt too scared to intrude when she'd seen the silhouette of Veronica still hunched over the bed. She gave it a last go in the evening but this time it had been Esther who headed her off, saying Johnny had taken a turn for the worse. Seeing Sam had upset his equilibrium. He was weak and needed to rest.

Sam didn't give it too much weight. She could see the sense in Johnny benefiting from a good night's sleep. Telling him now would only stir things up again. Anyway, there was too much uncertainty. Her scheme needed to succeed first. She wouldn't even tell Esther.

Today as they drove back to Grogan's house, the *matatu* was silent, each of them wrapped in thoughts of what lay ahead. It had all seemed terribly exciting last night when she'd planned it with Kamau and Dedan, but now it appeared foolish and unnecessarily dangerous. There were armed men at Grogan's house, not to mention a servant with a knife and a grudge. Sam was not feeling very brave.

When she'd rung Grogan yesterday he'd been incredulous she should be ringing, angry with her for running away after the altercation with his man. He was minded to put the phone down immediately. It had been 'bloody rude', not to mention a serious attack on an innocent servant.

Forcing herself to press on, she'd asked what he knew about photographs of a dead baby. A witness had come forward, she said, a new one, an insider from the colonial regime of that period. There were other documents as well which might be of concern from a legal standpoint. She was sure Grogan would provide some excellent context, so would he mind awfully if she popped over with a colleague to run over a few matters?

'What witness?' he'd barked.

'Confidential, I'm afraid.'

'You coming at this from the prosecution or the defence, Sam?'

'Neither,' Sam had replied. 'More of a duty call, really. But I suppose as I'm working for HMG it falls more into the defence category.'

The lie appeared to seal it and Grogan was mollified, if brusque. He was busy. He needed to be at the orphanage by four so they had a small window after lunch. Take it or leave it.

Persuading Grogan to see them had been the easy part. It was the next stage Sam was worried about. Somehow she needed to make him see it was in his interests to part with the two suitcases. Her plan was to argue she simply wanted to borrow the films to check against witness statements. She'd say she'd take them only as far as Nairobi, where there were proper screening facilities, to be returned

396

post-haste. It would all be unofficial – he was not to worry about them going any further. She might even promise to give him the baby letter in exchange.

It all sounded thin to Sam but if Grogan genuinely didn't know or had forgotten what was in the cases he might be amenable. Of course, it was highly possible that he wouldn't fall for any of it. He'd probably be suspicious of Sam, on the defensive over the baby material and the prospect of a new witness.

Which is where it got interesting. If Plan A failed, Plan B was undoubtedly the riskiest and stupidest part of the arrangement. If he didn't believe her, she was going to have to retrieve the cases herself.

Dedan had suggested how it might be done. It was so outlandish she'd thought he was joking, but Kamau had urged her to hear him out. Sam had flashed him a warning then – the two of them could not be allowed to start plotting and scheming without her.

'It had better be good,' she'd said.

'Oh it is Sam, it is explosive!' he laughed.

What was required at Grogan's place, Dedan explained, was a diversion. When he was young his grandfather Gatimu used to take the boys fishing. They caught a lot of fish, but not because they were any good at fishing.

'Gatimu looked like a sensible guy but he was a crazy man. We loved him! He used to make weapons for Mau Mau. After the struggle he kept a lot of his toys in a lead-lined tea chest buried under the chicken shed. When we went fishing he would fetch a couple of grenades and we'd chuck them in the river. Bang! Big explosion. Lots of water in the air; lot of fish on the surface.'

If Grogan didn't buy Sam's story she needed him and the knife-man Jordan, and anyone else inside the house, *outside* so she or Kamau could look for the cases unhindered. So, the second she decided her arguments weren't working she would signal to Dedan by sending him a pre-set message on her mobile. It would be easy enough to do from her pocket without Grogan noticing.

Dedan knew there were still at least five grenades in the tea chest. He would place them far enough away not to hurt anyone but near enough to worry everybody and make them think they were under attack from poachers or Samburu cattle raiders or whatever other enemy the paranoid guard-hiring Grogan thought was out to get him. When they heard the explosions the occupants of the house would come running.

'No,' said Sam, appalled. 'Absolutely not. We are not using grenades. End of story.'

'C'mon, Sam, it'll be fun. I was in the military for five years. I know how to set a fuse. It will be easy. No one will be hurt.'

'Nope.'

Kamau intervened again.

'Sam – seriously, we should do this. You spent half of last night telling me what an evil man Grogan was. Still is, presumably. I know you're doing this for your grandfather but think of all those veterans – alive and dead – who endured what Grogan and the others did to them. This may be our only chance. Hopefully we can persuade him, but if not we need to do whatever it takes to obtain the evidence.'

'*Whatever it takes?* Careful, you're beginning to sound like Grogan.'

'If they break the compact, then maybe we have to too.'

'Break the law to protect the law? That's just not a proper argument,' Sam said.

But even as she'd been saying it Sam knew she would end up agreeing. Grogan and his generation had gone too far. Invisible to the world, they thought they'd got away with it. Worse, they believed what they did was right.

The guards at the entrance to the house had been alerted to their arrival, motioning where to park the *matatu*. Dedan chuckled and told them he was just dropping off his passengers. He needed to see a guy and would be back in a short time.

As Sam feared, it was Jordan who opened the door.

Adhesive strips fixed a bandage across his nose. It was not a clean dressing, with evidence of seepage at the bridge, and he had to look past it, forcing him to squint out of the corner of his eye. Holding the door slightly ajar, he stared sideways at Sam, pupils glittering. He waited for them to go first and as she passed she smelled the milk and mint.

'We have been looking forward to seeing you again,' he said in a low voice, his fingers brushing her thigh so lightly it might not have happened. Sam stiffened. He laughed and Sam's stomach heaved and dipped at the folly of it. If Kamau had not been beside her she would have run straight out again. She reached for his hand and he gave a reassuring squeeze.

Then they were in the drawing room where Sam had watched the film. A log fire was burning in the grate but it did not take off much of the chill. Grogan was standing by his chair, hands behind his back. He wore shorts and his thin legs were encased in long beige cotton socks. He did not extend his hand.

'Who's your friend?'

'This is Kamau. He's the archivist who found the documents. I thought it would be helpful for him to be here if you had any questions about them.'

'Kikuyu?' he asked Sam.

'Why don't you ask him yourself?'

Grogan barked a short laugh.

'Good-looking chap isn't he? Amazing what you discover in the archives nowadays. Better show me what you found.'

She handed him the letter.

Grogan scanned the document, turning the paper over to look at the other side. He shrugged.

'Where'd you really get this? It's confidential – this kind of material never gets let out.'

'You don't deny it's authentic then?'

Grogan motioned them to sit down while he perched on the side of his chair.

'Look, what do you want, Miss Seymour? I've been speaking to your people in Nairobi. Apparently you've gone AWOL. Seems you might be changing sides. Clearly runs in the family. If you thought you'd pin something on me with this' – he waved the letter – 'you're barking up the wrong tree. Doesn't mean anything. I write to a policeman about a photographer. That was my job. Don't see the problem.'

'The problem is,' Sam said, 'that the photographer was Johnny and before he went you'd instructed someone – Graves, wasn't it? – to cut off a baby's head and stick it on a bamboo pole. A baby's head, Grogan? A little chilling, don't you think? Straying just a touch beyond propaganda? If you were prepared to do that it looks rather like you might have been prepared to do a lot more. Might not be seen in a good light by members of the public. Or a jury.'

Grogan stared through his thick glasses. He didn't move, and spoke very quietly.

'You could only know about that incident if someone told you. Graves is dead. The police officer I wrote to is long gone and I mentioned no such thing. That leaves one person.'

Sam stared back as bravely as she could. He was an old man and she had Kamau by her side. Yet she was scared of him. Just the way he spoke; sibilance barely masking the menace. She'd slipped up badly. She'd only showed him the letter because she'd promised it as a means of entry. She hadn't foreseen how Grogan would join the dots.

'I don't know what you mean,' Sam said. 'And, frankly, it's irrelevant. I showed it to you as a courtesy. If you don't have anything to say about it – fine. There's something else actually. More important.'

Grogan smiled tightly.

'No, no. Hang on,' he said. 'You have no fresh witness as such. I know them all. Apart from that defunct District Officer turncoat Nottingham helping the human rights brigade in Nairobi they're either dead or will be very soon.'

'Who's Nottingham?'

'Nobody you need concern yourself with. But if you haven't been speaking to him about it then you must have . . . '

Grogan's voice trailed off and he stood quickly, marching to behind the sofa where he put both hands on the edge.

'So what is it that's so much more important? I'd appreciate it if you were quick. I'm on a tight schedule here.'

Sam exchanged glances with Kamau. This was it and she was not hopeful.

She dived in with her plea to borrow the films, explaining how they might aid the legal process, how a loan would be temporary; how instructive a film showing the real nature of the camps would be to those who claimed they were centres of brutality.

'They might swing it, Grogan,' she said gamely. 'They might make all the difference. Prove your version of events.'

Grogan nodded slowly and chuckled to himself.

'Well, well. It *was* the films. Thought so. Clever girl. But perhaps

400

not as clever as you think. Every inch your grandfather's girl, though, I'll give you that.'

Kamau's face tightened and he sat forward in his chair. Sam prayed he wouldn't intervene. Grogan was reaching down behind the sofa.

He heaved a familiar-looking suitcase onto the cushions and walked round to the front. Unclasping the case, he extracted one of the round metal canisters, using his thumbnail to prise it open.

'This what you came for?'

He held it up to show Sam. It was empty.

Grogan repeated the exercise with another canister. And another, flinging the empty cases onto the floor.

'Tell me when to stop.'

Empty.

'Do you really think,' Grogan said, hurling the last of the film canisters onto the pile on the floor, 'that I am an imbecile? I remember possessing the arrogance of youth but it never blinded me to the obvious. I am seriously disappointed in you, Sam. How could you have possibly imagined that I would not have looked at the films?'

His words were punching the fight out of her. There was nothing left. She had failed.

'I don't begrudge the old *mzees* a few pennies,' he continued, his tone reverting to the old, breezy Grogan. 'Poor buggers have been through enough. But when I saw what was on here – what Johnny had really been filming, sneaky bugger – I thought it prudent to deal with them. Old film combusts in a very satisfactory manner, you know.'

He was pacing the room now, back and forth in front of them, a malevolent metronome.

'I don't know what you're really up to,' he snorted, 'and naturally I shall be telling Pugh of this gross intimidation of an elderly citizen. I suggest you don't even think of trying to scapegoat me. I will not be paraded as the sole representative in the dock when all I was doing was serving my country.'

Sam looked at her feet, appalled at how badly she had let Johnny down.

'If you do,' Grogan said, 'I will not only press charges on you for assaulting Jordan but I will drag your family name through the mud.

401

I'm the last man standing – d'you see? As a mere propaganda man in the Pipeline my hands are clean. Pity about Johnny's, though. Be a shame to let the world know what a violent torturer he was.'

'He was never a torturer.'

'How do you know? You don't. Or did Johnny write some self-serving bullshit about it in that so-called scrapbook you told me about? Must have if you're sitting here.'

Sam felt pinned to the ground. Everything she'd learned from Johnny told her that Grogan was lying, but how could she be certain? How could she *know* about the past if she hadn't been there?

'I don't see how the authorities are any more likely to believe you than my grandfather.'

'Really? Why don't you get your Kikuyu boyfriend here to have another look at the archives? If he did, he'd find an arrest warrant for a certain Mr John Seymour. No longer extant but that's not the point. He was a criminal, you see, and people don't tend to believe dead criminals when live witnesses can testify to how evil they really were.'

Grogan had taken off his glasses and was polishing them with a faded yellow cloth. The more he spoke, the more Sam saw the younger version, detached and cold. A man of logic but not of reason.

'That's how I'll spin it, Sam. Take your chances if you will but I'm quite good at it.'

'You're a liar, Grogan, always have been. You can't help yourself. Apart from you, Johnny would never have hurt a soul.'

'You sure? Let me tell about your grandfather. He was a coward. None of us liked what we were obliged to do but we did what we had to – so others didn't. That's the way it worked back then. It was called public service. But Johnny couldn't take it. He snapped. One evening he came steaming into my office screaming that he had to get out. He'd seen too much. I tried to calm him but he was too far gone. Went berserk. Had a go at me – the bugger actually stabbed me – before getting onto his motorbike and riding off. Ran away like a little boy. All hell broke loose. Arrest warrants put out. A wanted man. Johnny Seymour, the fugitive.

'It was ironic really, Johnny could have come back at any time. The government declared an amnesty for all violence during the Emergency. Idea was to reconcile with the Kikuyu, get them around the table, but it applied to everyone – Brits too. That means me as well, by the way.

'So that was your grandfather, Sam. A coward with a proven record of violence. Just the sort of man the Empire used to do its dirty work – isn't that the caricature your generation has written for us? You've got Tansy's blood in you so you may be made of sterner stuff but I wouldn't dream of dragging any of this up if I were you.'

Was that really how it had ended? Johnny was her grandfather, her family. She had to believe him. But Grogan made his version sound foully credible. How could any of them not be contaminated? Was it possible Johnny had swapped the roles around in his explanations, done the very things that he'd ascribed to Grogan?

Grogan was smiling now, his hands behind his back as if he were on parade, chin jutting, his face shining with certainty. She shook her head. *Of course.* She recognised that look from Johnny's description. He thought he was so bloody cunning. This was exactly what he'd done to Tansy and Johnny. Lied and manipulated and distorted.

But he'd missed something. She stood slowly, patting her jeans to make sure the mobile was still there.

'What about the other case, Grogan? What about the rest of the films?'

Grogan laughed derisorily.

'What films? The other case you saw in the attic might have been filled with film canisters but there was never actually any film in them. I got Jordan to look after you left. Nothing in there except stinking old newspaper!'

Sam smiled. 'Keen as mustard' Jordan was; Grogan said so when she'd first visited. But he'd also said his man was illiterate. Jordan couldn't bloody read a note if he tried.

Now she was certain.

'Oh good,' she said, reaching into her pocket.

'Good? How's that good?'

'It means Johnny's been telling the truth. So fuck you, Grogan.'

She looked at Kamau, grinned and pressed 'send'.

403

Chapter 50

Nyeri District, April 2008

The explosions started immediately. The sound had a spectacular effect on Grogan, who sprang into the air like a frightened eland before crouching down behind the sofa. Even Sam, who was expecting them, jumped a little. The noise was loud and increased in intensity with every succeeding explosion. Dedan must have planted the grenades much nearer than he should have.

'*Jordan!*' Grogan yelled. 'Get out there and see what the hell's going on.'

Behind her Sam heard someone running. Grogan, meanwhile, was bent double, peering cautiously out of the window. She followed his gaze and saw the two guards hunched behind their little hut. Dedan was rolling a cigarette, his sunglasses pushed high on his forehead. He laughed as Jordan sped past, heading to the source of the explosions.

But Grogan, still anchored to his position by the window, was not leaving.

'Aren't you going out there?' she asked. 'Could be trouble.'

Grogan didn't bother to look at her.

Kamau was standing by her side and he tugged urgently on her arm.

'*Sam! It must be now.*'

They had a minute, perhaps two. She nodded at Kamau and started for the door. Grogan whipped his head round.

'Hey – where the hell do you think you're going?'

'None of your business,' she said. 'I'm just going . . . '

Grogan blinked and coughed, half-pant, half-groan. He knew.

'*You're going for the other case!* What's in there? Sam, stay right where you are.'

404

Grogan covered the short distance to her side in a rapid spider's scuttle. He put his arm out, palm up, pushing against her shoulder. Kamau growled but Sam's actions were fired by adrenalin and she danced round Grogan with ease.

In retrospect it hadn't been a conscious decision, but instead of going to the door she went to the fireplace.

'Take this,' she said to Kamau, handing him the poker. 'Keep him in here. Don't hurt him unless you have to, but if you have to, hurt him as much you want.'

Later on Sam recalled very little except a feeling of hurrying with great precision, replaying her previous foray into the attic with fewer obstacles. She undid the catch on the ladder first time, was up the steps and into the loft in seconds. She found the light switch immediately, saw the solitary case instantly and within two minutes was back in the living room clasping it to her breast as if it were a baby.

At first she thought Kamau and Grogan were not in the room. But they were on the floor, Kamau kneeling on Grogan's chest, leaning on the poker with both hands, pushing it down onto the older man's chest. Grogan's face was red and he was squirming and panting, wriggling like a fat shrimp on a hook.

Through the window she saw Dedan holding Jordan by the arm, but then the servant threw it off and looked at the house, directly at her.

There were things she had to say to Grogan. She'd rehearsed them on the journey. But, seeing him floundering on the ground, there seemed no point. He was pathetic. An old man near the end of his life. A man who'd held great power and performed great wrong. She looked round the walls. Men his age had photographs of children and grandchildren. A wife. There was nothing here. The house was a shell. He was impotent, a victim of the past, impaled by history and memories as surely as her own grandfather and all the others.

But there was one final piece of business. She tapped Kamau on the shoulder.

'Let him go now.'

Sam stared down at Grogan. His glasses had fallen off and without the lenses his eyes had paled to an almost colourless grey.

'Listen, Grogan. You should have spent money on Jordan's education. The paper he saw in this case isn't just paper. Inside every

405

canister are the notes that Macharia wrote when he was in that hell-hole of a detention camp. Whenever he saw a guard strike someone he wrote their name down. Whenever he went into that damp room and met you with your fucking pliers he wrote it down. Every single obscenity you ever did is recorded for history.'

Grogan had stopped wriggling and lay flat, only his chest moved rapidly up and down as he sucked in breath.

'And remember this: you may think you have immunity from some fucked-up deal back then, but there is no statute of limitations on war crimes. *War crimes.* Think about it, Grogan. Your time has come.'

The blinking had slowed but Grogan's chest was rising and falling as if someone were pumping it with great force. She hoped he wasn't having a heart attack. She wanted him to dwell on the vastness of what she'd told him. At the door she stopped.

'Oh and by the way, you should know that the witness is Johnny. He's alive and well. In fact, he's better than you've ever been in your entire life. I'm going to see him now. And when I tell him about this he's going to enjoy every moment of it.'

Grogan's arm flapped up before falling back to his chest.

'No,' he whispered. 'He won't. He can't ... he was there ... none of us ever can.'

'Yes he bloody will. He absolutely will. You've lost, Grogan. Get used to it.'

And Sam, echoing Johnny before her at another crucial juncture, believed what she said with every ounce of her being, the notion that it might be otherwise, inconceivable.

Chapter 51

Nyeri District, April 2008

The dust cloud created by the *matatu* as it sped away from Grogan down the long private road was impressive, its swirling mass given added energy by Dedan flinging the van around, squealing the tyres to dodge bullets Sam hoped were imaginary. She and Kamau were in the back, being hurled from one side to the other, their eyes pinned to the rear window.

No one was following but it wasn't until they were at least five miles clear of the estate, bumping along a back lane no one could possibly discover, that Dedan stopped, pulling the van off the road into the cover of the trees.

'We did it!' he exclaimed, jumping out and executing a strange two-step shuffle. He put his big hand through the van window and turned on the sound system, flooding the trees with Tony Nyadundo's Ohangla rhythms. Sam and Kamau grinned at each other and embraced.

'We bloody well did do it,' Sam whispered. 'Thank you – you were amazing.'

'So were you,' Kamau said.

'I can't believe it. When those grenades went off I thought I was going to die. And then coming back to see you pinning down Grogan. He was like a stuck pig! Christ, did we actually do all of that?'

'Here,' said Dedan, handing Sam a hipflask. 'You did do it and you were magnificent. A leopard indeed. Let us toast our success.'

To any onlooker it would have seemed a mightily odd thing to have come across in the middle of the bush; two Kenyans and a British woman dancing and drinking and smoking as if they were at a party.

Later, as they lounged against the *matatu*, sharing the last of the flask, Sam could not hold it in any longer.

'I can't stand here with all that evidence only a few feet away from me. I've got to see what's in the case.'

With Kamau and Dedan looking over her shoulder, Sam placed the suitcase on the bonnet and snapped the catches. It opened easily. Inside were six of the round metal film containers. Sam picked up the first one on the pile. It felt cool to the touch and she allowed herself a brief moment of private congratulation. With Macharia's evidence the case for reparations would be immeasurably stronger. She couldn't wait to see Johnny's face when she showed him. She'd been feeling guilty about exhausting him yesterday but this would surely put the spring back in his step. Such a shame Tansy wouldn't be here to see it.

The canister was empty and she had a twinge of anxiety. Then she remembered it must have been the one Jordan had already opened. There were five left and these were still sealed with tape. She reached for another, trying to force it open, but she could not unpick the ancient adhesive. It was stuck solid.

'Try this,' Dedan said, handing Sam a curved panga.

'Looks suitably lethal.'

Dedan grinned.

'My ancestors used it to chop up their foes.'

Sam looked at the blade closer.

'Really? Look, "Made in Birmingham, 1988".'

'Are you going to open this or not Sam?' Kamau asked. 'Not sure I can take the suspense.'

The tip of the panga blade cut effortlessly through the tape and Sam used her fingernails to prise the container open. The airtight lid sprang off with a pop and Sam was hit by a foul, ancient stench. Fifty-year-old shit mixed with the worst body odour.

Dedan wrinkled his nose but Sam was smiling.

'Means we're on the right track. According to Johnny, Macharia wrote all his notes on toilet paper – and he hid them in the latrines. They're bound to stink.'

Daintily Sam used her forefinger to root among the scraps of paper. She was surprised at how light they were, parting under her finger as if they weren't really there. They didn't look like old newspapers either, more like shiny black negatives, gossamer-thin.

Something was not right. She selected one but it crumbled in her fingers. A larger piece at the side looked as if might be more solid. She managed to pick it up but as she unfolded it, it too fell apart in her hands. She found another and saw to her relief there was writing on it. But the words were tiny and the paper so thin it was almost impossible to decipher.

It looked like a list. She made out a name. *Schapps.* It was the only whole name on the paper. Letters were missing from all the others. 'Gav' something? And then 'rogan' – surely Grogan. She passed it to Kamau, but he shook his head.

'No – can't read it, sorry.'

She opened the next canister.

It was the same story. Some of the scraps still resembled newspaper but they had disintegrated. It reminded her of an old mouse nest. A den of dry paper, chewed by time. One after the other, they all crumbled. A tantalising word here or there but nothing whole.

With mounting anxiety Sam opened the next canister.

The same.

In desperation she cut open the rest, ignoring cries from the men to be careful. Not a single, whole note remained in any of them. Bacteria and time had consumed them all. Memories of notes were all that remained. History as homeopathy. Wisps of wisps.

She carefully pulled out the last tiny piece of paper. Slowly, holding her breath, she unfolded it. Maybe this one.

Nothing.

Dust.

A scrap stuck to her finger and she blew it into the air, watching it turn and swirl; a tiny black petal melting into the warm red earth.

Dust to dust.

There were a lot of people outside Johnny's house. Sam pushed through them, steeling herself, one of the empty canisters in her hand. She didn't know what to say to him.

'Tell him what seems right, Sam,' Kamau had said.

But what was right? No films; no notes. The past had promised to deliver its secrets but snatched them away at the last minute. She was ashamed. She *had* failed him. Johnny would never have the satisfaction. She began to understand about burdens.

She wouldn't say anything now; she'd wait until he was feeling stronger. Perhaps together they could make sense of it. She excused herself as she nudged past an old lady who was crying under the stoop. Who were all these people? Sam tried the door but there were more villagers on the other side. She stood on tiptoe in the doorway and saw Esther and Veronica by the bed. Esther spotted her and motioned to Sam that she would come to her.

Sam waited outside and lit a cigarette. People were looking at her strangely. She knew from previous attempts at conversation that few of them spoke English. She couldn't ask Kamau to translate as he and Dedan had stayed at the *matatu*, going through the canisters once more, unable to accept the truth of their disintegration.

'There you are, Sam. Where have you been? We've been looking all over for you.'

Esther smiled but she looked drawn and tired.

'What's going on here?' Sam asked. 'Why are all these people in Johnny's house?'

Esther stroked Sam's arm. 'Tell me first where you have been. Someone said you were with Grogan. Can that be true?'

'Yes, we were,' Sam said. 'I thought we could unearth some of the films that Johnny took but the bastard burned them all. And then I was stupid enough to believe I could find Macharia's old notes – the ones Johnny promised to get out of the camps.'

'Did you find them?'

Sam stamped out her cigarette. It was all hopeless.

'None of them survived. They'd all rotted away, turned to air. Oh Esther! I failed him. We were so near – with those notes we could have transformed the case. Johnny would have . . .'

'*Sam*, listen to me. You have to forget about that now. There are more important matters to consider. You know that Johnny is ill. I am sorry that I cannot shield you from this, but it is now worse than that.

'He is dying, Sam.'

'*Dying?* He can't be. You said he had months—'

'Last night he had a crisis. The doctor says he would have died many hours ago if he had not been waiting for you. He is not always lucid but all he asks for is you. He wants to say goodbye, Sam. He is stubborn. It is common for the dying to wait until their loved ones are there. And that is you, Sam. He loves you.'

Sam felt faint. She had only just met him, only scratched the surface of finding out about him. He couldn't be going now. It was impossible. How was she going to explain about the films? What would her father say?

'I can't, Esther. I've let him down. It was all for nothing. The films – his films – are gone. Macharia's notes turned to dust. Everything's gone. He was right, it's useless. Nothing I can say will mean anything.'

Esther's hand gripped Sam's forearm suddenly and tightly.

'*Sam*,' she said sternly. 'You must and you will go in there and say goodbye to your grandfather. Whatever you say to him will be a comfort. As for the films – you have to understand something very fundamental.'

She had started to lead Sam back towards the house but stopped before they reached the small crowd that had been gathering ever since word of the white *mzee*'s dying had spread. She grasped Sam's wrists in her small hands and gazed up at her solemnly.

'Listen to me now. This is important. Sam – it is wonderful that you have tried so hard. For your grandfather and for all of us. Like Johnny, you have laboured mightily to right a great wrong.

'But in the end this is a matter we Kenyans have to deal with ourselves. The help is appreciated – do not get me wrong, it really is. Personally you've helped me so much already just by listening and I am so grateful. But this is *our* struggle. No one can take upon themselves what is not theirs to take. We began this and we will end it.

'Now go, Sam, go and say goodbye to a wonderful man.'

Most of the lights in the room had been turned down and Sam approached the bedside in gloom. Veronica rose from the mattress and held Sam gently, resting her forehead on Sam's.

'Thank you for coming. He wanted to see you desperately. It means so much to him.' She smiled and pulled away and Sam could make out the tears running down her cheeks. 'And to me as well,' she added. '*Asante*, Sam. *Asante sana*.'

Sam sat on the bed, overwhelmed by sadness and the necessity of the moment. Johnny stirred and she grasped his hand. It was like a bird's claw, weightless. She stroked his parchment forehead. Hot and dry. He was far too thin; his skin so light it felt as if it too would come apart in her hands.

411

'Johnny,' she whispered. 'It's me.'

Johnny slowly turned his head on the pillow and opened his eyes. They fixed dully on Sam, but when recognition came they widened and he tried to sit up.

'You're here,' he said, speaking so softly Sam had to lean in so close she could feel the tendrils of his breath on her skin.

'Hey, hey, don't get up,' Sam said. 'Lie still, Johnny. It's OK.'

'You're here . . .'

Sam felt fat gorges of tears mass behind her eyes. He was so frail; hardly here.

'Look, Johnny. Look what I found.'

Sam held up the film canister in front of her grandfather.

'After all these years, the films. Your films! I found them at Grogan's. And Macharia's notes.'

She was crying now.

'We did it, Johnny. Together. You don't need to worry any more. We can do it. You kept your promise.'

'My darling Tansy. Thank you. Tansy . . .

Johnny's lips twitched, the words barely words, whispered sounds but Sam knew what he'd said and was glad.

'It's all right, Johnny. She's with you now. Tansy's here.

'It's all going to be fine.'

Postscript

6 June 2013

*Extracts from Foreign Secretary the Rt Hon William Hague's
statement to Parliament on the settlement of claims of Kenyan citizens
relating to events during the period 1952–63.*

[...] During the emergency period, widespread violence was committed by both sides, and most of the victims were Kenyan. Many thousands of Mau Mau members were killed, while the Mau Mau themselves were responsible for the deaths of over 2,000 people, including 200 casualties among the British regiments and police.

Emergency regulations were introduced; political organisations were banned; prohibited areas were created; and provisions for detention without trial were enacted. The colonial authorities made unprecedented use of capital punishment and sanctioned harsh prison, so-called 'rehabilitation', regimes. Many of those detained were never tried, and the links of many with the Mau Mau were never proven. There was recognition at the time of the brutality of these repressive measures and the shocking level of violence ...

The British Government recognise that Kenyans were subject to torture and other forms of ill treatment at the hands of the colonial administration. The British Government sincerely regret that these abuses took place and that they marred Kenya's progress towards independence. Torture and ill treatment are abhorrent violations of human dignity which we unreservedly condemn.

I can announce today that the Government have now reached an agreement with Leigh Day, the solicitors acting on behalf of the claimants, in full and final settlement of their clients' claims.

The agreement includes payment of a settlement sum in respect of 5,228 claimants, as well as a gross costs sum to the total value of £19.9 million. The Government will also support the construction of a memorial in Nairobi to the victims of torture and ill-treatment during the colonial era.

[It] is my hope that the agreement now reached will receive wide support, will help draw a line under these events and will support reconciliation.

The settlement I am announcing today is part of a process of reconciliation. In December this year, Kenya will mark its 50th anniversary of independence and the country's future belongs to post-independence generation. We do not want our current and future relations with Kenya to be overshadowed by the past.

Author's Note

In writing *White Highlands* I wanted, above all, to produce a novel that deals with strong, flawed characters, following them to their ultimate destiny or demise – in many senses, an old-fashioned story of love and adventure. But because the story is deliberately placed in a controversial historical setting that still resonates today, it is important to lay out what is true, what is fiction and, in a realm where context is all, the author's stance.

The campaign against Mau Mau was an intensely bloody and nasty struggle that saw tens of thousands of African Kenyans killed by hunger, disease and brutality. The precise number who died during this period is, like so many other aspects of this colonial conflict, hotly contested. Many were killed in what was effectively a civil war between supporters of the colony and Mau Mau revolutionaries. And it is certainly true that Mau Mau indulged in their share of atrocities, notably the Lari massacre. However, there is no way of escaping the fact that British forces and their colonial proxies caused the deaths of many thousands of Kenyans, possibly tens of thousands, either by creating the conditions in which they died or by directly killing and torturing. In contrast, the number of white settlers killed by Mau Mau was thirty-two.

What made the violence applied to Mau Mau more disturbing was the systematic manner in which force was applied. Aside from the shooting war in the forests, there was also the construction of a large 'gulag' of detention camps, in which suspected Mau Mau sympathisers were incarcerated and tortured, 'compelled', in the chilling euphemism of the day, to give up their oaths of allegiance on pain of beating or worse. Meanwhile, outside the camps, under the villagisation programme, established Kikuyu settlements were destroyed and women and children forced to live in new villages where they were required to labour on public works projects, often forced to submit to terrible treatment at the hands of Kenyan loyalists.

When, as a journalist, I began to interview Kenyan veterans I could scarcely believe the scale of this brutality, even after taking into account the possibility that some tales might have been exaggerated or falsified due to financial motives linked to their campaign for reparations. But story after story tumbled out, not just to me but to lawyers and historians actively examining the claims, and such records as there were seemed to back up many of the accounts.*

However, while the brutality was real enough, it is important to stress that none of the characters in the book, except obvious public figures, are real. While many lawyers, British and Kenyan, have done excellent work in seeking redress for Mau Mau veterans, none are characterised personally here. To my knowledge, there was no official mission of British lawyers sent to Kenya with the purpose of examining the strength of Mau Mau veterans' claims. A press office was run by the colonial government in Nairobi during the Emergency, in which there was a film section, but none of the men and women who staffed it are represented here. Any resemblance to any real people, living or dead, is entirely coincidental.

Many of the external events in the novel did take place but in some cases, the chronology has been altered to fit the novel's narrative. The scene where Johnny, Tansy and Macharia come across mass arrests of Kikuyu in Nairobi, for example, was based on Operation Anvil, which took place a year later, in 1954. The march by white settlers on Government House did happen as described and some of their actions are based on historical fact – burning the askaris' legs with cigarettes, for instance. The mission hospital at Kagamo is entirely made up. Of the many detention camps, Langata, Mackinnon Road, Manyani and Hola were real, but Umua is not. None of the warders or guards or general staff, British or African, are based on real people. However, almost every one

---

*There are now several excellent history books examining the period. Two of the best recent accounts are Caroline Elkins's *Britain's Gulag: The Brutal End of Empire in Kenya* (Pimlico, 2005) and David Anderson's *Histories of the Hanged: Britain's Dirty War in Kenya and the End of Empire* (Phoenix, 2006). Anyone wishing to delve further into Mau Mau should read anything by the brilliant John Lonsdale, Emeritus Professor of Modern African History and fellow of Trinity College, Cambridge.

of the violent acts described in the book did happen to someone at some period of the conflict. The Chief Secretary's Complaints Co-ordinating Committee, the CSCCC, whose minutes were given to Sam by Mattingly, was a real body that contemporaneously heard many of the complaints described in the book.

For decades numerous documents from the period were hidden away. But during the reparations campaign a large collection of official papers, known as the Hanslope Park archive, has surfaced, revealing fresh insights into Britain's dirty war against Mau Mau. As scholars examine the new material, more information is sure to follow. And if all this happened in Kenya, it is worth asking what more horrors are yet to emerge from other former British colonies that fought for their independence?

As a journalist I tried to raise the profile of this period with factual reporting, but as journalists know well, stories arrive quickly and disappear even faster; seemingly important at the time but swiftly consigned to 'tomorrow's chip paper', or its digital equivalent. Aside from greater longevity, fiction can, or should, be different. Story-telling can sometimes be enjoined to extend beyond being 'a good read' to play a part in the self-mythologising that helps frame identity, at both personal and national level. This need not be overly prescriptive or heavy handed: the beauty of fiction is that there are as many stories as there are writers and perhaps as many interpretations as there are readers. And of course, as many historians would argue, there may be any number of different 'histories' as well, depending on the viewpoint of both the historian and the epoch, movement or people being examined. This novel is only one small voice in all these discussions.

But if historical context is vital, rightly making us wary of viewing the past through the filter of contemporary morality, it is also true that the fifties were not the Middle Ages. While that decade may often seem foreign territory to modern eyes, it was not really such a different country. The people who inhabited those times flew in jet planes, watched TV, listened to the radio, went to the cinema, fretted about nuclear power. The Universal Declaration of Human Rights had been signed four years prior to the state of Emergency in Kenya. Those who served in Kenya during this period were in every important sense like us; in many cases, they still are us. There were good and bad people then, as in every era, but those who perpetrated the abuses belonged to a generation of Britons who had a close acquaintance with right and wrong. Less than ten years previously they had fought the 'good war' against the Nazis and had some experience with camps of one sort or another. The difference in Kenya is that they did not liberate them, but constructed and ran them.

Of course, these were not concentration camps or anything like it, but they – we – should surely have learned that when large numbers of men and women are put behind barbed wire, when they are whipped, starved, tortured and denied basic rights, no one should be surprised when large numbers die, nor that however many contorted legal reasons are used in justification, the humanity of the gaoler is diminished every bit as much as the gaoled.

Only if we recognise this and take heed can we head into the future with any hope of not repeating previous mistakes. Arguably this may be more germane now than ever. The tendency in some quarters to paint the past in romantic colours, conjuring a golden pre-European era when Britannia ruled the waves with fairness and blue-eyed compassion, needs to be resisted with hard-headed truths about how we actually did behave.

For as the saying goes, if you do not know where you came from, then how can you know where you are going?

Acknowledgements

For what is often a solitary pursuit, novel writing can be surprisingly collegiate, and I would like to thank the many friends, family and professionals who have helped me. But while happily acknowledging them, it must be stressed that any errors remain exclusively my own.

So, first, vast thanks to my wife, Sarah Lonsdale, who has not only read every word but has shown endless patience in allowing me to read draft versions to her. Her suggestions and encouragement have been invaluable. Thanks too to Tom and Livvy for their wonderful backing, their comments, and for enduring their father being locked away for hours with bad music emanating from his study.

Huge thanks to my good friends John Fisher, Hugh Dignon, Jeremy Lonsdale and Sue Swan for reading early drafts and being fantastically encouraging. And to Chris Niel and Amanda Davis for always being supportive, for having early faith and then persuading me to get out and see people who could actually get me published.

I have been enormously lucky with my agent Piers Blofeld of Shiel Land Associates. Not only did he find a great home for *White Highlands*, but he was extremely creative in shaping the book and guiding me through the shoals of such a sensitive subject. His advice, encouragement and good humour have sustained me through what has turned out to be a delightfully painless process. Thanks too to Lucy Fawcett, also of Shiel Land, who has been brilliantly encouraging as she took the manuscript out on the long screen road.

My luck in finding excellent, creative people to help extends to Little, Brown where my editor Richard Beswick has backed me from the start, his cool, sure hand steering *White Highlands* into becoming an infinitely better book than the one he was presented with. The same must be said for Zoe Gullen, senior project editor at Little, Brown, whose editorial eye misses nothing and whose deft expertise has not only saved it from innumerable errors but also helped shape the text into an enormously better read. And major thanks too to publicity manager Zoe Hood, for being so enthusiastic and professional in pursuit of publicising the book.

There are undoubtedly many others who I have not named, friends and professionals who have helped in a thousand different ways and to them I add a heartfelt thank you.

Lastly, I want to pay my deep respects to the men and women in Kenya who suffered so grievously at the hands of the British and their allies. Neither side had a monopoly on good or bad, but it is impossible to meet Kenyan veterans, as I was privileged to do, and not be struck by their great dignity and patience in the face of such appalling behaviour. More than money, they have always said they wanted acknowledgment of the crimes perpetrated. With reparations having been awarded by the British government, a start has been made, but we owe it to those men and women never to forget this shameful and dark period of our shared history.